C000273954

Debbie Horsfield was born in Manchester and educated at Newcastle University. An award-winning writer, she has many televised, published and performed plays to her credit.

MAKING OUT

Debbie Horsfield

CORGI BOOKS

MAKING OUT
A CORGI BOOK   0 552 13518 6

First publication in Great Britain

PRINTING HISTORY
Corgi edition published 1989

Corgi Books are published by Transworld Publishers Ltd.,
61 – 63 Uxbridge Road, Ealing, London W5 5SA, in
Australia by Transworld Publishers (Australia) Pty. Ltd.,
15 – 23 Helles Avenue, Moorebank, NSW 2170, and in
New Zealand by Transworld Publishers (N.Z.) Ltd.,
Cnr. Moselle and Waipareira Avenues, Henderson,
Auckland.

This book is set in 10pt Times by
Chippendale Type, Otley, West Yorkshire

Printed in Great Britain by
Cox & Wyman Ltd., Reading, Berks

CHAPTER ONE

February

It was the smell of smoke which woke her. In the half-light she groped for the alarm clock, then for Ray. His side of the bed was cold. She sniffed the air. What was burning? Where was everyone? The door to the kids' room was open, but their beds were empty. And that was definitely smoke coming from under the kitchen door. Panic rose in her stomach.

'Sharon! Nicky! . . . '

Jill was calling them even as the voice on the other end of the phone was saying, 'Emergency . . . which service do you require?'

'What's up?' The door of the kitchen had opened and Ray was looking at her with a grin on his face. Behind him smoke was belching out of the grill, while Sharon and Nicky, still in their pyjamas, were chipping charred scraps of bacon off the bottom of a blackened pan.

'Where's the fire?' Ray seemed to find the whole thing hilarious.

Ten-year-old Nicky pushed his way to the fore.

'It's not a fire,' he said, almost pityingly. 'It's breakfast.'

'Alright, you. Get back to bed.' Jill found herself almost manhandled up the stairs.

Minutes later she was sitting up in bed, forcing herself to eat the burnt offerings while Ray and the kids watched eagerly. It felt odd to be the centre of attention for a change – but then, it was likely to be an odd day all round.

'Dad . . . me mam's never been out to work before –
she won't know what to do.'

Nicky had yet to be convinced by the new arrangements.

'It's your dad you should worry about,' his mother
retorted. 'It's him can't tell a tea-towel from a tin of peas.'

'I'll manage – no problem.' Ray seemed alarmingly
confident.

'Time you were up,' he ordered. 'Those days are over.'

'What days?' she queried.

'Lay in bed till all hours, minding the world with your
head in the pillows.'

Jill smiled at him.

'You don't know the half of it yet, do you?'

Jill looked closely at herself in the mirror. Thirty-one,
handsome if not beautiful, generous, good-humoured,
intelligent – on the whole, she thought, not a bad face.
Since her marriage to Ray at eighteen, her energies had
gone into keeping house and bringing up the two kids.
Sharon, just twelve and already expert at 'being difficult',
hadn't coped well since Ray had lost his job. How would
she deal with this new state of affairs? And how would
Ray fare as he swapped his overall for a pair of oven
gloves? Jill felt a stab of guilt as she brushed on a trace of
lipstick. Then trepidation. Nerves. Even fear. But most of
all, the thought of getting out and earning her own living
filled her with sheer exhilaration.

Ray was in the kitchen, elbow-deep in breakfast debris
when she came to kiss him goodbye.

'Take it easy,' he warned.

Jill grinned at him. 'You too.'

The kids rushed to the window to watch her go. She was
trying not to let it show, but as she walked briskly down
the road, she felt like a trapped bird that had finally

escaped from its cage.

Jill paused outside the factory gates. Lyne Electronics, the sign said. Women clattered past in twos and threes, laughing and gossiping, but as Jill stepped forward to join them, a screech of car brakes and a woman's voice yelling, 'Are you sick a' life or what, y'dozy cow!' drove her back on to the pavement. Jill's only impression was of a battered silver object, pulsating with red fur and loud music, disappearing round the corner of the building. Barely had she recovered when, from inside the factory, came the sound of a buzzer for the start of work. The moment had finally arrived. Oh well, let's give it a go, she thought, and, taking a deep breath, she walked in through the doors.

'Rex Buckley – Company Manager.'

And I bet you've no shortage of admirers, Jill thought to herself as she eyed up her new boss.

Young, self-confident, well-dressed, the merest suggestion of five o'clock-stubble, he seemed only too aware of his charms as he perched on the end of his desk to greet her.

'My assistant, Norma . . . '

Jill was vaguely aware of a rather mousy-looking creature, scrabbling about nervously amidst the filing.

'Now we tip you in at the deep end here, so if you'd like to go with Bernie, we'll see if we can't find you some work to do.'

Jill stood up. Her nerves had returned. It was one thing to tell yourself that going back to work after twelve years was no problem. Getting to grips with the job and new workmates was another matter entirely.

Bernie was beaming paternally at her and permitting himself the chivalrous gesture of holding open the door.

As they went out into the corridor, she was rather alarmed to find his arm creeping round her shoulders in a gesture which she thought took a bit too much for granted considering they had only known each other for ten minutes.

Bernie, it soon appeared, not only seemed to think well of himself and his own importance, but also of the company.

'Oh, you've come to the right shop here, love,' he was saying. 'We're out there in the forefront of British technological engineering. Skill, productivity, efficiency . . . we've got it all.'

Then leaning closely towards her and squeezing her shoulder confidentially, 'You see, Jill, what matters with us . . . is *people*. If *you're* happy, *we're* happy. And a happy workforce is a busy workforce.'

I can see what your game is, thought Jill, as she tried to edge herself out of his grip.

'Now, I don't know how you feel about all this union nonsense but round here we don't go in for it much. In fact, the only industrial action *we* believe in is you girls whamming them components into little holes!'

And he chuckled appreciatively at his own wit. Jill managed a feeble smile in return.

Now they were coming out on to the factory floor itself. She could see benches of blue-overalled women, heads down, beavering away at the soldering iron, glancing up, eyeing her as she passed, giggling, whispering between themselves.

'That's the way, girls,' Bernie beamed, swaggering slightly to remind Jill that she was in the presence of 'the management'. 'Just one big happy family . . . ' he assured Jill, and Jill would have had no reason to doubt it had she not suddenly been barged right off her feet. Glancing up at Bernie, she saw that his complacent smirk had been replaced by a slight puckering of the brows.

'Alright, alright lad, where's the fire?'

The figure before him seemed in no mood to give a straight answer.

'Hey, I know what you said, okay? Ignore it, forget it – I did and I have, but she's gone and done it this time, and *you* wanna try going over there, 'cos where d'you put your face, that's what I'm asking – y'know what I mean? And what is that, right? That is harassment, okay? That is embarrassing, and I don't need this aggro, right? And *she* wants locking up, she does, and I don't think it's fair . . . '

He paused only for lack of breath. Jill was struggling not to laugh. Here was this tall, crucially clad West Indian boy, trying desperately to hang on to his Eddie Murphy cool, and at the same time quivering with indignation.

'Are we talking about Queenie here?' ventured Bernie.

The very name seemed to throw the boy into another paroxysm of lip-trembling.

'Hey, I can do without this aggro – y'know what I mean?'

By now even Bernie seemed to be having difficulty in concealing his amusement. The boy was clearly desperate to have his woes taken seriously, and Jill suspected this wasn't by any means the first incident of its kind.

'Righty-ho, lad,' nodded Bernie, and with an expression of utmost gravity, pulled out a walkie-talkie from his top pocket.

'Bravo Foxtrot to Delta Golf. Come in please.' His tone was grave with urgency.

'Yeah, what's the problem, Bernie?' Rex's voice came back in reply.

'Bravo Foxtrot to Delta Golf – we have a problem here – request immediate attention. Repeat, immediate. Over.'

Considering they were only about thirty feet from Rex's office, Jill couldn't help feeling that the walkie-talkie was rather unnecessary. In fact she could see Rex quite clearly as he left his desk, brow creasing with slight weariness as he took his jacket off its peg.

Jill glimpsed the suddenly animated figure of Norma reaching for the office intercom mike. Next minute Norma's shrill tones were ringing out over the factory:

'Telephone call for Mrs Fox! Telephone call for Mrs Fox!'

Almost imperceptibly there was a bustle to work and a hum of anticipation from the factory floor. All eyes to see what would happen next, Jill watched as Rex, buttoning up his jacket, made his way down the corridor towards them.

Bernie nodded towards the boy, who was still twitching with nerves and indignation.

'What is it this time, Simon?' Rex's voice sounded very restrained.

'It's . . . pictures,' stammered the boy.

'Pictures?' Rex was waiting for further explanation.

'Hey, y'know what I mean? . . . ' He clearly couldn't bring himself to be more precise. '*Them* sort of pictures.'

Rex glanced at Bernie. The word 'Queenie' was mouthed in reply.

'Ah,' Rex nodded. That seemed to explain it.

'I think we'll have a little look, then, shall we, Simon?'

The suggestion seemed to electrify him.

'No, no, that's okay . . . why don't I just, y'know, like . . . forget about it, okay?'

But Rex was already off down the lines of benches, Bernie at his heels, Jill trailing behind, and Simon bringing up the rear wailing to anyone who would listen, 'Hey, we can sort it out. We don't need to see her . . . we can just forget about it.'

They had arrived at Simon's office. It didn't take long to trace the source of his distress: nude male pin-ups with a passport photograph of Simon's head had been stuck on to the glass partition wall.

Jill stifled a giggle. Simon was hovering behind Bernie, keeping his face hidden, trying to look unconcerned. Jill noticed the glint of amusement in Rex's eye as he examined the works of art more closely. Suddenly, from behind the pane of glass rose a head of peroxide-blonde hair, and the face of a woman appeared, mouth carved out in lurid red lipstick, grinning obscenely at Simon's discomfort. The woman seemed oddly familiar. It took

Jill two seconds to place her as the driver of the battered silver rust-heap of a car which had nearly carved her into the gutter.

'Mind, they're a bit warm and no mistake.' Bernie was flushed with embarrassment, struggling manfully to maintain his look of gravity.

'Not from where *I'm* stood, doll,' rang the retort, in broad Scouse accents, from the woman behind the glass.

'Hey Simon!' she goaded, catching sight of the boy trying to edge off into the cleaner's cupboard. 'How's that for beef an' two veg!' And she jabbed at one of the more well-endowed specimens of manhood which adorned the window-display.

This was too much for Simon. His mouth creased in dismay and he was about to flee down the corridor, when Rex decided things had gone far enough.

'Alright, Queenie, you've had your fun. We'll see these off, shall we, Simon?'

With horror Simon realised that *he* was expected to remove the offending articles. Queenie, glaring at him, gimlet-eyed, daring him to approach the pictures, ensured that he stood rooted to the spot.

It was Rex who came to the rescue.

'Let's see if we can find somewhere for these where they'll be better appreciated.'

He smiled urbanely at Jill, then calmly strolled over to the glass partition and removed the pictures.

'I don't think we want to give our new recruit the wrong impression, do we, Queenie?'

Jill thought she could detect a slight snarl twitch at the corner of Queenie's mouth, but the lady herself obviously knew better than to argue. Besides, there was that irresistible glint in Rex's eye which made even Jill catch her breath and feel that there would not be many on this factory floor who would be immune to his charms.

'Right, Bernie, we've wasted enough time. I think we'll start Jill off here, alright?'

11

He was standing by a bench of five women. An empty seat in the middle was soon eclipsed by the daunting presence of Queenie.

Jill's alarm increased as the six women eyed her with varying degrees of suspicion.

'Alright, ladies, I'll leave you to it.' Rex turned on his heels and headed back to the office, murmurs of appreciation from the floor gathering in his wake.

'Alright, girls – chop, chop.' It was back to business with Bernie. 'Let's show Jill why this company leads the field in modern technological expertise.'

Muffled snorts of scorn and derision greeted his solemn posturing. It was becoming clear to Jill that Bernie was by no means taken as seriously by others as he liked to take himself.

'Now, love, you'll be seeing a lot of me around.' His assurance was not entirely welcome. 'We go in for what we call "hands-on" management here . . .'

Jill was conscious of a flicker of wry laughter from the girls. ' . . . which means we like to keep ourselves "in touch" so to speak, with the shop floor.' And to emphasise the point, his hand was suddenly very much 'in touch' with her waist, which he proceeded to squeeze proprietorially.

'Now Pauline here will show you the ropes.'

'Oh will she?' came the indignant retort. 'Not till she's put on supervisor's grade with supervisor's wages she won't.'

This siren was a decidedly exotic creature: glossy jet-black hair (definitely dyed, Jill thought), crimped, waved and sprayed stiff, with eyebrows and mascara to match. She was rather plain, though it was hard to tell how plain beneath the lashings of lipstick and powder which caked her features. A square, not to say solid, figure had not prevented her from squeezing into fashions which had seen better days on figures half her age.

Jill could hardly decide who was the most fearsome – this Pauline, or Queenie.

12

'Never mind her. You sit here, love.'

At last a more welcoming tone, this belonging to a kindly looking woman, almost grey, who motioned her to sit beside her. Gratefully, Jill accepted.

'Right, then,' growled Bernie. 'I'll be keeping an eye on you.'

The girls clutched each other in mock-terror. Rattled, Bernie was wisely making his retreat.

'Don't think I don't know what goes on,' he muttered (though it was clear to everyone that he hadn't the remotest idea) and, clicking his stop-watch menacingly at them, he bustled off, Simon scuttling behind him.

Jill glanced round nervously at her new workmates. They seemed a formidable-looking lot, still suspicious, slightly hostile, even resentful.

'Right, lovey, here we are, I'm Sally.' The oldest member of the bench had decided to take the new girl under her wing. 'This is Donna . . . '

A trim, conservatively dressed woman of about thirty-six, plain but pleasant-looking, smiled warily at her.

'Carol May . . . '

This one was a revelation. She was obviously in her late forties, but Jill had seldom seen a more glamorous-looking woman: masses of blonde hair, the face of a woman ten years younger and the figure of a teenager. She seemed very aware of her attractiveness, but totally at ease with it, even amused by it. She nodded casually across at Jill.

'Pauline, of course . . . Queenie . . . '

'I think we've met,' Jill ventured, a slight edge to her voice.

'You wanna watch that step, girl. You might've knackered me motor,' came the reply, leaving Jill in no doubt about Queenie's view of her arrival at this bench.

'And this is Klepto . . . ' Sally resumed.

'I'm sorry?' Jill wasn't sure she'd heard correctly. Carol May casually slid her cigarette packet away from the straying fingers of the girl beside her.

13

'She's a great one for "borrowing,"' she explained charitably, leaving Jill to draw her own conclusions about the tiny, olive-skinned Greek girl whose enormous eyes gazed vacantly out at her.

Jill glanced round at her new workmates. She'd already forgotten half of their names, and that was *before* they started to explain about the bits of wire and coloured plastic strewn across her desk. It all looked impossibly difficult – and yet, here was Klepto, apparently without a thought between her ears, automatically slotting the tiny components into place on the circuit boards.

Not too old to learn a few new tricks, she thought as she watched Queenie pick up her soldering and set to work with a skill which belied her air of couldn't-care-less. Jill knew they were all watching her, waiting for her to make her first mistake.

'So . . . ' she ventured, tentatively, 'what's it like here, then?'

Queenie put down her soldering and glared across at her, eyes narrowed.

'Bernie's a soft-head, Simon's a toss-pot, Rex is whoever-gets-there-first-so-join-the-queue, the place is ten years outa date, run like a pig's tea party, the work's piss-easy and the canteen brew's gnat's. What else d'y'wanna know?'

'Oh . . . no . . . thanks,' Jill stammered. 'I think that's fine to be going on with.'

In Jill's living-room the goings-on were far from fine. Ray was standing in the middle of the floor about to embark on his first ever encounter with the Hoover. It had already taken him three-quarters of an hour to work out how to use it, and another half-hour before that to actually find it. Then he had recalled having once seen Jill put it somewhere under the stairs, so having finally tracked it to its lair, he now had the beast assembled and ready for its trial run. He was about to press the switch when he realised the

14

living-room curtains were open and that he was actually visible from the road. He drew the curtains to. It was bad enough to know he was hoovering without actually being caught in the act.

The phone rang. In the silence of the house, the noise made him jump.

'Hello? . . . '

A weary expression crossed his face. The voice on the other end seemed to go on forever.

'Yes, mam,' he sighed when the voice finally paused for breath.

'Of course I'm managing. What d'you think I am?'

He replaced the receiver. The house was suddenly silent again. Funny how he'd never thought of it being like this when Jill was at home. Somehow he had always assumed it was noisy and cheerful and full of non-stop gossip and tea-drinking, with maybe the odd five minutes in between to hang out the washing or iron the odd shirt. In fact this wasn't at all the lively scene he had pictured while he was still at work, bemoaning his lot, cursing the management, swearing he would swap places with Jill any time. He was cursing now alright. And wishing more than anything he could swap it all back again. He turned on the radio and the TV and the hoover. Anything was better than silence.

Jill was wondering whether she wouldn't prefer to be back in the kitchen, facing the agonising decision of whether to do steak pie or fish fingers for supper. Instead she was standing in the canteen queue, dithering between a teacake and a jam tart, and finally being elbowed out of the way by Simon, who had clearly decided to change tack and try his hand at being assertive. His efforts were shortlived. He was suddenly seized from behind and pressed down to within an inch of the hot-plates on the counter, where his puckered, woeful face was smothered in bright red kisses from a triumphant Queenie. Struggling free, he

15

shot off down the corridor towards Rex's office, scrubbing his cheeks and roaring for his cards, Queenie's raucous laughter still vibrating in his ears.

Jill had not had a good morning. She had ruined three circuit-boards, spilt two trays of components and soldered Pauline's earring to the bench. To make things worse, Queenie had watched her every mistake with glee, and as the buzzer went for lunch, had cheerfully assured her that she 'wouldn't last a week.' It can only get better, Jill assured herself as she joined the other girls at their table for lunch.

They were an odd bunch, she decided. Donna, primly eating her neat little sandwiches out of her Tupperware box; Pauline, self-righteously nibbling on a pair of unappetising slimming biscuits and sanctimoniuously detailing the calorie-content of everyone else's lunch. Then there was Klepto, her nose in a paperback romance, mechanically stuffing crisps into her mouth, while Carol May toyed with a salad and Sally drank tea from a flask.

Jill sat down, feeling slightly dejected. Without being deliberately hostile, the girls hadn't gone out of their way to welcome her; indeed she was still made to feel very much the outsider.

A tray groaning with food was slammed on to the table beside her, shocking her out of her reverie. She surveyed the contents with sheer amazement: fish, chips, peas, baked beans, sausage roll, toast . . . not to mention the sponge and custard, chocolate biscuit and tea.

'Off yer peck a bit, are you, love?' remarked Carol May without a flicker.

'I'm cutting down, girl. I'm worried I might wake up one day and find that Chunky's been squashed to death.'

The whole table shook with laughter and Jill wished for the courage to join in, but Queenie's glare swiftly changed her mind and she applied herself zealously to the cheese-and-pickle sandwich.

'Well, come on, then,' Pauline was protesting. 'Where are they?'

'Well, give us a chance to feed me face,' retorted Queenie through a mouthful of puff pastry, and she shovelled another great forkful into her mouth before pulling out a large shopping bag from under the table.

'Cheap at the price, girls,' she proclaimed, emptying out an assortment of Valentine cards on to the table.

'Fell off the back of a camel,' she whispered confidentially to Jill, then grabbing a card displaying a reclining nude male pin-up, she waved it across the table at Donna and chuckled, 'How's that for old Action man – Simple Simon? That'll stick a bit of glow in his cheeks!'

Donna flushed and looked away. Queenie was about to pursue her advantage when Carol May intervened.

'You missed a treat, on Saturday, Donna – went for a run in the "Flying Ashtray".'

'Oh aye, some treat,' Pauline sniffed. 'Gets to the end of the street, sodding copper books us.'

'What for this time? Eight in a car?'

'That or them furry dice constituting a mobile fire hazard.'

Jill was utterly baffled by all this talk, but no one seemed about to enlighten her.

'You should come out with us sometimes, Donna,' Sally was urging. 'It'd do you good.'

'Oh, I couldn't – not on Saturdays. Gordon has his organ club.'

Queenie snorted with derisive laughter, spraying toast-crumbs across the table.

'It's his hobby,' explained Donna, addressing Jill to be sure of a sympathetic audience. 'Where he works they've a fad on these . . . electric organs. So come Saturdays, we take it in turns to lay on the vol-au-vents while the fellers give organ recitals.'

'So . . . er . . . is he any good, then?' asked Jill politely. She really couldn't think what else to say.

'Good?' exploded Queenie. 'He's that friggin' good

he's been at it hammer, tongs, spanner and nails the last sixteen years, and never so much as a whiff of morning sickness!'

Donna rose, tearful. 'One fine day, Queenie, someone's gonna stick you in the ground . . . and drape a bag of cement over you.'

And with that she left the table and ran out of the canteen. It was obvious to Jill that a very raw nerve had been touched somewhere, but once again no one troubled to explain it to her and she didn't feel able to pursue the subject. Sally was glaring at Queenie in disapproval.

'Well,' she sneered, 'no wonder he frigs off on his organ with *that* gob sagging at him day and night.' But Sally's continued glare put a stop to any further remarks.

'Here, give us this one, then,' said Pauline, selecting a Valentine card from out of the pile.

'Y'givin' that your Frankie?' Queenie was wide-eyed in mock-surprise. 'Where's it's hammer and sickle?'

Pauline scowled back at her. The joke was not appreciated.

'Go on, I'll owe you for it,' said Carol May, choosing herself a card.

'What? – that for your Col? Or is there a secret admirer?'

'Chance would be a fine thing,' came Carol May's retort.

Jill had plucked up the courage to make her own selection.

'Cash,' insisted Queenie. 'On the nail.'

'Joke, though, isn't it, Valentine's Day?' Carol May's voice was bitter.

'Speak for yourself,' Pauline sniffed.

'And hark at that,' jeered Queenie, eager to find some target for her malice. 'He'd divorce you if he could wed that bloody Scargill he's so fond of.'

'So where's *your* offering, then?' demanded Pauline, stung. 'Or is Casanova in the doghouse this year?'

With great pomp and ceremony, Queenie brought out a

18

cardboard box at least two feet square and about three inches deep, lifting the lid to reveal a huge shiny satin-padded card, bedecked with fat cupids and love-birds.

'My God, it's a duvet!' Sally shrieked. 'You'll want a pillow-case for that, not a box.'

And in the screams of hilarity that followed, Jill noticed Klepto slip a card into her handbag and quietly go on with her reading.

'I don't know why *I'm* bothering,' Carol May was moaning. 'He'd not notice us if I rowed naked down the canal wrapped in boiled maggots and fishing wire. Correction . . . ' she paused. 'He'd notice the maggots.'

'Aaagh, you wanna give that dickhead the elbow, girl,' Queenie protested. 'We're wasted on 'em all, the bloody villians!'

'You married, are you, love?'

Jill realised with a start that Carol May was addressing her.

'Oh yeah,' she smiled shyly. 'Two kids.'

'Feller on the dole?'

'Does it show?' Jill had thought she'd made a good job of keeping *that* quiet.

'Oh, wake up, girl, what makes *you* different?' Queenie was merciless when she got going. 'Mind, it's the best career going for fellers round here. Least it's reliable.'

'Oh, I'm just stopping till he gets started again.' Jill was keen to assure her.

'You'll have a long wait, love,' Carol May looked grim. 'Most of this lot here were only coming till the fellers got signed off. They've been here friggin' years.'

'Aaagh, they love it, that's why.' It could only be Queenie. 'Gets you out of the house, your own wage, a good laugh, a gutful with the girls on Friday nights . . . the fellers don't know what they're missing.'

Jill looked glum. She suspected Ray knew exactly what he was missing – and that he wouldn't want to be missing it for very long. She took a sip of tea. It was cold, stewed, and her jam tart was stale.

It was almost dark when she closed the front door behind her, almost sinking into the doormat with exhaustion and relief. Not that it had been a physical strain, but the toll on her nerves made her feel positively geriatric. Now at last she could relax, wind down. A hot bath, a quiet chat with Ray and the kids over supper . . .

Supper. Some of the tension was already beginning to creep back. Through the crack in the kitchen door she could see the chip-pan spitting and crackling, Ray poking at it with a long-handled spoon as if anticipating an explosion. He's got it on too high, was her first thought, and immediately she bit back the words.

I haven't to interfere. That's *his* job now. And she opted instead for the living-room, where she was greeted by the sight of Sharon and Nicky, sitting sulking, aiming kicks at each other under the table. She had barely time to digest this performance when they both caught sight of her, sprang to their feet and volleyed her with a hail of complaints.

'Mam, he says I can't have tea at Darren's . . . '

'Mam, he says I can't watch Thundercats . . . '

'Mam, why can't we have a gerbil . . . ?'

Jill threw her hands up in submission.

'One at a time, will you?'

The din subsided. Jill noticed the table had been laid upside down. She was determined not to comment.

'So, how've you been?' she asked breezily.

Sharon scowled back.

'There's nowt for tea.'

'Why ever not?'

'It's in the bin.' Sharon was almost triumphant.

'It's been exterminated,' Nicky volunteered.

Further speculation was halted by the entrance of Ray, proudly bearing a supper tray and ordering them all to the table. Jill watched in mounting dismay as enormous heaps of mashed potato, baked beans, chips and burnt sausages were heaped on to plates and handed round. Sharon scowled silently, prodded a blackened chip with her fork

20

and pushed the plate away. Ray's bottom lip began to curl. Jill knew what was coming.

'Looks very nice, love,' she said hastily.

'Something wrong with the cooker,' he snarled.'Turn your back five minutes, the bloody food's cremated.'

'Perhaps you had it too high . . . ' Jill couldn't resist, but already she knew it was a mistake.

'You do your job, let me do mine, alright?' Ray certainly wasn't going to make this easy. For a while they ate in silence, the kids chasing the odd chip round the plate, Ray shovelling back his food with relish as if to prove that it really was edible.

'How've you been?' Jill ventured at last.

'Oh, it's a piece of piddle,' Ray boasted. 'Just needs a bit of organising.'

Beside him the kids had started jabbing each other with their forks. Ray wheeled round and cuffed them lightly across the ear. Jill was twitching to intervene but forced herself to stay silent. Another pause. More sulking, more scraping of knives on forks. Finally Jill could bear it no longer.

'Aren't you going to ask, then?'

Ray looked puzzled.

'How *I* went on?'

'Oh yeah . . . ' Ray had remembered. 'How d'you go on, then?'

'I coped alright.' And her voice was tinged with pride.

Ray seemed oblivious. 'Well, don't get too settled. It won't be long.'

Jill was about to retort when Ray darted across the table and cuffed Nicky round the ears. A prolonged wail went up. A burnt sausage was retrieved from under a chair.

'Me mam never hits us,' Nicky howled, rubbing his ear.

'No, well your mam was soft then, wasn't she?' his father retorted.

'She wasn't. She just didn't have a mard head on all the time.'

21

This latest from Sharon was guaranteed to send Ray's temper rocketing. Suddenly Jill found herself tapping Sharon across the hand.

'Less of that, young lady.'

'Eh! D'you mind?' Ray leapt in and gave both the kids a crack across the head. A fresh bout of wailing broke out.

'Are you satisfied now?' he snapped at Jill. Jill could hardly believe her ears.

'Can we have a bit of hush, please.' Her voice suddenly rose above the rest of the commotion. Silence fell. What had got into her? They all stared at her in disbelief.

'When I come in from work . . . what I would like . . . is a bit of peace.'

And to her own amazement, she found herself gathering up her dinner and stalking out into the kitchen.

Open-mouthed, Ray and the kids watched her go.

'What's got into her, then?'

Ray had his suspicions, but chose to keep them to himself, while he vented his frustrations on a second helping of mashed potato.

'By *my* watch I make it two minutes and forty-two seconds *before* lunch.'

Queenie slipped into her handbag the sausage roll she had been heating up on her soldering iron, and nonchalantly replaced it with a circuit-board. Bernie eyed her narrowly, his suspicions roused, but other than an impudent grin he had nothing to charge her with. He turned instead to Jill, who after two days of confusion and misery was just about getting to grips with her first piece of soldering.

'Alright, my love? Settling in?'

'Yes, thank you,' Jill assured him, stiffening as he gave her waist an encouraging tweak and strolled off to pester some other bench.

'Alright, then, who's for a quick bevy?' Queenie demanded, counting the seconds till lunchtime.

Jill excused herself hastily. She didn't drink at lunch-times (Ray would be appalled at the thought), and anyway she had a few errands to fetch down the market.

'While you're there, lovey, you couldn't stick us a couple of quid on Friday's 2.30 . . . ?'

Sally was already getting her purse out. Jill went cold with panic. Then she noticed the rest of the bench had fallen silent.

'Two quid?' Carol May was saying. 'What's running?'

'I've a fancy for that Magic Mushroom,' Sally replied. 'I don't expect it'll do much, but . . . ' She shrugged. 'You never know.'

Jill was dimly aware of a ripple of interest from the rest of the girls.

'*I* might just have a quid on while you're at it,' Carol May ventured, seemingly casual.

'Yeah . . . me too.' The same tone from Pauline.

'So that's four on Magic Mushroom,' said Queenie, putting in a pound of her own.

'Five,' came a voice from across the bench, and Klepto's coin found its way on to the pile.

By now Jill was starting to suspect a conspiracy, and when Donna added her money to the stake (greeted by howls of amazement from Queenie), Jill knew something was definitely afoot.

'Do yourself a favour, love,' Carol May whispered. 'Stick yourself a quid or two on.' Then, seeing Jill still rooted with bewilderment, 'She knows what she's talking about, love. If Sal says back it, get your purse out.'

Jill reluctantly slid her own pound coin into the ring.

I'd best not tell Ray about this, she thought.

'Well?'

She looked up. They were all watching her expectantly.

'I'm sorry?'

'You were gonna place the bet for us,' Carol May assured her. 'What's the problem?'

Jill shifted awkwardly in her seat. This was going to sound so ridiculous.

'I've never done a bet before,' she stammered. 'I don't know what you do.'

'Oh, whadder-yer-like, girl? Where've you been all yer life?'

Queenie shrieked in disbelief. It was inconceivable to her that everyone shouldn't be as intimately acquainted with the interior of a betting shop as she was.

'I'll come along with yer, eh? – so you'll know what to do next time.' She gathered up the stash of coins. 'We'll not be long, girls,' she assured them. 'We'll take the carriage.'

Jill's eyebrows rose in alarm. Did she mean that 'vehicle' – for want of a better description – which had almost ended her career before it had begun? That mobile heap of rust and fake fur which any sane person would have consigned to the scrap-heap decades before?

'In tests,' Carol May was musing, 'nine out of ten passengers who expressed a preference said they would rather be dead.'

Jill felt a lump stir in the pit of her stomach.

'In fact,' Pauline sniggered, 'by the end of the drive, most of them were.'

The buzzer went for lunch. Jill reluctantly rose from the bench.

'Enjoy your ride, love,' Pauline smiled maliciously.

Jill peered nervously through the haze of smoke at the dingy walls and the lists of names and figures. So this was what she had been missing all these years. She would quite happily forgo the pleasure now, except that Queenie had put her in charge of the stake ('I'll only blow it on ciggies otherwise'), so here she was standing in the queue, being stared at by rough-looking, unshaven types, trying to match the brazenness of her mentor in front who was leaning on the counter and flirting outrageously with one of the regulars.

'Just missed your Chunky in here,' the admirer was saying.

'Well, he'd better be a bloody apparition, then,' Queenie's voice resumed its usual shrill tones.

'I've left word with that Job Centre he's to come with a job or he's coming out in bruises.'

And with that, she snatched the money from Jill's grasp, thrust a hastily scribbled betting slip at the clerk and stormed out into the street.

By the time they reached the market, Queenie's temper had cooled to a low simmer. Jill, buying eggs and tomatoes at a nearby stall, glanced uneasily at this formidable woman who excited both her admiration and her dread. She had moved across to a rail of children's clothes and was regretting the price of a blouse in Sharon's size when Queenie appeared over her shoulder.

'Get it on tick, girl,' she ordered, tearing the blouse from Jill's hand and gesticulating to the stall-holder.

'Hey, Andy! – ten weeks at 50p a shout!'

Jill hastily retrieved the blouse.

'Oh, I couldn't,' she whispered. 'We've never borrowed. Ray doesn't believe in it.'

'Well, he better start if he believes in keeping a shirt on his back,' came the reply. 'Go'way, girl, it's not immoral – it's a sign you're well off.'

Jill looked unconvinced.

'Oh aye,' Queenie assured her. 'The richer you are, the bigger the debt they let you run up. That's *my* philosophy – you suit yourself.'

And Queenie was fluttering a filmy black negligee for Andy's valuation when she suddenly appeared to go rigid with rage.

'God help us,' she spluttered. 'I'll swing for that one fine day.' And flinging down the negligee, she hitched up her skirts and sprinted across to the pub opposite as fast as her four-inch heels would allow her.

Jill trailed behind her, mystified. All she had seen was a ratty-looking bull-terrier slink across the street carrying

25

what appeared to be a handbag in its mouth. Now what could be so sinister about that?

Jill caught up with Queenie on the threshold.

'Right,' she muttered, flinging open the doors and marching in.

Jill peered gingerly over her shoulder.

The apparition at the bar looked like a fugitive from the early sixties. Dressed from head to foot in grimy, studded leathers, hair greased back off his not-so-young forehead, sideburns bristling down almost to his chin, this ageing rocker stood with his back to the door, a roving hand each on the backsides of the women standing either side of him. It was then that Jill noticed the dog. It sat crouched at the feet of this vision-in-leather, snuffling what now appeared to be a pile of handbags, but, on looking up and sighting Queenie, it beat a hasty retreat under a nearby table, dragging its booty with it. Jill was aware that a hush had gradually fallen and that everyone in the bar was looking towards Queenie. Everyone except for the Easy Rider.

'Oh aye,' he was saying, 'They don't call us Travolta for nothing. You're looking at a major force on the dance-floors of the north-west. What I can't do with the Bee Gees isn't worth doing.'

And he grabbed one of the women round the waist, swept her backwards to the floor, tango-style . . . and came up to find the face of Queenie beaming down at him. His unfortunate partner soon found herself in a heap on the carpet.

'Oh, hello, love . . . ' he was smiling feebly.

Jill realised this must be the celebrated Chunky she had heard so maligned by Queenie at work.

'Nellie's keen on taking a few dancing lessons . . . at the right price, of course.'

Nellie, however, seemed keen only to get out of the way of Queenie's aproaching foot, while Queenie herself advanced menacingly on her partner.

'Why, if it's a lesson you're after, doll . . . '

'Now, Queenie . . . ' The landlord's voice was fraught with dread. 'We don't want any bother.'

'Oh, it's no bother,' she smiled sweetly. Then seizing Chunky by the lapels, 'Lesson One: How to get your arse round that Job Centre before I tan it to match your bloody liver!'

'I'll . . . just see me pint off, love,' Chunky dithered.

'Oh, I would . . . if I were you,' rejoined his mate. Then suddenly her voice rang out across the room. 'Eh, you! Get over here!'

Jill watched as the dog slunk reluctantly over to its mistress, who snatched a purse out of its mouth and cuffed it fiercely across the head.

'Catch,' she said, throwing the purse to Jill, who grasped it, bewildered, feeling it was oddly familiar. It was only when she opened it and found the photos of Ray and the kids that things began to fall into place . . .

Queenie meanwhile was bidding a tender farewell to her partner. 'I want you down that street before the last gobful gets behind your back teeth!'

And with that she stalked out. Jill, following behind, just caught the tail-end of Chunky's remark to the assembled company. 'That's *her* sorted, anyroad.'

Queenie froze in her tracks. Jill watched with mounting alarm as Queenie, curiously rummaging about in her shopping-bag, turned tail and strolled back into the pub. Jill followed in time to see Chunky turn to face Queenie with a look of horror – to be rewarded by a tender smile and a box of six free-range eggs upturned on his forehead. Boadicea then wiped her hands on his shirt, blew a kiss to the landlord and calmly strode out of the pub.

Minutes later they were swerving in and out of the traffic, mounting the kerb, ignoring red lights and generally proceeding in a manner quite normal by Queenie's unorthodox standards. As the car screeched into a U-turn

27

half-way down a dual carriageway, a sigh escaped Queenie.

'Oooh, I can't resist him, though – d'y'know what I mean?'

'Ye-es . . . ' replied Jill, dubiously.

Ray's day could not have been described as 'action-packed', though he was obviously trying to make up for it this evening by terrorising a floral polyester duvet-cover with a raging hot iron. Jill glanced up from her task in hand – getting Sharon to stand still while she let down the hem of last year's dress – to observe Ray's newly cultivated look of long-suffering self-righteousness. In a corner Nicky sat picking his nose and flicking the contents into the budgerigar's cage. The television droned away in the background. No one spoke. Finally Sharon flared up defiantly.

'I feel sick.'

Jill nudged her to keep quiet. She knew what was coming.

'Me tea was burnt.'

Sure enough, that did it. Ray snapped, slamming down the iron.

'It might well be burnt when I'm stuck before a stove all day, and madam there can't be bothered to bring home a box of eggs like she's asked.'

Jill looked guilty at her omission, but Ray was spoiling for a fight and she wasn't going to provoke him further by rising to the bait. The silence resumed. Nicky completed the excavations inside his nose and cast about for something else to dig at.

'Billy Smith had two hundred quid on today.'

'I beg your pardon?' Jill got the impression this was all for her benefit.

'He had a ninety quid gold chain, seventy quid tracksuit and forty quid trainers.'

'Good for him,' Jill snapped, stuffing another pin into the dress and, painfully, into the base of her thumb.

'When can *I* have forty quid trainers?' persisted her son.

'When they don't cost more than a tenner.'

Nicky curled his lip and proceeded to vent his disappointment on one of the sofa cushions.

'We never have nothing new here.'

'When I'm back at work, love . . . ' piped up Ray in his most cajoling voice.

Nicky refused to be pacified.

'There *is* no work.'

'There is an' all work,' Sharon butted in. 'Janice Gibb's dad says, yes there is, only people's too bone idle to go and get it.'

Jill, stung by this injustice, sprang to Ray's defence.

'You tell that Janice Gibb, if I see her dad, it won't just be his head that's buried in the sand.' And she tugged at Sharon to stop the girl from fidgeting while she drove another pin into the hem.

'Can't I have a new dress this once, dad?' Sharon's wheedling had an immediate effect.

'Ask your mam, love. She's in charge of purse-strings now.'

Jill was not gratified to have the onus of saying 'no' shifted solely on to her shoulders.

'You know we've no money at the moment . . . ' she began, but Sharon suddenly jumped down from the chair in a fit of weeping and turned on her.

'Why is there no money? There used to be money. It used to be nice here. I hate it now. I hate you . . . ' (this, to Jill) 'I hate everything.'

And with that she ran out of the room, slamming the door violently behind her.

'Come back here now!' Jill was livid.

'Leave her,' Ray was urging, this time more gently.

Then Nicky announced with an air of great importance, '*I* hate everything too,' and marched out with such dignity that Jill found herself struggling not to laugh. She succeeded without any difficulty when she saw Ray's smug expression.

'I hope they're not going to be like that *every* time I go to work.'

'Well, don't look at *me*, love,' he shrugged. 'If you can't stand the heat . . . '

'I know . . . ' she decided to pre-empt his moment of triumph. 'Get back in the kitchen.'

Friday morning already. As she stood in the cloakroom buttoning her overall, Jill could hardly believe she had survived almost a week. And tonight she would actually be taking home her first wage packet. Not that it was much of a wage packet. Nothing to make a song and dance about. And Ray would have a face down to the floor, of course – her doling out the housekeeping to *him*. And then it would have been nice to wipe the scowl off Sharon and Nicky's face with a bit of something . . . but 'bits of something' never came cheap, and anyway the money was spoken for before she had even opened the packet, so there it was . . .

It was Klepto who interrupted her musings. She had barged in, expecting to find the place empty. Now she was walking off, hanging her head, trying to evade Jill's scrutiny.

'What's up with your face?' Jill caught up with her.

'I walked into something.'

Carol May appeared behind them.

'Walked into your father's fists, I'll bet. He's too handy with them hooks of his.'

'I'm saying nowt,' protested the girl.

'You've no need with a bruise the size of a duck-egg bawling across your cheek at us.'

Carol May glanced at Jill. 'He wants locking up, he does.'

Now they were interrupted by squeals of laughter as Pauline clattered down the corridor, preening herself, while Queenie and Sally spluttered with mirth behind her.

'It's not the length of the barrel, it's the power of the shot!'

'Well, the dirty dachsund!' Queenie was shrieking.

Klepto perked up at the sight of the large Valentine card which Queenie and Sally were tossing between them.

'Who's it from? D'you know?' she asked.

Pauline flicked back her hair and smiled coyly. 'Let's just say I've got me suspicions.'

'Oh, go on, tell us.' Klepto was desperate to know.

'Oh, 'scuse me, love, I don't think I can,' she pouted, trying to sound mysterious.

By now the group had reached their bench. Jill listened to their snorts of laughter and delight, wishing for the courage to join in.

'Give us a look at what your Chunky's sent you.'

Pauline's reward was a bared set of fangs.

'Don't mention that little grub to me,' spat Queenie.

'Oh, don't tell me,' Donna remarked innocently as she joined the group. 'He's never forgot what day.'

'He's got six hours to buy up Interflora or he'll forgot what friggin' *year*!'

Now Klepto slid a card from her bag and slipped it on to the table. Pauline snatched it up.

'Hey, who's that from?'

Klepto giggled shyly. 'Don't know.'

Jill knew at once. It was the card she'd seen Klepto 'borrowing' on her first day at work, and now here was the poor girl sending it to herself. Jill smiled sympathetically.

'Well, he's got very nice handwriting, that's all I can say.'

Klepto blushed and retreated behind her fringe.

'Well?'

Pauline was standing over Carol May, arms folded.

'Who's it from, then?'

The envelope stood propped up, unopened at her bench. Carol May looked round, saw six pairs of eager and expectant eyes, and slowly tore open the seal. A cursory glance was all she permitted herself before tossing the card on to the bench where Pauline and Queenie fell upon it like a pair of vultures.

31

'Who's it from? Who's it from?' Klepto was dying to be told.

Queenie and Pauline exchanged a significant glance.

'Not her old man, that's for sure!'

'How d'you know?' Klepto's naivity was touching.

'You ever met her old man?' came Queenie's dry retort.

Now the arrival of Simon promised to furnish new entertainment. He approached sheepishly, face quivering with resentment.

Queenie leered obscenely at him.

'It wasn't funny,' he growled.

'What's that, lover?' Queenie was all innocence.

'You know,' he muttered.

'Nah, cross me heart.'

Simon began to falter. 'It wasn't you lot . . . that sent it?'

A shriek of delight went up from the girls.

'Oooh, has he got a secret admirer?'

'*I* know who it is – that what's-it-called? – just started in Dispatch . . . y'know . . . blond, blue eyes . . . well-upholstered . . . '

Queenie winked at him suggestively. Simon brightened at the thought.

'What, y'mean that Wendy?'

'No, Stan I think his name is,' Queenie replied, and Simon's bottom lip finally gave way as he was seen heading off towards Rex's office, calling out for his cards.

The sound of the buzzer heralded the arrival of Bernie, who bustled up, brandishing a clip-board and clicking his stopwatch.

'Right, girls – would you believe I'm about to make your day? Today at four o'clock . . . we shall have the pleasure of a visit from none other than . . . the Chairman himself.'

'Go'way, not old Smiler?' Queenie jeered. 'What's his game?'

'Mr Beachcroft,' corrected Bernie, 'will be dropping in

to check on our progress with the new order – and I'm sure you'll all want to give him something to beam about . . . '

'Fat chance,' grimaced Pauline. 'Last time *his* face cracked, the *Titanic* sunk.'

'So if I know you, you'll be setting yourselves some pretty impressive targets for the rest of the day . . . '

A volley of sarcasm greeted this remark, but Bernie was in a fine mood today and breezed ahead, undaunted.

'And to save you the bother . . . why don't *I* set them for you?'

His face shone as he adjusted the figures on the day's target counter, relishing their scowls of discontent. The welter of protest soon subsided as the girls realised their energies would be better spent trying to reach the ludicrously high targets Bernie had set them. Jill bit her lip. When the pressure was on they *all* had to pull their weight. That meant heads down, no chattering, no skiving and definitely no mistakes. It was going to be a long day.

By early afternoon the target counter had ground to a halt – and it wasn't from overwork. All over the factory floor, benches were sitting idle. Queenie was expounding loudly her theories of economic growth, while a very anxious Bernie buzzed about like a neurotic hornet, trying to call Rex on his walkie-talkie.

'Bravo Foxtrot to Delta Golf . . . come in Delta Golf . . . do you read me?'

'Loud and clear,' replied Rex, standing behind his left shoulder.

'Now what's happened?'

'We're out of chip caps again,' flustered Bernie, dreading the blame for what was becoming an all-too-familiar occurrence.

'Bloody typical,' Rex fumed. 'That'll really cheer Beachcroft up, won't it? Alright, get on to Supplies. Sharpish.'

And Rex strode back towards his office, while Bernie

scurried away in the opposite direction, pausing only to glare at the girls and assure them they'd be back to work before they knew it. Queenie knew better. It would be at least two hours before the new batch of components came through. She lit a cigarette. Carol May stood up.

'Alright, Pauline?'

Pauline nodded. Carol May pulled a small hold-all from under the bench, and together they headed off towards the cloakrooms.

'Stick us down for me ends at three!' Queenie called after them.

Jill watched, utterly bewildered, but she knew better than to expect an explanation. Now Sally, unfolding her paper, suddenly cried, 'Eh, up! – the 2.30!'

They all glanced up at the clock above. The time was 2.28.

'Go 'ead then, Magic Muffin!' roared Queenie.

'Magic what?' Sally stared at her in disbelief.

'Magic Muffin – five to two favourite.' Queenie spoke as if addressing a child. 'Remember?'

'No, Queenie . . . five to two favourite is Magic *Mushroom*.' A sudden hush fell on the group.

'Give us a look at that ticket.' Sally's expression was frosty.

'Magic *Muffin*. Fifty to one.'

Queenie stiffened. 'I don't believe it!' She turned on Jill. 'After all that, you've went and stuck it on the wrong one!'

Jill was horrified. 'Me?' she repeated.

'Too right it's you. Where else are you trying to stuff the blame?' Queenie's eyes were like screwdrivers, glaring into Jill's, daring her to deny it. In that moment Jill knew it was a test of wills between them – and that if she didn't back down, she would be landing herself with one very formidable enemy. She stood up.

'Excuse me,' she murmured, 'I must get a drink of water.'

'Hang on a minute, love . . . ' Sally called after her.

34

'Oh, leave her, eh?' Queenie sneered. 'When you're in the wrong it's as well to know it.'

Sally glared back at Queenie.

'I couldn't agree more.'

Jill sat down on the toilet lid and took a deep breath. No tears. She was determined to deny Queenie *that* satisfaction. But how she could face the rest of them? What would they think of her? Her mind rambled on, annoyed, confused, wounded, till at last she became aware of voices coming from the washbasin area.

'So d'you know, then? Who your card's from?' That was Carol May's voice.

'Well, let's say I've got a bloody good idea.'

That was definitely Pauline. Jill decided she'd better make a move out of the toilet, and she arrived at the washbasins in time to hear Pauline whisper the word 'Rex' to Carol May. The effect was astonishing. Carol May choked, her laugh became hysterical, her eyes widened in disbelief and she repeated the name several times to make sure she'd heard correctly.

'Yes, well, don't broadcast it,' Pauline snapped. 'And mind, it's to go no further. Alright?'

'Oh, I wouldn't dream of it, love,' Carol May assured her.

Jill meanwhile was staring in amazement at the scene before her. Ten minutes earlier this had surely been the ladies' toilets. Now it appeared to be a hairdressing salon. Spread out along the washstands were all the tools of the trade – shampoo, conditioner, hairspray, mousse, combs, scissors, even a hairdryer plugged in and the radio playing – while Pauline was enthroned before the mirrors, having her hair set by Carol May. It was Pauline who looked up and noticed Jill hovering diffidently behind them.

'Checking up on us, then?' she sneered.

'Oh, no . . . I'm just . . . ' Jill faltered, then the sight of the radio gave her an idea. 'You couldn't get the 2.30 on that, could you?'

Blank looks greeted this suggestion, then suddenly the penny dropped.

'The 2.30! Pass it here!' Carol May grabbed the transistor and tried to tune it to the station. It was a cheap radio and nothing could be heard above the crackle of interference.

'Come on, Magic Mushroom . . . '

'No . . . it's not.'

Carol May and Pauline turned to Jill.

'We put it on the wrong one.' She took a deep breath. 'We've backed Magic *Muffin*.'

There was a groan from Pauline. Another quid down the drain.

'And who's fault's that?' she snapped at Jill.

'Sssssssshhhhhh!' Carol May had found the racing commentary.

She turned it up as loud as she dared. The race was in its closing seconds.

' . . . and it's Magic Mushroom from Ptarmigan . . . Ptarmigan from Eager Beaver and Dog's Dinner . . . Dog's Dinner in fourth place and Magic Muffin coming up behind . . . and in the lead it's Magic Mushroom . . . and Magic Mushroom's down! . . . Magic Mushroom's over and Eager Beaver's gone with him . . . and it's Ptarmigan in the lead now from Magic Muffin . . . Magic Muffin's coming up on the inside . . . and Magic Muffin takes the lead . . . and it's Magic Muffin by a head from Ptarmigan and as they cross the line it's Dog's Dinner in third place . . . '

Carol May switched the radio off. The women gaped at each other in disbelief.

'It won.' Pauline was stunned.

Suddenly Jill's eyes widened further. With deliberate calm she announced, 'It was fifty to one.'

Carol May dropped her curling tongs with a clatter.

'Magic Muffin,' Jill repeated. 'It was fifty to one.'
And she turned round and walked out.

Pauline and Carol May were cavorting with glee like a pair of fourteen-year-olds when the boom of the tannoy put a stop to further celebrations.

'Telephone call for Mrs Fox! Telephone call for Mrs Fox.'

'Oh, bloody hell!'

Carol May swept her hand along the washstands and scooped all the paraphernalia into a bag, while Pauline was busy at the mirrors, frenziedly trying to arrange a headscarf across her curlers in the most artistic manner. Then they both scampered out of the toilets and tore back to the bench, overtaking Jill en route.

Jill was in a daze. All the events of the week and now this . . .

She could hear Pauline and Carol May go clattering past, hissing to the rest of the girls on the bench.

'It won! Magic Muffin! It's won! Fifty to one!'

Then she was vaguely aware of erupting jubilation, and a great deal of hugging, kissing and dancing in which no one took the trouble to involve her. Jill sat down, and almost immediately the jubilee subsided as Rex appeared, Bernie in tow. But instead of delivering the expected rebuke, he merely strode past without saying a word, leaving Bernie to deal them a glare and the reprimand.

'Don't think you can take it easy. We'll have the next supplies through in an hour . . .'

Queenie sniggered behind her hand. Bernie sensed a mood of mutiny, and wisely made his departure before he lost all credibility. Queenie could hardly restrain her delight.

'Right, girl.' She turned to Jill. 'That just gives you time to collect before old Beachcroft sticks his beak in.'

Jill stared at her.

'That's the score, doll,' Queenie assured her. 'B-Group rules – new girls always collect.' And she fluttered the betting-slip across the bench.

Jill was dumfounded. 'Now? In the middle of the shift?'

Sally was about to intervene when she appeared to suffer a blow to the knee from beneath the table. Queenie smiled encouragingly.

'We've hit a stand-still, pet – the timing's spot-on. Go 'ead, love, we'll cover for you.'

Jill looked round at her workmates. They were all watching her, not hostile, but daring her, egging her on. Suddenly a flash of defiance made her rise to the challenge. She looked Queenie resolutely in the face, then calmly picked up the betting-slip and walked out. On the bench, mouths dropped to well below knee-level.

It was one thing to stand outside the door, squinting narrowly through the smoke and gloom to where the clerk presided at his grubby counter. It was another matter entirely to venture alone into this den of villains, knowing she held the key to a haul of nearly four hundred pounds – in cash. Jill edged her way in, ignoring the whistles and sniggers, and made straight for the counter. The clerk scowled slightly as he took her ticket, then without a word, began to count out the money. Jill opened a large zipped shopping bag and shovelled the wads of notes inside.

She was running for the bus when an impulse made her head back to the market. Fifteen minutes later she was paying the conductor and flopping down, relieved, on the back seat of the bus. A bunch of chrysanths and several other packages bulged out of her shopping bag. She felt very pleased with herself.

Queenie frowned and glanced ruefully at Jill's empty seat. Now and again you made a mistake – and this one had been a real beaut.

Heads were down all over the factory, hands scrabbling to fit components, target counters clicking over at a lunatic rate. Someone had told them to look impressive and impressive had been the response. Except for B Group, missing one of its workers, now lagging miserably behind its targets and the rest of the shop floor.

'He'll crucify her,' Donna was muttering.

'Never mind *her* – he'll friggin' lash the backside off *us*!' Queenie hissed.

'Well, that's torn it,' Sally announced grimly, as Rex loomed into view, accompanied by Bernie, Norma . . . and Mr Beachcroft. The irony of his nickname – 'Smiler' – couldn't be missed. This man had the sourest expression imaginable. And it was making straight for their bench.

By curious coincidence, so was Jill. Except that Jill, buoyed by her success and the thought of a pleasant weekend ahead, was tripping nonchalantly along, humming cheerily to herself. She collided with Mr Beachcroft at precisely the moment when he was bending down to examine some new electrical fittings behind B Group's bench. Jill clambered to her feet unaided, while four pairs of hands sought to steady the might of Mr Beachcroft. Bernie swelled with indignation. His one thought was to be stern, and to be *seen* to be stern. He cleared his throat and rounded on Jill.

'And where d'you think *you've* been, then?'

Jill was lost for words. 'I've just been to . . . '

'And what've you been filling *that* with?'

He pointed to her bulging shopping bag. It occurred to him she might have been pilfering from factory supplies – though why anyone would want to steal circuit-boards or electrical components he didn't stop to consider.

Jill shot a glance across to the girls. They were frozen, speechless with horror. Even Queenie was struck dumb, staring at her like a deranged gargoyle. They could lose their jobs. If they were implicated in this fiasco . . .

'Alright, what's going on?' Rex could no longer trust Bernie to cope with the situation.

Jill looked straight at Queenie. 'The girls sent us out to fetch something.'

'Fetch what?' Rex's annoyance was mounting.

The girls could hardly believe their ears.

Jill unzipped her bag, and still looking straight at Queenie, slowly brought out the bunch of chrysanths. Then she turned to Mr Beachcroft. 'On behalf of everyone here I'd like to present you with a small token of our esteem and say what a privilege it is to work for such a friendly, caring company.'

And there was a touch of irony in her last words as she glanced at Queenie to make sure the message had sunk in.

Queenie, however, was not slow to recover. She sprang to her feet, winked at Jill and broke into rousing applause, while the rest of the bench, quick to catch on, joined in. Bernie was beside himself with rage. Such unadulterated cheek, such blatant disrespect for the chairman of the company . . . but what was happening? Miraculously, Mr Beachcroft had broken into a smile and was actually patting Jill on the shoulder.

'Thank you very much, my dear,' he growled. And then to Rex, 'You've obviously got a good bunch together here.' Rex smiled urbanely.

'Happy equals Productive,' murmured the chairman with approval. 'That's the way.' Then he turned back towards the canteen, muttering to Norma, 'Now where are those Custard Creams you were telling me about?'

Jill sat down at the bench. Rex and Bernie were hastening after the chairman as the girls sank back into their seats. No one spoke. Jill eyed them all in turn. Then she placed the shopping bag on the table and grinned.

'Fancy a run out tomorrow?'

Jill and Carol May were collecting their coats. It was

astonishing to see how relations could change in the course of an afternoon.

'Where are you going?'

Jill felt she had the upper hand now. She could afford not to seem too eager.

'It'll be a surprise. You'll enjoy it, though,' Carol May assured her. 'We're all going – bar Donna.'

'Oh, we don't bother asking Miss Prim.' Queenie had just joined them. 'She's too busy with her vol-au-vent recitals.'

It was lightly said, but something in the tone told Jill she was now 'one of the girls', entitled to join in all the intrigues and rivalries of the 'inner circle'. She was flattered. It felt good to be involved. She was tempted to go with them tomorrow, but then there was Ray . . .

She hadn't given much thought to Ray at all recently. Somehow he didn't fit in too well with the picture of general joyriding and merrymaking.

'I don't know . . . I'd best not. Ray likes us at home.'

'Your loss, doll.' Queenie shook her head. 'Okay, who's for a lift?'

Jill hastily declined.

'How's he coping?' Carol May enquired, as she and Jill walked through the factory gates together.

'Oh God, don't ask,' Jill laughed. 'He keeps setting fire to things.'

'And you've been here a week? Be glad your home's not a pile of ashes by now!' Carol May smiled. 'I'll see you next week, love.'

There were three fire engines and two police cars. It was obviously a huge fire, Jill thought, as they screeched past her and turned the corner into her street. Her street. Her blood ran cold. She broke into a run. Rounding the corner, she turned sick at the sight of a barrage of blue

41

lights flashing outside her house. Sheer terror gripped her as she stumbled into the arms of the young police constable who was barring her way.

'Can't go in there, love.'

'I live there,' Jill sobbed.

A police sergeant came forward.

'Where are they? What's happened?' Sheer panic had made her hysterical. Suddenly she was weeping with relief as Ray appeared with the kids at his heels, all three eagerly watching as an elderly woman was wheeled out of the house next door.

'Alright, Mrs Skeggs?' Ray was shouting. 'Your daughter's on her way.'

'She's had a nasty fright,' said a fireman to Ray. 'It could've been worse, though. They're real buggers, these chip-pan fires . . . '

Ray suddenly caught sight of Jill's face and grinned. 'Alright, love? Bit of excitement we've had.'

Jill burst into tears. 'I thought . . . '

'What? It was *us* gone up in smoke?' Ray was scornful. 'We can cope on our own, y'know.'

Jill followed him up the path into the house. The kids had run on ahead. Obviously something more engrossing was going on than the mere fact of *her* arrival. In the kitchen Ray was defrosting four ready-meals while the kids sat glued to the TV in the next room.

'Knives and forks, plates out!' Ray called through to Nicky.

'Aw, dad . . . it's a good bit.'

'Do it!' came the reply.

Nicky's head appeared round the door. 'Two chocolate eggs and a can of pop?'

'You're on.'

Jill could scarcely credit her senses. 'Two *what*?' she demanded.

42

' 'Scuse me, love.' Ray bustled past on his way to the microwave.

'Oh, brill, Dad,' Sharon enthused, coming in and opening a bag of crisps.

Jill was about to snap at her for spoiling her appetite when she realised that Sharon was wearing a new jumper.

'Where d'you get *that* from?'

'Me Dad bought it,' Sharon looked smug.

'D'y'like me new socks, Mam?' Nicky rolled up his trousers so that Jill could appreciate the full effect.

'Me Dad says we can have videos tonight,' Sharon announced. 'It's good with me Dad at home.'

This was getting beyond a joke. Jill rounded on Ray. 'What is going on?'

'We're doing nicely, thanks.'

'Oh, I can see that,' Jill snapped.

'Did *you* get us anything, Mam?' Sharon goaded.

Jill paused. 'Well, I did, as a matter of fact.'

She reached for her bag. Suddenly Sharon and Nicky were remarkably alert. Jill retrieved two bags and gave one to Sharon. She fingered it, slightly sceptical, then peered inside. Her face lit up.

'Aw, Mam – brilliant!' And she rushed upstairs to try on her new dress. Nicky was wide-eyed with anticipation.

'Is it, Mam? Is it what I asked for?'

Jill threw him the package.

'It is! It's what I wanted!' and he sped out of the back door, roaring into next door's garden. 'I've got 'em. She got us me trainers!'

Now it was Ray's turn to protest. 'Where the bloody hell did those spring from?'

Jill smiled at him. 'You're not the only one that gets to play Santa Claus.'

'And where do *I* come in?'

'That's yours.' Jill was trying not to smile. 'There's your housekeeping.'

Ray stared at the notes on the table. 'How am I supposed to make ends meet on that?'

'The same way that *I* did.'

Ray was silent. Jill felt a rush of sympathy. It was murder for him, this reversal of roles. She sidled up to him.

'I see you forgot what day it is.'

'No.' He looked guilty, then: 'What day *is* it?'

Jill took an envelope out of her bag. Ray peered inside and pulled out a Valentine card. He looked sheepish.

'Well, read it.'

Jill watched as two ten pound notes fell out on to the table. 'It's a present. Come on, you can buy us a Babycham.'

Ray stared at her, uncomprehending. 'Yeah, but hang about . . . you don't come home with this much.'

'*I* don't,' Jill grinned. 'But Magic Muffin did.'

Jill put her bedside light out and slid her arm round Ray's waist.

To her disappointment he was almost asleep. She kissed the back of his neck. He turned round, surprised to find her still awake.

''Owt on tomorrow?' he murmured drowsily.

'No . . . ' Jill hesitated. 'Well, the girls *did* ask us . . . ' He was starting to frown. 'But I said I'd stop in with you.'

Ray was pleased with his small triumph. 'You'll not miss much.'

Jill wasn't quite convinced.

'Where are they off, then? Anything special?'

'Oh no . . . ' Jill turned over. 'Probably just tea and a natter . . . '

The noise was deafening. The crowd baying, seemed to sense blood. Grown men screamed, small boys grimaced and frail pensioners shook their fists. As usual, Carol May looked immaculate. Not for her this frenzied, unseemly behaviour. In the next seat along, Klepto was stuffing her fingers into her mouth, while Pauline clenched her teeth and Queenie hissed. A shout went up and Sally was on her feet shouting, 'Get stuck in, lad! Go on, bite his ear off!' Then the crowd erupted once more and nothing could be heard except the muffled grunts and the referee's voice counting, 'One-A, Two-A, Three-A . . . ' And then the bell.

CHAPTER TWO

March

Pauline stood sideways in front of a full-length mirror and breathed in. She would definitely be sending this girdle back. When you shelled out that sort of money, you didn't expect to find half your waistline bulging out over the seams. She turned up the tape and resumed what she liked to describe as her 'work-out', though it amounted to little more than bouncing up and down, rotating her wrists in time to the music, and exhaling strenuously in accordance with the instructor's voice. The major effort, however, was reserved for pouting at her reflection, and constantly changing position to see which angle flattered her most. Now she broke into a fit of 'aerobic breathing', attempted a press-up, and finally leapt on to the scales. The message was not good.

A boy of about sixteen, bleary-eyed and squinting, poked his head round the door.

'Me dad's just phoned.'

Pauline turned down the music.

'He says to tell yer he's called a union meeting round here for eight and there's to be beer and fish paste butties.'

Pauline pursed her lips in disgust.

'We don't have paste in this house. We have pâté.'

And she laid the stress on the second syllable. The boy seemed somewhat bewildered by the distinction.

'There's boxes come an' all.'

Pauline perked visibly at the news. 'High time, too. You can shift them up here later . . . and Darren . . . ' The boy was about to drift out again. ' . . . Don't tell yer dad, d'you hear? It's a surprise.'

Darren nodded sleepily and wandered off, presumably back to bed. Pauline teased out her first lock of hair and attacked it with a curling tong.

'Lyne Electronics, good morning . . . '

Norma handed the phone to Rex.

'It's them,' she whispered, handing over the receiver.

Rex's voice was steady, but anyone who knew him would see he was unusually tense this morning. Bernie was biting his nails. Norma started to polish the leaves of the rubber plant. The tension seemed to be catching.

Rex replaced the receiver. Norma and Bernie looked at him expectantly. He grinned and gave the thumbs-up sign.

The 'Flying Ashtray' screeched to a halt halfway up the bumper of the car in front. Queenie leaned out of the window shrieking like a banshee.

'Try letting yer Guide Dog drive, you dozy bugger!'

In the back seat, Jill closed her eyes and shuddered. It had been six weeks now, and she hadn't got used to Queenie's style of driving. To cover her mounting nerves she leaned across to Carol May in the passenger seat.

'D'you hear there's jobs going down the soap works? I might give Ray the nod.'

'He's had that, love,' came the reply. 'They're only taking women – and them just skivvies.'

'That's saved telling him,' Queenie smirked.

'How d'you mean?'

Jill knew exactly what she meant.

'You. Stopping here.'

'Oh, he doesn't mind me working now. He likes being at home.'

Queenie and Carol May exchanged a knowing glance. Well, if that was her story . . .

Suddenly Queenie erupted in a snort of derision.

'My God, what's *that* done up like a ninepenny rabbit!'

The object of her scorn soon loomed into the view, sporting leg-warmers and a skirt perched nervously, midway up her thigh. 'I don't know what's got into *her* with her big ideas,' Queenie scoffed. 'No sugar, no caffeine, friggin' leotards . . . she'll be drinking that fizzy water next.'

And she treated Pauline to a blast of her car horn, which left the skirt riding higher on the thigh and its wearer's pulse-rate rocketing towards the ton.

'Don't tell me. You want something that bit different, right?'

Donna knew it had been a mistake. When Pauline had her catalogue out, you kept your head down and your attention elsewhere, otherwise you were swiftly drawn into the net, release being obtained only at the cost of some heavy-duty purchasing.

'Just that cut above to sit on the side an bring a bit of class to the place? . . . Well, what can I say? I mean, *me*, I'm *always* gonna say FG54638.'

Donna's jawed dropped.

'Er . . . what *is* it?

Pauline looked at her in amazement. 'It's a Tudor brass filigree after-dinner mints holder.'

'Ah . . . ' Donna nodded in what she hoped resembled admiration.

''Course, it can be an acquired taste . . . but once you've got one, you wonder how you'd ever done without.'

Incredibly, Donna actually seemed immune to the magnetism of this particular item. Pauline sniffed haughtily. Some people's taste left a lot to be desired. She leaned across and ventured to entice Sally into a minor spending spree.

* * *

'Alright, ladies, we are now talking Big Time! We are talking New Frontiers in British Component assembly.'

The entire bench bristled to the chirp in Bernie's voice. Obviously a new order had just been clinched.

'Right Simon, get them little beauties dished out.'

Simon unloaded the trays of new components. The girls eyed them with suspicion.

'What we making?' Pauline demanded.

'Never you mind about that. All you need to know is from now on we'll be supplying to some pretty important people.'

'They must have money to burn, come crawling to *this* dive.' Queenie's faith in the company was touching.

'And meanwhile, yours truly will be on hand to make sure there's no temptation to nod off or overwork the old jaws. In other words . . . ' Bernie paused for effect. 'We want this order out by the end of the week.'

Howls of protest broke out. Bernie draped his arm round Pauline and muttered confidentially. 'And . . . er . . . perhaps I shouldn't be saying this . . . but we've had word there's a nice surprise in the offing if we meet these new targets.'

'And if we don't . . . ?'

'Let's just say that in that case we might have to find a change of scenery for some of you . . . '

Mutinous murmurs began to rise.

'Well, let's not get left at the "Off", shall we? Let's show them what this set-up's made of.' And patting Simon on the head, 'You keep those supplies pouring in. They'll be through 'em at a rate of decibels this week.' He beamed at them. 'Bloody decibels.'

'Jesus, we've earned a brew this morning. I'm dry as a buzzard's jock-strap.'

Queenie reached for a second mug and tossed back an extra teacake to replenish her strength. What was the big idea, setting such ludicrous targets? This place was in serious danger of losing its reputation as a 'holiday camp.'

Jill was grateful for the stiff April breeze as she wandered round the side of the factory, sipping her tea. The girls often came out here in summer – it was a sun-trap, and its view over the surrounding landscape was worth a second glance, even to the most jaded viewer. Steel and concrete vied for prominence beside slate and sandstone; past and present merging amid the rolling contours of the Pennine foothills; new growth springing from decay, and bold new ventures, scuppered by misfortune or mismanagement, falling into disrepair and back into decay again. It was a good place to get away from the claustrophobia of the factory floor. Now it seemed as if someone else had had the same idea. Jill glanced up to see Sally sitting on a low wall a few feet ahead, completely engrossed by some cards on her lap. She strolled across and looked over her shoulder.

'Secret admirers?'

Jill's voice had startled, but Sally's eyes welcomed her.

'To tell you the truth, it's birthday cards,' she grinned. 'Fifty-eight today.'

'Well, you've kept that quiet,' Jill teased her. 'Mind you, who needs reminding these days?' She sat down beside her. 'Let's have a look, then.'

Sally seemed to shift uneasily as Jill flicked through the birthday greetings.

'To Mam . . . To a dear friend . . . To Auntie Sal . . . To Nana on her 63rd birthday with love from Jamie and Kelly . . .'

Jill looked up, puzzled. Her eyes met Sally's. 'To Nana on her 63rd . . .'

Jill gathered up the cards and handed them back. 'I didn't realise you had grandchildren,' she said hastily.

'In Bournemouth.'

'You'll not see so much of them.'

'Not since Ralph shifted himself upstairs last year.'

Jill was very slow today. It took her two sips of tea to remember that Ralph was the husband who'd passed away last year.

50

'Oh . . . I'm sorry,' she mumbled.

'Oh, don't *you* be.' Sally patted her hand. 'He's a great one for skiving, that bugger. Now he's skived off up there he'll have Peter and Paul to skivvy for him instead of me.' She paused a moment.

'Mind, you can't help but miss it sometimes. Great gawnin' gap in the bed where his back-end used to be. I met him over there, y'know.'

She nodded across the landscape to where the crumbling façade of an old factory lingered in the final stages of dereliction. 'Oh aye, courted, wed, worked . . . *and* scooped a tidy lungful of asbestos every time you breathed.'

The thought seemed to amuse her.

''Course, you never had your Safety Regulations in them days. Mind, you never had much doings down the Dole Office neither. You fell over work round here once. Turn forty-five now, you're classed as senile. You keep young while you can, love. You're sold for scrap soon enough.'

It was said without a trace of sentimentality or bitterness.

Jill was quite unequal to a reply.

'And how's that feller of yours managing?'

Sally had sensed her discomfort.

'Oh . . . he's fine. Well, you know what it's like . . . you just get on with it.'

'That's the way,' Sally rejoined, but as they grinned at one another, both were wishing it could all be as simple as that.

'Alright, Ray! Still the man of leisure, eh?'

Sharon and Nicky took advantage of the distraction to stuff a couple of chocolate bars into each pocket. Ray smiled wearily as he recognised his former workmate Noz, and tried to look as if he were perfectly at ease with a shopping list, a supermarket trolley and a pair of roving kids.

51

'Seen this?' Noz sniggered to the simpering female beside him.

'Sends his poor wife out to work while he sticks his feet up.'

Noz peeled open a can of beer and toasted Ray. 'Cheers, mate. You take it easy while you can.'

And he piled another tray of cans into the arms of his companion and headed for the check-out.

Ray turned bitterly to his shopping list again. Cheese, ham, bacon . . . he was heading for the delicatessen counter when a trolley collided with his shins and an old lady smiled up at him.

'You don't mind me pushing in? I only want a couple of trotters.'

Ray smiled back feebly.

It was difficult to decide which was the most frustrating. Norma bashed irritably away at the typewriter. Was it people thinking that all secretaries were half-wits and treating you accordingly? Or people knowing that you weren't one, but still behaving as if you were? She hammered out the words 'Yours sincerely.' It was definitely the latter. Rex knew full well she was capable of running this office – as evidenced by the fact that she *did* run this office – but when the mood was on him, he would persist in crediting her with the intelligence of a pea-hen. Take now, for instance. Considering that the 'Personnel' file was her speciality, it was reasonable to think she could have something useful to offer to this morning's discussion.

But no, here she was, banished to the corner with a tray of audio-typing, while the debate was left to Rex – and Bernie, of all people. It was even more irritating not even to be able to *hear* what was being said. She really ought to be allowed the consolation of ear-wigging . . .

She quietly slid her audio head-set off and continued typing. That was a great improvement.

'Oh, no question – we've some useful hands among that last lot we took on,' Rex was saying.

'Oh, very useful . . . '

Bernie never had an opinion, Norma noted. His function was simply to agree.

'No, it's excellent . . . '

There he was, nodding again.

'But whichever way you look at it we need to do better. We've fifteen or twenty here not pulling their weight. They've got to go – simple as that.'

In the corner, the typing faltered momentarily.

'We're in a different league now, Bernie – and some of them still think it's Sunday knockabout. The question is . . . ' He was flicking through the latest sets of production figures ' . . . where to get the early baths in.'

'Oh, well, now . . . where? . . . I mean, . . . there's the question.'

Bernie had his usual fund of wisdom to offer.

'Never easy seeing of the Dead Wood Brigade,' Rex frowned.

'However . . . no point in hanging on, eh? Norma?'

His change of tone made her jump.

'Did you get me those Personnel files out?'

Norma flustered across with the papers.

'Right, then, let's see who we've got here . . . '

The eyes were wide, staring, almost manic. Pauline was battling to fix on a false eyelash, the crowning glory of a face which was now a cosmetic triumph against adversity. Emptying almost a whole can of lacquer on to the stiffened crests of her hair, she peeled off the homely quilted housecoat to reveal a tight-fitting, low-backed gown in mauve-pink Lycra.

'Oh yes, definitely . . . ' she preened, rippling with satisfaction. The next moment she froze. A door had opened down below, raised voices burst forth . . . and footsteps were definitely coming upstairs.

In one sweep she whisked the entire contents of the dressing-table top into a drawer, covered them with clothes, and, buttoning up the housecoat to its neck, gingerly opened the bedroom door.

'Where's yer bog, love?'

Pauline bridled in distaste. It was one of Frankie's union pals.

'The *lavatory* is across there.'

She shut the door on this uncouth specimen and resumed her elaborate preparations. A dowdy headscarf was fastened in place across the lacquered locks, the four-inch stilettos were replaced by a pair of mules, and the entire outfit concealed beneath an unimposing rain-mac.

The door to the living-room was still slightly ajar, and as Pauline crept downstairs she could see through the haze of smoke and the debris of beer-cans, the presiding figure of her husband Frankie, holding forth in his best table-thumping manner.

'And what I'm saying, comrades, is that our rights are being seriously undermined . . . by management providing, what is in effect, a smaller plastic cup for us to drink our tea out of . . . '

'I'm just off round me mam's, love . . . '

Pauline poked as little as possible of her head round the door.

'Well, don't stop till all hours,' growled her spouse. 'Eh! . . . and don't talk to no one on the bus!'

'I wouldn't dream of it, love.'

Pauline sighed with relief as she shut the door behind her. By the front gate she stopped, glanced nervously back at the house, then slipping on her stilettos, flung the mules under a bush by the wall. Out on the street now, she tore off the headscarf, and fluffing up her curls, ran to meet the taxi which stood waiting at the corner.

Jill sometimes wondered if she was in the wrong house. Surely she wasn't mistaken. Hadn't they used to do things like *talk* to each other, eat meals at the proper time, in the proper place, take an interest in one another's affairs . . . ?

But here was Ray, flat out in an armchair, nose in the paper, while Sharon and Nicky sat gawping at the box, dining out of a large bag of toffees strewn across the floor between them.

'Right, you lot! That's it. Teeth cleaned and time for bed!'

'Me Dad says we can stop up . . .'

Jill was in no mood to discuss it.

'Both of you. Bed. Now.'

They rose to their feet, scowling at the kill-joy and stamped upstairs to bed. Jill waited for Ray to speak. It was soon clear she could still be waiting next morning.

'What you reading?'

Ray looked at her with impatience. 'Jackanory.'

'Y'what?' She wasn't in the mood for riddles.

Ray turned the paper round for her inspection. Her face fell.

'I thought you didn't mind stopping home.'

Ray resumed his scrutiny of the Jobs column. 'You thought wrong, then.'

The taxi drew up just after midnight. The woman paid and was trying to tiptoe across the road when her heel caught in a grid and sent her plunging into the gutter. The taxi-driver sniggered as he drove off. *She'd* had a fair few tonight, he wouldn't mind betting.

Now she was grovelling under a bush, scrabbling to find something. 'Oh, bloody hell,' she cursed under her breath, and, fumbling with the doorkey, let herself into the house. In the darkened hall she took off her heels and examined herself in the mirror. The hair had long since lost its bounce and the make-up now looked worn and garish. But the sight which made her stiffen with horror was the appearance, just beneath her throat, of a large purplish love-bite.

She fell upon it with her foundation stick. Still faintly visible. It was polo-neck time tomorrow, but as for tonight . . .

'What the hell time d'you call this!' Frankie's voice bellowed out in the darkness.

'I missed the last bus,' came the feeble reply.

'Get up here now! And you can fetch us up those indigestion tablets while you're there.'

Pauline grimaced. Not only had she to face the music over her late return, there was also the operatic performance of Frankie's unsettled stomach to serenade her towards the morning.

The dark-windowed limousine pulled away from the factory gates and sped off down the road. Queenie, Klepto and Sally watched it go with mounting suspicion.

'Perhaps it's Fergie,' Klepto ventured.

'You can bet it's that villain Smiler up to some tricks,' Queenie muttered darkly.

Norma was hoping to slide past unnoticed when Queenie turned and pounced on her.

'Alright, spill the beans, girl. Who's he got sneckin' around that we should know about.'

'I've no idea,' flustered the girl.

'Well, I can recommend you *get* some idea, or I wouldn't care to be you when we find out.'

Norma was backing off, sizing up her escape routes.

'Give over, girl,' Queenie persisted. 'Rex must know. Do his desk over – have his case out. It's in your own interest.'

'Is it?'

'Oh, too right, girl.' Queenie smiled ominously. 'I guarantee it.'

Rex stood at the corner of the bench, arms folded. A revolution seemed to have occurred. Right across the factory floor, target counters were clicking round at a dizzy pace. Complaints from the girls that they'd never been made to work so hard were – for once – the absolute truth, and some of them were wilting visibly under the strain.

Queenie, surprisingly, was not one of them. Nor, in fact, was Jill. Both girls were performing remarkably well under the pressure, but the same could not be said for Sally. Many times did the fingers falter and the brow contract with worry.

Rex shook his head and frowned. 'Er . . . Pauline?'

The black lashes fluttered coyly.

'A word in the office if you don't mind.'

Pauline rose triumphantly. This would fuel suspicion. After all, she was a very attractive woman, and what if the man *was* barely thirty . . . ? She drew in her cheeks and caught her breath. This could be it. After that Valentine, he was finally going to declare himself.

'Sit down, Pauline.'

Not a very promising start. Rex was looking irritable.

'I wonder what you think's goin' on out there.'

Pauline simpered at him beneath veiled lids. 'Going on?'

'That bench of yours. D'you know how far behind targets you are?' What had this got to do with his passion for her? Pauline wondered.

'I can see you're not interested in bonuses – not on this sort of productivity . . . so I'm starting to think we've got the combination wrong . . . '

To hell with combinations, just ask me out, Pauline was thinking.

' . . . and whether we wouldn't get better results if we split you all up and put you on other groups.'

Pauline's jaw sank. What was he saying? 'Split us up?'

'I don't run a rest-home, Pauline. I've a customer waiting at the end of the week. And if these results don't improve dramatically . . . '

'But we don't want to go to other groups,' Pauline had finally flipped. 'You can't make us sit where we don't want! I'll have the union on to you!'

'I think you'll find the union doesn't exist *solely* for the purpose of making work one big skive.'

Pauline leapt to her feet. 'Well, that's what you think.'

'I don't want to go on other groups,' Klepto was wailing.

'Give over! We'll friggin' lash 'em with the union,' Queenie bristled.

'Contrary to some people's opinion, the union doesn't exist solely for the purpose of making work one big skive,' Pauline retorted pompously.

'Well, it's news to me, girl.' Queenie was indignant. 'What else do I cough up me dues for?'

'Chin up, Sal. They'll never do it.'

Sally was looking very down-in-the-mouth. Carol May waxed indignant.

'What's up with this place? Time was you drew a cushy wage, a good laugh and a decent kip round here. Now it's getting on for bloody Siberia.'

'Yeah, well, friggin' Mata Hari better sneck out something sharpish, before we *all* come down with chill blains.'

And Queenie prodded fiercely at her soldering as Bernie loomed across, clicking his stopwatch and declaring smugly,

'Now then, we'll soon see how much you lot want to stay together.'

The briefcase was open on Rex's desk, but the man himself seemed in no hurry to depart.

'How am I going to sneak a look if he stops here all lunchtime?' Norma thought.

'You get off to the canteen, Norma. I'll see to it here.'

That was it, then. No undercover stuff today. The

58

thought of Queenie's wrath filled her with dismay. Reluctantly, she collected her purse and went out.

Rex waited for the door to close, then picked up the phone.

'Hello? . . . hello, Princess, is mummy there?' In the pause that followed, Rex bit his lip, and a look suspiciously akin to guilt crossed his face.

'Stella . . . look, love, I'm going to be late . . . yeah, another bloody meeting . . . some Health and Safety business . . . '

Behind him the door opened and Norma crept back to retrieve a conveniently forgotten cardigan.

'Don't wait up for me, love . . . you know how they go on . . . '

Rex replaced the receiver. He looked less than satisfied with his performance.

'Just come for a cardie . . . ' Norma tried not to look the picture of guilt.

'Here.' Rex threw her the keys. 'You may as well lock up while you're at it.' And taking his briefcase and jacket, he strode out of the office. Norma watched him go, then made a beeline for the appointments diary. Here it was . . . Wednesday, 25th . . . But where was the meeting? The page was conspicuously blank. Norma raised her eyebrows and closed the book.

Sally sat hunched over her mid-afternoon cup of tea. It was really getting to her, this pressure of work. Suddenly she was starting to feel her age . . .

'You're wanted in the office.' It was Bernie whispering confidentially. Sally looked worried. 'Sharp as you can now.' And he ushered her out of her seat.

Jill and Queenie, approaching with their trays, watched her go with puzzled looks.

* * *

'Sit down, Sally.'

Rex's voice was kind.

'I've been thinking, Sally – you're getting on for . . . what is it now?'

'Fifty-eight.'

'Fifty-eight, is it? Well, we're none of us as young as we'd like to be. So how are you managing these days? Bit hectic, eh?'

Sally gulped. What was he getting at?

'I'll come to the point, Sally.'

Behind him Norma dropped a tray of filing.

'Between you and me, we need to streamline. We need to sharpen our act to *really* stand a chance of holding our own in the marketplace. Now you've been with us . . . what? . . . twelve years? It's a fair crack of the whip, y'know.'

Sally's eyes were getting moist. She certainly wasn't making this easy for him.

'I'm looking for twenty redundancies. Couple of years, you're up for retirement. Are you telling me you couldn't have more fun at home, now, with a nice spot of cash, than flogging yourself out there with that tribe of villains?'

Sally was dumb. It was what she'd expected, of course, but hearing it was still a shock.

'Think it over a couple of days, eh?'

Rex stood up and held Sally's chair for her. His voice was suddenly firm.

'Get used to the idea.'

Sally hardly knew where she was. In the corridor she felt the tears starting to rise and her pulse began to race.

'Who's coming, Mam?'

Pauline bristled with indignation.

'No one's coming. We're getting a bit of class round here for a change.' And she held the peach nylon festoons against the window to calculate their full effect. Darren shifted about uneasily. It was an unsettling transformation.

What were these paintings in aid of? – wild horses bathing in waterfalls? – what was all that about? And those fake ferns in wicker vases? And that fancy brass thing with the mints in it?

'And mind you don't stick your feet up here in future,' Pauline warned.

'Mam, that cheese in the fridge is off. It stinks.'

Younger son Jason stuck his head round the door. Pauline was fuming.

'It is not "off" – it's French – and it's to be had for tea on Sunday.'

'Well, I've stuck it on toast with sardines, but it's went all soggy and slid off. It stinks like a navvy's in-soles.'

Pauline was about to explode.

'Hey, what's all these?'

Jason was rifling through the After-Eight mints.

'What d'you think you're doing?' Pauline yelped. 'They're not put there to eat, y'know! God, you're like animals in this house.' Darren and Jason pulled a face. 'I'm off round yer nan's later, so you can see to your own tea.' She paused, and put the lid on the box of mints. 'And I've counted those, so if there's one missing when I get back, somebody won't half catch it.'

'I'm just saying . . . '

Jill spoke louder. Ray wasn't exactly a captive audience these days.

'You finally get settled . . . and now they want to shift you off somewhere else.'

She pecked his cheek and took her coat off.

'Where's the kids?'

'In there.'

Something in his tone of voice made her look up.

'What is it?'

He shrugged his shoulders. Jill followed him into the living-room where Sharon and Nicky sat, heads bowed, in silence.

'So what d'you reckon these little beggars have been up to?' His voice was almost triumphant. 'Only skiving school.'

Jill was appalled. 'I don't believe it.'

'No? Well, believe that if you can stop around long enough to read it.'

He threw a letter at her. Jill looked up at the kids, tearful, disbelieving.

'But why? I thought you liked school.'

They continued to stare at the carpet. Jill skimmed back over the letter.

'And what's this? . . . "wondering if there were any problems at home you might like to come and discuss . . . "'

'I wonder.' Ray's voice was heavy with sarcasm. 'Perhaps if they saw their mam a bit more.'

Jill jumped up, genuinely hurt. Ray was into his stride now. 'You're out by eight – some nights you don't get back till nine. They must be wondering what you look like.'

Jill was close to tears now. 'We've had overtime . . . '

'I'd sooner we starved if these got a look at their mam more than two days a week. I wouldn't mind a bit of a look-in myself.'

Jill was stung by the unfairness of it all.

'I don't hear much skriking when a decent dinner turns up – when new clothes get bought – when a few quid gets swilled down *your* throat.'

'It chokes us, d'you know that? Cap in hand to you all week – and now this palaver.'

Jill was reeling.

'I thought we were managing.'

'Did you?' Ray laughed in disbelief. 'We *will* manage, though.' His severity frightened her. 'The dole can cough up from now on, and you stop here where you belong.'

She sat back with shock. She couldn't give up her job now. How could he seriously expect her to? She looked to see how the kids were responding.

'Come here, you two.' She opened her arms to them.

They came over, dragging their feet, and allowed themselves to be hugged. 'It'll be alright now.' Jill was looking over their shoulders at Ray. His face was livid. So that was her game.

'You make your mind up, love. That job goes . . . or you'll find that something else does.'

And he snatched up his wallet from the table and walked out.

Pauline gave her hair a final spray and smeared on another stroke of lipstick. A pity this dress was so tight, but she couldn't wear the mauve Lycra two nights on the trot. Still, people said she did suit tangerine . . . She put on the coat but tonight the headscarf wasn't needed. Frankie was out.

Halfway down the stairs she froze. That couldn't be Frankie's voice. He wasn't due in till after ten.

'What the bloody hell's this lot come as?'

'Me mam's new idea . . . ' Darren was saying.

'As if we don't have bother enough without the front room done out like a Turkish brothel . . . '

Pauline didn't wait to hear more. She ran back into the bedroom and started tearing off her shoes, unzipping her dress, undoing her stockings . . . no time to change out of the black lace bra and suspender-belt . . . Everything had to be bundled into a drawer, the housecoat flung on, the hairspray brushed out, the lipstick scrubbed off . . . with barely enough time to smother her face in cold cream before Frankie walked through the door.

'God, I've worked up some muck today.'

He took his shirt off and sniffed at his armpit.

'Whiff that. Go on.'

'No thank you.' Pauline was panting from her exertions.

'There's eight hours solid graft gone into that. Perhaps I *will* have a bath after all.'

'You're in early.'

'They let us go.'

'That's handy.' Pauline tried to sound casual. She watched him strip off his socks and shoes, then stiffened as he came across to get a clean pair from out of the drawer.

'Hello, what's all this?'

To her dismay, Pauline realised her housecoat had fallen open and the lace of the bra was peeping through. She pulled it together hastily.

'No, come here, let's have a gander.' Frankie was intrigued. 'By God,' he enthused. 'You look like one of them video nasties. Early night, is it?' He gave her a knowing leer. Pauline started to do up the buttons.

'Give over, Frankie.'

'What's goin' on? My rights don't stop here, y'know.'

Pauline got up and tried to edge out. 'I've got earache.'

Frankie was at the door in a flash, barring her way. 'What's come over you these days?' Pauline was quaking. She dreaded to think what might come next.

'I get home, dripp'd to buggery. I think I'm in the wrong house with all that junk dangling about. Since when do we have After-Eight mints. You're getting above yourself, you are, lady.'

'I fancied a change.'

'Oh aye, and who coughs up?'

'It's from the catalogue,' Pauline faltered.

'Well, you can tell that bloody catalogue to come and fetch it back again. I'm up to here with goings-on behind my back.'

'What d'you mean?' Pauline wasn't at all sure she wanted to hear.

A pair of mules were slammed down in front of her face.

'Since when do these grow under currant bushes?'

'Oh . . . ' came the lame reply, 'I wondered where those had gone.'

'You can wonder where these have gone an' all.'

Pauline's mouth creased with horror as Frankie flung open the drawer and tipped all her precious cosmetics on to the floor.

'Since when do you need this sort of muck?'

'I like to look nice,' she stammered.

'What for? You're wed seventeen years, you can let yourself go. Don't make me laugh.' He tipped them all into the bin. 'I wonder what fancy man's give yer that idea.'

Pauline seemed about to faint with terror.

'He's not a working man, that's for sure. Not with money to burn on skinny bits of mint and scent enough to pong out Trafford Park.'

'There's nobody!' Pauline was desperate. 'Cross and hope to die!'

'Oh, there'll be no hope about it.' Frankie grabbed her wrist. 'If I catch you playing away, lady, I'll fetch you such a twagging, you'll want a new backside . . . '

He flung her aside and strode towards the door. 'And I doubt if they'll have your size in the catalogue.'

The door slammed with a resounding thud. Pauline sat still on the carpet, rigid with shock.

Queenie was not pleased this morning. They had come in to find the targets set higher than ever. Bernie had given them another roasting, she hadn't even had time to light her first cigarette and now here was Pauline giving them earache with her incessant plain-chant.

'I'll have 'em for this. I'll call a work-out. It's bloody slave labour, that's all.' She paused to insert a single component. 'I don't have to put up with this, y'know. *I* know people.'

Queenie slammed down her soldering.

'If you shoved half the sweat into *this* you put into moving that supersonic gob up and down, we might get the Queen's Award for Industry.'

'I doubt that very much, Queenie. Not by *my* calculations.'

Inevitably it was Bernie.

'We're out of red'uns again,' Pauline snapped.

'And that's not all, is it? Bernie cooed, slipping his arm round her shoulder. 'Time, my lovelies . . . is not on your side either.'

And he made a great show of adjusting his stopwatch and noting down the latest figures. Sally sunk lower in her seat and tried not to hear.

Mid-morning found them collapsed round a table in the canteen, gratefully knocking back the tea.

'God, I've sweat that much, you could float the *Queen Mary*.'

It was a three-teacake snack for Queenie, which gave a fair indication of the current stress levels.

'I don't think I'd want to stay if we got split up,' Donna remarked suddenly, much to everyone's surprise.

'Fine if you can afford the choice,' sneered Pauline, her mood not the least improved. And tossing her slimming biscuits back into her bag, she reached for a large éclair.

'Oh, what the hell,' she shrugged off Carol May's look of surprise. 'If we're going down we might as well sink like a sack of spuds.'

At this moment Jill arrived, bringing with her a reluctant Norma.

'It's what we thought,' Jill announced. 'Redundancies.'

'Sssssshhhhhhh!' In vain Norma implored them to lower their voices.

'It's *voluntary* redundancies,' she corrected. 'With "incentives" to clear out fast.'

'Why, the sneaking, conniving . . . hang on a minute . . . ' A thought had occurred to Queenie. She pulled Sally to one side. 'You've been in that office. Don't tell us he's been wafting his "incentives" at you?'

Sally shifted uneasily. Queenie pounced.

'He's got you down for the sack, hasn't he?'

'Retirement,' mumbled Sally.

'Oh, go'way girl – sack, retire, redundant . . . it all scrap. Well, we'll see about that.'

66

Sally watched in alarm as Queenie stalked off towards Rex's office.

'What are you going to do?'

'Never you mind. But if he gets away with his gear-bits intact, he can stick the bloody flags up!'

Norma, mouth agape with horror, tore back to the office like an electrified rabbit.

'Who is it, Norma?'

Rex hadn't even bothered to look up when the door burst open and Queenie erupted in to the room.

'It's . . . er . . . Mrs Reynolds.'

Norma scuttled back to her desk.

'See what she wants, would you?' Rex continued to play with his calculator.

'She wants a word with someone,' Queenie announced, fiercely.

'She'd . . . er . . . ' Rex was taking no notice of her.

'Well, I . . . er . . . think he's busy at the moment.' Norma's eyes implored Queenie not to pursue it.

'It's urgent.' Queenie's reply was unequivocal and Norma was coming adrift.

'She says it's er . . . '

Rex was unruffled.

'Have a look in my diary and see if I'm free.'

By now Norma was way out of her depth, caught between two powerful adversaries and totally unequal to the game being played.

'Well . . . you . . . er . . . *seem* to be . . . '

'Ask Mrs Reynolds to take a seat, will you?'

Queenie didn't wait to be invited. She prepared herself to unleash a volley of abuse, but to her great consternation, Rex was still twiddling with his calculator. Queenie began to get the uneasy feeling she was being out-manoeuvred. Finally, Rex looked up, smiled urbanely, and asked her how he could be of assistance.

'Someone here wants a right swivelling!' Queenie

strained to rekindle some of her former fury. 'Twelve years's hard labour – and now you wanna tip her out like an old fag-end.'

'I'm not quite with you yet.'

Rex was trying that one, was he?

'Go 'way, lad – Sally's for the chopper. We know all about it.'

'Ah . . .' Rex leaned back in his chair and studied Queenie awhile.

'Sally, I assume, informs you she's been offered early retirement?'

'Offered? Oh aye, if the poor bugger had any choice!'

'I take it she's also informed you that technically she should have retired three years ago . . . but that thanks to management turning a blind eye, she's been allowed to stop on, drawing a wage which, quite frankly, she's not been worth since I can remember. Now while you're here, perhaps you'd like to tell me why I should be wasting my time – and the company's money – offering her early retirement . . . when I could have her sacked on the spot for dishonesty?'

Rex's tone was pleasant, without the hint of a threat. Which somehow made it very threatening indeed.

'Now, a word to the wise, Queenie . . . Firstly, while I'm always open to discussion, it might be as well to get your facts straight before you come in reading the Riot Act . . . and secondly, unless this place pulls its finger out, Sally won't be the only one that's "retired" – except in *this* case, you might not find the company's so handy with its cheque book.'

He paused to let the idea sink in.

'And now, Queenie, I won't keep you. I know you'll be itching to get back to those components.'

Rex smiled affably as Queenie rose to go. One-nil to him, she thought bitterly. She hadn't a leg to stand on. And more to the point, neither had Sally.

*   *   *

68

'Well, I wish it were *me*, that's all.' She caught up with Sally and Jill on their way back to the bench. 'With all that loot, you'll be friggin' buzzin'!'

Sally knew what that meant. Her fate was sealed, and all she could do now was grab the money with both hands.

'Aye, it's a fair few coppers, I suppose.' And she wandered off to the bench, leaving Jill and Queenie staring grimly after her. Jill turned to Queenie and frowned.

'Hey, don't give me that, girl,' Queenie was on the defensive for once. 'She's sixty-three.'

Jill shrugged in resignation. She hadn't meant to accuse. She was trying to commiserate.

'I know.'

Queenie, Pauline, Donna, Klepto, Carol May, Jill . . . heads to the bench, hands frantic, faces beaded with perspiration. They were a good bunch, hardworking, good for a laugh, there when you needed them . . . Except now. This time there was no changing it. Even Queenie had failed. Twelve years had seen this company dragged squealing into the present, and here was Sally, another of its casualties. Bernie was bustling up, but still her hands stayed motionless. No point in killing yourself. Not on your last day.

'Right, you lot. In the office. Now.'

Bernie was looking severe. They stood up in silence and filed past him towards the office.

'I warned you this wasn't Butlins.'

Rex surveyed them all in turn, his expression pained, regretful, stern.

'I asked for results. This . . . ' he tapped a sheet lined with figures, ' . . . is what you've come up with. Now next time you'll not fall into the error of leaving it all to the last moment, because next time there'll *be* no "last moment".'

You'll find it's a very different ball-game round here from now on.' He paused.

'Alright, collect your bonus, get back to your bench.' And as if to nip in the bud the rising jubilation, 'Now you've proved you can take the pace, *that's* the pace you'll be working at in future.'

Jaws began to sag. Rex had got the response he'd aimed for.

'So make the most of your weekend, ladies. Next Monday, the fun *really* starts.'

They began to filter out, relief and glee mounting to a near-hysterical pitch.

'I know what *I* could use . . . '

'Couldn't we all?'

'Let's do one down the Ritz tonight – make a proper job of it!'

Roars of approval greeted this suggestion of Queenie's and they were all piling back to the bench when Rex called out behind them, 'Er . . . Sally? Could I have a word?'

Sally glanced at Jill and Queenie, then slowly stepped back into the office. The door closed behind her.

'First in grabs a table.'

'Be there about nine.'

'I might be late – I'll have to wait while me Dad's gone out.'

'Enjoy yourselves.' This last from Donna, who inevitably wouldn't be joining them but was good-humoured enough to wish them a good evening and slip Klepto a fiver for a round of drinks.

Jill and Queenie lingered behind by the lockers.

'Where is she?'

'Aaagh, she's snuck out the back way, sly beggar. Don't worry . . . ' She noticed Jill's look of concern. 'She's tough as old leathers, that girl. Oh, alright, then, I'll get on the blower.' Jill wouldn't be reassured. 'Don't panic – she'll turn up.'

But despite her own protestations, even Queenie seemed to feel uneasy. She picked up the phone and dialled.

The flowers beside the photograph had died. In its cage, the canary chirruped and pecked at its mirror. Drab and faded the room looked now, overwhelming the sense of emptiness and isolation. The figure in the chair sat motionless, staring at the telephone. The ringing stopped.

Jill was pleased with her new dress. It made her look younger, she thought. And those few missing pounds made all the difference. What would go best with that shade of lilac? – Choosy Cherry or Midnight Ruby?

'You're not going out?'

Why was Ray so bad-tempered tonight?

'It's only a works do.'

'I don't believe this.' She hoped he wasn't going to start slamming doors again. 'You're so keen to get shot of us, then?'

'Now what've I done?' Jill couldn't deal with his sudden moods. Ray stared stonily at her. 'Just forget it.'

And sure enough, the door slammed.

The Ritz had definitely seen better days. Despite the bravest efforts of its flashing lights and neon, the scuffed upholstery and the seedy alcoves gave the game away. Not that a venue ten times less salubrious would have disappointed Klepto. A dust-heap would have sufficed. She hadn't bothered to mention it to anyone, but tonight was her first-ever 'night out'. Seventeen was still an age when you stayed home and tended the family ironing board in her father's book. She had escaped tonight on the pretext of visiting her gran. It would probably cost her a broken nose if she was caught.

71

Nothing could be further from her thoughts at this moment as she lolled across the table, gazing eagerly around, trembling with excitement and fear at the thought of being asked to dance. She was not the only one. Jill had unexpectedly caused a few heads to turn when she walked in, and now she found herself wondering what she'd been missing for so long. When was the last time she and Ray had enjoyed themselves like this? She corrected herself. When was the last time she and Ray had enjoyed themselves full stop? Carol May caught her eye across the table and tipped her glass.

'Cheers, pet. You look fabulous.'

Carol May could afford to be free with her compliments; it would be difficult to look more fabulous than Carol May. Pauline was putting up a brave fight, but her spangled bolero and sequinned pedal-pushers could hardly compete. She consoled herself by sneering at the rest of the clientele and downing the remains of a lurid-looking cocktail.

'Go on, Klepto, your shout.'

The girl got up eagerly and set out on her odyssey to the bar with wide-eyed enthusiasm.

Jill saw Carol May glance at her watch.

'She *will* come, d'you think?'

'She heard where we said. Let's hope so.'

Pauline was too busy preening herself to notice their anxiety.

'My God, what *does* she look like?'

'She' was Queenie, out in the middle of the dance-floor, gyrating in a manner which could only be called 'abandoned'. Pauline resolved that *she* wouldn't be seen dead making such an exhibition of herself – which was just as well, as her trousers could never have taken the strain.

''Course, it's not really my scene, this,' she was saying. 'I like something with a bit more . . . '

Without warning, her voice trailed away, a look of horror came over her face, and as Jill and Carol May watched in sheer amazement, Pauline dived beneath the

72

table. There was barely time to register her departure, when the chairs on either side of them were pulled out and immediately occupied by two slightly balding Lotharios, kitted out as they might have been around their twenty-fifth birthdays, which by now were going on for fifteen years away.

'Mind if we join you? The name's Fred.'

'Fancy a beer? Yours truly, Manfred.'

'I don't drink beer.' Jill exchanged a glance of amusement with Carol May.

'Don't drink beer? Hey, I could live off beer, me – couldn't I, Man?'

'Oh, what? Can a duck swim, Fred?'

'Hey, Man, how much did I put away last night?'

'Seventeen pints, mate.'

'Seventeen pints, love.'

'And then he brought it all back up again!'

'I did! I brought it all up again! Hey, I'm a right crazy bugger, me, though – I'll drink anything!'

'He will an' all! Anything!'

Courtship rituals had certainly changed since she was young, Jill was thinking. Fred was offering her a cigarette from a monogrammed case.

'That's pure gold, that is. I'm a rep, me. I sell bacon.'

'Lovely,' Jill murmured.

'Hey, there's good money in bacon. What do I drive, Man?'

'You drive a Capri, don't you, Fred?'

'I drive a Capri, me.'

'Course, we've usually gone a bit more upmarket than here, eh Fred?'

'Oh, up town or what, Man? – where the money is? – spend it while you can, eh?'

And as if to prove to Jill how favoured she was to be receiving his attentions, he slid his arm round her shoulders, at the same moment as Manfred was completing an identical manoeuvre on Carol May.

'If you don't mind . . . ' Carol May good-humouredly removed the offending paw. 'I happen to be a granny.'

'Oh, eh, she's a card, isn't she!' Manfred was almost convulsed with laughter.

'And I suppose *you've* a husband and ten kids at home!'

Jill slipped from under Fred's grip. 'Two kids.'

The mood changed instantly. Fred pulled away from Jill as if she'd been convicted of carrying typhoid.

'We're wasting our time here, Man', he sneered. 'We've drawn a couple of has-beens.'

Jill and Carol May burst into laughter.

'Oh, what, Fred?' Man persisted. 'Crufts not in it?'

'Y'wanna see *his* bird, then,' Fred boasted. 'Fit or what, Man?'

'Say that again, Fred. Thighs like Maradona?'

Beneath the table, this innocent remark appeared to have an electrifying effect on Pauline. So far noticed only by Jill, she sped off on all fours, away from the table, and disappeared into the thick of the crowd.

Klepto was tripping back from the bar, wrestling with a tray of exotic cocktails, and wearing a vacant grin across her face. Suddenly her expression seemed to undergo the same transformation as Pauline's had five minutes before, and, without another word she plummeted to the deck, still clutching the tray of drinks. Jill, having glimpsed this latest development was beginning to wonder whether her Pina Colada hadn't been spiked.

Meanwhile, Klepto was proceeding stealthily ahead on all-fours, pushing the tray in front of her, when she rounded a corner and came face-to-face with Pauline.

'What the frig are *you* doing down here?' Pauline hissed.

'Sssssssshhhhhhhh!' Klepto implored, but her voice suddenly trailed away as a pair of legs loomed into view, blocking her path. Klepto glanced up. Glaring down at her was a young Greek in his early twenties, mouth curled, eyes cold: her older brother Nico.

Klepto smiled foolishly.

'Hello . . . '

'What d'you think you're playing at?' This was no display of fraternal affection.

'I'm just . . . having a drink.'

Nico seized the tray and slammed it on to a table, drinks cascading down Pauline's neck as she crouched on the floor.

'Get your coat,' Nico commanded.

Down at knee-level, Pauline decided the moment was ripe for escape. She clambered to her feet, removed a cocktail cherry from her cleavage and was making for the exit when a voice from behind stopped her in her tracks.

'Hey! – what *you* doing here?'

Pauline turned half-sideways, trying to keep her face hidden behind a curtain of hair.

'If you don't mind, I think you've made a mistake.'

Fred leapt up and rushed towards her.

'No, hang on – I've got me Capri.'

Pauline picked up her handbag and fled.

'I bet that's news to Frankie,' Carol May chuckled.

'Well, well, there's no substitute for passion, is there?' Jill giggled.

Carol May's expression was deadpan.

'I wouldn't know, love.'

At this moment, gripped by the wrist, Klepto's pleas were falling on deaf ears.

'Don't tell me dad.'

'What's it worth?' Her brother taunted, and was preparing to drag her away, when he was arrested by a light tap on the shoulder.

'Alright, lovey, on yer way.'

He swung round, angrily. 'You talking to me?'

Sally smiled affably at him.

'Just so we get a few things cleared up . . . your sister is my guest – and since we're pretty busy enjoying ourselves, I don't think we need any armed escorts to stir up the fun.'

'My sister is leaving now.'

'I don't think she is.'

'My dad's gonna wipe the walls with her!'

'Well, he should have a field-day, then, and use *you* on the ceiling.'

Sally's voice was as courteous as ever.

'You see, lovey, I'm stood at that bar trying to get a drink – could hardly miss you and Mr Universe, there.' And she nodded in the direction of the bar where a stunningly handsome Greek boy stood watching them keenly. Klepto's eyes popped out on stalks.

'And while it's no odds to *me* whose backside your hand's wrapped round, I think it might just be of interest to yer dad.'

Sally smiled pleasantly at him. His fist quivered in blind frustration. Sally shook her head.

'Any problems, Sal?'

Queenie's face appeared over Klepto's shoulder, wearing its most belligerent expression.

'I think we're all sorted, thankyou.'

But Queenie wasn't to be cheated of her contribution.

'Hop it, Zorba,' she gestured. 'Get back to yer mouth-to-mouth with Hercules there.'

Nico was in full retreat when Sally called after him.

'Just remind us, lovey – what's that lovely licorice stuff you go in for?'

'She means ouzo,' added Klepto, helpfully.

'Well, I wouldn't say no, lovey.' Sally paused. 'Not when I've got a lie-in from now on.'

A glance between the girls confirmed their fiercest hope. Sally was apparently coming to terms with the inevitable. At any rate, she was going to have damn good crack at it.

'And where've *you* been,' Queenie turned on her. 'I've rung you six times tonight.'

'Twelve years I've worked there, she's never so much as lifted a phone. Now I've bloody gone, the ringing's never stopped.'

'Knowing you, you'd took a dive over Trafford Bridge.'

'Then you *don't* know me, lovey,' Sally retorted. 'My eyesight's not that gash I'd drop for a canal trip without a barge.' She seized one of the cocktails off the tray. 'And I can still see to flop a few of these.'

It was a brave attempt but no one was fooled. It was ludicrous to think that Sally would take to retirement like a duck to a pond, but Sally was game and they were going to give her all the back-up they could muster. Queenie topped up the cocktail with the sinister-looking concoction in her own glass.

'Alright, get afloat, girls! While *she's* sticking her feet up, we'll still be shoving bits of wire in silly bloody holes.'

'You'll not miss much, Sal,' Jill assured her.

'She'll not miss those shifty, sneaky pack of wolves in white collars, that's for sure.'

'Sod 'em all, eh, Sal?'

They applauded the sentiment with raised glasses.

'So what y'gonna do with all that money, Sal?'

And Sally replied, quick as a flash.

'Count it.'

Bernie felt a headache coming on. The wine was partly to blame, but it had received some admirable assistance from his wife Nancy who was sitting beside him, and who'd been nagging him into a stupor all the way home.

The lights turned red. Bernie coasted to a halt.

'And I must say,' Nancy continued to drone on. 'The amount *you* put away, I'm amazed you don't start a reservoir.'

'We've had a rough week, love,' he pleaded.

The lights turned green. Bernie had just engaged first gear when his foot flew back to the brake. Into the road reeled a chain of women, garlanded with streamers, blowing hooters, and performing a conga. The spectacle had passed before he had time to register, and was now proceeding noisily down the street behind them. Nancy pursed her lips in disgust.

'You'd think folk had money to burn, the amount that gets washed down some throats.'

Bernie sat bolt upright, a flicker of recognition beginning to dawn.

'Well, easy come, easy go. They don't deserve jobs if that's where the wages end up.'

Bernie peered through his rear-view mirror and shuddered. 'Yes, love,' he murmured.

Halfway down the next street, the conga erupted into some imaginative gyrations and disappeared like a chorus of Bluebell girls into the night. The evening was still young.

CHAPTER THREE

April

A steady rhythm of bedsprings broke the early morning peace, as first light picked out the whiteness of a sheet and a shapeless mass of clothing heaped haphazardly over a chair. On the bedside table an empty beer can rattled, the muffled sounds grew louder; then suddenly, with a rustle, silence.

'Why've y'give over?'

Jill's voice broke the heaviness.

'I've gone off the idea.' Ray's voice was disconsolate in the dimness.

'Y'bin off it for months,' she observed, not without resentment.

'*Three* months, to be precise,' retorted Ray.

It was her own fault for being so bloody-minded about the job. He'd been waiting to fling that in her face, the kind of riposte he specialised in – that somehow carried with it a promise to sort her out, to make her come to her senses, to help him feel better. But somehow, when the words were out, he always felt worse than ever: irritable, ineffectual and deeply angry. And now loomed the prospect of another day, playing the captive skivvy in his own home, while *she* . . .

He sat up violently in bed and switched on the bedside lamp. Jill lay there beside him, head on the pillow, staring ahead, as his sour face turned on her.

'I shaped well enough before you started down that bloody cat-house.'

'We should bottle it, then.' Jill's voice was cold. 'It makes a great contraceptive.'

Norma arrived earlier than usual at the factory that Monday morning. Earlier, that is, than her usual more-than punctual self, which commonly found her in the office a good thirty minutes before everyone else. Advance punctuality, she called it. Others might label it sheer nosiness. For some reason she was looking smarter than usual, as she collected a large Datapost box from the security guard. Signing for it with characteristic efficiency, and glancing about her as if on the alert, she carried the box away down the corridor, with a self-importance which suggested she was in possession of some 'very important information'. Teasing open the door with one knee, she gained the sanctuary of her office and with elaborate care placed the box on her desk. Another precautionary glance, then she opened the seals, and delicately lifted out an object, copiously veiled in tissue. Moments later, careful hands revealed the source of all the mystery: a slightly jet-lagged Bonsai tree.

Ray was still in bed, staring at the wall, when Jill came back into the room, dressed and ready for work. For the first time in months she was forcibly struck by the sight of him – despondent, unshaven and run-to-seed. Her heart went out to him.

'Y'gonna stop there all day?' she asked.

'Sod-all else to get up for, is there?' he challenged, defiantly.

Jill snapped. 'I don't wonder you get no work. You've got "useless" tattoed in six foot letters across yer head.'

Ray laughed aloud – but his bantering tone belied the seriousness of his feelings as he told her, 'I might well when I get down the Social an' told I'm never really tryin'.'

Jill looked suprised.

'Oh, aye, the joke,' he continued. 'As if you'd *choose* this caper.'

Jill was putting on her make-up now, determined to stay out of the all-too-familiar wrangle that was gathering.

'I'd crease to see some of 'em try – runnin' house, mindin' kids, chasin' a wife who's face he's forgot, *and* fight a running battle with some clever betty who keeps tryin' to retrain yer to twiddle computers.'

'Perhaps you might like computers,' she ventured, hopefully.

'I trained as a fitter,' he thundered. 'I'm a bloody good fitter. And I'm not about to get palmed off playing tiddlywinks with microchips just because someone decides my job looks better on a bleedin' robot.'

'Ray . . . ' But she was already late. There wasn't time to console him.

'Oh, don't mind *me*, love,' he goaded, heavy with sarcasm. 'You get out there an' enjoy yerself.'

Jill sighed. There was no arguing with Ray in this mood. She decided to leave him to it, and quickly picking up her coat, she went downstairs. Ray sprawled back against the pillows, listening to the now-familiar sound of her closing the front door, and walking away down the path.

Norma's mysterious activities in the office that morning did not stop with the Bonsai tree. She was preparing, with elaborate care, a large tea-tray. She'd begun by buffing it up a little with her hanky (regretfully, that's all there was to hand), then laid out, very neatly, teapot, sugar, milk, cups, saucers, teaspoons . . . So far, nothing very out-of-the-ordinary, perhaps. But the plate of fondant fancies, placed strategically at the centre of the arrangement, was a rarity indeed. Into the middle of one of the cakes she proceeded to stick two tiny flags: the Korean flag, and with a touch of pride, the Union Jack.

*   *   *

The table was littered with fishing equipment. Revolting looking jars of bait, grubby pouches, old matchboxes, spools, pellets, small round lead objects, maggots crawling about in open tins . . . Carol May hummed to herself as she came into the kitchen. Even at this hour of a Monday morning, she still looked imperturbably glamorous. She lit a cigarette and drew deeply on it, enjoying the day's first drag.

She was brushing on mascara as Colin came eagerly into the room, cheerful at the thought of a day's fishing. Their wedding-day, twenty eight years since, had witnessed his last attempt to make the most of his appearance. This morning he was graced by a pair of old jeans, one of his several seedy pullovers, and a well-worn pair of scuffed shoes, taken from a selection which boasted many replicas but few improvements. Despite this, and rather surprisingly, he was physically well-made, could almost have been handsome if taken in hand – but if Carol May had ever had the interest, she'd abandoned it years ago.

Colin glanced up at his wife. Something in the more-than-usual care with which she was preparing for work made him give her a second glance. The moment passed without her realising it was there, and Colin started to amass his gear.

'Crackin', these, aren't they?'

He had picked up one of the plumpest maggots and was stroking it, almost affectionately.

Carol May was silent. She wasn't deliberately ignoring him – it was almost as if she hadn't heard.

'Right, I'm away, then.' He moved to kiss her – the usual peck on the cheek – but she hadn't noticed, and somehow had managed to veer away just as he leaned towards her.

With relief, she heard the back door close behind him. It was impossible to know what he was thinking. Perhaps *he* didn't care either. Did that make it better, she wondered? She wouldn't think about that now. It was too late to start feeling guilty. She swept her hand through her mane of hair, picked up her overall and went out.

The car pulled up outside the factory gates. Donna leant across to kiss her husband, tried to look serious – and broke into a giggle.

'What's tickled *you*, then?' Gordon was amused to see her looking so mysterious.

'Something . . . ' She grinned self-consciously as he nudged her for an answer.

'Go on,' he urged, trying to temper his curiosity, though catching the tone of her mood.

'I might have news for you later.' She was almost flirtatious. 'If you're lucky.'

Gordon leant across to kiss her, smiling broadly. Donna was momentarily thrown. What if someone was looking? She glanced round self-consciously, leaving Gordon in a rather odd position at her neck. It seemed to typify their relationship: this 'having-a-go' at being passionate, and always slightly missing. Even after years of marriage there was still an awkwardness, an inability to relax, to work out quite where the noses and chins should go. Gordon persevered, determined not to lose the impetus of the moment but just as Donna was finally surrendering, a deafening hammering on the window made them spring apart in shock.

'Go easy, girl, you'll eat no dinner!'

Queenie's contorted face, grinning obscenely through the window, was not a welcome sight. Furious, Donna leapt up, in two minds whether to pursue her, but Queenie was already off through the gates, roaring with laughter. Donna snatched up her handbag, and, venting her anger by slamming the door, stalked away into the factory.

Just inside the foyer, the 'Welcome Board' was receiving

83

the unprecedented attentions of Bernie. Brow furrowed as he consulted a clipboard, he was painstakingly selecting letters from a box and sticking up a message.

LYNE ELECTRONICS WELCOMES CHUNG DON WAN, CHU KIM SOOK, JUNG SOO PAK, HAN BONG YUN, CHUK LOO YUNG

So far it had taken him half an hour, and he was beginning to fear that at any moment he would run out of 'U's.

Donna paused. Such extraordinary names. Perhaps someone was playing a practical joke. But then she saw Bernie, and at once discounted the idea.

By the time Carol May and Jill, busy with their hair at the mirrors, saw her enter the cloakroom, her humour was completely restored.

'Glad *someone's* got it to smile about.'

Donna wasn't going to be drawn by Carol May or anyone. She merely smiled back and let herself into one of the toilets, while Carol May and Jill exchanged a look of surprise as if to say, 'What's got into her?'

The door locked, Donna installed herself eagerly on the toilet lid. Scarcely able to contain her excitement, she took out a small packet from her bag, and, quivering with anticipation , tore it open with trembling fingers. By now she knew the instructions more or less by heart, but still she double-checked: 'Wait 30 minutes . . . if the tip turns blue . . . ' *If* the tip turned blue . . . ? It *had* to turn blue. This time she was absolutely positive . . . She paused a second in dread of being overheard, then began to lay the contents out on the floor in careful preparation.

'Two quid apiece or three for a fiver!'

Suddenly the ladies toilets took on all the character of a market-place. A hard-faced woman in her late thirties, rough-voiced and singularly unattractive, stood fingering a handful of change. Behind her the washbasin area appeared to have undergone a startling transformation, festooned as it now was with elaborate displays of Easter eggs. Around the stall a din was gathering, coins rattled and eggs were changing hands at an alarming rate. Klepto ambled across, her eye drawn to a large silver box, wondering how to 'acquire' it without actually opening her purse.

'That's four pound twenty-five.'

The sour-faced woman seemed to know Klepto of old. In the doorway, Queenie uttered a snort of derision.

'How much?'

The woman glared across at her.

'What's up, love? Yer on a diet?'

Queenie's eyes narrowed. This woman had trespassed onto her patch, but she wouldn't be here long if *she* could help it.

'Oh, I can't take the cheap stuff, pet,' she smiled acidly. 'It gives us the squirts.'

The remark had the desired effect. Several women hastily put back the eggs they were poised to buy, and even Jill and Carol May were torn between amusement and disgust.

At this moment Donna emerged from the toilets straightening her blouse.

'Bin havin' a bath in there?' ribbed Carol May.

'Aaah, she'll not need one, the lather that tongue of his was gettin' up!'

Queenie was on form this morning, but Donna studiously ignored her, and began to wash her hands. This served only to provoke Queenie into continuing the pursuit.

'D'y'do home demonstrations, pet? Or just in public?'

Determined not to rise to the bait, Donna pushed past her, dried her hands, and walked coolly out of the door.

'Hey, don't tell us he's tryna get one in before his tackle gets outa practice!'

'Shift you, we've had it if we're late.'

Carol May, like Jill, obviously felt Queenie's parting shot had overstepped the mark. The sour-faced woman fired her rival a look of venom and bent down to pack up her merchandise, while Queenie, seeing her off guard, seized the opportunity – and strolled out carrying a huge egg under one arm. Jill and Carol May looked at each other and followed swiftly. Only a wide-eyed Klepto remained, when the woman realised her classiest egg was now missing.

'It wasn't me – honest!'

Klepto backed towards the door as a face like thunder advanced menacingly. With a yelp, she grabbed the door-handle, turned and ran for her life.

Norma stood expectantly outside the front entrance holding a 'LYNE ELECTRONICS' pennant. When no-one was looking, she practised the odd dry run, trying various gestures, weighing different phrases for best effect. It was important to make the right impression, she thought. Bernie picked nervously at his watch, while Simon scurried around gathering up stray bits of litter. Finally, Rex strolled up, apparently as cool as ever.

'All set?'

'No problem.'

Bernie gave a thumbs up, brimming with importance. It was clear that visitors of significance were due.

'Alright girls, red-hot offer-of-the-week, an' guaranteed to send the sparks flyin'!'

Queenie pulled out a box from underneath the work-bench and slammed it on to the table.

'It's another job-lot of electric blankets,' quipped a deadpan Carol May.

However, when a roistering fanfare revealed Queenie's latest 'offer', the effect was indeed electric. Shrieks of admiration and delight greeted a writhing mass of exotic lingerie: camisoles, french knickers, suspender-belts and countless other frilly specimens, the *coup de grace* being a magnificent red satin-and-lace basque. Queenie held up the labels for inspection.

'All the way from Gay Paree – see for yerselves – it's got "la" in it.'

A black lace teddy had cornered Pauline's attention.

'Well – well – isn't *someone* going to be a lucky boy, then?'

She winked knowingly at Klepto, but the gesture went unnoticed. Klepto was gazing enraptured at the red basque, stroking the satin, fingering the lace. Pauline turned her wit on Carol May.

'Nothin' for you, pet?' she queried, feigning surprise.

'Waste of time, love. No sense feeding the meter when the fire's gone out.'

Jill, meanwhile, had been drawn to a pair of satin French knickers, but finally put them back with a sigh.

'Kids want new shoes. What d'y'do?'

Pauline snatched up the knickers, almost triumphantly. 'Look at me,' she whooped, tempering her excitement with a hint of coyness. 'Y'best stick us down for these an' all. All that wear an' tear – y'can't have too many, can yer?'

Queenie and Carol May exchanged a glance.

'Go on, Donna,' rallied Pauline, rising in confidence and daring. 'Treat yourself.'

'Oh, that'll keep the chilblains at bay, will it?' Donna fought shy of the lace camisole which Pauline had lobbed at her.

'Go 'way,' exclaimed Queenie scathingly. 'You can afford it! Why's he workin' for a building society if he can't slope a few readies into his pocket now an' again?'

Donna flushed. 'It might've escaped your notice, but people don't usually get to be under-manager of the local branch by embezzling society funds.'

'Eeeh, no – is that right, girl!' sneered Queenie.

But her sarcasm failed to hit its mark.

'What d'y'want for this, then?'

Klepto flinched as Pauline wrenched the basque out of her clutching fingers.

'Fifteen quid.'

'Fifteen quid!'

'Hey, it's genuine Polyester, that,' retorted Queenie. 'You look at the label – I don't deal in tat, y'know.'

'I'll do you a tenner.'

Queenie snatched back the basque and bundled it away contemptuously.

'An' the workmanship gone into that?' she sniffed.

Klepto sighed with regret. If only she had the money . . . if only someone was feeling generous . . . if only, somehow, the basque could come into her possession . . .

Her quandary was short-lived, and further trading was halted by the sound of the buzzer. Hard on its heels came the sound of Norma's voice shouting across the tannoy: 'Telephone call for Mrs Fox! Telephone for Mrs Fox!'

Knowing that Rex was on the move, the girls fell swiftly to the task in hand, expertly clearing the desk of lingerie in a matter of seconds. Moments later, Klepto's mouth fell open and she began tugging at Donna's sleeve. Donna nudged Carol May, who in turn gave Queenie a prod, till the whole bench was alive to the sight of Mr Beachcroft – Old Smiler himself – leading a group of six oriental-looking businessmen across the factory floor on a tour of inspection. Rex and Bernie followed in close attendance – along with Norma, who dared not look at Queenie for fear of some reprisal, as if this were somehow her fault. The girls watched agog as the party made its way down the rows towards their bench, Bernie bustling ahead importantly, anxious to make sure they created the right impression.

'Shape up, shape up, ladies . . . Simon, chop-chop with them components now . . .'

Simon rushed nervously across, while Bernie began to

talk to Rex via his walkie-talkie, though Rex could not have been more than six feet away.

'B-group – Beta gamma . . . er . . . Beta groupie – A-Okay.'

Rex, with a trace of weariness in his look, nodded in acknowledgement, and proceeded to lead the party over.

'This is one of our manual assembly bays . . . ' he was saying, one of the visitors providing a simultaneous translation to the rest of the group, who instantly swarmed round the bench, chatting volubly. A pair of black satin knickers which had fallen out of Queenie's box drew admiring glances from some of the party, but just as they bent to investigate, Queenie's foot whisked the item sharply away under the bench.

'Alright, ladies, carry on now . . . '

Fortunately, at that very moment, Rex was moving the group along. The girls watched them go, expressions full of suspicion, till Pauline, with hushed tones, gave voice to what they'd *all* been thinking.

'I don't like the look of *that*.'

'So now we know why he's had us scaddin' around like hot cats lately,' deduced Queenie darkly. 'Fattenin' us up for *this* little lot!'

'What d'y'mean?' quizzed Jill in alarm.

'Why, y'know what it is, don't yer. Bloody take-over bid, that's all.'

'Oh, give over.' Pauline reckoned this had to be one of Queenie's worst jokes.

'Dead right, girl – or didn't yer clock bloody Chairman Mao an' his mates squinty-eyein' us up, makin' funny squiggles in their little red books?'

Could it be true? They all looked at each other, real alarm growing visibly in their faces.

'Well, *something's* going on,' observed Donna sagely.

'Not much, pal! – an' I should know. Our Marg's place got took over by bloody Nips. It's no ciggies, no gabbin', no breaks, twelve-hour shifts an' no overtime.'

Nobody liked the sound of this; they were looking

grimmer by the minute. Queenie continued ominously, making the most of the dire scenario.

'Mind, that's if we get kept on.'

'What d'y'mean?' repeated Jill weakly.

'Oh, they're not bothered with this redundancy pay-offs lark. Oh no, it's on-yer-rickshaws, pets, an' chopsticks to the lot of yers!'

Bernie, who had been hovering behind, now advanced upon the bench.

'Try not to overwork the old jaws, eh, girls? – no point givin' our guests the wrong idea.'

And there was just enough of a threat in what he said to convince them that Queenie's predictions might not be that wide of the mark.

'They won't make us work sat on the floor, will they?' moaned a fearful Klepto, keen to get the practical implications straight. The canteen was abuzz with talk of the morning's event. The girls of B-Group, like many another, sat huddled round a table, heads together, muttering treasonably.

'Oh, give over, y'daft sod,' chided Jill, laughing uneasily.

'Oh aye, you say that, but I've seen *Bridge on the River Kwai*, doll – I know what kind of working conditions to expect.' Queenie was hardly a font of reassurance, and Klepto's mouth was beginning to sag.

'You take no notice,' Donna commanded.

'And we'll have all that Jappo junk down the canteen – bamboo shoots an' raw fish an' funny tea with no milk.'

'I don't think so,' opined Donna calmly.

Such dissent was not going to suit Queenie.

'Well, if you know so much about it, tell us why not, then?'

'Because for starters, they're not Japanese.' She paused to let it sink in. 'Norma says they're Korean.'

This was greeted with mild surprise by some of the girls, but to Queenie it was all grist to the mill.

'That's right, Nips – slitty-eyed – foreign. They're all the same to me, pet – I'm not prejudiced.'

There was a nudge from Carol May, as a hush suddenly fell across the canteen.

'What's her game? – bloody Norma. She could've warned us,' hissed Pauline through her teeth. Norma was leading the Korean delegation to a table in the far corner, carrying before her the plate of flag-bedecked fondant fancies. On her way back to the office, Norma's route took her past the girls' table.

'I want a word with you,' growled Queenie.

Norma scampered past, glad to escape for now. She knew too well she'd be cornered sooner or later.

Donna glanced at her watch and rose from the table.

'Won't be long,' she said with feigned ease, as she left the canteen, making for the ladies' toilets.

'What's that about?' wondered Pauline, with raised eyebrows. Queenie was quick with a suggestion.

'Prob'ly old Gordon ringin' for directions.'

'What's he need *them* for?'

'Well, he's not found his way to base *without* so far!' Whereupon she roared with laughter at her own wit, not in the least daunted by the frowns of the others who didn't seem to find it quite so funny.

Another five minutes. Donna replaced the test-tube in its hiding-place behind the toilet, and rejoined her work-mates at the bench – where she discovered that Queenie's wit was by no means exhausted.

'I take it he knows what end to go for, does he?'

'I'm sorry?' This was all very tedious, thought Donna.

'I mean, he does get out his own half sometimes? Y'know, the number of no-score draws you two's bin clockin' up, it makes us wonder if he knows what the goal looks like!'

Donna turned to her soldering. Queenie ploughed on.

'Aaagh, what? – did I show yer up, Donna? Did I disgust yer?'

'You always disgust me, Queenie.'

Queenie's taunts threatened to grow ever more vicious, till she was halted in mid-bite by an unpleasant discovery.

'I don't believe it!' Heads looked up in alarm. 'Bugger me if some bitch hasn't went an' ripped us!'

'Y'what?' Jill hadn't quite grasped the *patois*.

'The friggin red job!' Queenie barked.

'Well, who'd've whipped it?'

'Some bugger has, that's all!'

And Queenie was set to overturn the bench in her search for the treasured item, till the sight of Klepto, working away, nose to the bench, suggested other possibilities.

'It's *you*, isn't it? – y'bloody tea-leaf! God, If I'm not sick of nailin' stuff to this desk to stop it walkin' into your bag!' Klepto was looking tearful. 'You've got till five to cough up fifteen quid or little Robin Redbreast – or you'll find yerself a tidy little heap on Norma's First Aid Box!'

'And who d'you think you're talking to?'

Queenie wheeled round to the sound of Donna's voice.

'Who's to say it couldn't "walk" to other benches? Who's to say it's "walked" at all? Don't assume because things "walk" into *your* possession, they take the same route to other people's.'

The girls nudged each other. What had got into Donna? All the same, it was rather impressive. Queenie was looking quite gobsmacked. It didn't take her long to fish up a retort, however.

'Oh, hello, Miss Educated? Miss Prim? – O level Needlework an' a degree in lookin' down her nose! Ask yerself – if she's so bloody clever – why ol' Gordon can't hit the jackpot without the aid of diagrams!'

Donna rose to her feet.

'What I *do* ask myself, Queenie . . . is how long before they invent a disinfectant strong enough to do the job on that mouth of yours. A decent dose of pesticide and we'd *all* feel a lot cleaner.'

And, shaking with anger, she abruptly walked out. As Jill got up to follow her, Queenie appealed to the bench at large:

'Now what've I said?'

She was met by a wall of frowns.

'Donna? Where are yer?'

Jill scanned the row of toilets, till muffled sobs led her to the right door.

'Donna . . . let me in, eh? . . . open the door . . . ?'

The sobbing ceased. There was a pause, then the noise of a lock being drawn back. Donna appeared in the doorway.

'It's negative.'

Her eyes were raw with tears. Jill stared at her, uncomprehending.

'It didn't go blue.'

Donna held up the test-tube. Suddenly the penny dropped.

'Oh, Donna . . . I'm so sorry.'

Donna's tears welled up again.

'She's right, then, isn't she? What a laugh! Donna's missed again, has she? Dear oh dear, nothing down for Donna!'

The bitterness in her voice gave way to despair.

'Why is there nothing down for Donna? What more d'you have to do?'

Jill hovered, feeling powerless to offer comfort.

'I've read that many books, and manuals, and diagrams . . . I could start me own clinic.' Donna laughed at the irony.

'So sure. This time I just *knew*.' She shook her head bitterly. 'I *thought* I knew.'

Suddenly she scrubbed the tears from her cheeks and jumped up.

93

'Where y'going?' Jill looked anxious.

'God knows.' But Donna sensed the genuine concern. 'Don't panic, I won't do anything daft.' Then her voice was scathing again. 'I'm too sensible.'

Unease did not subside as the day progressed – and neither did the direness of Queenie's predictions.

'*Now* look – they're measurin' up for barbed wire an' paddy fields!'

This, in response to the arrival of one of the delegates with a clipboard and pocket calculator.

'Oh, give it a rest, eh?' Carol May was beginning to tire of this incessant doom-mongering.

'Oh aye, sit still, clamp yer beak – let top office lob yer off sideways an' slam in a gang of yeller-bladdered kamikazes!'

'You'll be had up for that mouth one day' was Carol May's only response.

'We're took for mugs, though, aren't we?'

Looks of surprise greeted this outburst from Jill.

'Told nowt, gawped at like bloody chimps. I suppose we're meant to sit here and watch while the jobs get whipped from under us.'

'I'll skelp that bloody, Norma,' Queenie countered, glad to have an ally. 'There's friggin' loyalty! – snivellin', sneakin' scab – hand-in-mitt with Rex now. Don't tell us *she's* his floozy!'

Mercifully, the buzzer sounded for the end of work. Queenie snatched up her belongings and raced to clock off, pausing only to hiss abuse at a luckless Korean who unwittingly strayed into her path. Carol May hastened her away towards the exit.

'Don't you think you've done enough damage for one day?'

'Oh, go'way, girl,' Queenie blasted. 'I'm just warmin' up.'

* * *

The phone rang in the stillness of the empty office.

'Yeah . . . ? Rex's face relaxed into a smile. 'I'll be there. Give me ten minutes.'

He was fishing in his briefcase for the pocket shaver, when a noise outside the door gave him pause for thought.

'Yes, Norma?' he queried. 'Was there something you wanted?'

Norma blushed, still faltering on the threshold. How embarrassing to be caught in the act.

'Oh . . . I . . . er . . . didn't know you'd still be here.'

'I could say the same for you,' remarked Rex. 'What's the attraction in here? You seem fascinated with the place these days.'

Norma's blush deepened. She sincerely hoped he wasn't insinuating that she . . . how could she put it? – that her feelings towards him were anything more than those of any secretary towards her boss. She began to tidy the already-pristine racks of the filing cabinet.

'Seemed to go well today,' she ventured, after a convincing pause.

'Don't bet on it.' Rex seemed almost bitter. 'If I'm not mistaken, they've got us lined up for a "screwdriver job".'

'I'm sorry?'

'They build the stuff, fly it over here – we shove in a couple of screws and slap on a Union Jack. That's Beachcroft's idea of a partnership.'

'So it's all settled, then?' Norma thought it politic to feign unconcern.

'He'll "keep us informed".'

Rex took out his shaver and ran it across the stubble.

'Off home, then?' Norma inquired.

'That's right.'

'Could you drop me at the bus-stop?'

There was just the suggestion of a pause before Rex replied, 'I . . . won't be going that way tonight. I've some other business to see to first.'

'Oh? – with the Koreans?'

Was she being deliberately ingenuous? Rex decided to put his foot down.

'No. As a matter of fact, Norma, not with the Koreans.'

'I see.'

'I doubt that very much, Norma.' His change of tone startled her. 'And quite honestly, I'd start "seeing" a great deal less inside here if I were you.'

Norma discovered urgent business behind the Bizzie Lizzie.

Rex continued smoothly. 'I dunno, perhaps you'd prefer to be treated like a nine-to-five typist . . . However . . . ' he was beginning to frighten her, ' . . . if you want to continue to enjoy the privileges of your position, I suggest you take a bit more care to protect them in future . . . ' He patted on a suggestion of aftershave. 'Discretion being the better part of your function in this office.'

Norma glanced up, trembling, as Rex snapped his briefcase shut and put on his jacket.

'I'll leave you to switch the lights off.'

She watched him stride away down the corridor, and bit her lip ruefully.

That's torn it, she thought.

Jill switched off the TV and began to harvest the crop of empty beer-cans and crisp papers which had flourished around the sofa. A steady snore arose from the sleeping figure in the arm chair, and eager to avoid another confrontation, Jill was content to leave him to come to of his own accord. Which he presently did – but in a mood not calculated to endear himself to her.

' "Oh, and how was *your* day, love," ' he mimicked. " 'Budgie behave itself? Tea-towels good company?" '

'You'll get fat, you will,' observed Jill, seeing him stuff a fistful of crisps into his mouth.

'I'll want *summat* to cheer us up,' countered Ray. 'Great joke polishing formica all day.'

'I don't believe you sometimes.' Jill was almost laughing. You don't go out, you don't care what you look like – and how long since you played Sunday football?'

'Since I didn't fancy all that jaw behind me back. "There he is, Number 6 – washes his wife's overalls." I might well be playing sweeper – it's all I'm bloody fit for.'

Jill really did find this funny.

'Don't give me that, Ray. I've been there, I've done it – twelve years, remember?' She retrieved another beer-can.

'No wonder you wanna work. Out there's a doddle next to runnin' this shop. Now y'know what y'bin missing.'

She grinned at him, keen to show she wasn't really angry, but Ray would not be placated. He'd been waiting to play his master-stroke, and she'd just given him the cue.

'There's fitters jobs.' He paused for effect. 'In Folkestone.'

'There's what?' Jill wasn't really listening.

'J-O-B-S' he spelled. 'I know it's an endangered species, but it's not quite extinct.'

'Where's Folkestone?'

'Somewhere south.'

'Workin' away?'

'Well it's hardly commutable.'

'Give over, Ray.' The joke was wearing thin.

'What's so funny?'

'You'd never be here.'

'That'd make two of us.'

Jill was tiring rapidly. 'So when d'you start?' she teased.

'Monday.'

Jill almost reeled with the shock. 'Yer serious?'

'If I stop here, I go off me skull. That's serious.'

'But you can't just *go* . . . ' Her mind began to race. 'Who's to mind the kids? . . . who lets them in? . . . who'll get their tea . . . ?'

'They can have keys, get their own tea, mind each other . . . like every other kid round here's had to learn.'

'Not *my* kids.' Jill was steely.

'Oh, you're special, aren't yer?' Ray taunted. 'You're above all that? Well, get it through that skull, there's nowt left special round here.' He tried a gentler tack. 'It's half a chance I can't afford to miss.' Then back to the venom. 'And if it bothers you that much, you know what to do.'

'What?' But she already knew the answer.

'Stop work.'

It was past ten when Carol May took off her coat, examined her face in the hall-mirror, and went into the living-room.

'You're back late.'

Daughter Carol May looked up from the floor where her own three-month-old daughter – also Carol May – was being changed.

'I stopped off for a natter.' Carol May the Elder bent to kiss the gurgling infant.

'We've had our tea. He said we shouldn't wait.' And the daughter nodded towards her father who lay flat out in a chair, mouth agape, snoring.

'Water on?' Carol May seemed strangely preoccupied tonight.

'Havin' a bath?'

'You're not off home, are yer?'

'No, not yet.'

Carol May drew a paper bag from out of a drawer.

'There's something for yer.'

The daughter crouched to tear it open. A baby's knitted matinee-jacket fell out.

'Oh, mam . . . she whispered. But Carol May was already on her way upstairs.

She opened the cupboard and took out a large soft towel from the shelf. Scented oil, a long hot steep, the warm folds of a newly-washed bath-robe . . . she relaxed visibly in anticipation, her hand poised to turn on the hot tap –

then immediately stiffened. Beneath her, in a bath brimming with cold water, swam six large rainbow trout. She barely flinched. The towel, the robe, the bath oil . . . all silently replaced, she switched off the light and went downstairs.

Her daughter flashed a meek apology.

'I meant to warn yer . . . '

Carol May seemed not to hear.

'Col?' The snoring continued. 'Col?' She jogged his arm.

He woke with a jolt. 'Are those fish gonna be there all night?' There was no anger, no recrimination. It was all too familiar.

Colin missed her tone of enquiry.

'What d'you reckon? Crackers, aren't they?

'I'd think so if they were sat under a grill and sprinkled with almonds.'

Colin was appalled.

'They're not for eating,' he cried, as if the idea were a sacrilege. 'I've brought 'em to show Billy next door. He reckons he's caught whoppers? He's caught nowt compared to these.'

'I think someone else'll catch a whopper if them fish don't shift and sharpish.' His daughter was more alive than he to the mother's growing impatience.

'Can't it wait?'

'I want a bath. Col.'

'You had one this morning. Yer never out of it these days.'

Carol May turned to the door.

'So I'll just pull the plug out, shall I?'

Colin leapt up in real panic.

'No! . . . no . . . hang about . . . ' He paused as he went through the door, treating her to a look of real pity.

'Sometime I wonder if you really like fish at all.'

Carol May closed the door, her face deadpan.

'I sometimes wonder that meself.'

Carol May the Second was packing up her offspring and preparing to go. As her mother clasped her in a parting embrace, she pulled back and looked her full in the eye.

'Y'know you an' me dad . . . '

Carol May stiffened.

'Didn't y'never think about havin' more kids?'

'We thought about it.'

'And . . . ?'

Carol May returned her look.

'Thought about's all that's ever happened since.'

Gordon was practising his scales. The same notes, over and over, one after the other, slowly driving Donna to tears of distraction, till the china dog she'd been polishing fell through her fingers and shattered on the floor.

'Now look what you've done!'

She dived to the ground, scrabbling to collect the scattered pieces, as Gordon rushed to her side, alarmed by the tone of rising hysteria, and seized her by the shoulders.

'Donna? – just look at you. It's only a bit of old pot. We'll soon get you another.'

'I don't want another!' Donna's voice began to soar.

'What were y'gonna tell us?' Gordon had remembered the morning's promise.

'Nothing,' she said, dully. 'False alarm.'

'D'you know what I thought?' His voice crackled with mirth.

'I thought y'were gonna tell us you'd fell for it.'

'What?'

'An oven-job.'

This was the final straw.

'Why would I say a thing like that?' Donna snapped, and slamming the door behind her, she ran sobbing up the stairs.

The room was painted pale lemon. Neither a boy's nor a

girl's colour, but beautifully appropriate for both. The cot in the corner, the pram, the high-chair, the soft toys, the tiny clothes, all in their Sellophane wrappers – the story was told at a glance. Donna flopped down in a chair and picked up the battered old teddy – her own since childhood – from under the cushion. She held it a while, stroking its face, straightening its legs, till the corner of her mouth started to tremble and she hurled the bear with all her might into the corner of her room. Hours later, it seemed, Donna heard the knocking on the door. Gordon came in and sat down silently, watching her a long while before he spoke.

'They don't happen overnight, y'know.'

Donna felt the tears rising.

'Six years isn't "overnight".'

'You know what they've said down the clinic.'

'Relax.' Donna's voice was heavy with sarcasm.

'Well, then?' Gordon sidled over and tried to kiss her. She went rigid.

'What's up?'

'Not in here.' She was glancing round the room, flinching at the sight of piled-up babyware which seemed to carry with it its own reproach. 'It just seems a bit . . . calculated.'

Gordon pulled away. There was no helping her tonight.

'Perhaps we'd better have a brew instead. See what film's on, eh?'

But it seemed he'd got it wrong again.

'I'm not a kid, Gordon,' Donna flared.

Very well, then – perhaps it was time for a bit of plain speaking.

'No. And you might find you'll have to be more grown-up than you're prepared for.'

'Meaning what?' she flashed.

'Meaning if it *never* happens.' There, he'd said it, gently as he could. 'We might have to face that, Donna.'

'We *will* face it,' she countered, spiritedly. 'When it happens.'

'Well, then.' He was glad she seemed more resigned to the idea.

'*If* it happens.'

A tiny glass of cream liqueur rested on the table, the room lay in darkness except for the glow from the lamp and the phosphorescence of the fish-tanks. Carol May was knitting, her feet swathed in slippers, her limbs revelling in the luxury of a freshly-laundered bathrobe. The film was hastening to its heart-rending conclusion. Carol May took off her reading-glasses as the first pin-pricks of tears began to cloud her eyes. The knitting continued, hands busy, determined to persevere. Then the tears welled up again and the click of needles ceased. Why was she being so silly? It was only a film. Sobs were coming in great gusts now as the tears washed freely down her face. 'You know me,' she would tell the girls tomorrow. 'I like a good cry over a film.'

But they *didn't* know her. And her tears were not for the film.

Jill had forgotten it could be so good. Indeed she'd rather forgotten it could even exist. What had brought that on?' she wondered. Surely even the film, good as it was, could not have roused them to such heights of passion. Now as she lay back on the rug, her heartbeat beginning to subside, she tried to remember the last time they'd made love on the living-room carpet. It was just after Sharon was three, she thought. Ray rolled back and surveyed her with triumph.

'What d'you say to that, then?'

Jill smiled happily. Surely he didn't need to ask?

'Thought I'd show yer what you'll be missing.'

Jill reached out and kissed him.

'I know that,' she whispered softly.

'Y'don't have to.'

'What?'

'Miss it.' Ray lowered his lips to hers. 'I needn't go.' Another kiss. 'I could have a crack at one of them retraining schemes.'

'Would yer?' Jill's head swam with happiness.

'That's provided . . . ' He kissed her again.

Jill felt herself catch her breath.

'Y'never thought what we've bin missing these months?' Ray murmured. 'Me comin' in, you here, tea sorted, place like a palace . . . '

' . . . me to look after yer, me to ask you how it's bin in the big world today . . . ' Jill hadn't been slow to catch his drift.

'I like it like that,' he purred. 'I know where we are.' He bent to kiss her again. 'Y'don't wanna get rid of us, do yer?'

Jill pulled out of the embrace and started to gather her clothes.

'Why d'you need to work?' she challenged.

'Why? Because this place is doin' me head in, because . . . '

'Y'don't want to be stuck in all day – y'want to feel worth summat – y'like the company – y'want to give yer brain cells a bit of an airing.'

'Yeah,' he agreed. If she knew that, why was she asking?

'Perhaps that's what *I* want an' all.'

Ray shook his head in disbelief. 'You've only bin at it two months.'

'Ray, it took us two *minutes* to realise the perks of bringing in me own wage.' She must try to make it simpler. 'I can hold me own out there. I feel useful. I do a good job of work.'

'Y'did a good job of work here,' Ray reminded her.

'Oh yeah – dusting the ornaments? Programming the washer? Guess what, Ray, I found it about as riveting as *you* do.'

Couldn't he see? Why didn't it make sense to him?

'You've had your needs attended to for fourteen years. High time *I* got a look in.'

But it wasn't clear. It hadn't sunk in.

'What d'y'mean?' He was genuinely hurt. 'I take you out on yer birthday. I spend a fortune at Christmas.'

'Not on *me*, Ray. On a hoover, on an ironing-board, on a new mop . . . I was the best-kit skivvy this side of Salford.'

Ray was taking umbrage in a big way.

'Ray, I'm not talking about birthday cards an' bunches of daffs. I mean *me*, getting out, doing something – even if it's only chasing coloured blobs of plastic round a circuit-board.'

'Will y'give over yapping and hear some sense?' Ray's voice soared above her chimes of explanation. 'I've said I won't go. You stop work. I'll stop here.' Jill fell silent. 'I'm prepared to compromise.'

Jill felt her blood start to boil. That was his idea of compromise? She wanted to fly at him, grab his head and knock some sense into it. Again he offered, as if with pride at the thought of his gesture: 'I'm prepared to compromise.'

Jill stared at him coldly. 'I'm not.'

'Right, then. Just think on.' Ray snatched up his clothes and began to dress. 'You had the choice – it's *you* that's sent us packing.' He paused to fling the final barb. 'And *you* can tell that to them two up there.'

'Hey you! – get your arse across here!'

Norma looked up and saw there was no escape from Queenie this time.

'Watch yer ankles,' warned Jill, as she approached the bench.

Norma peered gingerly under the table and found herself staring into the muzzle of a very mangy bull-terrier. She flashed Queenie a look of panic.

'I'm mindin' it, aren't I?' Queenie announced. 'Chunky's got wind of jobs down Agecroft. No Dogs Allowed.'

'There's none allowed here,' remarked Pauline acidly.

'No, but a fair few seem to have slipped through the net.'

Pauline was stung. She retreated to her handbag and fished for her lipstick.

'There'll be murder if top office gets wind.'

'Who's gonna tell 'em?'

'Definitely not me,' thought Norma, catching the full blast of Queenie's glare.

Klepto broke out into a salvo of sneezes.

'I'm allergic to dogs,' she simpered apologetically.

'Aye, an' we're allergic to bloody Nips!'

Norma thought she was about to be seized round the neck. 'I'll not be a sec . . .' She backed off hastily.

'You'll not be *alive* if y'don't spill them beans an' sharpish all over this bench.'

'There's nowt to spill,' stammered Norma. 'You know as much as *I* do.'

'Well, what's the bloody game on?' Pauline struck in.

'I've no idea. It's just a visit.'

'Aaagh, give over, girl – nobody "just visits" from the other side of the friggin' world. If *you* don't know what Smiler's up to . . . '

'I don't!'

'Well, you'd better find out,' blasted Queenie. 'Or just in case he's not clocked it yet . . . we could always broadcast who it is sets *you* all-of-a-flutter not a million miles from here!'

Norma flushed the colour of beetroot, then reddened even further when Rex's voice was heard, ringing over her shoulder in tones of heavy sarcasm:

'If you could just spare me a few moments of your valuable time, Norma . . . ?'

Contorted with embarrassment, Norma stumbled back to the office, while Queenie rubbed her hands in glee, predicting confidently: 'I think she'll find she knows more than she thought she did.'

*   *   *

105

Klepto was painting on a mouth of 'Sultry Scarlet' when Donna appeared behind her in the mirror.

'I'm just testin', she assured her, half-afraid that Donna would step into her father's shoes and lash her with reprimands. But Donna had lipstick of her own to apply – a new shade – and rather more daring than the subdued shades she normally favoured. Klepto watched her a while, then, seeming to summon up the courage, she ventured to address her.

'Y'know that red thing?'

'Mmmmmm?' Donna was still busy addressing the mirror.

'It *was* me – borrowed it, I mean.'

'Yes, I know.'

'Y'know!?' Klepto almost leapt through the roof. 'But you went an' stuck up for us.'

Donna continued to paint her face. To Klepto, at this moment, she appeared stern and terrifyng. In reality, she was trying not to laugh.

'Where is it, then?'

Klepto opened her bag and reluctantly slid out the red lace basque, fingering it longingly.

'When I saw it, I just knew . . . if I could have that, I would never wish for anything else.' Donna was still frowning. Klepto persisted. 'See, why is it just in books that girls get to wear red lace bodices? This one here' – she pulled out a paperback – *Passionate Interlude* – 'all the girls wear them. And Angelique de Belleville gets hers ripped off.' Donna was shaking her head – she didn't understand. It was alright for *her* . . .

'See, it's alright for *you* – you've got Gordon – you're used to passion and romance and . . .

'Yes.' Donna was suddenly brisk. 'But what's to happen with this?'

Klepto was at a loss. Fifteen quid or no basque – that was the deal. And she certainly didn't have that kind of money.

'We'll have to find a way to sneak it back, then.'

'Will we?' Klepto was bitterly disappointed.

'Yes.' Donna remained firm. 'We will.'

Now a new thought occurred to set her trembling.

'Yeah, but I *can't*. She'll know it's me!'

Donna took the basque, gazed at it a moment – almost regretfully, it could be said – then tucked it into her handbag.

'We'll do it now – while they're still on dinners.'

'Yeah, but . . .'

'What?'

Klepto was not to be reconciled to her loss. 'I've never wanted 'owt so much as that. D'y'know what I mean?'

Donna said nothing.

'Y'don't think she'd forget about it, do yer?' Klepto was clutching at straws again.

'No. I don't think she would.'

This was the final knell. Klepto began to snivel.

'We can't have *everything* we want, y'know.'

Donna thrust the girl a hankie and left her to it.

The factory floor was deserted as Donna sidled up to B-Group bench and stooped to look under Queenie's chair. Sure enough, the dog was there, curled into a heap and snuffling at a purloined circuit-board.

'Hey!' Donna hissed. The beast raised its porcine snout.

'Here, y'little sod!'

The dog rose eagerly to snatch the proffered basque from her outstretched hand, wagging its tail in gratitude. Donna cast about for further offerings, and fell upon the half-opened packet of cigarettes on Queenie's desk. Slipping this extra booty into the dog's maw, she turned and calmly strolled out.

'Don't tell us me ciggies have walked now!'

It didn't take Queenie long to spot this new disappearance.

107

'It's just as well me teeth are real or they'd be off an' all!' Queenie dived about the desk, scattering components, burrowing through belongings, till Donna rounded on her with impatience.

'Do you mind? Some of us prefer to work.'

'Bugger that!' retorted Queenie. 'My lungs are cryin' out for pollution.'

And she continued to wreak havoc among her work-mates, till finally the whole bench was obliged to down tools and join in the hunt for nicotine.

'Oh aye? – Man's Best Friend, is it?' Carol May directed Queenie's glance beneath her chair. 'A tea-leaf *and* a pervert?'

Queenie's wrath erupted.

'I'll kill it! I'll have it by the gear-bits! You wait while we're home, y'bugger – you'll wonder what wall's comin' at yer next!'

She was dusting down the rescued basque when Donna strolled across.

'I'm glad that's turned up.' Donna's voice was serene. 'Fifteen quid, was it?'

And laying down three £5 notes, she scooped the basque from the table and folded it away into her bag.

Pauline's jaw plummeted. 'By God, the bacon *has* hit the roof, then.'

Jill turned to Donna and squeezed her arm approvingly. 'Good for you, love.'

Klepto's head drooped, and presently the snivelling resumed.

Norma was hoping she might avoid further interrogation, when Queenie finally ran her to ground in the ladies' toilets.

'Well?'

'Well what?'

'You know friggin' well what.'

Norma conceded defeat. 'There *is* something . . . '

'That's better.'

'There's a file . . . '

'I'm listenin'.'

'With letters in it . . . '

'Aye?'

'From Them. Marked "Confidential".'

'And?'

'That's it.'

Queenie shook her head. 'That's not it.'

The full horror of what was being asked of her now dawned on Norma. 'Oh no . . . no, I couldn't . . . '

'Hey, who's askin' you to read it? All you've gotta do . . . '

'No, I can't . . . It's on his desk. I daren't sneak it out. How can I?'

'Well, if you can't fetch it *out*, girl, we'll just have to send someone *in* for it.'

'What d'you mean?' Terror now gripped her.

'It's dead easy, pet – all y'do is sit there . . . '

Norma sat there, typing, beads of sweat gathering on her brow, as Rex pointed out the latest production figures to the Koreans clustering round his desk. Suddenly the door creaked ajar. Norma shot bolt upright in her seat and resolutely kept on typing. Seconds later her legs all but gave way, as a low growl arose from under her desk, and looking down, she saw the dog scowling expectantly up at her. Norma seized the Confidential file, thrust it beneath her chair, closed her eyes, expecting at any minute to hear the order for her dismissal – then opened them again in time to see a mangy tail disappearing out of the door. She rushed to the coffee machine and pressed for '3 sugars'.

' . . . very impressed with your latest figures . . . delighted we could reach agreement over our proposed deal . . . our first batch of components should reach you by the end of the month . . . '

Queenie snatched the file from Jill's grasp.

'So that's the game, is it? Pollutin' British goods with bloody Nip rubbish!'

'It's a bloody insult, y'know!'

'I like the way we're kept informed.'

'We won't have to learn Japanese, will we?'

This last, a wail from Klepto, sent the crescendo of protest spiralling even higher, till, alarmed by the mounting hysteria, the dog beneath Queenie's seat began to bark.

'Shut that bloody dog up!'

All hands launched themselves to grab its muzzle.

'Bolt that kisser, y'little bleeder!' encouraged Queenie, all to no avail. The dog twisted round and wheeled away under the bench, Pauline and Donna in hot pursuit.

'Get it!'

'*You* get it!'

The shouting soared, the barking defied all attempts to silence it, till over the tannoy came Norma's tones, almost hoarse with panic: 'Telephone call for Mrs Fox! Urgent telephone call for Mrs Fox!'

Queenie flew towards Klepto. 'Get on the floor!' she ordered.

Klepto started to gibber.

'Get on the floor!' hissed Queenie, helping Klepto into position with a sharp stab of the foot. 'Now bark!'

'Y'what?'

'Start barking!'

Another threatened footprint to the face saw Klepto finding unknown reserves of canine impersonation. The dog, alas, was determined to turn her virtuoso performance into a duet.

'Now twitch!'

Klepto felt a sneeze coming on.

'Twitch, divvy – yer havin' a fit!'

And so the sight which greeted Bernie when he marched across from Rex's office, was a twitching, sneezing, barking mass, writhing across the floor.

'She's havin' a fit, poor lamb.' Carol May assured him.

A snarl arose from beneath the bench. Encouraged by the end of Queenie's boot, Klepto broke into another volley of frenzied barking. Bernie stepped back in panic.

'Get her to Norma! We can't have her in here like that. It might be catching!'

'I should say so,' Pauline concurred.

'I never knew she went like that.' Bernie was way out of his depth.

'It's her you-know-what,' whispered Queenie. 'Time of the month.'

'Oh . . . er . . . right . . . say no more . . . righty-ho . . . '

Bernie flushed scarlet and eagerly made way for Rex.

'Okay, what's the problem?'

As Bernie was muttering in his ear, Queenie spotted Norma signalling an escape route, and dispatched the dog towards the exit with a boot to its hindquarters.

'Poor love's beside herself,' sighed Jill, bending over the invalid.

'Simon!'

The boy came running in response to the summons.

'Y'better carry her off to see Norma.'

'Me? Carry?' Simon's embarrassment scaled new heights.

'That's what I said.'

And now Klepto was to suffer the further indignity of being mangled into something resembling a rugby tackle, and then unceremoniously dumped as Simon overbalanced and plunged to the ground beneath her.

'Give over, daft-head.'

Donna's intervention spared Klepto further blushes, and gave Jill the opportunity to slip across to Norma's office and return the file to her trembling grasp.

'Alright, alright, y'never seen a fit before?' Bernie was determined to impress the Koreans with the power of his authority.

The girls repaired to their bench.

111

'I want them all assembled in the canteen for five o'clock,' Rex instructed.

There was no time to assess the significance of that remark before Jill returned, mission accomplished, and the panic subsided to sighs of relief.

'What's the big idea, then?'

Bustling to take his place in front of the assembled workforce, Bernie found his way barred by Pauline. He flashed her a smile of condescension.

'I think we can safely say we've pulled off a major coup here. I think we are talking yet another first for Great Britain in the world trade stakes. Pushing forth the frontiers of technological expansion . . . '

Rex's arrival put a stop to this oration. 'Right, ladies, there's no mystery. This company's in serious trouble.'

He was cold and unsmiling. The girls felt a chill descend.

'You all know we're one of only two companies turning out our type of product. Till two months ago we could undercut Blains of Greenock by twenty per cent. Now Blains are undercutting us by fifteen per cent. As a result, we're about to be put out of business.'

Murmurings rose from the shop floor. Rex continued. 'Our Chairman Mr Beachcroft has worked out a deal with Yongchon Electronics which allows us to undercut Blains by a further ten per cent. We'll continue to work as usual, but we'll be importing certain components from Korea and we'll also in effect be Yongchon's first export outlet in this country.'

Something about his coldness gave the impression he personally did not favour the deal. But this was not the place to offer up dissent.

'That's all, ladies. Thank you.'

A hush fell as he headed for the exit, accompanied by Bernie and the Korean delegation, but as the door closed, mayhem, led by Queenie, broke loose.

'Why, what did I tell yer? It's Pearl Harbour all over again!'

'Least we've still got jobs,' Jill pointed out.

'Oh aye, we'll soon see what that's worth when they start flyin' their Kung Fu sessions at us first thing in the morning!'

'Where is Korea anyway?' Pauline wanted to know.

'It's some pit over east, full of junks, chop suey an' little yeller midgets that can't talk properly!'

Donna could keep silent no longer. 'Since they've been good enough to keep us in business, we could at least learn to treat them with a bit of respect.'

'I won't waste me breath,' declared Queenie. 'I was here first. If they wanna work with me, *I'm* the one wants treatin' with respect. An' that goes for the rest of yer if you've any sense.' And she paused before firing them her parting shot.

'Ask yerself why the Giant Panda's nearly extinct!'

Klepto scraped back her hair and tied it into the knot so favoured by her father. Still smarting from Donna's betrayal, the afternoon's events had barely registered. Dogs, Koreans, components, fits . . . but it was Donna who occupied her thoughts still. Donna ought to be ashamed of herself, Donna who should be afraid to speak to her ever again.

'When's yer birthday?'

Yet here was the iniquituous Donna actually having the nerve to address her.

'Why?' she snapped back.

'It's come early.'

Donna thrust a brown paper bag into her hand and disappeared onto the toilets. Suspiciously Klepto lifted a corner and peered in.

Carol May was the first to notice the foolish grin.

'What *you* lookin' so pleased about?'

Klepto twisted, smirked, looked coy, then turned her back and appeared to be fiddling with the buttons on her overall. The girls had gathered, intrigued by this performance, till Klepto whipped round, flashed open her overall and revealed, in all its gaudy splendour, the red basque. Cheers of laughter rang out, soon to be joined by rounds of applause, as the passing Korean delegation chanced upon the spectacle and added its own approval to the gathering hubbub. Bernie thought it polite to avert his eyes.

Jill turned in her sleep and woke with a start. He'd gone. Where was he? 5.55.am. What was he doing up at this time? She threw on a dressing-gown and tiptoed to the door. He was standing at the bottom of the stairs, bent over the hall table, apparently scribbling a note. Jill saw the suitcase beside him, and stared down the stairs.

'Go back to bed.' He looked up and saw her look of anger.

'I don't believe it. You were just gonna go.'

'A lift came up.'

'Now?'

'I need to get me digs an' that sorted.'

'When was this arranged?'

Ray screwed up the note he'd been writing. 'Last night,' he admitted.

Jill was incensed. 'You were just gonna nob off, without sayin' ta-ra? – without us even tellin' the kids what's happening?'

'Sssssh!' Ray implored her to keep her voice down. 'I thought *you* could tell 'em. They'll only get mard. I hate them skriking. I can't handle it.'

'Oh, and I can, I suppose?'

Their voices had brought Sharon and Nicky to the top of the stairs.

'What's happening?'

'Who's going?' Nicky had spotted the suitcase.

Miraculously, Jill and Ray suddenly became light and cheerful.

'Yer dad is, love. It won't be for long. He's off to Folkestone, diggin' the Tunnel. Aren't you excited for him?'

'Why's it exciting? Why can't he stop here and dig?' Sharon, as ever, knew how to throw cold water on all Jill's efforts.

'Because he doesn't like what's on offer round here. He wants summat to suit his skills. Don't yer, love?'

'Yes, love,' Ray concurred brightly.

'And he'll phone us every night, and send us cards, and we'll see him every weekend . . . '

'Not *every* weekend, love.'

Jill's smile slipped.

'I thought you said . . . '

Sharon came to the rescue. 'He might as well stop here for what that'll cost.'

Jill resumed her catalogue of delights. 'You'll have tea round yer nan's, we'll have all that money coming in, no more creeping for hand-outs . . . '

Nicky started to cry. 'Who's gonna take us to United?'

Jill and Ray rushed to soothe him. 'I *will* be home some weekends, love . . . and why not see if yer mam will take yer?'

'Me mam's embarrassin',' Nicky wailed. 'She don't even know who Brian McClair is.'

Jill grabbed the baton with desperate jollity. 'Well, we shall learn who he is, shan't we? We shall get up off our backsides and move with the times. And if there's nothing down for us here, we shall go out there and look for it. Y'know what they say – it's an open market, a free country . . . '

'Who says that? Jackanory?' Sharon was scathing, but Jill forged on.

' . . . and what counts is making sure this family's alright, with decent standards of living – and we shan't

115

let a few hundred miles get the best of us – will we, love?'

'No, love,' Ray was beginning to feel he had all the dignity of a jack-in-a-box in this little charade.

'We aren't a family, are we, though? – if we're stuck here an' me dad sods off to the seaside.'

Sharon had that uncanny knack of undermining every point you tried to make.

'It won't be any holiday for him, love – you can be sure of that.'

A car horn sounded. Rather too eagerly for Jill's liking, Ray picked up his bags.

'I'm off, then.'

He submitted bravely while the kids wept, complained and clung to him. Unable to look Jill in the eye, he kissed her on the cheek and ran out.

Sharon continued to chime out the glad tidings. 'Eddie Beak's dad went workin' away. His mam's just got her divorce.'

'Is it 'cos of me?' Nicky was saying. 'Is it 'cos I done bad at school?'

' 'Course it's not,' Jill assured him. 'It's . . . '

' 'Cos of her,' Sharon accused. ' 'Cos she won't stop home an' mind house for us like he's asked her.'

'It is nothing of the sort,' Jill flared.

'It is an' all. It's just 'cos you want yer own way, so you've made him go, and now we won't see him for ages . . . '

Now Sharon started to cry and Nicky pealed in with his own contribution. Jill was beside herself with indecision. Suddenly she opened the front door and shouted. 'Ray . . . !'

Jill was running down the street, dressing-gown flapping behind her.

'Ray . . . !'

She must ask him to stay. She must swallow her pride,

suppress her own feelings, anything . . . but she mustn't let him leave.

The car was beginning to pull away as she ran up and hammered on the window. To her surprise she realised Ray had more than one fellow-traveller. Six bodies squeezed into the car, all seeming remarkably chirpy for such a dismal errand, all looking as if they were embarking on a day out instead of leaving home and family for God knows how long. The reason for their cheer appeared to reside in the opened cans of lager which nestled in their laps – Ray's included – and the breezy patter of the early-morning DJ.

Ray wound down the window – and tried to wipe the smile off his face.

'What's up, love?'

'I wanted to ask yer . . . ' Jill faltered. Ray's mates were grinning at her. She must look a sorry sight.

' . . . to remember to phone us when yer settled in.'

Behind her Sharon loosed a huff of contempt. Before her Ray was smiling, patronisingly, patting her on the hand. 'I'll see what I can do, love.'

Then the window was wound up again, the car moved off; Ray picked up his lager and smiled with relief.

Standing on the pavement, Jill watched him drive away. She recognised that smile; she knew its source. It was something to do with having your cake and eating it.

She turned round to see Sharon scowling, Nicky weeping, and the empty house beckoning.

CHAPTER FOUR

May

'I am well known for my sparkling wit and sense of humour.'

Any minute now, Jill thought, I'm going to brain that girl.

'Men are often intimidated by my intellect.'

'You'll be intimidated by a lash round the arse if y'don't nail that gob of yours an' sharpish!'

Queenie voiced what the rest of the bench had been thinking for the last twenty minutes. Computer Dating was Klepto's latest notion. Had this been a Monday morning – when energies ran high and patience was at a premium – it might have gone down better – but timing being one of the girl's lesser virtues, she'd chosen the tail-end of Friday afternoon, when a long week and short tempers combined to yield her a less-than-lukewarm reception.

'God, I'm paggered.'

Queenie flung down her soldering and lit a cigarette. B–Group had not performed well this week. The number of faulty circuit-boards had rocketed, and Bernie's habitual jig of rage was turning into a veritable war-dance. Elsewhere, the components supply had dried up, the Pick and Place machine was on the blink, the office switchboard lay strewn in a mass of wires across Rex's desk, and workers and management alike were counting the minutes to the start of the weekend.

Everyone, that is, except Jill. Could she focus her

thoughts, she would have to concede that the coming weekend promised more problems than pleasure. Ray was due home – and what had once been keenly anticipated, of late had become – dare she say it? – almost a chore, a hiccup in her well-organised schedule. How they had reached this sorry state, she couldn't quite remember, but there they were – and she'd found herself unusually preoccupied with the problem this week.

'Yer wanted.'

Jill was back to earth with a start as Bernie muttered in her ear.

'In the office – if you please.'

Jill frowned. Whatever Rex wanted, she could have done without it right now.

Queenie watched her go with a look of suspicion.

'What's all that about?'

Bernie, for once, was happy to enlighten her.

'It's about the dross coming off this bench, Queenie – some of it so gash, it wouldn't look out of place on your car.'

And he strolled off, swelling with triumph, leaving Queenie, for once, speechless at his sheer audacity.

'Okay, let's hear about it.'

Jill stared back at Rex, uncomprehending.

'Some problem? Something upsetting you?'

She shifted uncomfortably. 'Why d'you ask?'

'Because all those rejects, all the faulty circuit-boards . . . come back to *you*.'

'Me?' Jill gawped in disbelief.

'Like it or not, Jill, that check-up system's accurate to a T . . . and you're the one it keeps pulling out. Now I don't know how long it's been going on, but it stops right here.' Then, more gently, 'C'mon, Jill, you're a good worker. If something's bothering you . . . leave it at home, eh?'

Jill was stunned. Not for one moment had she imagined her domestic problems could be affecting her work . . .

119

The arrival of Simon halted further speculation. He burst through the door like a derailed 125 and flung himself on Rex's desk.

'It's one of *them*!'

Rex's eyebrows raised itself in query. 'I beg your pardon?'

'Here! Now! Just come in!' And he gestured towards the far end of the corridor where there now stood a small, immaculately dressed gentleman of distinctly Korean extraction. Simon thrust a card into Rex's fist.

'That's all we need.' Rex handed the card over for Bernie's perusal.

'Mr Kim Soo Yung . . . ?'

Norma stopped typing and looked up, horrified. 'Yes, but he's . . . '

'Correct,' Rex intervened. 'The son . . . of the president . . . of our Korean partners.'

'But what's he doing here?' Bernie flustered.

Rex eyed the visitor with ill-concealed resentment.

'I think I've got a pretty fair idea.

And, buttoning his jacket, he went out to greet the new arrival, leaving behind him a frenzy of activity, as Norma, Bernie and Jill attempted to return the office to a convincing state of efficiency.

'Mr Kim Soo Yung . . . just "dropped in" for a visit on behalf of our Korean partners, Yongchon Electronics . . . '

Rex was standing beside the visitor at B-Group bench, his civility strained to the limit.

'I'm sure you ladies will be elated to answer any questions Mr Kim might care to ask about productivity, attitude, morale, etc . . . We regret he couldn't give us any advance notice of his visit, but I dare say they do things differently in Korea . . . ' Then nodding to his second-in-command: 'Thank you, Bernie – if Mr Kim would like to accompany you to the machine room . . . '

All heads swivelled to watch them go, but scarcely had

they turned the corner when Queenie's own particular brand of racial tolerance burst forth in its most vibrant form.

'Bloody shifty, sneakin', slit-eyed pair of sharks!'

She turned to address the factory at large. 'Just dropped in? Oh, who's he kiddin', eh? Our Marg's got overrun by friggin' Nips. Glide in, no warning, try'na skelp yer with yer gear-bits exposed! Never trust a bugger that builds houses outa paper and goes to work in pyjamas!'

Rex treated Queenie to a rare smile of approbation. 'Ever considered a career with the foreign office?' he enquired.

Norma stood at the wages hatch, rigid with nerves. Behind her left shoulder, the inscrutable face of Mr Kim peered down as her trembling fingers handed out the packets and ticked off the names. No matter that this man had been effusive in his greetings, charming in manner, faultlessly courteous – to Norma he was a VIP – and a foreign one at that! – and nothing she'd learnt at Mrs Biddle's Typing School had prepared her to be in a presence of such magnitude.

Further down the wages queue, Donna was in a quandary. Jill's behaviour had been puzzling her these last few weeks. It was out of character, it didn't ring true. She might just try a few enquiries . . .

'Back tonight, is he?' she ventured, rousing Jill out of her now-customary daze.

'Oh . . . yeah . . . about ten.'

'You'll miss him, eh?' Donna pursued. 'Folkestone's a fair trek.'

'Oh, I don't know – I'm getting quite keen.' Jill affected unconcern. 'All this independence. Saves us living in each other's pockets.'

Donna looked sceptical.

'Oh yes,' Jill persisted. 'Actually we've not gone on so well in years. It's worked wonders.'

'That's handy,' Donna remarked. 'Not like *some* folk, then?'

'How d'you mean?' Jill didn't like Donna's tone.

'Never known what's slipped through their fingers till they've seen it slung round somebody else's neck.'

'Oh, I don't think so, Donna,' retorted Jill, hotly. 'We're not still kids, y'know.'

'Don't soft-soap 'em, girl – that's the trick.' Here was Queenie with another fount of wisdom. 'Never let 'em think they're indispensable. Why d'you think I've never let him get his woolly nine carats round *my* wedding finger? And you look at us, eh? Marital bliss without the maritals!'

Jill smiled feebly. Advice was cheap – particularly Queenie's. Real solutions came a bit dearer.

Norma trembled as Rex brushed past her wrist and fished out a wage-packet. Was there some problem? Normally Rex kept well away from the hatch at wages time. Now he checked through the figures, looked up at the recipient and handed over the packet. Carol May stood silent, impassive. Her eyes met his but their expression registered no change. Then she turned and walked back to her seat. Problem apparently solved, Rex, too, vacated the hatch and repaired to his office, leaving Norma writhing under the vigilance of Mr Kim. Queenie's fist now snaked across the counter and seized the proffered brown envelope.

'Ninety quid for forty hours graft! – I won't know where to stick it all!'

And leaving a bemused Mr Kim to wonder why the blame should somehow be laid at *his* door, she stomped back to the bench.

*   *   *

With a shudder of relief, Norma reached for her coat and fished thankfully for the bus pass. Ahead of her lay A Quiet Weekend, thank you very much. A little light gardening, a spot of chutney-making . . . her modest schemes would soon relieve the tension of the last half-hour, spent trembling in the company of the Orient.

'Any plans for the weekend?'

Rex's enquiry made her jump, but before she could respond, Mr Kim's voice was heard, replying amiably, 'None at all. I'm entirely at your disposal.'

Rex cursed silently under his breath.

'Ah, well . . . now . . . you've rather caught us on the hop, turning up out of the blue . . . so I doubt if we can manage to lay on our usual lavish hospitality . . . '

Mr Kim smiled agreeably. 'I'm sure my father would consider you'd made every possible effort.'

The threat apparent in this innocent remark, though unperceived by Norma, did not escape Rex. As she buttoned up her coat, Norma was aware of Rex elaborately rifling through his diary in search of a free half-hour.

'Well, it looks as if I'm tied up with company business the entire weekend,' he sighed in tones of regret. 'However, I'd be very happy to put my assistant Norma at your disposal.'

In the doorway Norma froze, rooted to the spot.

'I suggest we get on to the Britannia for our usual suite,' Rex was saying. 'And if we could organise a car to take you and Mr Kim into town . . . ' Rex turned to Mr Kim. 'This young lady's, as it were, our "hospitality expert".'

Mr Kim looked intrigued.

'A very skilled, very capable young person . . . knows the business intimately.' Rex drew the visitor to one side and whispered confidentially, 'I'm very happy to put her *entirely* at your service, Mr Kim. I don't think you'll have any complaints.'

Behind him Norma's eyes widened in panic.

'Now if you'll excuse me, Mr Kim. I've one or two

things to check up on before the weekend . . . ' Rex shook hands with the visitor and abruptly left the office.

Mr Kim turned to Norma, confusion and concern mounting by the second. How had Rex described her? Their 'hospitality expert'? What precisely did that mean? In his own country the term embraced a wide range of services, not to mention pleasures . . . But in England . . . Nothing he had learnt at the Harvard Business School, or from his more widely travelled colleagues at home, had prepared him for this. He would play it by ear, he decided. He would wait to see what was expected of him and take it from there.

'So . . .' he ventured to the owl-eyed creature quaking in the corner. 'You and I go to the hotel together. And then . . . ?' Norma groped behind her for the door.

'Er . . . 'scuse me a second,' she gibbered, and easing herself into the corridor, broke instantly into a gallop.

Extreme circumstances required extreme measures, and in the event there was only one way to turn. She turned.

'Go back *where* with him?' Queenie's shriek could have shattered lightbulbs. 'He's only got you down for one of them geisha girls! Tryna slope his sleazy oriental grip on defenceless, decent, Queen's English-speakin' women! *I'll* give him hospitality!'

Norma felt her pulse start to race. 'What y'gonna do?'

Queenie's smile was pure evil. 'Entertain him.'

Mr Kim stood outside the factory entrance clutching his suitcase. Beside him hovered Norma, beady-eyed alert to the smallest twitch of his eyebrow. A rumble like the approach of thunder, a cloud of fumes, a quiver of furry dice, and round the corner roared the 'Flying Ashtray',

124

scattering pedestrians, mounting the curb and almost detaching Mr Kim from his foot.

'Right, pal! – forget the funny stuff! In the back!'

It wasn't the most polite invitation Mr Kim had heard, but it was certainly the most persuasive. Queenie threw his suitcase into the boot, stood aside to let Norma scramble gratefully into the passenger seat, and finally slammed the door on Mr Kim as he sat cowering in the back. Not that the leg-room could be called deluxe from where he was sitting, cumbered as it was by empty lager cans, old take-away tins and . . . what was that old piece of fur coat festering in the corner? He tried to move it to one side. It emitted a low growl. He started back against the seat as the fur-coat raised its head and bared an impressive set of teeth.

'You mind that friggin' dog,' Queenie snarled. 'It's worth money, that is,' and jamming her foot to the floor, she swerved round an oncoming lamp-post and plunged out into the traffic. Mr Kim closed his eyes and prayed.

The receptionist shook her head. 'I'm sorry, madam, we don't seem to have a Mr Foo Yung down here.'

Norma flushed with embarrassment. 'No . . . well . . . y'won't, you see, because he's only just . . . '

'Whaddayamean, don't seem to have!' The chandelier rang to the chimes of Queenie's voice. 'D'you know who that is stood over there?' and she directed the receptionist's attention to Mr Kim who was gazing forlornly at a display of weeping figs, still clutching his suitcase. The receptionist apparently did *not* recognise the illustrious visitor, till a hiss in the ear from Queenie sent her scurrying to the book – with miraculous results.

'Ah, yes . . . here we are . . . if His Royal Highness would just like to sign . . . '

Queenie turned to Norma with a snort of triumph, Mr Kim beamed with relief, and even Norma's expression was hovering on the brink of a smile, when suddenly, a chorale of shrieks went up from the hotel lobby, and sixteen elderly American ladies, checking in at the start of a poetry-reading tour, scattered in all directions. The reason for their exodus soon became evident. Down the steps and out of the hotel leapt the dog, bearing between its jaws six assorted handbags. Queenie looked at Norma. Norma gaped at Mr Kim. And within seconds they were standing outside on the pavement, smarting from the threats of the manager, who'd had the temerity to suggest that the dog had been *trained* to carry out such raids!'

'We could always try the Holiday Inn . . .' Norma ventured feebly.

But Mr Kim had other ideas.

'No, no, no, please – the Holiday Inn is not necessary. I would much prefer your own hospitality.'

Norma was beside herself with panic. 'No, but . . . I've got nothing in . . . there's no room . . . only one b—'

She checked herself in time to avoid the dreaded word 'bed', but found Mr Kim apparently determined to foist himself upon her.

'No, please . . . it would be an honour. I'm very keen to learn more about your country, your customs – to get to know our British partners a little better.'

'Oh aye, that's yer game, is it?' Queenie broke in. 'Well, have it yer own way, pal. You wanna hob nob with the Great British worker? You shift yer lallies back in there.'

Kim clambered obediently into the back seat of the 'Flying Ashtray.'

'So now we are going to . . . ?'

'Give yer the time of yer life, pal!' Queenie vowed darkly, lunging back into the traffic in a flare of exhaust fumes.

By seven o'clock, Jill was in the kitchen, doing a very respectable impersonation of an octopus. One hand

126

stirred the casserole, another wound a lock of hair round the curling tongs, another seemed to be unwrapping a bunch of pinks, while a fourth arranged the whole display in a vase and went back to tending the stove. Jill was excited. Suddenly the thought of seeing Ray again made her feel as silly and self-conscious as a seventeen-year-old. She was determined. This weekend was going to be good.

The Flying Ashtray cruised to a halt in a grubby car-park outside a grubby block of flats. Queenie, no longer standing on ceremony, helped the dog out with her toe-cap, and stalked off into a side-entrance, pursued by the hapless Norma. Mr Kim remained to struggle with his suitcase.

Chunky looked up from the habitual debris of the living-room floor and grinned.

'We're blinkin' made, love.'

Queenie's eyes narrowed in suspicion.

'It's hot, that is. It's that bleedin' hot, you could fry eggs off it!'

Queenie's glare took in three wooden crates open on the floor. 'Somebody's arse'll be friggin' *roasted* if I don't hear some decent explanations, startin' now!'

But Chunky was not so easily subdued. 'All the way from Tenerife – strictly hush-hush – exclusive A1 merchandise . . . '

Queenie approached the nearest box. The corner of her mouth twitched but her expression never faltered.

'I'm waitin'.'

The calm voice struck a chill through Chunky.

'What for?' he enquired.

'To hear how the frig you've managed to land us with three ton of walkin' pie crusts.'

'Contacts, love. I know people.'

'Let's hope to God they never know me,' his mate blasted. 'The villains that fleeced a div-head like you for a heap of pet-shop chuck-outs!'

'No, no, y'can't get stuff like that these days,' Chunky assured her. 'We'll make a killing.'

'Oh aye, one of us will,' she growled. 'Y'better hope it's you.'

And she continued to glower at the sight which met her eyes – no less than six dozen assorted tortoises, clambering and scraping in the bottom of their crates.

Chunky's sudden look of surprise reminded her of another painful fact of life for the weekend. Norma and Kim were peeping diffidently round the door.

'Oh aye, lad, we'd better mind our manners now. We've got guests.'

And Queenie spat the word as if it were a streak of catarrh.

Norma thought of her chutney, and inwardly wept.

Jill had gone for the 'casual look' this evening. In other words, it had taken her about an hour and a half to achieve this appearance of effortless style. She rearranged her position in the chair – if Ray came in now, she would look better from this angle – and flicked the switch on the TV. The nine o'clock news was finishing. Half an hour to go. Her excitement rose – and she tried simultaneously to digest the two conflicting pearls of wisdom offered by Donna and Queenie: 'Don't take him for granted,' and 'Don't let him think he's indispensable.' Both contained the seeds of wisdom, neither told the whole story.

Well, hopefully the conflict wouldn't arise. The weekend was going to be a success.

'Mam, is he here yet?'

Jill wasn't the only one too excited to sit still.

'Back to bed, you two,' she ordered.

'Can't we stop up?' Nicky was pleading.

'No, you can not. It's too late for you. And you'll have something to "aaagh" about if you're not back inside them covers before I get this slipper off my foot!'

But her tone belied her. Excitement, not anger was speaking. She went over and pecked them goodnight. 'Off you go. He'll come up and see you.'

And, mollified, they trouped off upstairs, leaving Jill to retouch her 'natural looks', which were starting to melt.

Norma perched rigidly on the edge of the seat and sipped her tea. From the depths of the armchair Queenie was watching Chunky with mounting irritation. He glanced up at her and smiled feebly.

'They do like their exercise.'

Which was supposed to explain why sixty samples of illegal merchandise were now crawling about the carpet, being chased into columns of size and shape by their new owner.

'They don't *do* much, do they?' observed Norma.

That was a mistake. Queenie felt her hackles start to soar.

'Probably still a bit jet-lagged,' Chunky ventured.

The same might be said for the visitor who now poked his head round the door. Chunky, sensing a fellow-victim, nodded amiably.

'Alright, mate?'

'Thank you, yes . . . my room is . . . charming.'

''Y' won't see facilities like this where *you* come from,' Queenie grunted inhospitably.

'No, no . . . our style is certainly not so . . . "individual" as yours.' Kim's smile was not without irony.

'Fancy a bite to eat, mate?' Chunky's relationship with his stomach was basically one of affectionate indulgence.

'That would be delightful.' Kim hadn't eaten since the flight. 'Do we dine here or in town?'

Queenie's temper exploded.

'We don't "dine" anywhere, pal. Round here yer eat what's goin' an' bloody like it.'

Kim smiled amiably.

'I'm entirely at your disposal,' he assured her.

Which was his first mistake.

Jill leapt to her feet as the car drew up, then subsided with disappointment as it pulled into the gates across the road. She glanced at her watch. He was half an hour late.

'There yer are, pal,' Queenie announced with a sneer. 'Here's some of your lot.'

Mr Kim was standing beneath the lurid yellow neon sign which dismally proclaimed 'Wong Yip Chinese Chippy.' Should he bother to explain the differences – socially, culturally, politically, geographically – between China and South Korea? No, he decided, taking in Queenie's scowl of hostility. On balance, probably not.

'This'll make yer feel at home, eh?' she persisted, elbowing him into the queue.

As a matter of fact, it didn't. The rowdiness of the inmates, the seediness of the decor, and the collection of congealed batter behind the counter – none of this rang a bell.

'So, this is your "dining out"?' he inquired, good-humouredly.

Queenie rounded on him in a flash of molars.

'Why, what's the matter with it? What do *you* have, then?'

'Oh, we are more . . . "formal".' Kim picked his words with care. 'Not so . . . "relaxed".'

Queenie sprang aside as one of the more vocal specimens further up the queue suddenly reeled outside and proceeded to vomit against the front window.

'Yeah, well, we don't all get *that* relaxed,' she sniffed in disgust, then stopped short. She didn't have to apologise for this dump. If he didn't like it he could lump it.

Kim smiled back good-humouredly. Queenie began to be intrigued. What was the matter with him? Why wasn't he complaining? Couldn't he see what a pigsty it was? She would try a different tack.

'So what does the wife say to it, then? All this gaddin' off, hob-nobbing with civilised people.'

'It's part of my job. She understands that.'

'Ah, so yer *are* married, then?' she crowed, with a glance at Norma.

'And I have three lovely children,' he beamed, pulling out a photo from his wallet and handing it to her.

'Aaaaaaaaahhhh.' Norma melted instantly.

'Get a grip, woman!' Queenie glanced briefly at the photogenic cherubs and their picturesque mother, and tossed the photo back.

'I bet y'don't breathe a word of what you get up to on yer "business trips",' she jibed.

'My wife and I have no secrets from each other.'

Queenie was flabbergasted. 'What? – y'mean you just . . . like . . . *trust* each other?'

'But of course. Don't you?'

Queenie roared in disbelief. 'Trust *him*? Go'way, lad – I know his tricks like the back of me hand. He's a sneakin', conniving little rat.'

'Ah, that makes a difference.' Kim was disarmingly sincere. 'My wife is not a rat. I hope she could not marry a rat either.'

Queenie was starting to founder. Was there no way of goading this man? She mustered another attack.

'And who's idea is it to send you sneckin' over here, try'na catch us with our kecks half-mast?'

Kim reddened slightly. 'My father likes to keep an eye on his investments. To see how British industry *really* works.' He paused. 'My father's methods would not always be mine. For instance, I would have preferred to announce my arrival in advance.'

131

'Yer not the only one, pal.'

'I've no complaints,' he turned to Norma with a smile. 'I think I'm in good hands.'

Queenie was baffled. This man was too gracious, too amiable for words, and yet, from the little she had observed of his progress round the factory, he also appeared uncommonly smart. She would have to keep a tight rein on herself. Already she was finding it difficult to be rude to him. A kind of grudging respect was beginning to dawn. If she wasn't careful she might find herself starting to *like* him! They had reached the head of the queue, the spoils of the Wong Yip cuisine dispersed before them. How was it she'd never noticed before? Queenie wondered. The charred stumps of sausage, the lumpen vats of gravy, the dog-eared chunks of batter . . . how could anyone in their right mind regard this fare as edible, let alone base their entire diet around it? She glanced at Kim. He was bearing up admirably.

'What would you . . . er . . . recommend?' he enquired politely.

'A coupla Rennie's an' a blindfold?' she volunteered.

The ladle hovered over a cauldron of curry sauce.

'Next please?'

'Steak pie, sausage, chips and peas, four times.'

Queenie was having second thoughts.

'D'you do stomach pumps an' all, pal?'

By eleven o'clock Jill's good mood had evaporated, along with half the casserole. She dumped the fossilised remains, still steaming, into the sink, and switched off the oven. Back in the living-room, plates and table-settings were snatched up, as she blew out the lingering stubs of candle. Her 'effortless' glamour was now looking effortlessly frazzled. She told herself she didn't care.

*   *   *

The English Banquet.

Queenie stood in the doorway, saw the outspread detritus, the festering pools of curry sauce, the leaking cartons, the chip-spattered newspaper . . . and glowered. That spectacle was bad enough, but what really got to her was the sight of Kim, still dressed in his suit and tie, arranging his own modest meal with whatever small ceremony was possible, amidst the chaos, while Chunky, oblivious to all but the call of his stomach, sat gawping at the snooker, a meat pie in one fist and a beer can in the other. Now and again a gravy-sodden chip was thrown in the direction of the dog, who often as not ignored it, preferring instead to scavenge from Norma, who was attempting to pick her way through the grease with a plastic fork.

Kim was behaving with great equanimity. He was a guest, this must be some local ritual, he would look as if he was enjoying it.

Chunky belched and drained a carton of mushy peas into his throat. Queenie erupted.

'Hey, lad!' She dealt him a whack across the ears. 'Do we not have plates in this house!'

She marched off into the kitchen and could be heard trying vainly to unearth some clean crockery.

'What's up with *her*, then?' Chunky gaped.

Kim was all eyes for the snooker and politely did not hear.

The taxi drew up on the dot of midnight. Ray paid the driver and crossed the street. The living-room light was still on. He was glad she hadn't gone to bed.

Jill sprang up from the chair in delight, glimpsed the clock on the mantlepiece . . . and felt her irritation kindle.

Ray stood in the doorway, grinning like a ten-year-old, waiting to be kissed . . . and Jill heard herself snapping in response: 'What time d'you call this?'

133

'Bloody train come in two hours late.'

'Yer tea's ruined.'

'I'm not that peckish, love.'

'If I'd known I'd not have bothered.'

'Kids asleep?'

'At this hour? I should hope so.'

Ray was remarkably composed this evening. Even as she stalked about, plumping up the cushions, tidying the ashtrays, he watched her passively, waiting for that kiss. Jill caught a glimpse of herself in the mirror. Her face had given up the struggle and now looked merely grim. Behind her, Ray stood patiently, still hoping. Something was different about him tonight. What was it? She felt her resentment stir.

'New clothes,' she flashed.

Ray grinned with pride. So it had been worth all the effort. She had noticed.

'That's what Folkestone does, is it? You'll be getting too grand for us next.'

Ray could hardly believe his ears. 'Great stuff.' He pouted. 'Welcome home, love.'

'Don't be so sure.'

Jill bounced out of the room and slammed the door. Ray shook his head in disbelief.

'I'm not.'

At the top of the stairs she halted. What's the matter with me? she thought. Why on earth am I behaving like this? And then, How dare he have new clothes? And her frown returned.

Saturday morning saw the Flying Ashtray parked up against the back door of the building with its boot open. Presently Chunky's head emerged, scanned the street for prying eyes, signalled to Queenie who was peering through a hole in the net curtains, and disappeared back indoors. Seconds later he re-emerged, bearing one of the crates, which he bundled into the open boot. Norma appeared next, followed by Kim, each struggling to manoeuvre their own boxes into the car. Finally Queenie strolled out, not deigning to lift a finger in assistance, her role being one of lofty supervision. A mat of bedraggled fur, leaping into the car through the back window, completed this picturesque group, which clambered into its seatbelts and sped off.

By mid-morning the car-boot sale was in full swing. Norma peered gingerly out of the back window and shuddered. How had it come to this? Here she was, a pillar of respectability, embroiling herself – and the company's guest – in an illegal activity, with the added ignominy of knowing that the blame would be heaped entirely at her door if Rex ever found out. Round the outside Queenie prowled, lowering at Chunky, and raging at the thought of spending a hard-earned Saturday propping up the wall of a car-park.

One person only appeared to be enjoying himself. Kim strolled about inspecting other merchandise with a keen and practised eye. So this was how they did things in England?

Chunky pulled out a can of furniture polish and began to buff up the shells of his exotic merchandise. Queenie raked him with a glare.

'Where's its head?'

'Well, give it a chance,' Chunky blustered. 'What you've got to remember – where these come from it's night now – it probably thinks it's still in bed.'

The approach of potential custom saved him from a cuff across the ears, and he broke into sales patter, thrusting a hapless reptile under the nose of his would-be clients.

'Fifteen quid apiece, two for twenty-five! An asset to any garden – hours of non-stop fun . . . nah, y'don't know what yer missin'!'

Queenie sprang on to the bonnet and opened a flask. It was going to be a trying day. Was there a pub near here?

She thought she remembered seeing one near the far entrance of the car park . . .

She stopped short, half-thinking her eyes deceived her. There on the far side of the car park, Carol May was standing.

'I didn't know she came to this sort of thing,' Queenie mused, still watching, perplexed. But Carol May didn't appear to be buying. In fact it was almost as if she were waiting . . .

'I'll see if she fancies a quick cuppa.' Queenie raised her hand to wave but almost at once let it fall to her side. A man was approaching Carol May, now leaning over her shoulder, now smiling as she turned to him. Queenie whistled in disbelief. Rex, of all people. But here? With Carol May . . . ? She ducked down behind the car as the pair walked off to where Rex's car was waiting. He held the door as Carol May got in, then climbed behind the wheel and drove towards the exit.

Queenie shook her head in grudging admiration.

'Ooooh, you stuffy get.'

Then, turning as the car disappeared, she realised Kim had been watching too. He glanced at her, with a look of conspiracy which told her the secret would go no further.

Jill was crying as she left the cinema, blinking at the daylight and gratefully accepting the proffered handkerchief from Ray, who in turn let slip a muffled sniff. By contrast, Sharon and Nicky emerged dry-eyed and scornful.

'Bambi? God! It's embarrassing!' Sharon muttered. 'I hope nobody's seen us come out.'

Jill turned to let them catch up.

'Did you enjoy it, love?' she asked Nicky.

'Couldn't we not've seen *Nightmare On Elm Street*?'

Ray rubbed his hands, determined, in the face of mounting odds, to whip up some enthusiasm.

'Right, then – what d'you fancy next? *I* know . . .

Sharon's faced dropped. Now what was he going to do?

Parents were so embarrassing sometimes. Ray was half-way up the street, Jill behind him, urging them to get a move on. Sharon turned to Nicky with a look of resignation.

'I s'pose we'd better,' she shrugged.

The car pulled off the lane, and on to a rough dirt-track which ended in a small copse. Rex turned off the ignition. In the passenger seat, Carol May waited silent, impassive, staring ahead.

'Alright?'

Rex's voice was disarmingly matter-of-fact.

Carol May nodded. She opened the door and got out of the car.

Rex did likewise. Then calmly, without fuss, without a sound, they each opened a door and climbed into the back seat.

'I'm due back at five.'

A pause, then: 'He's fishing till eight.'

They sat motionless, side-by-side, staring ahead. Then, without a word, she turned to him, a flicker of anticipation crossing her face. He took her face in his hands and pulled her towards him, almost devouring her with his mouth. Her arm snaked round behind his neck, then slowly, she reached down and began to undo the buttons on his shirt.

'There you go, sonny – hours of harmless pleasure!'

Chunky was endeavouring to interest an evil-looking small boy in a bargain buy.

'Special rates for first-time buyers!'

The boy and his parents wandered away. The tortoise, in company with most of its comrades, remained in the box. Into the car, a handbag bulging from its jaws, scrambled the dog. Norma shot up and hissed at Queenie through the window.

'How long are we stopping?' She knew better than to

remonstrate about the dog's anti-social behaviour. 'No, it's just that . . . I've chutney to see to at home . . . '

Queenie's smile was almost pleasant. 'Fine. You scad off with Chairman Mao, then. We're not stopping yer.'

'Oh . . . well . . . no . . . I'll give it a bit longer, perhaps . . . watch how you go on . . . '

Norma retreated into the comparative anonymity of the red furry seat-covers, and pulled the headscarf tighter round her face. There was no sign of Mr Kim. God knows what hazards *he'd* be stumbling into.

Ray put on a party-hat and grinned.

'This is the stuff, eh?'

Sharon groaned and hid behind the menu. A sour-faced waitress sloped across and dumped four plates of hamburger and chips on to the table, tucking the bill under a leaking ketchup dispenser. Sharon pushed her plate away.

'Bad f'yer, them are. Got cholesterol.'

Ray stopped eating in mid-bite. 'Can't please some people.'

Jill seized at her fork and dug into her chips with as much relish as she could muster.

Rex lit a cigarette, took a long, slow drag, and passed it to Carol May. She lay back against the seat and drew at it, inhaling deeply. Handing it back, their hands scarcely touched. There was no necessity. Reassurance, reflection, all conversation seemed an irrelevance. Rex took another drag and began to button his shirt.

'Next Thursday?'

She took the cigarette from his fingers.

'What time?'

'Get it engraved . . . spray it to match yer curtains . . .

'lovely table decorations . . . everyone a gem . . . '

Chunky's patter was scraping the barrel now, but with an hour to go and a total of three sales in the bag, desperate action was called for.

From her vantage-point on top of the bonnet, Queenie was watching Kim, who was standing at a neighbouring stall which sold electronic equipment. In fact, he didn't seem to be taking all that passive a role, she now observed. He appeared to be demonstrating the attractions of a small pocket cassette recorder, to the delight of the stall-holder and the evident interest of a rapidly swelling public.

'We make these,' he was telling them. 'I can recommend them unreservedly. These are just a few of the features . . . '

And as the crowd closed in, Queenie could observe a fluttering of ten pound notes, and within minutes, the dispersal of the flock, along with the entire stock from the boot of the grateful stall-holder, who was beaming at Kim and shaking his hand vigorously.

Queenie spat. Her aim landed suspiciously close to Chunky's foot.

Now Kim was making his way back to them, smiling with satisfaction. Chunky's woeful face greeted him.

'How are you doing?' Kim enquired.

'Still a few left to shift,' came the feeble reply.

At this point Kim caught sight of the cardboard on which Chunky had scrawled 'Exotic Reptilia – £15 each or 2 for £25.' Kim shook his head.

'It's a joke.'

Chunky failed to raise a guffaw.

'It's too much. You price yourself out of the market. How much did you pay for these?'

Chunky lowered his voice.

'Fifty quid the lot.'

'Okay . . . ' Kim was busy with his pen. 'Now we'll see.' And he turned to show Chunky the cardboard which now read: 'FANTASTIC REDUCTIONS! £6 EACH OR TWO FOR £10!'

Chunky was horrified. 'Eh! Eh! Y'can't do that! I've an honest livin' to make!'

'You make no living at all if you charge these prices,' Kim retorted.

Queenie, clambering off the bonnet to remonstrate, found herself elbowed aside by a family of eight, who now descended on the Flying Ashtray and emerged thirty seconds later bearing away four tortoises. Within minutes Chunky was surrounded by eager punters, clamouring to thrust their £10 notes at him. Kim retired from the throng, Chunky's voice soaring above the rabble:

'Fantastic offer . . . giveaway prices . . . all the rage in Casablanca . . . years ahead of its time . . .'; though as Queenie approached to supervise the operation, he leaned aside, still lamenting, 'Fifteen quid *each* these are meant to be!'

'Why don't you chubb that kisser, div-brain. How many did *you* shift?'

'I was on the point . . . interest was perkin' up . . .'

'Get that second box undone before my foot perks up your backside!'

She stepped back and noticed Kim watching her with a look of mild reproach.

'Go on, lad, say it – you'd never speak to *your* missus like that.'

Kim smiled amiably.

'It's not for me to pass judgement.'

'This is how we do things over here, lad. Y'gotta let' em know who's boss.'

'Ah . . . you like to be boss?' This was interesting.

'Not much, pal! Who doesn't?'

'And at work too?'

'Oh, go'way. I'd lose me drinkin' arm to land inside old Bernie-lad's boots.'

'Ah, he is a good boss then?'

Queenie roared with laughter. 'Oh, give over, eh? – there's no such thing. Great sneck tryna catch yer on the hoof? – beakin' over shoulders till you mar a decent day's

140

work wondering where he's gonna sting yer next! Boss equals bastard, mate – it comes with the job.'

'So if *you* are boss . . . ' Kim pursued. 'What then?'

'Then I get me own back,' Queenie rejoined. 'Then it's *my* turn to play blue murder with them poor sorry buggers on shop floor.'

'But what's achieved then?' Kim sounded incredulous.

'What d'you think's achieved? Satisfaction for this girl here!'

Kim shook his head. 'But that's just a vicious circle.'

'That's right,' Queenie agreed. 'That's how we do it over here.'

Kim looked puzzled. This was all new to him. 'In *my* factory we have no bosses – only workers.'

'You'll get bog-all done then, pal,' Queenie assured him. 'Y'want some bugger breathin' down yer neck, else nobody does a tap.'

'In *my* factory, the workers are bosses, the bosses are workers . . . Our profits increase sixty-seven per cent in two years.'

Queenie's mouth dropped open, but she had barely time to consider the wisdom of Kim's policies when a smartly dressed woman pushed past her and accosted Chunky.

'I take it you realise you're breaking the law?'

'Geraway!' Chunky feigned disbelief.

'Illegal imports? Cruelty to animals? I wonder what the RSPCA would make of it?'

Queenie was across in a flash. 'Oi! Hop it, hamper-mouth! We don't need your sort scaremongerin' the payin' public away.'

But the lady was not to be daunted. 'Someone should get onto Immigration. How d'you know they haven't got rabies?'

'They don't bite.' Chunky held up a specimen for inspection. 'No teeth, see?'

'No, but they could give you a very nasty suck.'

Queenie stepped in. 'Any second now there could be a very nasty accident.'

The lady retreated. 'You should be ashamed of your-self!' she flared at Chunky.

'Pet Supplies, fourth boot along!' Queenie rejoined. 'They do a crackin' muzzle in your size!'

And she chortled with triumph as the lady disappeared into the crowd.

Nicky was feeling sick. This was his fourth ice-cream in as many hours and his stomach was starting to rebel.

'Hang on, love – you forgot yer Flake.'

What had come over his Dad? Once you'd be hard pushed to prise a boiled sweet out of him – now he was choking you with the stuff. His mother seemed inclined to agree.

'You spoil them kids,' she was saying.

'Can't spoil me own, who can I spoil?'

'They've to learn they can't just *have* all the time.'

'Oh aye, they could learn that, lookin at *me*,' Ray quipped.

'*I* fancied a good time this weekend. See what fancy did.'

Nicky ran on ahead. Any minute now this would start to get boring.

Ray dragged his feet.

'You know your trouble?' Jill pursued. 'You still think yer eighteen. Self to please, mam to skivvy and no claim on yer wage but what goes down yer throat.'

Ray took refuge in a sulk.

'I should've stopped in Folkstone.'

'Well, if it's that exciting . . . '

'It's a sight more bloody fun than bloody earache and long faces!'

Jill was livid. How was it, once again, the blame was being dumped on *her* shoulders? She turned on Ray with a vengeance. 'You want it all, don't yer? Me in the kitchen . . . me in the bedroom . . . mam, missus, money coming in . . . '

Ray had halted. The vehemence of her attack took him by surprise.

'Well, *I* work an' all now,' she went on. 'I've a tongue in me head, I've something up here – I can't just be what you fancy, when you fancy, *and* go out and bring the bread in.'

Ray rose to the bait. 'And where do these two come in? Dumped round yer mam's, fetch their own tea, come home to an empty house . . . '

'They can manage.'

'I wonder.'

'If you wonder that much, stop home and watch.'

'It's *you* should stop home and watch.'

'Oh, I thought it might be.' Jill's voice was cold. 'You can't have it both ways, Ray.'

'Can't have it *any* way, seems to me.'

'And whose fault's that, then?'

'And whose *is* it, then?'

They'd reached deadlock. Reasoning was out of the question. They trudged along side by side, both stung, both determined the other should give way first. Finally the anger subsided, and all that remained was bleak weariness.

Chunky had clinched his thirty-eighth sale when he saw the policeman approaching. The young constable was having his ear bent by the well-dressed lady and she was proving impossible to placate. Chunky stopped in mid-bark, seized the tortoises from the grip of bemused customers, shovelled them back into the box and started to hammer the lid on.

Queenie leapt to her feet. It must be the pressure – he'd clearly taken leave of his senses. And she seized the crowbar and tried to lever the lid off the box again. Chunky, meanwhile was tearing up 'FANTASTIC REDUCTIONS' and grappling to lock up the boot. But even as she prised up the lid, Queenie was scrabbling to nail it down again. The approach of the Law had caught her eye, and bundling livestock and personnel alike into the car, she stuck her foot down and headed for the exit in a cloud of sparks. The Long Arm of the Law reached for its notebook and jotted down a registration number.

'So now we celebrate.'

Queenie slowed to a meagre 72mph and turned to look at Kim. 'Y'what!'

'As your saying is, we've made a killing,' Kim replied. 'You know this place?' He handed over a card for Chunky's perusal.

'Twenty-two Queen Street? Just off Deansgate, innit?'

'But this time I'll be host and you'll be my guests.'

Norma suddenly remembered urgent business at home. 'If I could just be dropped off by a bus stop . . . '

But the plea appeared to go unheard, for the next second the speedometer rocketed to 82mph, an oncoming cyclist narrowly avoided his Maker, and Queenie shot off down a one-way street yelling 'Hang on to yer shreddies, petals! – I know a short cut!'

'So . . . ' Ray's voice was resolvedly chirpy.

'So . . . ' Jill rallied to hit the same note.

'So I'll most likely give it a miss next weekend.'

'Fine.'

'I'll post the money. No sense spendin' all that hard-earned just to catch a couple of hours at home.'

'No.'

'So, you'll manage?'

'Oh, I'll manage.'

'Right. That's that, then.' Ray picked up his hold-all and jacket. 'I'll ring yer.'

'That'd be nice.'

And that was it. Those stilted, awkward, desperately cheerful words constituted farewell for at least a fortnight.

Jill was astounded. How on earth had they come to behave like strangers? Was there nothing Ray would say to make it all okay again? Funnily enough, Ray was wondering when Jill would come to her senses and say the magic words. So there they stood, awkward, fumbling, till Ray mumbled something about missing a train, pecked Jill a perfunctory kiss and in a moment was gone.

The entrance to the Yung Chon Garden Korean Restaurant resembled the doorway of an opium den, but as a beaming Mr Kim led his party down the stairs, quite another picture emerged. Stylish decor, tasteful lighting, formal dinner settings and polite nods from the kimono-clad waitresses all conspired to overawe the unfamiliar guests.

'The manager here,' Kim was explaining. 'His family is friends of my family at home.' And as if to confirm his story, the manager himself emerged from the office, and rushing towards Kim with outstretched arms, embraced him, shook his hands, called upon his wife to embrace and shake hands, summoned his daughters, the waitresses, the chef and all the kitchen staff to offer greetings, till a shout went up from a neighbouring table, and twelve Korean businessmen sprang to their feet, clamouring for Kim's hand, as the ritual began all over again. Queenie began to feel uncomfortable. This man whom she'd vilified, abused, insulted . . . never at any time had he ceased to be courteous, charming, liberal and good-humoured. And here he was – the toast of the town, evidently – introducing her to fellow-countrymen as his 'good friend and colleague'. Queenie would have to take herself in hand. Feelings dangerously akin to a sense of shame, and a liking for her oriental friend, were beginning to take root. And that, she decided, would never do. But now Kim was presenting her to the party of business men – more 'friends from home', as it turned out (Korea must be a small place, Queenie surmised), and actually inviting her to preside, in the seat of honour, at a full

Korean banquet. Queenie smiled graciously – and hoped Chunky wouldn't let the side down by some outrageous *faux pas*.

But clangers didn't drop much louder than Chunky's next impropriety. As Queenie turned – intending to utter instructions to good behaviour – her eyes lit on the large wooden crate he was carrying.

'What the frig's that doin' here?' she rasped.

Chunky lowered his voice. 'Dear stuff, this, y'know. Can't be too careful with foreigners about.'

Queenie resisted the urge to brain him against the side of the table, and glided across to take her place in response to Kim's nod of invitation. Chunky slid into a seat beside the wall where he could keep an eye on his swag, while Norma found herself sandwiched between two over-attentive Sumo types who seemed to regard her as their own personal spoils of victory.

Kim was hovering beside Queenie's chair as she came to the top of the table. With amazement she realised he was holding it for her to be seated. She couldn't remember the last time someone had held a seat out for her. Correction. She couldn't remember the last time she'd ever waited that long. Now, as the food began arriving, Queenie felt the old prejudices raise their heads.

'What d'yer all eat over there?' she queried. 'None of them bird's beaks and feet an' nests an' that . . . '

Kim smiled complacently. 'Wait and see,' he urged her. 'You'll enjoy it. Please . . . allow me.'

And he began to serve her from the ambrosial fare, superbly cooked and sumptuously laid out before them. Queenie sniffed, prodding the food with her fork. There was no way she was going to enjoy this – foreign food didn't agree with her. But as her teeth clamped on the forkful of Hot and Sour Prawns, she was forced to concede that this time she and it were in full accord. Kim took her approval with keen delight, now suggesting this dish, now recommending that, and Queenie was obliged to give a grudging 'thumbs up' as she reached across the table in search of more oral gratification.

'I'll say that for you's inscrutables,' she munched, through mouthfuls of delicately-spiced vegetables. 'Y'can't half fettle up a decent dinner.'

'So now we have a chance to compare our national cuisines,' Kim replied with smile.

Queenie withered. She hoped he didn't think the offerings of the Wong Yip constituted the best Britain had to offer. But no, he'd obviously forgotten that culinary debacle, for here he was raising his glass to her.

'Cheers, pal,' she toasted.

'No, no, no,' he corrected. 'In Korea we say "dupsida"!'

And as he rose to his feet, tapping his glass, the whole table fell silent, eager for his oration.

'I would like to propose a toast,' he raised his glass. 'To my English hosts – for showing me a typical English weekend, as lived by the typical English family.' He bowed in turn to Queenie, Chunky and Norma. 'Dupsida!'

And the whole table rose and toasted them in unison.

Queenie was into her fourth glass, when Kim called on her to return the compliment. Struggling to her feet (this liqueur, whatever-it-was, had crept up unawares and rather ambushed her), there was a twinkle in her eye as she addressed the whole assembly, but more particularly, Kim.

'Yer's've come over here to get the benefit of the Great British expertise . . . and me little pal here's turned out a nifty sharp learner.' (Kim bowed in mock gratitude.) 'In the interests of East–West relations, I'm prepared to concede you might not have it *all* to learn. So since we've gone all oriental – an' just to prove I'm a bit of a linguist meself – the toast is . . . Dupissda!'

And though she couldn't remember saying anything that should cause such an outbreak of unbridled hilarity, she was very glad of the opportunity to knock back another drink.

* * *

Jill finally came downstairs, to find Sharon and Nicky, as ever transfixed by the TV screen.

'Right! Get that rubbish off!' she commanded. 'We seem to have lost the art of conversation in this house.'

And she started to bustle round in exemplary fashion, tidying away any traces of the abortive weekend. Sharon eyed her with suspicion.

'When's me dad back?' she queried.

'Not for two weeks,' came the brisk reply.

'Why can't he come next weekend?'

'He's busy.'

Sharon looked sceptical. 'Well *I'd've* bin nice if he'd come home.'

'You'll want some practice, then. You've lost the knack lately.'

'I'm in good company, then, aren't I?'

'Right!' she spun round, half-inclined to box the girl's ears. 'I've had enough lip off you, lady. It's high time we had a different tune round here.'

'Like what?'

'Like no moaning for yer dad – like no long faces an' carry-on like we've nowt better to do. If he wants to go chuckin' his charms about Folkestone, we shan't be sat up losin' kip for him.' She was in full swing now. 'And y' better get used to baby sitting – 'cos I'll be off out a lot more from now on.'

'Out where?' Sharon was indignant.

'Where I please.' She glanced across at Nicky whose face bore its own distinctive brand of ill-humour.

'Alright, what's the mard lip for?'

'I'm starvin'.'

'Well, what d'you fancy?'

Nicky sensed an opening. 'Barbecue ribs, double chips, banana milk-shake an' a giant choc-ice.'

'Right, get yer coats on. Let's catch the place before it shuts.'

'Choc-ice *and* milk shake?' asked Sharon, incredulous.

'Why not?' demanded Jill with forced bravado. 'We don't have to ask yer Dad before we can treat ourselves.'

'We'll get heart attacks,' Sharon fired.

'Well, that'll just serve him right, then, won't it?'

Sharon and Nicky traipsed out to get their coats. Clearly their mother had gone mad and it was best to leave her to it. Jill, meanwhile, continued to whirl round the room like a dervish, tidying, clearing, re-arranging . . . It was only when she came to the mantelpeiece, that the sight of her wedding photo cause a temporary hiccup – but it was soon obscured by the rubber plant, and so ceased to give offence. Then a quick glance in her compact-mirror, a defiant stroke of rouge across the cheekbones . . . and she was ready for anything.

In the hour that had passed since Queenie's sixth glass, the Yong Chon Garden had grown considerably livelier. Kim and Chunky now stood astride their chairs, arms round each other, voices raised in a Korean drinking song – the punchline of which was the downing of yet more alcohol. Aided and abetted by the rest of the table, which was getting rowdier by the minute, they crooned their way through a dozen songs – and as many bottles. Or rather, Kim did. Chunky, with no idea what he was singing, confined himself to a few tuneless warbles and a great many more 'punchlines' than the songs seemed to warrant. In the red corner, Norma was battling gamely against efforts to force-feed her with chopsticks, while Queenie lay sprawled out, her head across the table, arms still beating time to the music. In the midst of this wassailing, the wail of police sirens could scarcely be heard, so it was with considerable surprise, a few minutes later, that Chunky looked up from his fifteenth glass and saw seven police officers, two immigration officials, three dogs, and an RSPCA inspector standing in the doorway.

'That's the ones,' yelled a voice, and seconds later

Chunky found himself being manhandled from his chair, handcuffed, and bundled into a black maria. The next few minutes seemed to blur, but somehow he was vaguely aware of his crates being carried out and driven away at high speed, an Alsatian slobbering down his front, an overwhelming urge to throw up . . . and then, oblivion.

Kim, on the other hand, was sufficiently *compus mentis* to inquire what the charge might be, and to be told by a grave-looking PC, 'I think you know fine well, sir?' Then, consulting his notebook. 'Smuggling, sir?'

Perhaps the most tragic figure in all this drama was that former pillar of the community, Norma herself, who all but leapt at the throat of the officer-in-charge, piping hysterically. 'No, no, it's all a mistake! – you can't arrest *him*!'

'Oh aye, here's another one,' sighed the officer, and two WPC's sprang from the shadows to bustle Norma into the back of the van, which presently sped off into the night, Chunky recovering briefly to protest: 'Nah, you've got it all wrong . . . these are *English* tortoises . . . they're bred under glass in Macclesfield . . . '

Back in the Yung Chon Garden, Queenie stopped singing, slid back further in her chair . . . and started to snore.

'Whaddayamean, "can't be seen!"'

Barely two hours later, Queenie had staged a remarkable recovery. Admittedly a little raddled in the lipstick department, she now stood terrorising the officer-on-duty, who would never again think manning the desk down the station was a soft option.

'You'll be sparkin' off an international incident!' Queenie threatened. 'You watch – they'll have the kamikaze's over in no time,' and despite the protests of her quivering victim, she seized the telephone and dialed directory enquiries.

'Too right, pal,' she muttered to the voice at the other end. 'I want the Foreign Office.'

Norma was reacting badly to her term of imprisonment. Scarcely had she been inside the cell for three minutes when she felt an attack coming on . . . of self-preservation.

'It wasn't *my* idea,' she protested. '*I* never said . . . *I'm* not gonna lose me job . . . '

Kim turned to her with a complacent smile.

'That will not be necessary, I hope. Indeed, I am most grateful to you . . . ' Norma's jaw dropped ' . . . for enabling me to see how British justice operates.'

Presently he was able to witness its workings at closer quarters, as an inspector came in, eyed them all with suspicion, and asked for Mr Kim Soo Yung. Kim stepped forward.

'There appears to have been a mistake, Inspector. I am here on a government exchange mission. I think it would be . . . "unfortunate", . . . if the Korean press got to hear of this incident . . . '

The Inspector fixed him with a look of contempt. 'Oh, is that right?' he sneered. And for nearly thirty seconds they glared at each other, neither flinching, neither speaking, till finally the Inspector turned to his PC.

'Return Mr Soo Yung's personal belongings,' he ordered. Then, with a significant nod. 'And his wallet . . . '

And he flashed a triumphant smile at Kim, who, understanding perfectly, returned a polite bow.

Queenie was threatening a second Pearl Harbour, when a door opened and the prisoners were released into the foyer. She stared at them, scarcely crediting her own eyes.

' 'Yez are loose?'

'Oh yes, it was most enlightening,' Kim assured her. 'I compare our Korean with your British justice . . . and,' (patting his wallet) 'I find we are not so unsophisticated after all.'

Norma blanched as Mr Kim strolled into the factory at 9.10am on Monday morning, while Rex and Bernie were doing the rounds.

'Good morning, Mr Buckley,' he beamed at Rex. 'You had a productive weekend?'

'Er . . . yes, very useful, thanks. And you?'

'Oh . . . it was very quiet . . . very relaxing.'

Kim glanced across at Queenie. She was working away, bent over her soldering. Her smile was inscrutable.

CHAPTER FIVE

June

Skylarks sang in the bright, hazy June morning, as along the crest of a disused railway embankment, a lone figure pursued his daily run – or rather stagger – for at this moment he appeared to be hitting severe breathing and co-ordination difficulties, stumbling and flailing as he now was, clutching his chest painfully and rasping for air. Closer inspection revealed an interesting choice of costume, considering the season – tracksuit, anorak, shorts worn outside the tracksuit, mittens and balaclava – this must be a serious sportsman.

Klepto was humming to herself as she cooked breakfast. Or rather four breakfasts, all identical, all very elaborate, and none of them hers. Now it was the turn of the eggs to be flipped out on to the waiting plates, and, this task performed, she expertly balanced the platters along her arm and carried them through into the dining-room.

Rex let himself into the deserted office and lit up a cigarette. These days he was usually in early, often ahead of Norma. That said less about the attractions of work than about the quality of his home-life. Little peace and less sleep had been his problem last night. Right now a stiff injection of caffeine was called for. He slipped outside to the coffee-machine. It spluttered into life and disgorged its usual noxious brew. Rex shuddered and went back into the office. In the depths of the factory a small, bearded figure arose, clicked a stop-watch and scribbled a sum in his notebook.

The jogger was fighting for breath, his legs crumpling beneath him as he staggered down the embankment and on to the main road. Only another two miles. How long could he stave off the impending heart-attack? Still, what better way to go, than in the pursuit of physical excellence?

The argument was gathering pace as a fist banged the table and a volley of Greek expletives ricocheted to and fro across the room. Mercifully, Klepto was not their target, nor even their subject. The family business was the matter in hand – and father, and elder brothers Georgiou and Nico, would as soon think of including Klepto in the discussion as they would consider thanking her for the breakfasts she had cooked. Younger brother, Tino, smiled sympathetically and was handing her the empty plates, when a hand knocked her sideways and thrust a coffee pot in her face.

'It's empty!'

Her father dealt her a blow to the ear which sent her reeling back against the wall.

'You half asleep or what?' barked Georgiou.

'You better wake up fast, before you wake up to the back of my hand,' added Nico – needlessly, she thought, since she had felt the backs of two hands already this morning. Without another word, she retrieved the coffee pot, and rubbing her ear, returned to the kitchen.

There was a rattling on the door. Glancing up, the woman saw a dark, hooded figure, breathing heavily against the frosted glass – and started to scream. The door was unlocked – seconds later, he would be in the room. She grabbed the deterrent nearest to hand – which happened to be a bowl of cold, greasy dishwater – and flung it at the oncoming figure. He stopped, the corner of his mouth began to crumple, the balaclava peeled back . . . to reveal the woeful face of Simon.

The mother threw up her hands in horror. She was a large woman, solidly-built, a match for any intruder. Now, however, she was dabbing at the boy's face with a tea-towel, bleating with maternal anxiety.

'What you playin' at? – you try'na catch your death, standin' in all that water?'

Simon tried to wriggle free.

'Oh, hey, give over, mam . . .' he squirmed. But all to no avail. The dabbing, clucking and cosseting went on until the boy could make his escape to work.

There was a man in the ladies lavatories. Norma made this unsettling discovery when she tried the door of the end toilet and found it occupied by a beard. Later she had to suffer the indignity of having her ablutions timed and the results noted down for posterity. Back in the office, fortified by a couple of wine gums, she watched with Rex and Bernie as the beard himself – one J.F. Parrott – paced the factory floor with slide-rule and tape measure.

'But he wasn't due till ten . . . ' Norma protested.

'Eight o'clock he shows up – no introduction, can't answer questions – any queries, we'll "have to get in touch with our Korean partners".'

Rex was seething; Bernie indignant.

'They've cheek to spare, them bloody Nips! "Efficiency Experts"? Since when do *we* need checkin' up on? I wonder what they think *I* do all day?'

Rex was starting to wonder, too, when Norma suddenly gulped and started to choke on her custard cream.

'Look who it is!' she spluttered. 'But we're not expectin' him! He's not down in the book!'

Despite her protests, it had to be admitted that Mr Beachcroft required no appointment to visit his own factory – and as he was this very minute opening the office door, there was little to be done except put the kettle on.

'How long's *he* bin here? Owt on he shouldn't be knowin' about?'

The Chairman was viewing Parrott's antics through clenched teeth.

'I'm pleased to say we're working to maximum efficiency, Mr Beachcroft,' simpered Bernie.

'Aye, well, we'll see about that.' Beachcroft always took Bernie with a large dose of salt. 'I've just tipped up a tidy pile of brass to stick the cat among *his* pigeons. Where's that tea, then, Norma?'

'Milk or lemon?' flustered the secretary.

'Lemon? How long's that bin on offer? I take it we're not so free with that sort of muck down the canteen?'

'I think the girls will tell you we're free with very little round here,' Rex assured him.

'That's the way,' growled the Chairman. 'Now then, for your information – in precisely four minutes and twenty-three seconds, we've a Dr Carlyle arriving . . . '

Rex looked blank. Was the name supposed to mean something?

' . . . and Dr Carlyle goes by the name of "Human Resources Manager". Now they tell me these chaps do wonders with the work-force. Harry Prescott got one in for two weeks last March and his profits went up twenty-three per cent in three months . . . '

Rex could imagine what was coming next.

'Now we've got ours for a week, an' as I've paid through the nose for his services, we'll want some heavy-duty co-operation all round. Mind, we're not so keen we want the place coming to a standstill. Whatever he wants, he can do a bench at a time. Right . . . ' consulting his watch – 'I'll be off, then – let's mind we get our money's worth.'

*　　*　　*

'I don't understand,' wailed Norma when the Chairman had departed.

'What we're talking,' Rex replied, 'is a Chairman's answer to an oriental prayer. Up profits, increase productivity, and preferably before lunch, so His Nibbs out there can rake up the odd good word to relay back to our "colleagues" in the East.'

Bernie muttered darkly.

'Well, Doctor Carlyle-whatever-he-is can keep from under *my* feet if he knows what side his cake's iced! It takes more than fancy titles to impress *me*.'

Whereupon a knock at the door ushered in a small, rather pretty girl of no more than twenty-five, dressed in a high-fashion suit and an enormous hair-bow.

'Good morning.' She put out her hand to Rex. 'I'm Tamsin Carlyle. How d'you do?'

'Right ladies . . .'

The Monday-morning gossiping subsided as Rex addressed the assembled workforce.

'I'm here on behalf of Mr Beachcroft to introduce you to Dr Carlyle . . . who's going to show you how to "fulfill your potential" and "feel good about yourselves".'

Queenie stubbed out her cigarette, folded her arms and glowered.

'Fulfil my friggin' backside! Our Marg's had this palaver! Work harder, longer hours, less money – an' kid yerself yer enjoyin' it!'

'Well if it perks things up for the workers, it gets full marks in *my* book, thank you.' Now and again Pauline remembered she was a shop steward.

Queenie humphed, but Bernie's arrival with Dr Carlyle

157

– and for some reason, Norma and Simon – saved her the trouble of a retort.

'Budge up, budge up – room for a couple of small ones! Go on, Simon, they won't bite!'

Simon sidled in next to Klepto, evidently judging her to be the least malevolent of all the bench.

'Right, girls, your turn next for what they call a Counselling Seminar. This young lady's in charge . . . ' He noticed Queenie's glare of antipathy. 'You'll need to keep your wits nailed on here – alright, my love?'

'Yes, thank you,' replied the girl, coolly, moving away from Bernie's comradely embrace.

'Right, then . . . I'll . . . er . . . leave you to it . . . '

The girl drew up a chair.

'Hello, I'm Tamsin . . . '

Greetings ranged from uneasy smiles to downright hostility.

'My job is to help you find ways in which you can feel more positive about yourselves, develop your strengths, discover skills you didn't know you had . . . okay?'

Several nods but little comprehension.

' . . . and what we're going to be doing this week is learning about ourselves by *talking* about ourselves – about our aims and aspirations, learning how to trust each other, how to expand our "comfort zones", giving and receiving "feedback", getting familiar with our body language . . . '

She paused. How much of this was actually getting through? She would start with the easy bit.

' . . . so, anyway, what we're going to do to begin with . . . is to learn how to relax . . . '

Incredulity was mounting by the second.

' . . . and what I'd like us to do . . . is to close our eyes . . . and try to visualize what it's like to be the hairs on the top of the skull . . . '

Queenie cast her eyes to heaven. 'And may the Lord pickle yer while vinegar's cheap!' she prayed.

* * *

'To *my* mind she raised a lot of very interesting issues.' Pauline had decided that 'expanding comfort-zones' were right up her street. 'I'm all for "openin' up" once in a while.'

'She must be friggin' wrecked, givin' her gob that work-out – an' you lot sat there like dicky-tinsel, gawpin' at her!'

Queenie was scathing, but her real scorn was reserved for Pauline. 'An' *you* seem to have trouble nailin' yer grid shut, not openin' up!'

Tamsin had reached the head of the coffee queue, where her request for 'a cup of hot water, please' drew further contempt from Queenie – not least when Tamsin dipped into her case and produced a box of herbal tea-bags.

'Oh, Rosehip and Hibiscus Blossom,' noted Donna, with interest.

'She'll have us eatin' privet leaves next,' snorted Queenie, helping herself to double caffeine rations.

'Er . . . 'scuse me . . . '

Tamsin felt someone tug at her sleeve.

'Y'know what y'said about "knowing what yer worth" . . . ?'

She turned to see Klepto smiling shyly up at her.

'Well, what if *you* think yer worth one thing . . . an' everyone else thinks yer not?'

Tamsin smiled back. 'Well, than you have to find ways of making sure that everyone else sees you as you see yourself. D'you see what I mean?'

'Sort of . . . '

Queenie leaned over and hissed in Tamsin's ear: 'Don't bother knockin' too hard there, girl – there's nobody bin home for years!' Then, elbowing Klepto aside, she barged her way to the front of the queue.

'I wonder if that's what they call "assertiveness",' remarked Jill, drily.

'No,' opined Donna. 'I think that comes under the category of good old-fashioned rudeness.'

159

*   *   *

B-Group was seated in a circle, holding hands and gazing into the eyes of the person opposite. Or at least some of them were. Simon and Klepto were having great problems encountering each other's glance, while Queenie refused to eyeball anything except the underside of her thumbnail, which she was excavating with a hair-grip. Despite these minor set-backs, Tamsin continued to forge ahead with enormous optimism.

'So what we've been trying to do,' she enthused, 'is to build a rapport, and create an atmosphere in which we can really open up and learn to trust each other, okay? So that in the end what we're doing is working with complete confidence in one another, towards a common aim. Okay?'

A few eager nods, a hint of scepticism, a single dose of sheer hostility – she was certainly having *some* effect.

'So what I'm going to ask you to do – okay? – is to close your eyes and think really hard about your best-kept secret.'

A few eyes flashed open, alarm registered on several faces. Tamsin continued.

'Something you've done you might feel bad about? Something you've always secretly wanted? Something you've never told another living soul?'

She paused to let them rifle through their memories.

'Okay . . . Now share with us . . . trust us . . . we won't think badly of you, we won't reject you . . . '

Klepto's eyes were screwed tight in concentration, Queenie's were glazed over with boredom.

'I want you to keep your eyes closed . . . and when I touch you on the hand, I want you to share your secret with us . . . okay?'

All eyes were closed but Queenie's. Behind the bench stood Rex and Bernie, newly arrived to eavesdrop on the progress. Tamsin motioned them to be silent, then she reached across and touched Jill's hand. Jill started, panicked, then flustered.

160

'Oh . . . oh, I don't know . . . I can't think.'

'Take your time,' soothed Tamsin. 'There's really no pressure.' And she tapped Pauline on the hand.

'Oh, well . . . ' Pauline was bursting to begin. 'What can I say? I can't name names, can I? And when yer a married woman, it puts you in a tricky position . . . but if I let slip what a certain person not a million miles from here felt about me, an' how close we've come to actually doin' something about it . . . well, I think there'd be one or two surprised faces, if y'know what I mean.'

Pauline's 'revelation' having revealed practically nil, Tamsin moved across to touch Queenie's hand, which in a flash was retracted with a disdainful 'Pass!'

Carol May felt the tap on her wrist and toyed with the idea of *really* giving the girl something to think about. In the end she opted for half-measures, designed to titillate and ward off all in the same breath.

'Twice in my life I've thought about suicide. The first time was on my wedding day.'

Tamsin waited, expecting more. Rex, too, was agog – and terrified – to hear the second half. It didn't come. Tamsin passed over and brushed Donna's hand.

'It was two years ago. I stopped outside Tesco's.'

Queenie huffed and muttered 'riveting.'

'I saw this pram. I looked inside. I saw this . . . He was tiny . . . he was just so lovely . . . y'couldn't resist him . . . They shouldn't be left like that – anything could happen – anyone could just . . . '

A hush had fallen. They could hear each other breathe.

'I went to the park, I watched the ducks – everything you always think you'd do . . . '

One by one they were beginning to open their eyes.

'I put him back. She must've been in there ages, his mum. She never even missed him.'

Absolute silence. They stared at each other open-mouthed. Donna, alone, still kept her eyes closed. Tamsin was reeling visibly – nothing at Business School had prepared her for this.

'That's really . . . er . . . thank you . . . thank you for sharing . . . that's been . . . really terrific . . . I think we'll leave it there for today, shall we? I think we can see how sharing like this has brought us closer together . . . helped us to understand each other a little better? Thank you, Donna, you can open your eyes now.'

Donna looked up. Strangely enough there was no shame, no embarrassment, only a sense of calm, as if it had all been somehow therapeutic.

Tamsin rose, eager to recover in the sanctuary of the office. 'Well, we'll carry on with this tomorrow . . . '

'Yeah, but I wanted to say . . . '

Simon jumped up, but Tamsin had already disappeared.

'What?' Klepto at least was eager to hear his testimony.

'I think I'd like to kill me mam!'

Klepto's heart went out to him – she knew just how he felt – and they continued to ogle each other till Norma pushed passed, declaring to no-one in particular, 'Not all typists are thick, y'know.'

Elfrieda was not a vicious woman, but when it came to protecting her child from the villanies of the outside world, she was a veritable tigress. Which was how she came to be rifling through his top drawer, on the look-out for – she didn't know what – 'just checking', she would have said – when she came across that symbol of all decadence and delinquency, the bottle of aftershave. There, in this shrine of innocence, this temple of homage to Daley Thompson, Frank Bruno and Whitney Houston, lay the ultimate desecration – Brut. Wrapping it in toilet-paper, she bore it away downstairs and slammed the dustbin lid on it.

Klepto had mislaid her bag of crisps – seventh packet of the day, still the cheese-and-onion to go – and was wandering back to the bench to hunt them out. Presently

her eye was caught by something more tempting –
Tamsin's briefcase, open on the desk. Klepto could not
resist. Out came the Herbal Teabags, out came the
Filofax . . . but what really fixed her attention was a
leather-bound edition, exquisitely-illustrated, of Dick-
ens' *A Tale of Two Cities*. Klepto flicked through the
leaves with genuine excitement. Mills and Boon had
nothing on this. Such delicate print, such beautiful
pictures . . .

'Hello.'

Klepto leapt up. 'I wasn't pinchin' nowt.'

Tamsin smiled back at her. 'I know you weren't.'

Klepto relaxed slightly. 'It's lovely that, in't it?' She
stroked the book almost tenderly.

'You've read it?'

'Oh no, I don't read books like that. I'm too . . .
y'know . . .'

'What?'

'Daft. Y'know . . . like dim.'

Tamsin looked at her in disbelief.

'Oh, I am, though,' Klepto assured her. 'Me dad says.
And me brothers. And everyone really.'

'You manage the work here alright.'

'Oh yeah, but *anyone* can do that. Me dad says.'

Tamsin shook her head. 'You don't really believe that?'

'Oh, yeah, I'm fit for nowt, me,' she announced
cheerfully. 'I'm not like *you*, dead clever, standin' up in
front of people, tellin' them what to do, actin' dead
confident, an' . . . '

Tamsin began to laugh. 'D'you realise how long I've
been qualified? Two months. I've no real field experience, no practical knowledge of what it's like to work in
industry. I can *look* confident – but when I get up there in
front of everyone . . . I'm terrified.'

Tamsin was grinning at her. Klepto smiled back uneasily.
Why was the girl telling her this? Clever, well-spoken
Tamsin, baring her heart to stupid, tit-brained Klepto? It
was all too confusing. To cover her awkwardness, she

163

turned to the book, examining its cover, dipping through its pages.

'Me mam had books like these,' she said. 'Me dad slung 'em all behind the fire.'

'Why don't you borrow it?'

'Me?' Klepto gazed in amazement.

'If you'd like to.'

'I'll bring it back.'

'No rush.'

'No, but I *will* though . . .'

Tamsin laughed at her protestations. 'I know you will.'

The two exchanged another smile. Rapport had been established, a friendship sealed. Klepto glowed with happiness. Someone had actually taken her seriously.

'I suppose you'd call her one of those "feminist" types.' Donna and Jill were walking down the factory steps on their way home.

'I mean, she's very independent, isn't she? Very . . . knows-her-own-mind.'

'Well, good luck to her,' Jill remarked. 'I wish I'd known *mine* at her age.'

Donna now caught sight of Klepto, ambling along with her nose in a book.

'What've y'been up to this time?'

She recognised the book as Tamsin's.

'I've borrowed it,' Klepto announced.

'You'll be had up one of these days . . .'

'No, *she* borrowed it me . . . She *did*.'

Donna looked dubious. 'I hope you're telling the truth, young lady.' Klepto drew herself up indignantly. 'I'm not still twelve, y'know,' she retorted.

'That's where all this "talk" gets you, is it?' asked Donna, as they watched her flounce off down the road.

Simon, at this moment, jogged past, breathing 'aerobically', dressed in running gear identical to the morning's.

Queenie, cruising past in the Flying Ashtray, leaned out of the window and yelled, 'If *she's* got all the answers, how come smart-arse here's still wearin' his kecks inside out!'

And doing a cautious 0–60 in 8 seconds, she roared away, leaving the onlookers to peer through the usual smoke screen.

Wednesday morning saw Pauline sporting an enormous bow *à la* Tamsin and attempting to educate her palate to Peppermint Tea. Leaning across to Donna, who was reading the *Telegraph*, she remarked in a newly 'cultured' voice, 'They do cost, yer "quality" papers, but y'get what y'pay for.'

Queenie flapped her tabloid with great display and announced, 'Great little rag, this – "My sex romps with 80-year-old Swedish gay vicar, by Elton John's disabled budgie".' Then, archly, to Donna, 'I could make meself a tidy pile, floggin' 'em some of those Jacka's she's had you lot comin' out with.'

'Yes, I've no doubt,' Donna sniffed. 'That's just about your level – exploiting people's privacy.'

'Privacy!' Queenie guffawed. 'I've had more friggin' privacy down Family Planning, with me arse round me ears an' fifteen friggin' medical students pokin' at us!'

Pauline drew herself up with dignity. 'I don't hear any other complaints. The rest of the bench seem satisfied – I, as official shop steward, am satisfied – the management is satisfied . . . an' if it's frettin' yer that much . . . I can recommend a hot infusion of Lemon Verbena. It calms the nerves summat crucial.'

'Hey, leave me out of it!' Queenie beseeched. 'You wanna make a prize dicky of yerself, you stick in there. She's havin' no effect whatsoever on *me*.'

'No, I can see that,' Pauline observed.

*　　*　　*

'You've heard the latest?'

Carol May had broken away from her *tête à tête* with Rex and was making for the bench.

' "Optional" session tonight after work?'

Jill was up in arms at once. 'And where's that bright idea come from? – nobody with kids to sort, that's for sure.'

Queenie snorted at the mere idea. 'I'm up to here gettin' me ear bent by that lippy mare, without stickin' in for extra time with no extra friggin' cash to butter the crumpet!'

Suddenly Queenie dived to attack her day's work. 'Oh, here we go – me ear's smokin' already!'

Now Tamsin appeared, looking faintly apologetic. 'So how d'you feel about this extra session?'

A sharp outburst of breath gave her some idea of Queenie's views.

'Mr Beachcroft was anxious to cram in as much as possible.'

'I'll bet,' sniffed Carol May.

'I hope you'll come. I know it's a bit awkward . . .' She turned to Jill. ' . . . specially for those with kids. I think you'll find it worthwhile. I really feel we're starting to make a lot of headway.'

Pauline swelled with self-importance. 'Well, *I* think it depends on yer priorities. Some of us feel we've something of a duty to our potentials.'

Tamsin ignored the splutter of derision from Queenie's corner. 'I'll look forward to seeing as many of you who can manage it.'

Jill and Donna were in two minds. Klepto glanced round the table, rose to her feet, announced, 'Well, *I'm* going,' then repaired to Chapter Six of her book.

Simon gazed dolefully at his supper. This was not lettuce. This was not the lean meat and green salad he'd asked for. He picked at a chip – one of a small mountain – and retired behind his *Running* magazine. Elfrieda emerged from the kitchen, carrying her own hearty meal of three cream crackers.

'Mam . . .' Simon had been waiting to press this point. 'Has someone bin rootin' in me bedroom?'

'Now who'd' a bin doin' that?' came the innocent reply.

'Me aftershave's missin' '

'Aftershave! – at *your* age! – the very idea!'

'I'm nearly twenty, mam.'

'Your father was a one for aftershave. See where it got him.'

Simon couldn't imagine.

'Livin' in some flat up Salford with a young floozy half his age.'

And not half bad, from what *I've* seen, Simon thought.

'We don't need his company, eh?' cooed his mother, piling bread and butter on to his plate. 'We don't need anybody. We got each other.' She caught sight of Simon's untouched plate. 'You tellin' me there's something wrong with that food?'

'Aaaagh, mam – I've said I'm off chips – y'know what I mean? – I'm in trainin'.'

'All that gaddin' about? You think I'm gonna sit there an' watch you faintin' of malnutrition? You thank the Lord you got a mam to look after you.'

'I don't need looking after,' the boy protested.

'I think it's fittin' for *me* to be judge of that.' She lifted a forkful of chips to his mouth. 'Just to please me, eh?'

'I can't now. I'm late.' Simon got up to leave the table.

'What's late? Where you goin'?' She seized him round the wrist. 'You don't bolt your food – you don't give yourself ulcers – you chew each mouthful 'least fifty times.'

'It's work, innit?' Simon asserted. 'We're tryna raise a bit of consciousness, y'know what I mean?'

'An look at me,' his mother wailed. 'What do I do? I get no company all day, I look forward to this evening, I take two hours cookin' his tea . . .'

'Aaagh, mam, it's just the once . . . '

'You can go out any day. How long's your mam gonna be around, eh?'

'Y'bin sayin' that for twenty years, mam.'

'You don't need to go,' she wheedled. 'You stop here, we have a nice quiet evening, put our feet up, treat ourselves . . . '

Simon slumped back in his chair. Elfrieda picked up a chip and dandled it before his mouth.

'You gonna eat it just for me, eh?'

Business must be bad. In fact, to judge from the fist-waving, expletive-ranting exploits of the Demetriades family, they were about to go bankrupt. Tino sat watching his elders in silence, making little contribution to the discussion. On these occasions he took a leaf out of his sister's book, sat back and observed – it saved a lot of earache – both literal and metaphorical. The clock on the side struck seven. Where was she? Half an hour to get there – that was no problem – but the discussion appeared to be winding down – and how she would manage to slip past unless they were still at each other's throats was extremely problematic. They were getting up, they were preparing to go out. Tino heard the stairs creak; she was on her way down; she would walk straight into them; he could hardly bear to watch . . .

Suddenly Georgiou rapped the table again, more vitriol poured forth, the business seemed to take a turn for the worse . . . and Klepto stuck her head round the door.

'Just off round me nan's,' she muttered, and edged out again. Her departure barely registered. A wave of the hand dismissed her and the argument resumed.

Klepto shut the door silently behind her – and ran.

Court shoes clicked down the deserted corridors as Tamsin Carlyle, eagerly armed with files and folders, made her way to the canteen – or rather, the Seminar Room, as it was now grandly titled. She was looking forward to this evening's session. Real progress was being made, she felt. All the doubts, the misgivings, the anxieties she'd felt on completing her course two months ago were finally beginning to subside. She could see a real value to what she was doing: helping ordinary, unambitious, unfulfilled women to uncover and exploit their real potential. It was very exciting. She hoped there'd be a decent turn-out tonight, so they could *really* start to advance. She opened the door to the canteen . . .

From her seat on the middle of the front bench, Klepto looked up from her third bag of crisps and grinned. Tamsin's face fell. Klepto misreading the cause, spluttered through a mouthful of Salt 'n Vinegar, 'I've had no tea.'

Tamsin shook her head. It wasn't the sight of Klepto's bulging cheeks which so disheartened her – but the fact that they were the only pair in the room!

'I'm not supposed to be here,' Klepto munched.

'Why not?'

Surely *she* wasn't about to depart as well?

'Me Dad – he'd jump the wall. He thinks I'm at me nan's.'

And what does your mother say?' queried Tamsin, putting on a brave face.

'Says nowt,' chomped Klepto. 'Said nowt for five years.'

'I'm sorry?'

'Come in from school one night, – she'd done a flit – nobbed off with two weeks takings. Soon be back, me Dad says. I knew she wouldn't, though. Cobbed off, in't she? Sick of gettin' used for target practice.' Then, with a rueful shrug. 'Now *I'm* his bulls-eye.'

Tamsin's mind raced: could she recall any 'useful advice' to be dispensed in these kind of circumstances? No, she couldn't call any to mind – perhaps she'd missed that lecture. She would have to rely on her own common sense.

'Why don't you leave?'

Even as she said it, she realised the impracticality of the suggestion.

'What? – y'mean, get married?' Klepto wondered.

'I mean, get away.'

'Get where, though? There's nowhere – not round here. Anyway, I'd be useless on me own.'

'Why should you be? You're not stupid.'

'Yeah, but . . . .'

'Your dad says.'

'He does.'

'And *I* say you're not. *Now* who d'you believe?'

Klepto paused a moment. This was a puzzler. Then . . . '*You*, I suppose.'

'That's better.'

Tamsin was pleased. Progress had been made.

'Yeah, 'cos if me Dad's bin tryna knock some sense into me for years, *some* of it must've stuck.'

'No, no, no,' Tamsin wanted to say. 'That's not what I meant.' But she was saved the trouble by the welcome sight of Norma, followed by the less-welcome arrival of Bernie.

'I say, I say! – bit of special coaching, eh?' He was winking at Klepto. 'Let's hope some of it rubs off!'

Bernie's attempt at wit was not especially to Tamsin's taste, but she went through the formality of welcoming the jester, and more particularly, of assuring Norma how pleased she was to see her.

'Don't be givin' her big ideas now,' Bernie warned. 'She'll be gettin' too grand to brew up next!'

Norma drew herself up haughtily.

'I don't intend to be brewing for you all me life,' she rasped.

'I should think not,' seconded Tamsin.

'No, indeed,' chuckled Bernie, missing the point entirely. 'Get some feller to devote yerself to, eh? That's the idea – remind me to write yer a reference.'

Not deigning to reply to this impertinence, Norma got out her notepad and pencils. She was intending to take copious notes this evening.

Jill and Donna poked their heads round the door. 'Have we come to the right place?'

'Grab a seat. We're ready to start,' Tamsin encouraged.

'Not much of a turn-out,' Jill whispered to Donna.

'You surely didn't expect Her Majesty?' Donna smirked.

'No, but I *did* think Carol May . . .'

The door opened and Rex appeared – albeit briefly – to beckon Bernie into the corridor.

'I hope you'll be more than this,' he remarked to Tamsin.

And Tamsin looked as if she hoped so too, when happily another dozen or so latecomers bustled in, to swell the ranks to a more respectable size.

'I'll be off, then,' Rex muttered to Bernie.

'Yer not stopping?' Bernie was surprised.

'Prior commitment,' came the enigmatic response. 'I'm leaving you in charge.'

Bernie swelled with pomp and circumstance, and swaggered back into the Seminar Room, leaving Rex to collide with a ludicrously coiffured and over-dressed Pauline, who clearly felt that 'going up in the world' was meant to include her hemline and hairstyle.

'Oooh, I do beg your pardon,' she fluttered, treating Rex to her sultriest expression.

'No problem,' Rex returned, scarcely seeming to notice her. But that, she assured herself, was simply because the flame of his passion was too fierce to be trusted to a single fleeting glance. Throbbing with the heat of the moment, Pauline, adjusted her neckline and strutted into the canteen.

'Okay, everyone. Nice to see so many of you here tonight.' Tamsin was relieved to count twenty faces among her audience.

'Now, what we're going to be looking at this evening . . . is The Future.'

Bernie nudged Norma in the ribs. 'Crystal balls next, is it?' he quipped.

Norma moved her chair a couple of inches to the left.

'Where do we all see ourselves in five years' time?'

A few murmurs, a few wisecracks, but essentially the same story – few had thought further than the months ahead, Christmas perhaps, next year's holiday maybe. The Future was something which didn't bear thinking about. It would take care of itself. What could *they* hope to do about it?

'Okay, now let's make it interesting. Where would you *like* to be in five years' time?'

That was more like it. All kinds of wild dreams and fantasies could be given full rein. Tamsin looked at Klepto.

'Any ideas?'

Klepto blushed. 'Up there.'

'Oh, now surely it can't be as bad as all *that* here.' Bernie bridled at the suggestion of any imperfections in his areas of operation.

'No,' disclaimed the girl contemptuously. 'I wanna be an air hostess.'

'A what!' A neigh of derision burst from Pauline's nostrils.

'I know I won't be, though.' Klepto was already sinking back into self-deprecation. 'They don't take dummies.'

'Anyone else?'

Tamsin was anxious to shift the spotlight from Klepto's lofty ambitions.

'Four kids an' a garden centre?' Donna giggled.

'Oh God, I don't know . . . I don't know *what* I want,' came Jill's fairly accurate appraisal of her present state-of-being.

'Richard Gere an' twenty-five score-draws,' Pauline boomed.

'*I'd* like to change desks.'

Norma's quiet assertion broke through the babble. 'I want the one nearest the door.'

'That's Rex's desk,' Bernie reminded helpfully.

'That's right,' came the terse reply, sending a ripple of surprise through the gathering and a look of bemusement across Bernie's face.

The dusk deepened as Rex toyed with his car keys and flicked the light on his watch. 20.17. He'd been waiting since quarter to eight and there was still no sign. Perhaps there'd been a change of plan, perhaps something had come up. It wouldn't be the first time he'd been left shivering in a dreary car-park, without even the satisfaction of being able to make a phone-call. He'd give it another five minutes, then call it a day and head off home for another slanging-match with Stella . . .

He heard the footsteps even before they turned the corner. He tried not to look too eager, but his eyes betrayed him. She was wearing a simple grey woollen coat with a flash of scarlet beneath. His pulse hammered with desire as he went forward to embrace her.

'No, not here.'

She pushed him away, and without looking at him, got into the car.

It was crazy to be meeting here – the factory car-park – even after dark. She couldn't think how she'd allowed herself to agree to it. Rex climbed in beside, her, groped for her hand. She withdrew it.

'Can we go?'

The ignition fired, the car hummed into life. Soon they were speeding off the main road towards open fields and farm lands. Carol May lay back against the head-rest and relaxed.

*   *   *

'Now, how can we achieve our aims?'

Tamsin scanned the sea of eager faces, all clamouring to divulge their fondest daydreams.

'Well, we can start by making what's called an "Action Plan". Small steps, bite-size chunks, one at a time, to set us on the road to making it all happen. So let's start by listing our positive qualities. Now Klepto . . . '

She stopped herself. 'I'm sorry, I can't keep calling you that. What *is* your name?'

'Ariadne,' mumbled the girl, a blush rising in her cheeks.

'Now Ariadne wants to be an air hostess. And I bet a few of you could think of a hostess they'd less like to fly with!'

She paused to let the muffled snorts of laughter settle down.

'Think of an air hostess and what comes to mind? Charming, level-headed, calm under pressure, good at languages, pretty handy with the in-flight dinners . . . '

More sniggers erupted. Tamsin was laughing too. 'And what do we have here . . . ?'

General mirth was now at its height.

'Well, what we actually have here is someone who does a decent job of work day-in, day-out . . . '

Tamsin wasn't laughing any more. ' . . . who's learnt to run a home and cater for a family of five with complete efficiency. Who's extremely patient, very good-natured, always calm – even under the most trying domestic circumstances . . . '

Klepto was suddenly gazing at the linoleum. It was difficult to listen to, this kind of testimony.

' . . . not to mention the kind of ribbing she comes in for among her "friends" at work . . . '

Pauline was silenced. Jill and Donna flushed.

' . . . who speaks Greek as well as English, who's so convinced of her own insignificance that she's bursting to learn . . . I won't carry on. I think we can see her serving those Duty-Frees already.'

Klepto's toes were curling. It was very kind of Dr Carlyle, but really, she'd rather people would stop gaping at her. Let's hear someone else being made a fool of instead.

Tamsin turned to the front row and smiled. 'Okay, now what about the rest of you? Can we start with you, Jill . . . ?'

Jill was standing at the bar trying to order a round of drinks. Or rather she was standing by the bar trying to order her thoughts into some semblance of clarity. What she had discovered about herself, her hopes, her dreads, the things she yearned for, the things she wouldn't admit . . . it was going to take some unravelling, this puzzle she had set herself.

'Sounds so easy, doesn't it?'

Donna's voice broke through her inner turmoil.

'Relax, unwind, don't become obsessed, be yourself . . .'

Only Donna could envisage what a tall order that would be.

'Well, how's this then?' Jill countered. 'Create your own space, demand the respect you deserve, find out who you really are . . .'

She was flicking through her 'Action Plan.' It all seemed too much like hard work.

'If we knew that, we'd none of us need to be here,' declared Donna.

'Try tellin' Ray I need space,' Jill offered. 'He'll tell us to go an' stand in Sedgeley Park.'

Klepto rose from nowhere in heated defence of her champion. 'Well *I* think she's brilliant,' she announced. 'I'm goin' straight home an' tell me Dad I'm not doin' tea for him any more.'

Donna shot out an arm to block her exit. 'I don't think you will, young lady. We want you back in one piece tomorrow. Bite-size chunks, remember?'

'I know,' argued the girl, 'but I'd rather stuff meself sick now an' get it over with.'

But Donna was firm.

'You heard what she said. Wait two weeks before you decide *anything*.'

'Two weeks is ages. If I don't tell him now I might forget.'

'If you *do* tell him now, you can forget flying. You'll be on your way up there without the aid of wings.'

Klepto wrenched herself free of Donna's restraining grasp. The message hadn't pleased her – but it had sunk in.

'I'm going to get some crisps,' she snapped, and stalked off to the other side of the bar. Jill shook her head, not in anger but in admiration.

'I wish I had her nerve. I feel like somebody's chucked a load of balls in the air, an' I'm stood here waiting to see where they land.' She laughed. 'And whether I come out with big ideas or a cracked head!' Another laugh. 'Funnily enough, I quite fancy the idea!'

It was now absolutely impossible for Tamsin to remain where she was, hovering behind the pillar. She'd been there from the moment Jill had broached her feelings of confusion to Donna. Coming back from the loo, and catching her name in the conversation, she'd stood concealed, fearing to hear ill of herself and her efforts, hoping to be rewarded by a few words of appreciation. On the whole she was not dissatisfied. She came forward now, accepted the half of lager Jill was holding out for her.

'Cheers.'

Jill and Donna raised their glasses. 'Cheers.'

Klepto appeared, crunching resolutely into Smokey Bacon. Her face was troubled, perplexed. Like Jill's. Like Donna's. Tamsin began to feel uneasy. They hadn't told her it was going to be like this. No one had ever discussed the advantages of letting sleeping dogs lie. And what she had unleashed in these women might never be at peace again.

Jill didn't want it to be. She was buzzing with possibilities, tremulous with excitement. Now it had actually been said: she was worth listening to, she had a right to be taken seriously. If Tamsin was to be believed, she was capable of so much more than she had ever given herself credit for. She couldn't wait to see Ray on his next weekend home – not for ten days, alas, but it would keep.

I'll show him, she thought. I'm not some brainless housewife – only fit for keepin' clean shirts on his back an' decent dinners on the table. From now on I start makin' the most of meself – an' stop apologising for it.

There was a spring in her step as she marched up the street under a cloudless night-sky. Not a moon in sight, just a powdering of stars. It was a good night to be deciding your future on.

Jill let herself in and hung up her coat. The living-room light was on. Strange, because she'd told Sharon to be in bed by ten and it was now well after eleven.

I'll have that little monkey if she's bin up watching videos, thought Jill, opening the door ready to castigate the offender – but instead of loosing forth a reprimand, her mouth fell open.

Ray looked up at her, saw the new skirt, saw the lipstick, saw the glow in her cheeks, and his scowl deepened to an all-time low. Jill was reeling; the shock of seeing him there was almost physical – it knocked her sideways. Seeing her dumb and open-mouthed, Ray's suspicions were confirmed. Already he'd detected a new tone in her letters, and in her voice on the phone the other night. Now she was rolling in at half-eleven, dolled to the nines and not even having the grace to think up some excuse. What sort of mug did she take him for?

'So where've y'bin?' he demanded.

Jill finally found her tongue. 'What're *you* doin' here?' she gasped.

'Who's bin mindin' the kids?' Ray's voice was positively vicious.

'Sharon's big enough,' she stammered, suddenly realising – with no small resentment – that she was being backed into a corner.

'Why didn't yer phone?' she asked.

'So you could get yer alibi sorted?' came the retort.

Jill was losing patience. 'I've bin at work.'

Ray laughed aloud. 'You've what?'

'We've had special sessions.'

'Oh, I bet,' Ray sneered. 'I see it stuck some colour in yer cheeks.'

'I'm sorry?' Jill couldn't believe what she was hearing.

'An' here's me thinkin' I could trust yer.' He laughed bitterly, as if the idea were utterly preposterous. She was livid.

'I beg your pardon.'

'See what thought did, eh?'

Ray threw himself into a chair, pointing an invisible gun at his head and flicking the trigger.

Jill's temper surged, but her better instinct told her to stay calm.

'I see,' she replied, her voice like steel. 'Here's you thinking you could trust me.'

In his chair Ray pouted like a censured schoolboy. Jill suddenly flipped. 'Who d'y'think you're talkin' to Ray. Trust me? Trust *me?* Who am I, Ray?'

Ray was suddenly thrown off stride. 'What d'y'mean, who are yer?'

'I mean, who am I? Who do *you* think I am?'

'You know who you are.'

'Do I?' Jill was something else now. A creature of fire, a veritable Titan. 'I'm starting to have serious doubts. I wonder if I've *ever* known. An' I wonder if you've the foggiest.'

Ray was foundering. 'Yer me wife, aren't yer?'

'I'm not "your" anything Ray.'

He looked at her in disbelief. She was changing out of all recognition – he didn't even know if he liked her at this moment.

'Yer talkin' broken biscuits, you are.'

'Not to me, Ray. To me I'm making perfect sense.'

He stared a while at this unfamiliar woman, then turned the full heat of his sarcasm upon her. 'Good for you. Let sense keep you warm, then.'

He waited for Jill's response.

'And what's that supposed to mean?'

Then he flung down his trump card. 'I'll finish gettin' me stuff together.'

Only then did Jill notice the half-packed case gaping open on the table.

'What stuff?' she faltered.

'I've got things here,' he reminded her. 'I came home to see if I had something more. Now what's worth havin'll fit in this suitcase.'

Jill was baffled. 'What's got into yer?'

'Got into *me*?' Ray shook his head in amazement. 'Time's got into me. Time on me hands, done a bit of brainwork – what I need, what I don't need, what I got down there, what's goin' for us here . . . Not a lot, is it? And *you* don't exactly look like yer pining away for grief.'

'I've managed.' Jill was stung by the injustice of his taunt. 'I've *had* to manage. I'm not bound to shut up shop and go round wearin' weeds for yer.'

'Who y'wearin' *that* for, then?' he sniped, smearing his hand across the blusher on her cheeks.

'Me.'

'Oh aye, tell us another.'

Jill was finally past tolerance and past caring. 'Because you're not Number One, Ray? Because I think it's time for *me* for a change? Well, if you don't like it . . . '

'What? I can what, then?' He didn't wait for her reply. 'Nah, well don't bother, 'cos I *am* doing. Don't let me cramp yer style.'

179

'I won't,' she flashed defiantly.

Ray snapped the suitcase shut. She'd left him no choice – and suddenly he wasn't at all sure he liked the sound of that. Dramatic gestures were fine, but she wasn't supposed to take them lying down. In his plans he'd always imagined her backing down at the last moment.

He couldn't realise how close she was to falling in with his plans. As she watched him toying with the lock, frowning like a spoilt child, her heart lurched and she began to melt.

'When y'comin' back?'

Quick as a flash, but too quick, Ray sensed victory. It was too sweet to resist. 'Dunno, do I?'

Jill was faltering. 'Look Ray . . .'

He was already polishing his trophies. 'Yeah, what?'

His arrogance, his stubborn pouting face, his tone of triumph . . . Jill felt herself growing cold again. He was watching her, half-mocking, a sneer sidling up the corners of his mouth. She was determined. She would disappoint him.

'Nothing.'

He hesitated barely a second, then snatched up his suitcase, shot her a look of bitter reproach, and walked through the front door.

Jill stayed where she was, too stunned to utter a sound. At the top of the stairs Sharon and Nicky stirred from their vantage-point and started to howl.

Mr Parrott stalked down the corridor, attached to a measuring-wheel, and almost drove Donna into a cleaners' cupboard.

'What *is* his game?' she asked Jill, brushing the mopheads out of her hair.

'God knows,' Jill shook her head. 'An' I doubt if Beachcroft does either.'

She hoped the bags under her eyes weren't too obvious. A night spent explaining to Sharon and Nicky that mummies and daddies didn't *always* agree – and wasn't that a healthy thing, really? – had left her red-eyed and bleary. Donna, however, seemed unaware, and if she could just stay clear of Queenie's scrutiny . . .

But now another person had her problems – or rather griefs, to judge from the tumult of sobbing coming from the bench. Jill glanced at Donna. Their thoughts were identical. She'd gone home last night and told her father, in the face of all their advice, and *this* was the result.

Klepto was lying face-down on the bench, face burrowed into outspread arms, weeping uncontrollably. Donna leapt to her side, drawing an arm across the heaving shoulders and whispering gently, 'What is it, love?'

Klepto raised her tear-stained face, gazed at them sorrowfully, stifled a sob and whimpered, 'He's dead.'

Jill and Donna went white. Endless horrific possibilities suggested themselves. Klepto lapsed into another bout of grief as Carol May joined them.

'Who is?' Jill implored her.

Klepto's sobs redoubled. 'Sidney.'

The girls stared at each other in confusion. Sidney? – was it one of her brothers? Some other relative? Surely not her father . . . ?

Pauline arrived in time to witness the spectacle. 'What's up?'

'Sidney's dead,' Carol May whispered in an accent of deepest regret.

'Sidney's dead,' repeated Pauline to the approaching Queenie, in similar tones of awe.

'Poor love,' added Jill, giving Klepto a squeeze of sympathy.

'Who the frig's Sidney?' hissed Queenie.

Klepto raised her head and treated Queenie to a look of utter contempt – as if the question were totally unnecessary.

'He's from the book.'

There was a clanging of dropped jaws and a rash of expletives. Klepto was oblivious.

'I never thought he would, though,' she sobbed. 'He

did, though.' Another sob. 'He let his mate go free . . . an' then he went up on the thingy, wi' the saw-thing on it . . . ' Her hand dipped in imitation of a guillotine. 'An' then his head got chopped off . . . an' I haven't cried so much since E.T. went home.'

And she dissolved into another flood of tears.

'Aaaaaaagh, whadder-yer-like, girl!' Queenie thundered. 'You'll do yerself a damage, all this readin'. It's not natural.'

Klepto rose to her full height of five feet. 'I could be an air hostess if I wanted,' she proclaimed. 'I've made a plan.'

Tamsin had arrived in time to catch the tail-end of this outburst. Now Queenie turned on her with a vengeance. 'So that's *your* work, is it? Puttin' soft ideas in her head?'

'Such as?' Tamsin challenged.

'Bloody readin'? Bloody air hostessing? She can't afford ideas like that – not on *her* IQ. It's pushed to cope with green men at zebra crossings!'

'Well, maybe if she pushed it a bit more, she'd give you *all* a surprise.'

Tamsin was getting a little fed up with Queenie's constant negativism. Moments later she was under siege as Queenie pelted her with bitter invective.

'Oh aye, shim in, girl – chuck around yer grand advice, set us buzzin' with big ideas. A week's time, you sail off again – where are *we*? Stuck here with all the pieces, try'na stick back what you've kicked to buggery!'

She turned to girls as if to enlist their support. 'Raise our friggin' consciousness?' she jeered. 'All she's raised is one piggin' great stink you'll spend the next six months try'na rub off!'

Never had Tamsin been more grateful for the sound of a buzzer. Reeling from Queenie's onslaught, she bent over her case, pretending to sift through some documents, while the heat of her cheeks cooled and her shattered self-confidence grappled to restore itself.

Queenie was right. That was what was so irksome.

What right had anyone to stroll into this, or any group, armed with clever theories and glib solutions? – only to depart at the end of the week, leaving behind confusion and disruption, planting seeds that could never flourish, shattering peace-of-mind, and undermining security. It didn't occur to her in this dark hour of self-doubt that many women round the table blessed her for coming – that the positive effects of her four days of counselling were already being felt in some quarters. All she could think of right now was saving face and looking for another career as soon as today was over.

The girls were scrambling into place around the bench as Norma and Simon arrived to join them for the final morning's session. All were agog to see how the Human Resources Manager would handle the dissenter. In the event, she cleared her throat, took a deep breath, and looked straight at her assailant.

'I'd . . . er . . . like to thank Queenie for making her views known . . . I think it's good when people feel they can be open and honest about what they're thinking . . . it's good for me to get feedback from you, so *I* can learn, so *I* can grow too . . .'

People were starting to shuffle in their seats and Tamsin sensed she was on the verge of losing credibility. Thank goodness the next item was likely to prove a popular one. She pulled out the day's project notes and spread them across the table.

'Okay . . . what I think we're ready for now, is to look at our feelings about work . . . and about our working environment.'

Those feelings didn't bear close scrutiny, judging from the hum of disapproval buzzing round the bench.

'So let's start by writing down some practical suggestions for improvement.'

This was more like it. A rush of enthusiasm greeted this proposal, and soon, the only sound heard was the scraping of pens on paper, and the sucking of nibs upon issues which required extreme concentration. Donna's first suggestion was the early removal of Mr Parrott, whose recent habit of leaping up from behind items of furniture – waving a piece of equipment (function unclear) which resembled a dowsing-rod – was proving to be a major distraction. Pauline's suggestions were more mundane: a hair dryer for the ladies cloakroom and toilet-tissue which didn't feel like the sandpaper on the floor of a budgie's cage.

Tasmin surveyed the new-found energy with satisfaction. At least she was going out on a positive note, and who knows, with any luck she might just win a few well-deserved improvements for the girls.

'After all,' she remarked, with a twinkle in her eye. 'Even looking at it from Mr Beachcroft's point of view, a contented workforce is usually a productive workforce.'

Queenie, reaching for her third side of paper, glanced across at her – and winked.

Mr Beachcroft was turning an interesting shade of purple. It was four o'clock; he'd dropped in, hoping to be told what a marvellous asset Dr Carlyle had been, how production was already up twenty per cent and that the girls were composing an anthem in praise of the company. He'd been greeted instead by a list – and it was this same item which was lending his complexion such an apoplectic tone.

'Rubber plants!' he blasted.

'Yes, that came up a lot, apparently – lack of greenery.'

Rex's face, studiously impassive, threatened to betray at any moment, an overriding desire to laugh.

Mr Beachcroft was in no such danger. 'Comfy chairs? . . . Rest Room? . . . Longer Breaks? . . . No Management Harassment?' – what the bloody hell does *that* mean?'

Norma coughed significantly. Bernie whistled and kept his hands resolutely in his pockets.

'New canteen . . . crèche! . . . '

The Chairman looked in imminent danger of spontaneous combustion.

'An' I've bloody paid to be told I've to shell out for all this palaver before I can expect a better score off them benches?'

Rex smiled a disclaimer. It was all most regrettable, his expression said.

Mr Beachcroft thought so too. 'Modern management techniques? – y'can bloody keep 'em,' he growled.

'Of course, it might be felt . . . ' interjected Norma, still busy at her typewriter.

'Who asked *you* to pipe up?' Beachcroft rounded on her.

The expected crumple never came. Norma continued to type – and talk.

' . . . that a gesture of "good intent" would do just the trick for making the workers feel their views were being taken seriously.'

'Gesture of good intent?' he fulminated.

'A few Weeping Figs, armchairs in the rest room, a decent coffee machine . . . '

The Chairman was astounded at Norma's audacity.

'Have you heard this one?' he demanded of Rex.

'Very astute, my assistant,' muttered Rex confidentially. 'A trained psychologist.'

Norma was treated to a second glance, then a third, and even a fourth. Beachcroft didn't like what he saw, but he was forced to view the secretary in a different light.

'And you think that a few bits of green an' a decent cuppa would make all the difference?' he asked Rex.

'It's how it *looks*, Mr Beachcroft,' assured the manager. 'It looks generous . . . even if it costs less than the price of a weekend's golf.'

Beachcroft's eyes narrowed as he observed Rex closely. Was the man being insolent? It was hard to tell – he always had that nonchalant, slightly mocking look about him, but something in his tone suggested less than the reverence a

Chairman demanded of his minions. He would keep an eye on this fellow.

Norma, meanwhile, had stopped typing and appeared to be waiting for his decision. Where had *she* sprung from? he wondered. Hadn't he remembered her as a bit of a mousy thing. Yet here she was, notepad at the ready, expecting his instructions. He must try to curb his generosity to an absolute minimum.

'Six rubber plants an' a new drinks machine.'

Norma's hands made straight for the phone.

'An' that's the lot. An' if I don't see some results comin' off that floor next week . . . '

'Get that down, would you, Norma? Six rubber plants . . . '

But Norma was already ahead of him. 'Good afternoon . . . Lyne Electronics here . . . yes . . . I'd like to order six of yer best rubber plants . . . immediate delivery . . . '

The Chairman winced, as if already feeling the pinch in his pocket.

'An' if you wouldn't mind signing this, Mr Chairman . . . ?'

Rex was holding out a piece of paper for him.

'An' what the bloody hell's this?'

'Just your authorisation for the girls to be paid that extra session's-worth tonight . . . '

Beachcroft was beginning to bare his teeth.

'I think Dr Carlyle mentioned it . . . ?' resumed Rex pleasantly. 'Best way for quick results, co-operation from the workforce, etc, etc. . . . '

The Chairman stabbed angrily with his pen at the dotted line, tossed the paper back at Rex, and stalked out of the office.

Rex smoothed out the creases, smiled urbanely and handed the slip to Norma. 'Get that off to wages, would you?'

'With pleasure,' came the brisk reply.

*　　*　　*

Once round the kitchen floor with the mop, a quick wipe across the work surfaces, peel the potatoes . . . she would be done by 6.30 – that would just give time to finish the ironing, set the oven, lay the table . . . and hopefully, slip out – on the pretext of visiting nan – while they were still arguing over the pudding. Fingers crossed, it would work out as well as Wednesday – they would barely notice she'd gone. She giggled to herself. She was getting quite good at this.

'So what d'y'call this, then?'

She spun round to see her brother Nico standing in the doorway, a smirk of triumph across his face.

' . . . more privacy . . . fairer distribution of household chores . . . enrol at night-school . . . '

Klepto's eyes widened in panic. He was reading from her 'Action Plan'. She flew at him, leaping to grab the folder from his hand, but each time she came within an inch of it, he snatched it away, lifting it high out of her reach, all the time dancing round her, tapping her face and tugging at the bow in her hair.

'Give it us!' she pleaded, panic-stricken lest her father should come in and ask to see what the fuss was about.

'No way, no way,' taunted her brother. 'So this is what yer up to on the quiet, eh? Gettin' above yerself? "Take driving lessons . . . learn French . . . " Y'don't need French for sweepin' up kitchens.'

'I'm not gonna be sweepin' kitchens,' protested his sister.

'Oh, we'll see what me Dad says about that.'

The mere mention of her father sent Klepto into paroxysms of fear.

'Give it us, please,' she begged. 'I need it.'

'How much?'

So it was back to the old extortion game.

'Ten?' she ventured, hopefully.

'Twenty.'

'Fifteen?'

Nico folded up the file and put it in his pocket. 'Forget it.'

'But . . . I'll have nowt left after me Dad's took his money.'

'Aaah, you'll have me cryin' in a minute.'

Klepto hated him at that moment. It was bad enough to be shelling out two-thirds of her wages to her father, without the further loss of her overtime bonus. She thought of making one final appeal to his sense of decency – wherever *that* lodged itself – but the slam of the front door and the babble of voices rooted her to the spot. Nico was smiling, holding his hand out for the money. Hands trembling with panic, she fished four £5 notes out of her wage packet and thrust them at her exultant brother. He smiled down at her – and calmly threw the file out of her reach into a corner. She dived after it, retrieving it just in time to meet her father's face as he came through the door. Utterly guileless, the girl found concealment quite beyond her. The file seemed to burn her fingers; her face was a picture of guilt.

'What's up with you?'

Brother Georgiou homed in at once on her terrified expression.

'Nothing!' she protested.

But Georgiou had already spotted the file, held trembling behind her back, and snatching it from her, carried it across to his father who stood glowering in the doorway. Klepto was close to hysteria – but there was worse to come.

'I have a right to my opinions . . . I should speak up for my own point of view . . . just because he is my father doesn't always make him right . . .'

Georgiou stopped reading. A look of utter disbelief had crossed his father's face.

'Read me that last one again.'

Georgiou was delighted to oblige. Klepto closed her eyes and waited for the blows to fall.

'What's this trash? Eh? Who d'you think you are?'

The first fell across her head, delivered with the back of her brother's hand. The second followed hot on its heels, courtesy of a rolled-up newspaper. Kelpto cowered, trying to shield herself with her hands.

'I just fancied a change,' she was whimpering.

'Change? You'll change your ideas pretty sharp if you've any sense!'

'She wants night-school! What's she gonna do with that? I bet that's where she went on Wednesday.'

'I went to me nan's.'

'Look at him!' Nico grabbed her hair and dragged her round to face their father. 'D'you think he was born yesterday? Eh?'

She was met by the unrelenting iciness of her father's stare, as he advanced towards her, fist clenching and unclenching, mouth twitching with mounting rage. He grabbed her by the neck, forcing her face close to his and hissing into her ear.

'You! I tell you something. From now on, you're watched, okay? You try goin' out there – you even *think* about it – you make sure you're lookin' after that shoulder.'

Klepto was starting to feel physically ill.

'We got this friend – he in't so soft as we are. He'll be out there, watchin' you for us – every step, every minute – where you go, who you meet . . . I hope you don't meet *him*, that's all.'

Klepto started to cry. Her father flung her aside. 'Let's have your key.'

She stared at him blankly. 'Give me the key!'

The message sunk in, she fumbled in her purse and reluctantly handed over her doorkey. Her father tore it from her, shaking his head in disgust.

'You bin spoiled too long, you have.'

He turned and walked out of the room. Georgiou strode across to her, snatched up the 'Action Plan' and shredded it to pieces before her eyes. Then he too, followed by Nico, quitted the room. Only Tino, who had entered unheard, sat watching unseen, now remained to steal a protective arm round his sister's shoulder. But not for long. Anxious to leave her no comfort in her distress, Nico had returned to yank his younger brother away and consign his sister to a night of misery.

The front door slammed, keys were heard in the lock outside, footsteps retreated down the path, then there was silence. Klepto rushed for the stairs, raced up, into her bedroom, in time to catch a parting glimpse of her father and brothers turning the corner of the street. Then, in sheer rage and frusration, she seized a whole armful of her Mills and Boon library and hurled them across the room. It was meant to make her feel better – but it failed. She sat down before her dressing-table, weeping into the mirror, her bow undone, and hanging askew across her head, till at length the sight of a book on the corner of the table seemed to provide more tangible consolation. It was *A Tale Of Two Cities*. Steeling herself to pass over Sidney's tragic fate, she flicked through the pages, stopping now and then to peruse a favourite illustration.

It had the desired effect. She stared critically at herself in the mirror; it was not a welcome sight. Her face was red and swollen from crying, her eyes puffed and bloodshot – but somehow she forced her crumpled expression into a smile. Minutes later she had scrubbed her face clean of tears and was starting to dab on a dusting of loose powder.

A heart was being sculpted out of shaving foam on the bathroom mirror. Dressed only in a pair of yellow-hearted boxer-shorts, and rapping to the beat from his ghetto-blaster, Simon was permitting himself a romantic flight of fancy tonight. It was, after all, a rather special evening – in more ways than one. Not only was he about to take his first-ever razor to the fluff just appearing on his chin, but he had finally admitted to the fact that he had been trying to conceal from himself for some weeks now: Simon was in love.

190

Tonight, at the extra session, he would see her. He would never declare himself, of course. He was still coming to terms with the fact, without having to endure the ordeal of *speaking* about it. But still, he would make the effort – she was worth dressing up for. He shook the can of shaving foam and was about to spray a name on to the mirror beside his own, when the door opened behind him and without so much as a knock, Elfrieda bustled in.

'It's only me.'

Simon snatched a towel from the rail and draped it round his loins.

'Oh, hey, mam – I coulda bin in the nude, y'know what I mean?'

Elfrieda chuckled with laughter and dug him in the ribs. 'An' as if I haven't bathed you enough years to know what goes on down there!'

If Simon could have blushed, he'd be scarlet by now. More cause for alarm was looming – Elfrieda had spotted his artwork on the mirror.

'An' what d'y'call that caper?' she demanded.

'I'm shavin',' announced her offspring.

'Shavin'!' The thought seemed to appal her. 'You'll do nothin' of the kind.'

Foam and razors were whisked away as Elfrieda turned her attention to the foaming heart.

'So, some little fiend's had a go at you, has she?'

'What d'you mean?' stuttered her son.

'Some young madam tryin' to snitch him away from his mother's hearth? Well, we'll soon put a stop to that.'

The heart was wiped from the mirror in a sweep of the hand. 'You can forget this lark, alright? And that scent you bin buyin'. You gonna need lookin' after a bit better from now on.'

Simon's spirits sank.

'You get dressed an' quick. We in't gonna be late.'

'For what?' asked Simon.

'Five minutes. And put a tie on.'

His mother tossed her head and flounced out of the door.

191

Simon called after her, 'For what, mam?'

But his plea fell on deaf ears – and in any case, he could imagine, only too well, what his mother was planning.

Klepto surveyed her face in the mirror. It was a patched-up job, to be sure – the blotches and tear-stains were still visible beneath the powder, but at least she looked more presentable. A pair of sunglasses, slipped into her bag from her top drawer, would complete the salvage operation. Now it was time to make her move – into a pair of high-heeled shoes, into her coat, and over to the window. Dusk was falling outside as she leaned out into the street, checking the coast to right and left. The shape beneath her bedcovers seemed dead to the world, and so it should. It was a pillow. Klepto waved goodnight to her sleeping partner-in-crime, switched off the light, and edged herself out backwards on to the window-sill.

First one leg, then the other, not assisted by the precarious heels, or the handbag slung round her neck, Klepto gradually manoeuvred herself down on to the shed roof below. One step, two step . . . suddenly a strangled scream sent her blood curdling. She was ready to faint with fear – but it was only the unfortunate cat from next door, waking with a start to find his tail impaled on a stiletto heel. She continued her descent, down across the shed roof, then, feeling gingerly behind her with her foot, she lowered herself down onto the dustbins beneath the shed, and finally reached the ground. It was now almost dark. In the shadows of the back yard, she gathered herself, straightening her skirt, smoothing out her tights.

A hand shot out of the darkness and wrapped itself round her mouth, stifling the scream in her throat. She felt herself beginning to black out, when the hand detached itself, and wheeling round, she came face to face with Tino.

'Sssssssshhhhh!' he exhorted her.

'Don't tell me dad.'

It seemed an unnecessary plea. Her younger brother had no intention of betraying her.

'Where y'goin'?'

'It's only work.'

'You best have this.'

He took out something from his pocket and pressed it into her palm. It was a bundle of four £5 notes.

'Go on, it's yours.'

She hesitated.

'Yeah, but where d'you get . . . ?'

Tino grinned at her. 'His pocket. He does you, I do him. Fair enough?'

Klepto threw herself at her brother and hugged him to her.

'Go on,' he smiled. 'You don't want to miss it. Hey . . . '

Klepto turned back.

'You better have this too.'

He held out a key – a front-door key. 'I take his other pocket too!'

Klepto took the proffered key. It was a risk. She might be caught coming back. But it was worth a try. She kissed her brother, and next moment she was running down the street and into the night.

The church was half-lit. Only the lights around the altar were switched on, so the purple cassocks and the white ruffs seemed to be picked out in a kind of luminescence. This particular House of God led a very active life – and never more so than tonight. Friday night was choir practice night, and right now the rafters were ringing to the jubilant chants of a 40-strong gospel choir, whose Hallelujahs and Bless My Souls set the shadows dancing and the communion cups vibrating. And the head soprano whose resonant tones soared above all the rest, was Elfrieda.

Her soul was in her voice as she trilled around the upper

reaches of the scales, pausing only reassure herself that the lost sheep – now reclaimed and stationed among the treble section – was behaving himself. Simon dragged at the ruff round his neck. It was too tight, it itched, it smelt of stale aftershave. Worse than this, his cassock made him look like an overgrown pixie, he'd forgotten the harmonies to nearly every piece they'd sung tonight . . . and the time was coming up to 7.30pm. Elfrieda had launched into a variation of her own, and the sheer jubilance of her outburst appeared to whip the surrounding choir into such an ardour of ecstasy, that they seemed almost possessed. The fervour mounted, rose to fever pitch, was sustained a good five minutes beyond what could be thought humanly possible, then closed to a chorus of hand-clapping, arm-waving and general embracing. Elfrieda mopped a lace handkerchief across her brow, turned to the trebles . . . and discovered one was missing.

Klepto was running down the factory road, heels clattering, out-of-breath, desperate not to miss the start of the session. The night was cold and clear, the road was badly-lit, and she could hear the echo of her footsteps and the heaving of her breath a long way off. She paused. Was it the echo? Or was it . . . ?

She turned and looked back, squinting through the shadows at the road behind her. A figure was running. A dark figure, breathing harshly, heaving towards her out of the darkness. It was then that she realized she hadn't escaped after all. This was he, the man, her father's paid assassin – for at this moment she was certain that she would barely escape with her life if he ever caught up with her. She broke into a sprint, but her shoes encumbered her and sheer terror made her legs feel as if she were running through water. Another twenty yards – she might just make the factory gates – at least then she could shout for help.

But he was gaining on her, she wasn't going to make it,

she was five yards away, two yards . . . and then she stumbled. Hands loomed out of the shadows and grasped her shoulders. This time the scream was on her lips, when suddenly a voice behind her, flustered anxiously, 'No, hey, it's cool – y'know what I mean?'

Klepto was torn between embarrassment and relief; and now her pursuer – Simon himself – seemed to catch some of her diffidence, as he fumbled to help her to her feet, muttering into his collar, 'No, here . . . let me . . . er . . . '

Klepto blushed and gingerly grasped the outstretched hand, 'Oh . . . er . . . thank you . . . '

Then she hastily dropped it as if it were a toasted brick, pulled her skirt off its perch on her backside, retrieved her sunglasses and hastened into the factory. Simon reharnessed his 'cool', straightened his tie and slouched in behind her.

The new drinks machine was proving to be a great success. Queues stretched round the corner waiting to sample the Superior Blend Leaf Tea and the Freeze-Dried Mocha Roast Coffee. Mr Beachcroft was scowling at the spectacle through the window in Rex's office, while Rex himself sipped gratefully on the first decent brew he'd tasted here in years. The Chairman flinched at the sight of six large rubber plants being manoeuvred into position by Bernie and Norma.

'Ppphhhah!' he spluttered. 'Bloody daylight robbery.'

Rex appeared over his shoulder, smiling amicably.

'Looks very nice to me, Mr Chairman' he remarked.

'That bloody woman!' countered Beachcroft, seeing Tamsin in conversation with Jill and Queenie. 'I'll brain that Harry Prescott, tellin' me it's an investment!'

But it was the drinks machine which really made his blood boil.

'D'you know how much them things cost these days? I bring her in for sharp, cheap results an' where's it leave us? – divin' into me own pockets to butter up the likes of that lot? Well, I'm buggered if they're gettin' another tuppence off me. I don't pay to give 'em a good time, y'know. This is a place of work, not the bloody dodgems!'

Rex repaired to his cup of coffee. He would not describe himself as a philanthropist – not by any stretch of the imagination – but Beachcroft's cynicism rather sickened him and he would rather not be drawn into the conversation. In the event he was saved by the arrival of Norma.

'Tea's up, Mr Beachcroft.'

She handed him the steaming beverage in a plastic cup.

'What the bloody hell d'y'call this?'

'Straight from the machine, Mr Beachcroft,' Norma assured him. 'It does biscuits an' all. I thought I'd better order the best.'

Next moment she thought she'd better order an ambulance, but the Chairman had apparently suffered only a mild seizure, and would, she was sure, be fully recovered in time to tell the assembled party how much gratitude they owed him. She exchanged a smirk with Rex and went out again to attend to the rubber plants.

Klepto was retouching the blotches under her eyes when Tamsin came into the ladies' behind her and started to comb her hair at the mirror.

'I'll miss it here.'

Klepto had forgotten she was leaving. Now the thought struck her painfully. 'Why can't y'stay?'

Tamsin laughed at the suggestion. 'I think Mr Beachcroft will feel I've done enough damage for the time being.'

'No, but I'll tell him – you've bin dead good – we've learnt loads off yer.'

Tamsin smiled to herself. If only she could explain to the girl.

'I don't think it's been entirely a one-way process.'

196

But Klepto was already thinking of herself, and the significance of Tamsin's remark escaped her.

'Thing is . . . I've only just started me "Action Plan". How will I be it after you've gone?'

'How will you be what?'

'An air hostess.'

'You don't need me to tell you. You know what to do.'

Klepto was not convinced.

'Yeah, but . . . I can't go to nightschool. I'm not clever enough.'

Tamsin was adamant. 'You are *not* stupid. That book you read – people read that at university. They study it for exams.'

Klepto was agog. 'At university?'

'That's right. So I'm sure if you can get through that in a week, you can deal with a few evening classes.'

Klepto considered the point, found sense in it, and permitted herself a small grin. Then suddenly another thought occurred to her.

'I nearly forgot!' She opened her handbag and retrieved a book. 'This.' It was *A Tale Of Two Cities*.

Tamsin shook her head. 'You keep it.'

'Me?'

'It's a present.'

'Honest?'

Tamsin grinned back at her. 'Honest.'

'Dr Carlyle tells me you've made a lot of headway this week.'

The Chairman was addressing the assembled work-force.

'Well, I'm glad to hear it – an' I look forward to seein' some tangible evidence. Rubber plants don't grow on trees, y'know – an' my wallet's got a good deal lighter since this morning.'

'I'm surprised y've not had heart failure!' muttered Queenie, with another wink at Tamsin.

'However – as I've always said – money put to good use is money well-spent – so I trust I'll get some good news in return when next week's production figures come in. Carry on, then, ladies.'

Tamsin stepped forward. There was a trace of irony in her voice as she addressed the gathering: 'I know you'd all like me to thank Mr Beachcroft on your behalf for the very positive way he's responded to some of your requests . . . '

A smattering of applause broke out but quickly subsided.

'Now tonight we're moving on to a *visible* demonstration of the power of trust and mutual support. Mr Beachcroft, if you'd like to stand aside while we demonstrate the need for total co-operation and commitment when people are working together. Now, as we discussed, I'd like us all to stand in a circle please . . . '

The workforce rose and filed into place.

'Okay, now this is what I'd like us to try . . . '

A few quiet words of explanation and encouragement, and the group would be ready to perform.

Beachcroft meanwhile was souring rapidly, muttering to Rex who stood beside him, 'Bloody party games now, is it? She'll be wantin' jelly an' buns for them to take home next!'

Tamsin turned to the Chairman. 'I think we're ready, Mr Beachcroft, to demonstrate for you that well-known business maxim – "A chain is only as strong as its weakest link." After three, everyone . . . one, two, three . . . '

With perfect timing the circle sat, all 120 women, on the knee of the person sitting behind. The chain held. Tamsin applauded, Rex and Bernie joining in.

'Yes, yes, very impressive,' growled the Chairman grudgingly, glancing at his watch and wondering how long the limousine would be.

'And now if we could have the management as well?'

Rex and Bernie moved to take their places, as the circle re-assembled for the final exercise.

'And I think for a perfect demonstration of how the ideal structure works, could we have the Chairman?'

Rapturous applause greeted this suggestion. Beachcroft cursed silently, but escape was not in his power. He made his way to the circle and squeezed in between Norma and Pauline.

'Okay, everyone . . . one, two, three . . .'

The circle sat – all except Beachcroft, who dithered, then swayed. The circle tottered slightly, seemed as if it might hold, then Beachcroft toppled, bringing the whole structure – writhing, and shrieking with laughter – down on top of him.

From behind a screen J. F. Parrott appeared, narrowed his eyes and scribbled ominously in his notebook.

CHAPTER SIX

July

It was Friday morning at number 27. Somewhere a radio could be heard, and a full-blooded female voice grooving to the beat. Then, from the bedroom, an early morning smoker's cough, with a rasping boom like a truck back-firing under water. In the kitchen, a slice of toast hopped out of the toaster.

'Give that here before I box the grid off yer!' bellowed the woman's voice, as the dog scurried, shamefaced, into the lounge, bearing the piece of toast in its mouth. Chunky stumbled out of the bedroom, still coughing severely, and looking as if he'd had a fight with a mangle. Half-blind with sleep, he groped his way towards the bathroom, hardly noticing Queenie as she appeared in the hall calmly eating the slice of toast. She would have made it to the bathroom before him, but for the dog which happened along carrying a half-empty take-away carton (from last night's supper): finding the progress of his feet unexpectedly halted, Chunky flew into the bathroom with a sort of lilting dive, leaving Queenie locked outside, itching to apply her foot to the underside of his chin.

'Shift, you – I've gotta get me face on.'

No sound was heard, so Queenie huffed and retreated to the hall mirror, till finally the flush of the toilet announced an end to the proceedings, and Chunky re-emerged into the hall. At that moment, a loud rap on the front door stopped them both in their tracks. Still half-dead from sleep, Chunky began to move gropingly towards the door.

'Whaddayerlike, div-brain!' hissed Queenie through her teeth.

'I'm seeing who it is.'

'An' what if it's that friggin' villain of a milkman flyin' more of his bills at us?'

'We don't owe *him* an' all?'

'Only about six months,' she replied with withering sarcasm.

Another rap rang out across their whispers; there was nothing for it . . .

'Who is it?' ventured Chunky gingerly.

'Recorded delivery,' came the answer from outside.

This was a bit of a poser. It was risky to accept delivery (that had been regretted all too often); but then, refusing meant never knowing what it was, and *that* was unbearable. So, his curiosity marginally getting the better of his apprehension, Chunky started to unbolt the door.

'Right, lad, y'can count me out.' Queenie was fleeing into the kitchen, as the open door revealed the postman grinning genially.

'Alright, mate? Expectin' another summons?'

Chunky, still scarcely able to see for sleep, was not responsive to the postman's humour. 'Gi's it here, then,' he mumbled, reaching out as the postman suddenly saw the dog appear and whisked his sack up over his shoulder.

'You'll have to sign for it. Eh, it's prob'ly another of them eviction jobs!' persisted the postman jovially.

'Don't sign nothin', interjected a sour-faced Queenie pacing irritably through the hall. The postman was not to be daunted. 'Mornin', Mrs Reynolds,' he nodded cheerily, handing her the post.

Queenie scowled.

'Y'never know, it could be yer Pools win!'

Chunky perked up, and hastily signing for the letter, he fingered it with anticipation.

'In my experience, it never is, though!' continued the postman with a chuckle as he turned to go. 'Yer lookin' bonny today, Mrs Reynolds.'

Queenie shot him another acrid scowl. Chunky was now handling his letter as if he thought it might explode.

'It's touchin' how all the final demands land in *my* name' glared Queenie, shutting the door on the street.

'It's your house, love,' he smiled good-humouredly, trying to mollify her. His reward was an impatient jab.

'Well, read it, dickhead, let's hear the worst.'

Chunky smiled benignly, opened the letter, and with furrowed brow, began to read. Suddenly his face became wreathed in smiles of a different character.

'Me Auntie Jessie's snuffed it!'

'Oh, well bear up, lad,' responded Queenie dryly. 'Don't prostrate yourself with grief!'

'Nah, but . . . she's left us summat,' he babbled, transported with delight. Queenie looked up, suddenly interested.

'How much?'

'I'm to see the solicitors.'

'Well, what y'waitin' for? Get yer geek scrubbed an' yer suit aired!'

All signs of sleep had quite vanished from Chunky's features. Indulging himself with a hop and a whoop, he scuttled off to the bedroom to 'air' his long-neglected suit.

'Eh! She might've left us her gold fillings!' he chuckled.

'Yeah, well you mind y'friggin' bite 'em first,' warned Queenie. 'We don't wanna land up with any ol' junk.' Then she flicked through the array of final demands – and casually threw them in the bin.

The streets were chaotic with the traffic as a car came swiftly round the corner and pulled up by the curb. Rex got out, looked up and down the pavement, and stepped into the adjacent public callbox. Extracting some change from his pocket, he lifted the receiver, and dialled hurriedly, still glancing round, evidently uneasy at the thought of being seen. Suddenly his call was answered.

'Hello? . . . Hello . . . no, don't go . . . no look, I know what we said – but if I could speak to you at work I wouldn't need to ring you at home . . . look, y've got to see me . . . tomorrow . . . well, Saturday . . .' Then all at once his tone changed. 'Is he in? . . . is he there? . . . look, I'm goin' off me skull here . . . hello?'

The phone went dead. Frustration showed on Rex's face as he carelessly replaced the receiver.

Colin was busily engaged with his tropical fish-tanks when Carol May came back into the living-room.

'That for me?' he queried casually, gazing at the sprinklings of dried food as they slowly sank or were nibbled at by the fish.

Carol May glanced at him. Did he suspect? What had he heard?

'Wrong number,' she replied calmly, her face absolutely deadpan. The cool exterior was effective as ever, but the trembling of her hand as she reached for a cigarette almost gave her away.

The buzzer sounded. Soon women began flooding into the canteen, eager for the refreshment of the mid-morning break. Within minutes, however, the atmosphere had become one of gloom and misery. The canteen counter was bare, and a sign stood on the till saying 'CLOSED DUE TO STAFF SHORTAGES'. The end of a hard week and not even the comfort of a decent cup of tea! The girls clustered hangdog round the drinks machine, Klepto hammering at it in an attempt to make it work.

'I don't remember seein' *that* manoeuvre in the instructions,' remarked Donna, wondering if reducing the machine to shavings of metal would be a positive step.

'No, it works – I've done it loads,' persisted Klepto earnestly, and with one final hit, the machine whirred into action and produced a cup of tea.

'I wouldn't mind if it was worth the effort when it

came!' was Carol May's conclusion as she pursed her lips at the vile brew.

Pauline came bustling up, looking affronted and gesturing at the till sign.

'What's the big idea?'

'One's on holiday, three's gone sick,' reported Jill morosely.

'Not much! – an' convalescing in Torremolinos from what *I've* heard.'

She thrust her money impatiently into the slot. Nothing happened. The coins had jammed.

'You've to kick it.' advised Klepto, by now the acknowledged expert. Pauline proceeded to give the machine a kick. Still nothing.

'Y've broke it,' Klepto observed, staring with pained expression at the machine, as at a sick animal. Several loud moans came from women further down the queue.

'Well, that didn't last, did it? I thought this was meant to be the best on the market.'

Pauline turned and noticed the once-proud rubber plants, now thoroughly dead. 'An' what variety d'y' call that?'

Jill was the first to draw her own conclusions. 'What gets *me* – if productivity's up, an' the money's pilin' in – how come we never see any of it?'

There were widespread murmurs of agreement.

'Other firms get bonuses – we get cold, powdered tea an' a pile of dead rubber,' she continued, as Queenie arrived, poised to feed her money into the machine. 'Save yer money, love – it's finally bin put out of its misery.'

'Oh, fly us a ciggie, then, will yer? I'm skint till wages,' craved Queenie, seeing Carol May take a packet out of her handbag.

'S'me last pair.'

'Why, *you're* knockin' them back a bit, aren't you?'

Carol May shrugged; to which Pauline, with a knowing wink, attached great significance.

'Oh, it's like *that* is it?

'Like what?'

'Trouble in't sack?' whispered Pauline with another meaningful look.

Carol May made no response, but casually lit a cigarette. For a moment there was an awkward silence, then suddenly Jill pulled out her own cigarettes, offered them round, and lit one herself.

'Hey, what's come over *you*?' Pauline eyed her suspiciously, still hot on the scent of scandal.

'I fancied a change.'

'I thought your Ray didn't approve,' chipped in Donna.

Jill bristled. 'An' where does *he* come into it?'

'Dead right, doll,' sided Queenie. 'Bloody lads? There's none worth two tanners to rub together. I wouldn't get stuck with one if y'paid us.'

Just then the buzzer went for the end of break. As the girls began to filter back, they caught sight of Rex . . .

'Mind you, I could be persuaded,' added Queenie salaciously, with a roll of her eyes.

'Not *that* type, love. They cost too much.' Carol May's tone had a reflective edge; she didn't mean just the money.

'They *all* bloody cost – it's whether yer paid enough to make it worthwhile,' mused Jill, as they all trooped back to the benches.

Carol May's remark had struck a real chord.

Chunky was standing outside the factory gates. Why he appeared – as ever – to be loitering with intent was hard to pin down, but somehow, even when he was 'just waiting', he contrived to look guilty and furtive. Suddenly he caught sight of Queenie, who came striding across with a great sense of purpose.

'Well?' she demanded.

'Nothing.'

'Whaddaymean, nothin'?'

'It's all bin left to me wife.'

'What wife?' mouthed Queenie, temporarily floored.

'Aye, well, there y'go,' he returned, with a crestfallen sigh. 'She were a right dozy get, our Jessie. Musta forgot I never re-wed.'

Already six steps ahead of him, Queenie assumed her most casual manner. 'Er . . . what has she left this wife, then?'

'Fair bit of jewellery, pair of brass cupids, five hundred nicker . . . '

'Right, that'll do,' she cut in, her tone almost military in its decision. 'Get in the car.'

'Eh?'

'You shift them lallies off an' get us a licence.'

Chunky was starting to get confused. 'A what?'

'Oh, whaddayerlike, you?' she scolded, jabbing him with her forefinger. 'D'y' think I'm about to kiss ta-ra to a stash of swag for want of a skinny bit of paper?'

Suddenly it began to dawn on Chunky. 'What? . . . Y'mean . . . get wed?' he stammered in disbelief.

'Well, don't stand there catchin' flies – y've been on at us to do it long enough.'

Chunky was beside himself with joy. 'Y'mean . . . y'will?' he stuttered, trying to embrace her.

'Oh, go 'way, will yer?' retorted Queenie, slapping at him. 'I'm only gonna say it once, an' that'll be down the Registry tomorrow mornin'.'

Chunky just stood there, helpless with delight; Queenie was less susceptible to the claims of sentiment.

'Well, shift, dickhead – before I change me mind an' pagger the gob off yer!'

And with this, she propelled him headlong towards the car. Rex, who happened to be passing at that moment, received an unusual salutation.

'Hey! – I'm gettin' married!'

Though Chunky had never met the man in his life, he called out to him, unable to contain his rapture.

'Congratulations . . .' returned Rex dryly. 'I think,' he added, with barely concealed amusement, as Queenie whacked Chunky across the head to hasten him on his way.

With Chunky dispatched, Queenie lost no time in legging it round the factory to where the rest of the group were sunning themselves on a back fire escape. Pauline drew particular notice with her unbuttoned overall, and sleeves rolled up for maximum exposure, but the array of bodies draped across the ironwork suggested she wasn't the only one engaged in serious tanning. Something was about to make them sit up.

'Right, girls,' announced Queenie, her arms outstretched in anticipation of applause. 'Me number's up – I'm gettin' married.'

There was a moment of silence while the joke sank in. '*You* are!' hooted Pauline.

'Give over!' chided Jill with a smile of disbelief. Donna was emphatically incredulous.

'I don't believe it!' she gasped, almost scornfully, wondering at the idea as at a bad dream. But this wasn't Queenie's normal style of cabaret.

'When?' queried Klepto, straight and earnest, looking Queenie in the eye.

'Tomorrow.'

'Oh aye,' chortled Pauline. '*And* the three bears?'

'Oh, that's nice,' flashed Queenie. She'd expected to be taken a little more seriously than this.

Jill still thought this had to be a catch, and was looking for the punchline. 'What's come over *you*, then?'

'Hey,' interjected Klepto with a sudden gasp. 'Y've not . . . y'know, like . . . "got to", have yer?'

Queenie gazed skyward for assistance. 'If God give this girl a brain, he musta robbed a gerbil.'

'Well, *I'm* chuffed f'yer,' said Carol May warmly, and gave her a hug.

'Flags out, that's one from six – I *must* be doin' well!'

Queenie's sarcasm finally sunk in.

'No, but if yer serious . . .' faltered Jill.

'Serious? I must be friggin' *critical*, lashin' meself to that minty little woolly-back. But what can y'do?' Here Queenie assumed an acid smile. 'I seen your examples before us an' I thought I might as well geg in!'

It had hit home now, and it was a tough mouthful to chew on; not a single one of the girls could be said to be entirely happy about her relationship. 'Happy' was not a word one tended to use in that particular context.

'So . . . tomorrow, then,' ventured Pauline, still reeling but trying to sound pleased.

'Yeah, an' I wanna full turn-out. If I'm gettin' sunk, I'm goin' down like a friggin' viking – fun, games, feast an' friggin' fireworks!' This was rousing stuff, despite the accompanying air of threat.

'I best get me hat out of mothballs, then,' said Donna nonchalantly.

The girls looked round in amazement. This unexpected gesture of support was a turn-up in everyone's book, though Donna herself was not unaware of the sensation she'd caused. Even Queenie was speechless.

Collection time at the wages hatch always guaranteed an early queue of women waiting restlessly for Norma to open up. When she did so that afternoon – most punctually, of course – Pauline had positioned herself strategically at the head of the queue to capture each one as they collected their treasured brown envelope. Presently, it was Hetty's turn at the hatch.

'Contributions for the blushing bride?' smarmed Pauline, pointedly rattling a tin in her direction.

'Blushing? Oh aye, that I *would* pay to see,' rejoined Hetty dryly.

'You'll be able to see tomorrow then, won't yer?'

Pauline spoke through almost closed teeth and a sort of plastic grin – the fruits of her efforts to conceal how much she hated Hetty. The woman tipped out the change from her wage packet, and with bad grace donated 50p. Pauline was about to proceed to the next candidate, when Hetty suddenly leaned across to her.

'Here, you're a mate of theirs – what's *his* game then?' she queried.

'I beg your pardon?'

'Gettin' roped to *her*? I'd stick a muzzle top of any weddin' list where *she's* the bride.'

'Well, there y'go, love – some people have funny tastes.'

Pauline paused for a maximum effect, then adopted a tone of acid pleasantness. 'Take *your* feller, f'r instance.'

And smiling broadly, she shook her collecting tin and rattled off down the queue.

Friday afternoon break was a special point of the week in the ladies' toilets. The place took on the tussle and shout of the stock exchange, as women crowded in to promote or settle business. This was the time of the week when money changed hands: debts were paid off, new debts run up, payments were made to various weekly clubs and catalogues, schemes and products were touted. Toiletry activities were incidental. This Friday 'down the lavs' found Hetty holding court over one side of the toilets, amassing money for her 'Christmas Club'; and glaring at Pauline who was busy collecting money on her catalogue. Jill pulled some coins out of her purse to settle her bill.

'They've fell to bits, them shoes, y'know – he's only had 'em five minutes,' complained Jill.

Pauline knew her wares like an expert.

'Well, if he will walk in them – they're not walking shoes,' she sniffed.

'Can I pay mine *next* week?' begged Klepto, looking very bleak.

'That's three weeks you owe now,' Pauline made a note in her little book.

Bristling at the apparent competition, Hetty called over from her side of the toilets.

209

'Any more f't Christmas Club? – Make yer money work f'yer!'

'Work for *you*, y'mean, sat in your Post Office account!' returned Pauline from her corner, rising to the bait.

Queenie emerged from one of the toilets where she'd been counting up the wedding collection.

'Stingy beggars,' she muttered. 'It won't even pay for the friggin' licence.' In her hand she had several scraps of paper, which she now thrust at Klepto. 'Here, y'can sling a few of these around.'

'What is it?'

'Me weddin' list.'

'You don't waste much time,' remarked Carol May wryly.

'Yeah, an' I don't want any junk. Knock-off by all means, but no paki.'

'At Greek weddings they all pin money on the bride's dress.'

Klepto's point-of-information was touching but not altogether relevant, opined the general assembly.

'Well, don't tell Chunky,' retorted the bride-to-be. 'He'll have us divorced an' married twice a month.'

'Too late anyway,' sighed Jill, as she pointed to Pauline's catalogue. 'I've pinned *my* last coppers to madam's bible there.'

'What y'wearing'?' probed Klepto, looking at Donna for inspiration.

'Never you mind,' came Donna's coy reply.

Queenie was mouthing silently to Carol May, 'Is she bringin' Gordon the Organ?'

But Donna had seen Queenie's reflection in the mirrors.

'Yes, I think so, Queenie. If you ask him nicely he might do yer a Wedding March.'

Queenie was dumbfounded. Donna calmly continued.

'I shall need a lift if there's any room goin'. Our car's in f'r'its service.'

'Yer on, doll,' answered Queenie quickly. Donna looked slightly apprehensive; there was bound to be a catch . . .

'I need somebody sound to make sure ol' goofy doesn't get lost on his way down the Registry – you two's'll be just the trick.'

'But who's taking *you*?' demanded Donna with puzzled mien.

'Go 'way, girl – yer lookin' at a bride on the eve of her weddin'. I can't be kippin' under the same thatch as me fiancé.'

The girls roared with laughter at Queenie's new-found sense of delicacy.

'Tonight I'm stoppin' with me maid-of-honour,' she announced proudly, and, to cap it all, presented Carol May.

'Yer wanted in the office.'

Norma had approached Carol May and muttered close to her ear.

'Oooh, what've *you* bin up to?' whooped Pauline, eager to drum up more scandal, though Carol May wasn't the least bit fazed.

'I won't be a tic,' she said, calmly going out.

Queenie took the opportunity to flourish her wedding list again.

'Right, dolls, get these scattered.'

'Why, what're *you* gonna do?' enquired Pauline.

'What any girl with half a tap of sense'd do under the circumstances,' grinned Queenie, making for her locker and pulling out a bottle of whisky. 'Get herself friggin' rat-arsed.'

Whereupon she up-ended the bottle and strolled out, taking a long lingering swig.

Norma remained buried in the wedding list. 'Where d'y'get Space Invader machines?' she queried.

*　　*　　*

To anyone watching through the window of Rex's office, it appeared to be a perfectly normal conversation between employee and employer. Carol May was sitting in front of the desk, Rex appeared to be working. Inside the room, the reality wore a different complexion. Rex's voice betrayed considerable emotion, though his face managed, more or less, to conceal it. Carol May remained impassive throughout.

'You've no business to fetch me in here.'

'I'd no choice, had I?' he quavered, without looking up. Someone passed the window; he started scribbling furiously, anxious to keep up the right impression.

'Can y'do tonight?'

'I've Queenie round. She's stoppin' the night.'

'Five minutes?' he persisted.

Carol May was growing impatient.

'How can I!' she remonstrated testily.

At that moment, Norma happened to return. She immediately sensed an 'atmosphere', and went to sit at her desk.

' 'Scuse me.'

'Right, then – I'll be round at eight o'clock,' declared Rex, suddenly brisk and business-like. Carol May looked alarmed.

'Let's hope we can have it all arranged to Queenie's satisfaction,' he added, improvising with remarkable fluency. 'Norma, we'll be fixing up a few things for Mrs Reynold's wedding, so I'll want you to get over to the florist's right away and see what sprays they do.'

Norma suspected this was just a ruse to get her out of the office, but she went anyway. Rex waited till the door was safely closed behind her.

'I can't handle this.'

'Oh, an' I *can*, I s'pose?' returned Carol May with caustic sarcasm.

Rex got up. He looked as if were about to do something

212

desperate, like grabbing hold her. Sensing this, she moved towards the door. 'I'm due back.'

And before he could argue, she had left the office.

A long week over, the girls were filtering out of the factory in twos and threes, keen to get home. But the thought of Queenie's wedding, a phenomenon indeed, was still very much to the fore in their minds.

'Don't forget yer carnations,' reminded Pauline. Klepto, on her way out with Jill and Donna, gave a little wave of acknowledgement.

'I'm glad there's a weddin',' she reflected. 'I've bin dead cheesed off since me holidays.'

'What time *is* it tomorrow?' wondered Jill, catching sight of something.

'Eleven o'clock,' replied Donna, her expression quizzical.

'Well, I hope someone knows the number of a good builder.' Jill pointed. 'State of the bride, she'll not stay up without scaffolding . . .'

Donna and Klepto followed her bemused gaze, and discovered Queenie, large as life, but less animated, lolling spread-eagled against the fence, dead drunk but still drinking, humming a tune to herself. She was covered in tinsel and streamers; balloons dangled and flapped from various limbs; and littering her clothing were scraps of confetti.

'See yer tomorrow, girls,' nodded Jill with a grin to Donna and Klepto, as they passed the spectacle on their way out of the gates.

As Queenie basked on in her drunken haze, Simon began to advance, giggling hysterically at his own daring, all set to pin a strand of his own tinsel on Queenie's overall. Queenie's off-guard state had evidently made him unusually bold. As he leaned forward, teetering over her sprawling

213

body, and stifling snorts of hilarity, Queenie suddenly sprang to life, ferociously alert.

'Do one, div, before I glorm yer head off!' she spat.

Simon shot backwards, and tried to retreat coolly out of the gates.

Queenie eyed Hetty and a group of other women who were just passing.

'Alright,' she growled. 'Who's next?'

They hurried off, frowning with distaste at Queenie's behaviour. Queenie laughed, threw her head back, and took another long swig at the bottle.

Chunky was in the bedroom laying out his suit. It had had its heyday during the *Saturday Night Fever* era, and its style owed much to John Travolta. Now, however, it was looking a bit the worse for wear. Chunky inspected the suit with a gaze of nostalgia and excitement. His face, usually so reminiscent of a startled rodent, was radiant with happiness, glowing at the thought of impending bliss. He jigged round the room, crooning to the melody of a Northern Soul love song. The dog sat waiting for a chance to pillage. When the telephone rang, Chunky danced across to it.

'Hello . . . eh, Kip, me ol' mate – what y'doin' tomorrow?' The dog scuttled swiftly across and seized a pair of gold-plated cuff-links.

'What'm *I* doin'? . . . I'm gettin' wed, mate . . . she's finally give in . . .' There was an awkward pause. 'What d'y'mean, have *I* forgot?'

There was a silence during which some dreadful penny dropped.

'Can't y'get someone else to drop it? . . . Because I don't fancy gettin' pulled on the way to me own weddin' wi' a car-boot full of knock-off . . . look, Kip, I know . . . I'll owe yer one . . . Give over, Kip, it's bloody miles away . . how'd it be if I done *two* dumps *next* week? . . . what d'y'say to that, eh? . . .'

He paused to hear the response.

'Tomorrow or else . . . Or else what? I see. Just "or else".'

'That's torn it,' he added, and put the phone down.

Queenie was standing on a chair in the kitchen, hands on hips, while Carol May made final adjustments to the hem of a magnificent dove-grey satin creation which Queenie was trying for size. At the kitchen table sat Colin, hunched over his tins of maggots and bait, overcome with nerves at the thought of another person in the room. Queenie preened and strutted at her reflection in the mirror.

'There's no gettin' round it,' she concluded. 'It's marryin' beneath us. He better friggin' realise what it's costin' me to make him legal.'

'I'm sure you'll see that he does, love,' replied Carol May with a wry smile.

Queenie resolved to drag Colin into the conversation.

'D'y' like me frock, then?' she asked, making a kind of mock-coy bob.

'Y'll have to ask *her* – it's not really my line,' trembled Colin.

Having to talk to a stranger was dodgy enough; having to talk to Queenie was worse; but not being the subject of angling capped it all. Queenie looked contemptuously at his fishing tackle and sniffed.

'I don't know how y'cope, love – it looks that fascinatin', s'a miracle y'don't get heart-failure.'

Colin tried to bury his head again.

'Oh, y'get used to it, y'know,' he bumbled defensively, 'once y've got over the first excitement.'

'I'm sure,' commented Queenie dryly.

Just then, there was a knock at the door. Carol May was about to go when Colin sprang up, eager to escape.

'Be them bloody Jehovah's again!,' he exclaimed with an uneasy laugh, and went out to open the door.

Carol May remained impassive as Colin's voice was heard from the hall.

'Whatever yer sellin' we don't want nowt.'

'Is Mrs. Reynolds in?' came Rex's voice.

Not trusting Colin to deal with this matter any further, Carol May went to the door, and beckoned Rex in.

'Y'better come through.'

Rex strolled in, followed by Colin, who immediately retreated to his fishing tackle. Rex had never met Colin before, and he looked at him now with thinly-veiled contempt. Carol May noticed him glance round at the room, at Colin, at the fishing tackle, at the fish tanks. She felt unexpectedly irritated, ashamed, resentful. Rex had made no attempt to conceal his scorn.

'Evening, Queenie,' he greeted breezily. 'Just to let you know – the flowers are due at nine, the room's booked from twelve . . . an' you'll be takin' care of food an' booze, I'm told.'

'That's the one,' confirmed Queenie.

Rex glanced at Colin in disbelief. Carol May caught his eye, then looked away. The temptation to lure Colin into conversation was too great.

'Y'll not be joinin' us tomorrow, I hear.'

'Oh . . . no, no – "otherwise engaged",' stammered Colin.

Queenie snorted with derision.

'Oh, no disrespect to Mrs Reynolds there – if it's a toss up between a "do" in a church an a "do" on't canal bank, I'll take me rods any time.'

To cover his embarrassment, he picked up a maggot and stroked it affectionately. This was too much for Carol May.

'Oh, give over, Col,' she pleaded.

'Well, I'm sure yer friend there knows the score right enough,' rejoined Colin, waving a hand at Rex. 'I dare say *he'd* not be traipsin' off to no weddin' without his wife's stuck her penn'orth in – has she, eh?'

Rex's reply was a superior smile. Carol May was desperate to get rid of him before he went any further.

'I'll see you out, then,' she urged firmly.

'Nice meetin' you,' smiled Rex, turning to Colin.

'Any time. Come again,' was Colin's flustered answer.

'Thank you,' oiled Rex. 'I might just do that.' Then, turning to Queenie: 'Y'look "innocence itself", love.'

'Oh, not me, lad,' she quipped. 'I missed out innocence. I passed Go an' went straight to the age of consent.'

Rex smiled to himself and strolled out. Queenie was left on the chair, watching Colin perform more stroking rituals with his maggots.

As Rex came out into the hallway, Carol May took care to shut the kitchen door behind them. As she accompanied him to the door, Rex suddenly grabbed hold of her and made as if to kiss her. She pushed him away.

'What's the matter?' he whispered.

'Not under this roof.'

'Yer wasted on him.'

'I'm still *wed* to him,' she corrected, halting Rex with a peremptory look. She closed the front door behind him, breathing a sigh of relief as she listened for the sound of his footsteps, and the revving of his car in the dark street outside.

The wedding-day dawned. By 9.30, a sprightly figure in a dazzling white suit was lacing up his blue suede shoes and fixing a red carnation to his lapel. From the kitchen, came the sound of the dog rifling through the bins in search of breakfast – the master being presently so preoccupied with his hair-gel that the dog could have got away with anything, except possibly the theft of a comb. His coiffure completed, Chunky now picked up a large battered suitcase from the hallway, and checking the corridors for inquisitive eyes, staggered out to the 'Flying Ashtray' and loaded it into the boot.

Filthy, battered and rusted as the vehicle was, Chunky had nevertheless made a concession to the occasion by bandaging a few strands of frayed ribbon to the aerial, and lashing a silver horse-shoe to the front bumper. The dog, too, was sporting his own distinctive brand of sartorial elegance – a studded diamante collar and a pink carnation tucked under his chin. The groom and his companion now leapt into the car, and with the aid of a minor firework display from the region of the exhaust pipe, the wedding-party got under way.

Jill was fixing a collection of small birds to the brim of her hat when Sharon came in with the post. The girl watched keenly as her mother flicked through the bills and double-glazing circulars till she came to the critical envelope.

'Who's gettin' married, mam?' Nicky interjected. 'Is it that man with the dog?'

Jill was too engrossed in her letter to register his questions.

'I hope there's stuff to eat. Will there be chips? I hate them things wi' puff pastry.'

When Jill started to bite her lip, Sharon decided it was time to interfere.

'Who's it from? Is it me dad? Is it, though?'

'Never you mind,' came the distracted reply.

'What's it about?' Silence from Jill. 'About divorce?'

'Yes, it's about divorce,' snapped Jill, losing patience. 'Are you satisfied now?'

'I don't agree with divorce,' scowled Sharon.

'Well, who's askin' yer to?'

'You an' me dad are.'

'Alright, clever.'

Jill was determined to put her foot down here and now.

'Everyone gets divorced now, don't they mam?' suggested Nicky, helpfully.

'Well, everyone's daft then,' rebuked his sister.

'Come on, shape yourselves. Get yer coats on.'

Activity was the only way to end this conversation.

'I don't like weddings,' Nicky moaned.

'I do,' declared Sharon. 'I like the one's that last.'

'What'll last, young lady, is a great box across them ears if you don't stop jabbin' on!'

Jill grabbed her gloves from the table, and had the misfortune to glimpse her own wedding-photo, now semi-obscured by the philodendron. Eighteen, innocent, ignorant and hopeful . . . she was none of those things now. 'Thank God,' she exclaimed – but failed by a whisker to convince herself.

Gordon looked at his watch for the fourth time in three minutes and remarked yet again, 'Any minute now.'

As the 'Flying Ashtray' roared into view, Donna adjusted her hat and trusted Chunky had thought to brush the dog-hairs off the back seat – but when she glanced through the window and noticed that the dog was on the back-seat, she half-considered flagging down the nearest taxi.

'Hop in,' beamed Chunky.

The dog's response was less welcoming. Gordon found himself sharing the rear accommodation with a set of bared fangs – which nevertheless took his mind off the journey quite successfully, thereby saving him several heart attacks.

'I thought we were heading for Jackson's Row,' remarked Donna, seeing the signs for the City Centre ignored, and their route diverted in the opposite direction.

'Spot of biz to do first, love,' Chunky assured her. 'Just deliverin' some bits for a mate – not take a mo.'

Donna checked her watch, then the expression on Gordon's face. Cautious optimism still prevailed. She herself was less sanguine.

A monstrous construction of white lilies and gypsophelia

had been delivered to Carol May's doorstep. The maid-of-honour had taken delivery of this floral feat of engineering, and was now zipping the bride into her gown.

'Oh, well, I knew they'd catch us one day,' sighed Queenie as her curves were gripped by the dove-grey satin and her features obscured by the veil of her tiny pill box hat.

Carol May, gorgeous in soft peach, gave the maiden a final inspection, pronounced her 'a stunner', and ordered the chauffeur to fetch the wedding-car. Queenie seized her bouquet, picked up a large battered suitcase, and teetered out on six-inch heels to the waiting vehicle.

'You'll have to budge up a bit – I daren't let me bait come a cropper,' apologised Colin.

Queenie was not overjoyed to discover she was expected to share the back-seat with several tins of maggots, but Carol May had taken the precaution of providing some liquid refreshment of a fortifying kind and Queenie was soon sprawling happily among the fishing rods warbling the first verse of 'Love Divine'.

'All that f'r a pair of brass cupids!' Carol May observed.

'I know,' agreed Queenie. 'I must be off me friggin mong!'

Jackson's Row was already buzzing with wedding guests when Jill arrived with the kids. Norma greeted them on the steps to the Registry Office.

'I've bought them a wok,' she confided. 'Y'don't think they'll have one already?'

'No, love,' Jill laughed, recalling what she knew of Queenie's eating habits. 'I think yer on solid ground there.'

'I hope it's me one day,' sighed Klepto, already dipping into her box of confetti.

'I shouldn't be in too much of a rush,' counselled Jill, breaking off in a hurry to get the benefit of Pauline and

Frankie's arrival, which was distinguished by the enormity of Pauline's hat and the loudness of her costume.

'Very nice, love,' murmured Jill.

'I didn't go to town too much,' Pauline proclaimed. 'Y'don't like to overshadow the bride.'

'No . . .'

'Mind, there was no danger of that at our weddin', eh?' Pauline nudged her husband. 'Y'couldn't get a look-in wi' me in me white tulle an' guipure lace.'

'I dunno . . .' sniffed Frankie. 'I thought y'looked more like the front room nets. I kept thinkin' you'd hang better in somebody's parlour window.'

Pauline frowned and seemed to be digging Frankie in the ribs, but the charmer carried on regardless.

'I've had this suit since the day I were wed,' he informed Jill. 'If y'look y'can still see the mark where I threw up during the signin' of the register.'

'Frankie!' Pauline turned to the outraged onlookers. 'He's only kiddin' of course!' she hastened to assure them.

Now their attention was claimed by the arrival of Simon and the statuesque Elfrieda, who propelled her son past the sniggering rows of guests and secured for herself a vantage-point from where she could criticise and pontificate to her heart's content.

'An' who might that bold little madam be?' she demanded, as Klepto was caught stealing a shy glance at her son.

'Oh . . . I work with her,' stuttered Simon.

'Oh, I can just imagine. I know her type of old.'

And leaving Simon to wonder what the precise 'type' was, she pulled out a handkerchief, spat on the corner, and proceeded to scour his neck with it.

'Mam! I can see to meself!' he protested.

'An' that would be the day!' retorted the zealous matriarch.

The advent of Bernie and his wife Nancy drew many facetious remarks, the majority of which were targeted at Bernie's swaggering gait (made more pronounced by the lack of leg-room in his trousers), and Nancy's plumed head-piece, with the pursed lips that scowled beneath it. This pair, accompanied by the supercilious Hetty of Easter Egg fame (and wearing a bonnet reminiscent of a nest of chickens), made their way haughtily through the gathering crowd to a position of vantage which accorded with their notions of superiority.

'Just look at them hats,' growled Frankie. 'That's the kind of get-up puts the Tories where they are today.'

'Where did you get married, mam?' enquired Sharon, pointedly.

'Eccles Parish,' came the reply.

'I'm goin' back there an' tell 'em y'didn't do it.'

'Do what?'

'Stop together till death do part.'

'I think we'll go and find ourselves a seat, shall we?' suggested Jill testily, guiding Sharon away by a few judicious tweaks of the ear.

As she steered the kids past Bernie's contingent, she caught the ladies gossiping in their usual charitable vein.

'I wonder if she'll wear white.'

'Oh, she'd have the effrontery.'

'White's very dated these days,' remarked Jill.

'No sign of the groom yet,' Nancy was smirking.

'If he's any sense he'll be down the docks boardin' the next boat to Brazil.'

Chunky was not celebrated for his good sense, but as yet Brazil was not his destination. Which was just as well, since he probably wouldn't have got there, judging by the mess he was making of this simple delivery errand. Travelling in the 'Flying Ashtray' was a hazard at the best of times, but when the driver was wrestling with the wheel and a tattered sheet of directions, the odds against survival narrowed considerably. Donna glanced down at her watch, then out at the trees and open fields, and leaned across to Chunky.

'You'll have to get your skates on, y'know.'

The map was still flapping as Chunky peered narrowly at the road ahead.

'There's meant to be a turn-off here somewhere . . .'

All heads turned to watch the arrival of Rex and his wife Stella. The manager had taken care to surpass even his usual devastating style and was looking like a cover-shot from the latest Next catalogue. Stella, meanwhile, caused a few raised eyebrows of her own. Rumour had accorded her a plain face, a dumpy figure and all the style of a fishwife. The reality was a slim, well-dressed, extremely attractive woman, who only required a little more awareness of her own considerable charms to make her a dangerous rival.

'Bridegroom not here yet?' inquired Rex of Norma.

'I can't think what's happened,' flustered the secretary.

'I'm sure last night's boozer can.'

Nancy and Hetty had descended like vultures at the first scent of bad news.

'Oh dear, an' here's the bride.'

A shout went up, and the crowd surged forward to see Bernie step across to open the door of the bridal car. Gasps of admiration and disbelief greeted the dazzling amazon, who emerged like a butterfly from its chrysalis into rapturous applause, and a premature cascade of confetti from the over-eager Klepto. Hetty and Nancy alone were less than fulsome in their praises.

'Dove-grey, y'notice.'

'Well, I think it's the very least she could do.'

Carol May climbed out next, exchanging a brief glance with Rex, and permitting herself a cursory appraisal of her unsuspecting rival, who was being viewed for the very first time. Queenie turned to acknowledge Colin's muttered felicitations.

'Y'can come in, y'know – there's fish in the sarnies.'

But the angler declined hastily and made off with all possible speed towards the nearest canal.

Rex drew Carol May aside.

'He's not here yet.'

'Oh Lord . . .'

They don't hang about, these places. Someone best have a word with the Registrar.'

Carol May nodded her agreement and together they hastened up the steps to break the news without first alerting Queenie. Glancing down at this attractive couple now hurrying towards him, the Registrar opened his arms and boomed, 'Aaah, the bride and groom.' And he turned on a small pocket cassette recorder which very distortedly blared out the opening bars of the Wedding March.

'Er . . . no . . . not exactly,' murmured Rex, though wishful thinking had its part to play in his glance at Carol May.

'No, it bloody isn't!' bellowed a more forthright guest, namely Hetty, whose attachment to Stella's cause was more than the lady herself had looked for, or even welcomed.

'The . . . er . . . bride's over there,' clarified Rex. 'And the groom's not shown up yet.'

'Ah . . .' The Wedding March came to an abrupt halt. The Registrar leaned confidentially towards Rex and whispered, 'What's the story? Spot of the old frostbite round the toes? Ha! ha!'

'I'm sorry?'

'Cold feet! Ha! ha! ha!'

The Registrar was a keen fan of his own wit.

'I think we should keep this quiet from Queenie as long as possible . . .' Carol May was suggesting.

But at that precise moment a shriek of 'He's not what!' broke out from the bride's direction, and all such precautions were thus made redundant.

'I always say, better now than after we've put the rings through their noses!' joked the Registrar tactfully.

Queenie's sense of humour was curiously lacking. 'That miserable, minty little scab! I'll give him friggin' late! I'll lash him such a twaggin', he'll be up there friggin' early to meet St Peter!'

'What exactly are we looking for?'

Donna decided the time for passive observation was over.

'Left, first right after the roundabout – a pub called the Old Pack Horse . . . '

'That's handy,' observed Donna through gritted teeth. 'We've yet to come across any roundabouts, and there's only about thirty Old Pack Horses in Greater Manchester.'

'Aye, but it says here on the map . . . I'm sure I took it down right . . . '

Gordon stared dolefully out of the window. To his left the hillside sloped sharply downwards to a quarry. To his right, the cow pastures tapered away to the horizon, and ahead of them was a duck-pond.

'Well, I can't see us finding any Old Pack Horses along here,' he observed drily, as the road became a dirt-track which skirted the rim of the quarry.

'Perhaps I best turn an' go back a bit,' deduced Chunky.

'It mightn't be a bad idea.'

Chunky slammed on the hand-brake, threw the car into reverse . . . and came to an abrupt halt.

'No problem,' he assured Donna, as he pumped the accelerator, pulled out the choke, rattled the ignition, and failed to produce a spark. Several more attempts, some of them Donna's, yielded the same sorry response.

'Now what?' Chunky demanded.

'Looks like the ignition points have gone,' observed Donna shortly, and leaning down to release the bonnet, she jumped out of the car and was prodding about inside the engine while Chunky was still dithering with the handbrake.

'I think we'll have to look at the distributor,' diagnosed Donna, as Gordon leaned over to offer a second opinion.

'Yeah, but . . . what does that mean?' gibbered Chunky.

'It means . . .' returned Donna, with deliberate calm, ' . . . we won't be going anywhere for the time being.'

Bernie was the bearer of grim tidings.

'He says they can't wait no longer.'

Another party was assembling. The bride pushing seventeen, and eight months pregnant, the urgency seemed justified.

'That'll bring back memories for a fair few here,' remarked Nancy, looking at the girl's vast stomach. Carol May, who knew this to be directed at her, looked away and tried to remember that weddings were supposed to be happy occasions.

'He could've had an accident,' consoled Jill, as Queenie's rage slipped into top gear.

'Accident! He'll friggin' wish he had! There'll be nothin' accidental about the shreddin' he'll get when I get me talons into him!'

Suddenly her temperature rose several hundred degrees. 'Eh! Where d'y'think you're geggin in!'

The expectant mother was being helped up the steps towards her overdue matrimony.

'Now don't get het-up . . .' Carol May urged vainly. 'You've missed yer booking. This lot's next in.'

Queenie's complexion took on the hue of an overblown peony. 'I'll friggin juice him for this! I've grit me gob, gagged me better judgements, all to wed some little skunk who can't be arsed to fly his grid in at the right time!'

'There's bound to be some perfectly good explanation . . .' offered Jill feebly.

'Oh, is that right? Well the only explanation I wanna hear is the one scrawped above his gravestone!'

Klepto's face quivered with disappointment. 'Have we all got to go home, then?'

The crowd seemed to hold its breath, waiting for

Queenie's wrath to descend on the hapless girl. It never did. Queenie caught sight of Nancy's smirk of satisfaction, and Klepto's head was saved.

'No, we friggin' do not go home! There's all that scran an' ale to get sunk into!'

A few guests looked taken aback, wondering if this was quite 'the form'.

'Well, you please yourselves,' Queenie jeered. 'I'm frigged if I'm missing the best bit!'

And diving into the throng – which parted before her like the Red Sea – she carved a track to Rex's car, and without waiting for an invitation, leapt into the back seat.

'She'll bloody skin an' fillet us! She'll chew us up an' use it for confetti!'

Chunky's fairly accurate appraisal of Queenie's present mood was currently being ignored by Gordon, who stood beside the car, awaiting instructions from Donna – who was lying beneath it.

'Right, I've sussed it.'

Donna emerged and looked expectantly at Chunky. 'Where's yer tools, then?'

'Me what!'

'Yer tool-box, mate,' explained Gordon patiently. 'Where d'you keep it?'

'I dunno . . .' Chunky was hopping about from one foot to the other. 'I don't know nowt about cars.'

'Give us them keys.'

Donna marched round to unlock the boot.

'No, no!' Chunky protested. 'Y'can't go in there!'

'If she can't go in there, then we can't shift from here,' Gordon assured him.

'I need a hand to get this unloaded.' Donna was already wrestling with the suitcase.

'No, no! – y'can't! – it's private property,' cried Chunky, flinging himself upon the battered container.

'Look here, d'you want to get to this wedding or not?'
Chunky seemed chastened by Gordon's reprimand.

'Right, well make yerself useful – hop off and find a
phone-box – let 'em know what's goin' on.'

'A phone-box?' Chunky wailed in disbelief. 'Round
here?'

'Well you'll not find one perched on yer arse, will you?'
flashed Donna, much to the surprise of Chunky and the
amusement of Gordon.

'She'll roast us, though . . . she'll bloody tan an' leather
us . . .'

Chunky's lamentations were heard several hundred
yards down the road as he trudged off into the distance in
search of British Telecom. The dog, shrewdly enough,
opted to stay with the car, where he stretched himself out
under a hedge and dreamed of stealing American Express
cards.

'Right, then . . .'

Donna rolled up her sleeves and fished the tool-box
from the boot. It creaked open to reveal a bent hammer, a
couple of rusty nails and a twisted screwdriver.

'Now what?' bewailed Gordon.

Donna dived into her handbag and produced the
ultimate weapon – her Swiss Army knife.

'Here we go, then . . .'

She tucked up her skirts and dived back under the car.

Queenie's choice of reception-room had not been for-
tuitous. Admittedly, choice had hardly come into it – at
twelve hours notice it was the best they could do – but still,
the dingy lighting, the crumbling paintwork, the lurid
decor and the dilapidated furniture all contributed to the
impression of a jumble sale that had seen better days. As
Queenie burst into the room, the DJ, who was chewing on
a leathern sausage-roll, sprang into life and flicked his well-
worn copy of 'Congratulations' on to the turntable.
Queenie ran at him like an enraged ox, and breaking her

bouquet across his skull, suggested he might care to 'Cut that bleedin' racket f'r a kick-off, pal!'

Behind her, the rest of the party was pouring into the room, Bernie lugging the mysterious suitcase.

'Stick it here, doll – over here!' directed Queenie, as a few guests clustered around to view the contents.

'Right, then – get yer laughin' gear round that lot!' invited the should-be bride.

It had been suggested that Queenie's trousseau was on display at the far corner of the room, but when Hetty and Nancy pushed their way through, intending to pour scorn on the bridal lingerie, they found a very different kind of fare before them. Piled-up in stacks, tossed willy-nilly across the bottom of the suitcase, lay sausage rolls, pork pies, sandwiches curling at the edges, boiled eggs squashed beneath battered cornish pasties . . .

'What's your gobs saggin' for?'

Queenie had noticed the look of disgust of the faces of Hetty and Nancy.

'Y'wanna think yerselves lucky there's plates laid on.' The two were swiftly elbowed aside, however, by less discerning palettes, and soon the rapidly-declining wedding-breakfast was giving Queenie some cause for alarm.

'There's not a lot goin' gash, is there?' she reflected. 'Pauline, doll, leg it down the chippy an' get us thirty papers of fish an' chips.'

Pauline had no intention of 'legging it' anywhere in this skirt, but she grudgingly took delivery of a £10 note and accepted Bernie's offer of an armed escort.

Queenie now strode onto the dance-floor, ordered the DJ to bump up the noise level, looked around for someone to 'do the honours' with her . . . and homed in on Simon.

'Try it now.'

Gordon turned the key in the ignition and waited for the spark. It came.

'I think we've cracked it,' he shouted to Donna.

'How's the time?'

Donna clambered from beneath the chassis. 'Nearly one. Not bad going, eh?'

This remarkable pair brushed the grease from their hands and looked at each other. Covered in oil, dirt and grass-stains, the sight seemed to send them into hysterics, for presently they were rolling across the grass shrieking with laughter.

'Funny what y'can do when you set yer mind to it,' smiled Gordon, crashing to a halt on top of Donna, and covering her neck with kisses. Another minute, and al fresco marital relations might have ensued, but a volley of sound from the boot of the car made the lovers spring to their feet in panic.

'What in the name of Nelly's that?'

Gordon flung open the lid of the suitcase – to reveal hundreds of digital watches, all playing a tune to commemorate the present hour of one o' clock.

'I see . . .' he remarked.

Donna was only grateful that Queenie could not.

Rex was dancing with Carol May. It was dangerous, he knew. It was tempting fate, it was playing with fire. Already all eyes in the room, including his wife's, were on the elegant pair as they waltzed their way round the dance floor, but Rex was feeling reckless today. It was worth taking the risk.

Queenie, meanwhile, was perched beside the DJ, rifling through his Oldies collection and stuffing herself with chips and liquor.

'She must be havin' butterflies, poor love,' commented Jill, with more than a trace of irony.

'To think I was young and in love once,' remarked Frankie.

'Were yer?' Jill found the whole idea quite incredible.

'So they tell me. I can't remember. To me it just felt like

indigestion.' He turned to Jill with a belch. 'Fancy a dance, then?'

They were joined on the floor by Norma, who observed tartly, glancing across at Hetty and Nancy, 'I don't know why people bother to dress up when they wear a face down to the floor.'

Stella was thinking the very same thing, but since she was stuck with the pair of harpies, there was little she could do but make the best of it.

'Has he asked you to dance yet?' interrogated Nancy.

'Oh, I can't any more. I've a bad back since our Lauren was born.'

'That's handy for some people,' mouthed Nancy to Hetty.

'Well, I wonder how long we're to sit here like piffy?' complained her faithful sidekick.

'He might still show up,' replied Stella, hopefully.

'I think that's wishful thinking, don't you?' came the smug retort.

Chunky trudged miserably up the track and collapsed under the front wing of the Flying Ashtray.

'Five miles to find a bloody phone – an' when I gets there the bloody pig's ripped out!'

'Well, not to worry, mate!'

Chunky looked up to trace the source of this cheery voice. On the other side of the car, reclining in the shade, lay the oil-smeared, begrimed figures of Donna and Gordon – with faces grinning like Chesire cats.

'In y'get, then,' Donna invited.

Chunky dithered, still bewildered.

'Well, come on, daft-head – we haven't got all day.'

The penny finally dropped. Chunky's lip began to wobble.

'Y'mean . . . you? . . . that? we can just . . . ?'

'Yer button-hole's wilted,' chided Donna, assisting him into the backseat with an elbow to the ribs. Chunky fumbled for his sheet of directions, but found himself relieved of the paper by Gordon.

'I'll navigate,' he announced.

Donna was already waiting behind the wheel.

'Yeah . . . but what about . . . ?'

Chunky was still grovelling to get into the front seat. Donna spun round.

'Sit still! – the pair of yer!' she ordered the man and his dog.

'Right, Donna – left at the main road an' first right at the lights . . .'

Donna turned the key in the ignition. It fired first time.

Thirty minutes later they were leaving the beauties of the nature behind and heading for more urban landscapes.

'So far, so good,' beamed Gordon. 'Now all we need is signs for the City Centre.'

The Department of Transport did not oblige, so sighting a young policeman strolling along the road ahead of them, Donna pulled the car in to the side and Gordon wound down the window. In the back seat a strange fit of convulsive coughing appeared to have seized Chunky, but Gordon opted to ignore it.

'Excuse me . . . are we on the right road for the City Centre?'

The young officer turned, took in the spectacle of a battered heap of rusted metal, and leaned politely across to Donna.

'Is this your car, madam?'

'No, Constable,' came the blithe reply. 'It belongs to the gentleman in the back.'

'I see . . .'

The gentleman in the back was suffering from fits, the constable observed. It was making him feel a little uneasy.

'Would you mind if I had a look round, sir?' he asked Chunky.

A kind of strangled yelp escaped from Chunky's throat. Gordon beckoned the young officer to his side and whispered confidentially.

'He's a bit overwrought. We're on our way to his wedding. You know how we lads get . . . '

The policeman did not know, never having been a part of the process himself, but he could sympathise with the suffering of a fellow human being.

'Well, if you can assure me that everything's in order, madam . . . '

'Oh, what a question to ask on a man's wedding-day!' quipped Donna – to an outburst of laughter far more raucous than the feebleness of the joke required.

Chunky was beginning to breathe again. The policeman was about to wave them on their way, when from the boot came a deafening encore of the digital alarm chorus. The policeman glanced at Donna and got out his notebook. In the back seat, Chunky was trying to bury himself beneath the dog.

'Registration number?'

The constable walked round to the front of the car, his pen poised. Gordon leapt out of his seat and drew him aside.

'We don't like to mention it . . . it's his wedding present – meant to be a surprise – extra-loud alarm clock.' Then, in an even lower voice: 'He's a bit deaf, y'see, Constable – today's his one ray of hope f'r' a decent future. If y'could just see his lovely bride . . . '

The officer was weakening. Donna sensed his indecision, and suddenly took it upon herself to exclaim, 'Oh my God! Nearly two o'clock! He'll be late! He'll miss his own wedding ceremony!'

'So if you wouldn't mind, officer . . . ' wheedled Gordon. 'The quickest way into town . . . ?'

The young constable was floundering. He knew he was being duped, but he'd only been on the beat for two weeks and wasn't used to dealing with this sort of hardened criminal. He put his notebook away and smiled feebly.

'Er . . . first right after the lights . . . straight on till you see the signs . . . '

'Bless you, love, you've been a treasure.'

Donna jammed her foot to the floor, and roared away at such a rate that anyone might have thought she was Queenie.

Barely twenty minutes later she was gazing dolefully round the deserted Registry Office while Chunky toyed with a faded bloom he'd rescued from the floor. Tears were beginning to well up in his eyes.

'They've all nobbed off,' he snivelled.

'I say, Donna – what a turn-up.'

Gordon had spotted happier sights – draped with a dust-sheet, seldom used, but still there in all its potential glory – an electric organ.

Donna had scarcely time to share his raptures when the Registrar himself appeared.

'More candidates for the Conveyor-Belt of Love?'

'The wedding booked for eleven o'clock . . . ?'

'Ah . . . Reynolds–Buttercup . . . the blushing bride-groom lost his nerve . . . they've all adjourned to the reception. Bit peeved, the bride was looking.'

Chunky groaned. The Registrar beamed, happy to be bearer of joyous tidings, and strolled back to his office. Chunky groped blindly for a handkerchief. Never would his chance come again. He had blown forever the right to call Queenie his very own Mrs Buttercup . . .

'I'll handle this,' announced Donna suddenly.

'Where y'goin' . . .

Chunky watched her depart through gathering mists of tears.

'Excuse me . . . ' Donna had caught up with the Registrar. 'I wonder if you'd be kind enough to spare a couple of minutes . . . '

*   *   *

Queenie lay sprawled out lengthways on the floor, hiccupping noisily, but still managing to force down another can of lager. Out on the dance-floor, Simon was resisting the gesticulations of Elfrieda to return to his seat and quit the side of Klepto in whose arms he was now waltzing. Stella and Nancy, picking their way through the throng to reach the ladies toilets, had to step over the outstretched legs of Queenie – Stella stifling an amused giggle, Nancy snorting with distaste.

'So . . . it's definite then?'

Nancy turned, powdering her nose in the mirror to accost Stella head-on. The wronged wife met her gaze boldly, then turned to retouch her eyeshadow.

'Well, y'don't stay wed to one man for eight years an' not read him like the back of a book.'

'Y'don't know who it is, though?' persisted the inquisitor.

'Not yet,' replied Stella, a trifle wearily. She was by no means appreciative of this impertinent prying into her affairs.

'Hmmmmm,' observed Nancy, significantly.

'I know one thing, though,' Stella rejoined. 'She'll not get him. Oh, he might get his bit of helter-skelter with her, but what he wants in the end is a nice safe ride – feet up, seatbelts, waitress service . . . he knows when he's well-off.'

'It'll end in tears,' predicted Nancy.

'Oh aye, an' they'll not be mine,' declared Stella. 'I'll give it till Christmas.'

Then she turned and walked out of the toilets, leaving Nancy open-mouthed and fumbling for her powder-compact.

'And serve her right, the little slut,' shouted Nancy, determined to pronounce final judgement on the matter.

Carol May waited for her to depart before she opened the toilet door. 'The little slut.' So this was what she was

235

reduced to – listening to slander in toilet cubicles. She approached the mirror to salvage her complexion, but the tears had already welled up in her eyes and the mascara was ruined. She wiped away the blackened smears, and left the rest of her face to shift for itself.

Rex knew at once that something was wrong. Her face across the room was deathly. The way she shrugged off Jill's concerned enquiry convinced him something terrible had occurred and he was by her side in seconds.

'What is it?'

'I'm alright.'

'Tell me.'

'I'm alright.'

Carol May felt his arm stealing round her waist, then looking up, saw Stella, Nancy and Hetty watching them – the latter pair with eyes of absolute venom. Stella, herself, was not by any means a vicious woman, but her senses told her she was being threatened and it brought out the worst in her.

'Don't you think you've done enough fraternising with the shop-floor for one day.'

Nancy was behind her in a flash.

'That's right,' she confirmed. 'Y'know what they say in management – start slummin' with the workers, they don't respect you.'

From off the floor, the apparition that was Queenie rose like an avenging angel.

'An' who're you callin' slums, girl?'

Nancy drew herself up indignantly as Queenie continued, 'Have y'seen yerself lately? – a gob like that should have a condemned notice nailed to it.'

'Oh, an' I suppose you think because yer all done out like a dog's breakfast, I'd be above takin' yer on!' shrieked Nancy.

'Why don't you drop yer drawers an' let yer arse talk some sense!' retorted Queenie.

'D'you hear that?' Nancy had flipped. 'D'you hear that – comin' her foul-mouth gab at me! How dare she!'

236

Queenie not only dared, she goaded Nancy to such a pitch of rage that the woman forgot her good manners and actually launched herself at Queenie's throat. Queenie was not the girl to stand back and watch. Flourishing her claws, she leapt on Nancy, circumcising her hat, scything her buttonhole and lacerating her tights, till half the room was clamouring to separate the gladiators – and might not have succeeded, had not Klepto run screaming in the room, yelling hoarsely at the top of her voice, 'Phone call! Phone call! We're to get down the Registry an' sharp! They're waitin' an' rebooked for three o'clock!'

For a split second the room stood still in stunned silence. Then Carol May took charge.

'Alright! Wedding at three! Everybody out!'

Then the stampede for the cars begun.

Queenie was scrambling into Rex's car when Carol May noticed her flowers were missing.

'Can't get married without a bouquet,' she insisted. 'Wait there – I'll fetch them.'

She ran back upstairs. The bouquet was still where Queenie had left it – or rather where it had landed after richocheting off the DJ's skull. Carol May snatched it up and ran back towards the stairs. At the top she halted to let someone pass. It was Stella. The two women gave each other a long, appraising look. There was no malice, no jealousy, only a kind of understanding, of complicity, even of sympathy. Then the moment passed, and Carol May ran away down the stairs and into the car.

Chunky was getting nervous. An hour ago his heart's desire would have been to see Queenie walk through the door of the Registry Office. Now he was not so sure. In fact, as the clock approached three, and the screech of car-brakes could be heard from the street outside, he began to feel an overwhelming desire to be several miles hence.

'Oh no y' don't,' commanded Donna, pulling him back into his seat. But the dog knew what was good for it and had already retreated beneath a table.

Outside in the road, a convoy of cars was attempting to triple-park on double yellow lines. Queenie leapt from Rex's vehicle and stormed up the steps, followed by a stampede of guests. In the doorway, she halted. At the far end of the hall sat Chunky, trying to burrow down behind Donna. Carol May arrived in the nick of time behind Queenie's left shoulder.

'Think of the cupids,' she hissed.

'I'm thinkin',' replied Queenie through clenched teeth.

'Ah . . . Mrs Reynolds?' The Registrar was beaming in avuncular fashion. 'You see we've run him to ground for you.'

'Do y' do funerals an' all, pal?' enquired the bride.

'So . . . if you happy band of pilgrims would like to make your way through to the Promised Land . . . ?'

The pocket-cassette hovered at the ready, but was mercifully forestalled by the unexpected strains of an electric organ issuing from the Ceremonial Room. Donna glowed with pride. Gordon was on form today.

Elbowing Chunky aside, Queenie marched in behind the Registrar. Chunky scuttled meekly in her wake, followed by Rex and Carol May, the chief witnesses. Behind them thundered the rest of the guests, hot and dishevelled, clattering and bumping into their seats.

When a comparative silence had fallen – broken only by the occasional hiccup from Queenie – the Registrar opened his service book and commenced . . .

' . . . will you love her, comfort her, honour and keep her, in sickness and in health, and forsaking all others, keep only to her as long as you live?'

Chunky broke into a fresh bout of sobbing.

238

'I will.'

'Edith Marjorie Beatrice . . . '

Queenie swayed slightly and hiccupped again.

' . . . will you take this man to be your lawful wedded husband? Will you serve him, love him, honour and . . . '

'Oh, go'way lad,' interrupted Queenie. 'Why else would I be stood here?'

The Registrar, struggling to retain some shred of dignity, now turned to Chunky.

'The ring?' he whispered.

'The what?'

'The friggin' ring, gonk-brain!' hissed the loving bride.

Chunky went white. In all the commotion he'd completely overlooked this minor detail. Queenie wasn't prepared to wait a moment longer.

'Gi's yer hand,' she ordered Carol May, and swiped the ring off her wedding-finger. 'I'll owe yer one.'

'No rush,' replied Carol May.

The ring was now stuffed into Chunky's quivering fist, then Queenie held out her finger to receive it.

'Well, get a move on, then!' she snapped.

Blinded by tears of joy, Chunky squinted to read the card held for him by the increasingly nervous Registrar.

'I, Charles Clifford Alfred, take Edith Marjorie Beatrice to be my lawful wedded wife . . . ' He was seized by another fit of weeping. ' . . . to have and to hold from this day forward, to love and to cherish, till death do us part . . . '

Tenderly, he moved to place the band of gold on Queenie's finger, but the ring was too tight, and Queenie tore it from Chunky's grasp and stuffed it onto her little finger.

'Anything else?' she demanded of the Registrar.

'Well . . . er . . . I . . . er . . . now pronounce you . . . husband and wife.'

The whole room broke into cheering, stamping, clapping and whistling. Chunky's face began to crumple. He leaned forward to receive his first married kiss, but was slapped away by Queenie.

'Pull yourself together!' she growled, and stuffed a handkerchief into his face.

Now Bernie rushed to the front, flourishing his camera.

'Snaps out on the front steps!' he announced, then leapt aside as the rush for the exit commenced, all the while accompanied by a thirty-second version of the recessional wedding march from Gordon on the organ. The Registrar scampered after the departing multitude, imploring feebly . . .

'If I could just ask you not to throw confetti on the steps outside . . .'

Confetti was coming down like a snowstorm. In some places guests were wading ankle-deep. Queenie was content to bathe in a shower of champagne foam, till she found her progress hampered by the presence of her bouquet.

'Let's get shot of this friggin' wreath!' she announced, flinging it into the adoring crowd and felling Simon to the ground with a single blow from its lilies. Recovering gamely, Simon proffered the wilted blooms, not to Elfrieda who was mentally clearing a space on the sideboard, but to the blushing, tittering Klepto, who was so overcome by the gesture that she ran away into the crowd giggling hysterically.

'Bride and groom . . . best man, bridesmaid . . . can we have a bit of order here, please . . .' urged Bernie – though needless to say without having the slightest effect. The whole party was attempting to cram itself onto three steps at the top of the flight. The Registrar, scrabbling about with dustpan and brush, was deputed to the role of official photographer, and at the command of 'Cheese and biscuits', the entire assembly grinned broadly at the camera.

'What're you lookin' so chuffed about?' snapped Queenie to the simpering, blubbering Chunky.

'Me wife!' he sobbed. 'Yer me wife!'

Queenie seized a handbag and whacked him across the ears.

'Don't you come that lip with me, lad!' she warned.

Then the camera flashed again and the moment was caught for posterity.

CHAPTER SEVEN

August

It was breakfast-time in Hawaii. Palm trees swayed against a cloudless azure sky, waves of surf broke upon endless miles of golden strand – and in the foreground, a woman strapped, too tightly, into a corset of flab-reducing electrode pads, was painting her legs with fake-tan lotion. For this was, in fact, not Hawaii after all but the attic of Pauline's house, and the vistas of golden beaches were only as real as the gigantic poster pinned to one wall. The woman was real enough, however. So, alas, was the flab she was trying to massage away, and the pasty whiteness of the legs she hoped to disguise. On her face she wore a pair of goggles – not for flying or deep-sea diving – but to protect her eyes from the vicious ultra-violet rays of the facial tanning lamp. A glance round the room proved it to be as far removed from the South Seas as could be imagined. Old lamp-stands, a discarded chip-pan, rolled-up bits of carpet, cardboard boxes full of old shoes . . .

It had, nevertheless, one major advantage over all the other rooms in the house – it could be locked from the inside.

Just what a bonus that was, could be appreciated only by a closer scrutiny of the cupboard to the left of the coconut grove, which seemed to house the entire contents of a pharmacy counter. Slimming pills (Dosage – one per day only), tanning pills (one per day - do not exceed stated dose), anti-cellulite pills (Will only work in conjunction with a calorie-controlled diet), Vitamin E pills, contraceptive pills . . .

Pauline, however, had her own special relationship

with these various lozenges, which brooked no interference from any instructions on the packet. Two Vitamin Es, two anti-cellulites, three slimming and four tanning pills were quickly washed down with a glass of low-calorie meal replacement milk-shake. Now came the moment to view the effects. By dint of a rigid adherence to this particular regime for nearly three weeks, Pauline had contrived to gain four pounds, half an inch round the hips, an increased appetite for 'union meetings', and a livid orange tinge to her face and neck. Oddly enough, it was the colour transformation which seemed to please her most – it added an aura of glamour, it carried with it the air of the jet-set, it gave her a certain mystique . . .

'Eh! Pauline! What the bloody hell y'doin' in there – redecoratin' yer arse?'

There was no mystique at all about Frankie – which was doubtless the root of the problem. The immediate concern, however, was to rip off the electrode pads, secrete the goggles, the tanning-lamp and the chemist's shop, and be halfway down the stairs before he decided to pay her an uninvited visit.

'Were y'calling' us love?' she simpered when she met him downstairs on the landing. Her blandishments were brushed aside.

'What's up wi' yer face?'

'What d'y'mean?'

'Y've gone a bloody funny shade these days.'

'I've . . . caught the sun,' stammered Pauline.

'Oh aye? – bloody clever in this weather,' growled the tender husband as she tried to edge past him into the bedroom. The inquisition wasn't yet over.

'You got scent on?' sniffed Frankie. 'Get it scrubbed.'

But, thoughtful to a fault, he kindly saved her the bother by spitting on his handkerchief and scouring Pauline's neck with it.

'Eh! – an' y'can tell that bloody union – if it's to hang on to yer as shop steward, it can give over keepin' yer out till all hours of the night.'

Pauline flushed guiltily.

'I'll tell 'em,' she assured him.

'Quarter past twelve last night,' he blasted.

'It's a good cause, in't it?'

'I wonder.'

Pauline's look of guilt increased, but she wasn't about to provoke her husband by asking him what he meant. She didn't want to get into *that* business again.

Mr Beachcroft had a surprise in store for Lyne Electronics – or more specifically, for Rex. At the unearthly hour of 8.15 this Monday morning, he delivered the newcomer – in person – by limousine and escorted her into the factory. 'She' was a smartly-dressed woman in her early forties, carrying a briefcase, and a look of disdain which boded ill for anyone who chose to cross her. As it turned out, many people would have no choice.

Samantha . . . Sarah . . . Stacey . . . Stephanie . . . Stella . . . Susan . . . Donna shook her head. She didn't like any of those – there was nothing that really stood out, or seemed to go with their surname. Well, perhaps it was all a bit premature anyway – as was the booklet of knitting patterns for bootees and matinee jackets – since, up till this point they hadn't got beyond the temperature charts and the ovulation counts. Which was how Donna came to be sitting up in bed with a breakfast tray before her and a thermometer dangling from the side of her mouth. Presently she took it out and shook it – how many times she'd done this already didn't bear thinking about. Still, here they were – nearing 'that' time of the month again – and if only she could relax, instead of thinking how much depended on it . . .

Downstairs Gordon was practising his scales. There'd been a flurry of activity on the organ this week. In a couple of days time, she would make sure Gordon gave himself a night off . . .

'So this is where you'll be based . . . '

Norma looked up from her early-morning pruning of
the office cactus collection, to see the Chairman showing
an unfamiliar face into the room.

'It's quite compact,' he was saying – which was something of an understatement. 'We don't go in for palatial
settings. You'll find all you need right at your fingertips.'

'And this is my secretary, I take it?'

Norma found herself appropriated by the newcomer in
a manner she didn't quite care for.

'Ah, now then . . .' The Chairman was caught on the
hop. 'We didn't envisage takin' on anyone extra. This
young lady deals with all the management business.'

'Ah, does she now?'

Norma seemed to rise in the woman's opinion.

'Bella Grout. Pleased to meet you.' She held out her
hand. 'I'm the new Executive Manager. I'm sure we'll find
we've a lot in common.'

Norma wasn't sure of anything right now, except that
since this woman appeared to take her seriously, she
might as well give her the time of day. Rex, she felt, would
be less enthusiastic. Bella smiled thinly and continued in
an ingratiating tone,

'Now, I think you an' I should have a nice cup of tea
together, and you can put me in the picture about how
you've been used to running things round here.'

Norma caught the Chairman looking at Rex's empty
chair.

'His Nibbs not here, then?'

'I . . . think he'd something to attend to,' volunteered
the loyal secretary.

'He's a sight to attend to, an' attend he will if he's a
scrap of nous left. I've sweat bloody guts for this Korean
tie-up, an' we'll not have it jeopardised at this late stage.'
He turned to Bella. 'I want this firm runnin' like clockwork

from top to bottom.' He prodded at the wall chart which was showing a healthy rise in production figures.

'We've tickled round the bottom . . . now let's get them brooms goin' up top.'

But Bella had already started as she meant to go on.

'I'll work from here for the time being.'

And, opening her briefcase, she made herself at home behind Rex's desk.

8.55 am found Jill walking to work. At least, she hoped she was walking to work – quite frankly, her mind was in such a daze, she could have been going anywhere. But the sight of the factory gates and the beaming face of Bernie in the doorway, reassured her she'd come to the right place. Or had she?

Who was this woman frowning at her and demanding her name?

'Bella Grout – Executive Manager' – or so the name-tag read – but she couldn't recall anyone of that name or status being around before.

'Name!' The demand was repeated.

'Barraclough,' intervened Bernie, pointing out Jill's name on the list.

'Sign here,' ordered the woman.

Jill obliged with some indecipherable scribble, then found herself being manhandled into a curtained booth, where three flashes in rapid succession told her she'd had her photograph taken. Barely had the snapshots come out of the machine, when Bella was sticking one onto a card, writing Jill's name and sealing it in plastic. Then, as the buzzer sounded, she handed Jill her identity-badge, and informed her she was late. Jill opened her mouth to argue.

'That's fifteen minutes,' the Executive Manager informed her.

'I'm sorry?'

'Every minute late docks fifteen minutes' pay.'

'But I was here . . .' protested Jill, turning to Bernie for support. But Bernie was not the man to stick his neck out, and Jill found herself elbowed aside as Mrs Grout attacked the next group of latecomers. Feeling more dispirited than ever, she wandered into the factory, examining the rather startled features on her new name tag – and decided this was one innovation she could have done without.

Rex seemed to share her opinion. He was watching, with ill-concealed fury, as two maintenance men struggled to manoeuvre another desk and chair into the already-overcrowded office. Rex's prime position had been usurped and his desk shunted sideways to make way for Mrs Grout's rather superior item of furniture, which Norma was even now stocking up with stationery supplies. When she reached across and took one of the phones from his desk to supply Mrs Grout, his wrath threatened to get the better of him.

'Mr Beachcroft says she's to have one of yours for the time being,' explained to Norma, seeing her boss about to throttle her.

'By all means,' came the acid reply. 'She can have the whole bloody shop for all *I* care!'

And as he stormed out of the office, the slam of the door set the cactus-tray quivering. Seconds later Simon was sent sprawling as Rex cannoned into him coming through the swing doors on his way out of the building.

'What's up with him?' Simon asked when he brought in the post for Norma's perusal.

'I think it's the report.'

'What report?'

'That feller we had in testin' tea-cups an' that for the Koreans. I don't think it was very nice about . . .' – she could never bring herself to utter Rex's name – '. . . about the management.'

Simon shrugged. As long as *he* hadn't been singled out for rebuke . . .

'So Mr Beachcroft's brought in Mrs Grout to sharpen things up a bit.'

'That bloody woman!' Simon had already fallen foul of the new Executive Manager. 'She's doin' me head in. She's got us countin' every circuit board in the shop now! How long's she gonna be stoppin'?'

Norma looked grave.

'I think it's envisaged she's a permanent fixture.'

It was to be hoped not, if today's most recent innovation was anything to go by: clocking on and clocking off for tea-breaks was the latest bright idea – and it wasn't going down too well on the shop-floor.

'Well, what else can they lash us with?' growled Queenie. 'Short of leashin' us to the bench an' slashin' wages to cover the cost of sittin' us there. They'll be chargin' us rent next!'

'I feel like I'm half-price in't Sale,' complained Klepto, tugging at her identity-badge. 'Why do we need these? I already know who I am.'

If that was the case, it was more than Jill knew. Just now she'd retreated to the privacy of a toilet-cubicle to reread the letter she'd already read six times this morning. It was in Ray's handwriting – but Ray's message seemed to offer little consolation and less hope. She closed her eyes to stem the flood of tears, told herself she was being silly – and almost convinced herself. The letter was refolded, stuffed back into the envelope, and Jill marched out of the toilet, determined to prove herself unmoved by Ray's tidings. Joining Donna at the mirrors, she began to paint on a smiling pair of lips in her most vivid shade of crimson. Donna, being neither blind, stupid or slow, noticed immediately.

'You alright?'

Jill flushed, then replied with great bravado, 'Oh, don't you fret about *me* love. I've just won the Pools. I'm about to become a free agent!'

248

'Oh?' Donna's voice was deliberately calm. 'You're goin' for the divorce, then?'

Jill's mouth seemed to tremble and she may well have divulged other feelings, but at that moment Pauline's tangerine features appeared round the door, and Jill decided to play the Merry Widow.

'Line 'em up, girls! Bring out the spare fellers! I'll have a nose in that catalogue, love. I'll be needin' a few new outfits soon.'

'You've not took yer ring off, then?'

Donna's quiet voice shattered her show of confidence.

Again the tears began to sting her eyes, but Queenie's timely arrival deferred their appearance on her cheeks.

'I'm frigged if I'm queuein' round the block for friggin' stewed gnat's juice! – I need something with a bit of nip to it.'

And in one movement she took out a steel comb, prised open the lock of the cleaners' cupboard, and was rifling through the mops and dusters in search of her alcohol cache. Her treasure hunt came to an abrupt halt.

'What friggin' tea-leaf's bin in here!'

'Now what's happened?'

'That's what.' Queenie stood back to reveal a top shelf bereft of everything but a brace of scouring pads.

'Half a bottle of gin an' two tail-ends of vodka just done a runner, that's all.'

Queenie continued to burrow around till a prolonged bout of coughing from Jill made her turn and look for the cause of the eructions. Bella Grout was standing in the doorway, arms folded, watching Queenie's excavations with interest.

'Yes, in here,' she called out to someone behind her. 'It's alright, they're just on their way back to work.'

Pauline suspected this remark was intended for her, accompanied as it was by a swift glance at the watch and a scowl in her direction. Pauline, in fact, had taken no strong liking to this woman. Indeed, after the quite unnecessary dressing-down she, as shop steward, had received this morning, it would be no exaggeration to say she quite detested her.

'Well, don't sit there like a lump of cold pudding!'

Bella was addressing, not Pauline, but the reluctant Simon who stood hovering outside the door, fearing to trespass into this females' sanctum. Nevertheless, at Bella's insistence, he edged across the threshold, twitching nervously as he passed Queenie.

'Well, what's the problem?' Bella demanded.

'Hey, this in't usually my territory – y'know what I mean?'

'I think *I'm* the person to decide that,' fired the lady, directing Simon and his toolbox towards the cleaners' cupboard. 'Well, let's get started. That's the door. We want two new locks – and you can leave the keys with me.' Then, turning to the girls with a poisonous smile: 'You ladies seem very keen to get some more wages docked.'

Quietly seething, they began to file out, but not before catching the next remark addressed to Simon. 'And that's another thing down in the report. Theft of toilet rolls from Ladies'.' She shot a look of accusation at Pauline. 'From now on we'll be issuing one roll per toilet per week, and after that they can make their own arrangements.'

'Oh yeah, but Rex . . . Mr Buckley . . . said that . . . '

Simon's babbling was cut short.

'Mr Buckley has a lot on his plate at the moment,' replied Bella, coldly. 'I'm sure he'll be grateful to have this matter taken out of his hands.'

'I wouldn't bet on it,' muttered Pauline, who felt herself to be better acquainted with the manager's feelings than any Mrs Grout could be. In this instance, however, she happened to be right.

'Have you seen the report?'

'Oh yeah, d'y'think he'd let *me* get me hands on it?'

On a disused upper floor of the factory, Rex and Carol May were discussing the infamous report – and its consequences. For once, it was Carol May who was trying to fold Rex into her arms – less from an excess of passion, than from a desire to soothe away some of his anger.

'So what has he said, then?'

Rex broke away and rammed his fist against the wall.

' "There's a feeling among our Korean partners that the middle management's a bit overstretched – I'm bringing in someone to help you out." Quote. Unquote.'

'Well, then?'

Carol May was less aware of any threat than Rex seemed to be. He himself was far from sanguine.

'Help us out of a job, more like. Seven years bloody Siberia down the drain.'

'It needn't be.'

Rex would not be pacified.

'I know him. I know how he operates. He wants maximum results on minimum outlay – and anyone – barring himself – is totally dispensable. I've had it up to here.' Rex was steadily working himself up into a frenzy. 'I get home, I've got Stella givin' me earache – "I'm never in, the kids don't see me." *You* can't make yer mind up. I book us a weekend away – you dish out the same old excuses . . .'

'Like a husband?' came the retort.

'Well, it's a bit late now to start feelin' guilty!'

'I couldn't agree more.' replied Carol May quietly.

Rex was silent. She watched him as he paced the empty floor, biting his lip, tearing at his nails. One thought was uppermost in her mind at this moment – how dearly she would like to slap his face and tell him to stop behaving like a spoilt child. But then, she reflected, it was the child who'd attracted her in the first place – reckless, impulsive, passionate and somehow lost, a world apart from Colin. And also her, if it came to that. It was a fact she didn't care to be reminded of too often – not so much the age difference, but the fact that he was totally unsuited to her, he was not her type at all, she couldn't even say that she *liked* him. And yet . . .

251

'So *now* what do we do?' he demanded sullenly.

Carol May glanced at her watch – she was late back for work.

'It seems we've *all* got our work cut out, doesn't it?'

She made a move for the door.

'No, don't go.'

Rex was barring her way, desperate to keep her another minute.

'I'm late already.'

'What about tonight?'

She sensed that was coming. She knew where his priorities lay. She would not be bullied.

'I'll let you know.'

Bella was still unclear about the overall geography of the factory, but one thing she *did* know – that staircase at the far side of the shop-floor was out-of-bounds to workers, and led to a floor no longer used by the company. So when she saw Carol May slip through the door and hurry back to her bench, she decided investigations were in order. Until she saw Rex take the same route barely thirty seconds later. At this point Mrs Grout decided a mental note would suffice. There would be plenty of time to make the most of her information later.

'Shape up, shape up now girls – it's for yer own good!'

Bernie was doing his celebrated impression of a sheep-dog, rounding up the girls and shepherding them back to their seats.

'Where've I heard that before?' Donna wondered.

'Pearl Harbour? – just before the kamikazes dived in?' suggested Queenie.

Bernie's arms continued to flag down the latecomers.

'If I fancied runnin' marathons, I'd stick me shorts on,' observed Pauline tartly.

'That'd be a sight for sore eyes,' enthused Bernie,

giving her bottom a complimentary pat – just in time to be caught in the act by the hawk-like Bella.

'If you're that short of something to man-handle, there's a few items of furniture want shifting in here.'

Pauline bristled.

'I don't know what you're used to round here,' continued Bella, 'but where *I've* come from they'd call that Sexual Harassment. Mind you . . .' with a sneer at Pauline – 'I can see there might be cases where it's less an imposition than a charity.'

And with that parting jibe, she sailed off to her desk, leaving Pauline and Bernie speechless with indignation. Rex, coming back to the office at the same moment, surveyed them with mild surprise and flung out a harsh reminder.

'I wouldn't stand still *too* long. Y'might find they buried yer.'

Leaving Pauline to soothe her wounded pride, Bernie bustled back into the office and handed Bella his latest set of timings.

'That's as good as you'll get anywhere,' he announced pompously.

Mrs Grout surveyed the figures.

'I think not, actually. Ah, thank you Norma . . .'

Rex looked up to see where *his* cup of tea had got to, but Norma apparently served no-one but Mrs Grout these days, judging her to be a far more likely instrument of promotion than he had ever pretended to be.

'Ten minutes tea-break,' continued Bella. 'That's two minutes from shop-floor to canteen, two minutes back again – I generally find six minutes is ample time to knock back a cup of tea.'

'But after you've queued an' that . . .'

Bernie was surprised to find himself taking the girl's part against this invader.

Mrs Grout slipped into a gentler vein.

253

'Bernie, if it was left to me, they'd still be on their fifteen minutes, no problem. But we're out to impress here. We're here to *out-do* our oriental pals. So we'll have to come down hard on those dawdlers and skivers, I'm afraid.'

She didn't *seem* to be afraid. She looked to be rather enjoying it all, as far as Bernie could tell.

The office hotline began to ring. Norma intercepted it.

'Lyne Electronics . . . oh, hello, Mr Beachcroft . . .'

Wearily Rex looked up from his desk and held out his hand for the call.

'It's for Mrs Grout,' Norma announced, and passed the phone to the triumphant Bella, who calmly took another sip of tea before cooing into the receiver.

'Mr Beachcroft? . . . yes, I think we've made some progress . . . we've got our work cut out, of course, but I think with the right attitude on everyone's part . . . oh, I'm sure there'll be no shortage of co-operation . . .' She smiled across at Rex. 'I think we all value our jobs too much. Thank you, Mr Beachcroft, we'll do our best.'

She replaced the receiver with a smirk of satisfaction.

'And now . . . Norma? – do we have last month's sales figures to hand?'

Norma had her finger on them immediately.

'Well, well . . .' Bella was shaking her head in admiration. 'I can see the ladies are going to run a sharp little team round here.'

Norma was preening herself, as Rex and Bernie exchanged a look of complicity. The men were certainly the underdogs in this new set-up.

Frankie was belching into his third helping of curry, his nose in the evening paper. Feet up, fast asleep and snoring loudly, his two sons kept their normal early evening vigil in front of the telly until it was time for the pubs to 'get going'.

'Bloody women managers?' Frankie put down his

paper and thumped the table. 'He wants floggin', that bloody Chairman of yours – keepin' grown men out of a job. She sounds a lippy little bitch to me.'

He took another forkful of Beef Madras.

'Y'wanna work to rule – that'd knock the bant out of her.'

The remains of the Prawn Vindaloo were shovelled onto his plate.

'I hope *I* never catch her, that's all. There's only one way to deal with her sort.'

And failing to unearth any further popodoms for demolition, Frankie retired to the sports section and let out another belch.

Pauline appeared in the doorway, wearing one of her oldest coats and a woollen headscarf.

'Just off, then.'

Son Jason roused from his slumbers.

'Aw, mam, I need a shirt ironed.'

'Shirts can wait. I've these ructions to discuss with shop-floor.' She simpered hopefully at Frankie. 'Y'needn't wait up, love. We'll have a fair session.'

'Half-eleven,' came the firm reply.

Pauline knew better than to argue the point. She was lucky he hadn't said ten o'clock.

'An' mind none of them bosses gives yer a lift back.'

'Oh, I wouldn't dream of it, love,' Pauline assured him, crossing her fingers behind her back – for of course, if *Rex* ever opened his car doors to her . . .

'And mind you give 'em what-for from me!'

'Right-o, love . . .'

Pauline closed the living-room door, collected two well-stuffed carrier-bags from just inside the porch, slipped a pair of curling-tongs into her handbag, and let herself out.

Next morning found her sporting another of her polo-neck jumpers. Frankie had received a lukewarm response to his

255

offer of a lift, and now his passenger was sitting tensed and wary, with a thick woollen scarf wound tightly round her throat.

'You're very quiet this morning, lady.'

'I've caught cold in me neck,' Pauline murmured. 'I think I'm a bit under the weather.'

'You'll be under my foot if y'come creepin' home at all hours one more time. If I didn't know better, I'd say there was summat goin' on.'

Pauline was grateful for any diversion at this moment – which made her pleased to see even Bella Grout arriving in her flashy new company car. She pointed out the culprit to Frankie.

'That's her from top office.'

Frankie leaned out of the window and surveyed the approaching figure.

'She's got a grid on her like a bag of spanners.'

He shouted across at Bella.

' 'Scuse me, love – where've I seen your face?'

Bella looked up, preparing to assure the man he was mistaken.

'Crufts, wannit?' bellowed Frankie. 'Or advertisin' Pedigree Chum?'

'Give over, Frankie. I have to work here, y'know.' Pauline had no wish to draw attention to the fact that this lout was her husband.

But Frankie would not be silenced. 'If *I* was your feller, I'd sling yer across me knee an' lash the arse off yer!'

Bella had already departed out of earshot, but not without noting the identity of Frankie's companion. Another justification, she mused, for her near-instinctive feelings of hostility towards Pauline.

Pauline herself was at this moment delving into the back of the car to retrieve a large cardboard box.

'What the bloody hell's that?' came her husband's enquiry.

'Oh, it's Donna's order from the catalogue.'

Pauline seemed in a hurry to depart.

'Eh! Just come here!'

With reluctance Pauline turned back.

'This meetin' tonight – yer back by twelve – or that backside of yours'll be a bloody pumpkin when I've done wavin' me wand across it!'

'Right you are, love,' replied Pauline meekly, and gratefully raced off into the factory.

Jill caught up with her at the door to the cloakroom. 'What brought *his* rash on?' she asked.

'Oh, he's had a mard head since he got up.'

'That's summat *I* don't have to put up with – Ray with a cob on every mornin'. It's a real treat, just havin' yerself to please.'

'For how long, I wonder.'

It was Donna who threw in this last aside as she sped by on her way to the clock. Jill scowled after her, wanting to ask her what business she had . . . but what was the point? Donna was insufferable these days and another blast of her self-righteousness was the last thing she needed. In any case, the buzzer had gone, and the sprint to clock on had begun.

'Stop! Stop! That'll do! We're not in the charity business.'

Bella's jurisdiction extended even to the canteen, where she was presently overseeing the pouring of tea and making sure that the prescribed levels of liquid (half an inch from the top of the tea-cup) were adhered to. Elsewhere, the buzz of gossip was capped by the sound of a drill being bored into the wall, followed by a series of hammer blows and a howl of pain from a stubbed finger. Simon was nailing a No Smoking notice to the wall, and Queenie was choking on clean air. Back at the table, the girls sat hunched over their lunches, watching the latest outrage with mounting fury. All except Pauline. Now a non-smoker and herb-tea drinker, these changes could not affect her – her attention could be put to better use elsewhere, namely the pages of the modelling magazine

257

she was reading, and upon whose dubious style she had based her own exotic appearance. Only Carol May was absent, and Queenie was not about to draw attention to the fact.

'I thought them Koreans went in for democracy.'

Donna's voice of dissent provoked a few surprised faces.

'Well, if that's it, they can bloody sling it.' Jill could bury the hatchet and agree whole-heartedly on this one.

'Oh, whadder-yer like you two!' Queenie riposted.

'D'y'think that's all Korean caper? That's smart-arse Smiler doin' a snidey, try'na geg in with their bosses. Only he's gone an' puked in his own handbag yet again. An' as for that . . .' She glared across at Bella. 'I'll mince the gob off it if it starts on *me*!'

Pauline passed Jill her purse. 'Get us another tea in, will yer?'

'Where y' goin'?'

'Out the back f'r a quick sun.'

Bella was passing at this moment. Pauline turned in her direction. 'I trust we can still breathe fresh air without gettin' it docked off wages.'

The girls watched her departure with amazement.

'She's sailin' a bit near the knuckle, in't she?' Jill wondered.

Donna turned away, murmuring to herself, 'She's not the only one.'

Queenie alone heard the remark, and turning to follow Donna's glance, saw Rex and Carol May entering the canteen together. Queenie glanced back at Donna – to be met with a look of utter frankness. So Donna, too, had guessed. It could have been worse, Queenie decided – it could have been someone who would take advantage of the knowledge. Like Bella, she thought, with a grimace. The woman was watching Rex and Carol May with eyes of steel. Carol May was laughing at something Rex had said.

'Aye, eat it while it's hot, eh?' Queenie muttered. 'While there's still no friggin' law against it.'

Pauline had got diverted on her quest for the sun. Or perhaps she had always intended to head for the toilets. It would certainly seem so, judging by the cardboard box she was carrying – Donna's catalogue order, wasn't it? On closer inspection, perhaps not. Pauline was struggling to prise over her head a full-length, turquoise sateen dinner-dance dress. This feat performed, she was standing in a cubicle, wrestling with the zip and wondering whether it wouldn't have been better after all to go for the size 14 which was kinder on her curves. Now it was done at last – the zip hauled up to the top of the dress. She had breathed in tight – did she dare to breathe out again?

A knocking on the toilet door made her almost burst her seams.

'Hello? . . .' she called tentatively.

'Somebody smoking in there?' came Bella's acerbic voice.

'Er . . . no . . . just usin' the facilities,' blustered Pauline.

'Three minutes to clockin' on,' came the brisk retort.

'Thank you,' called back Pauline graciously.

Bella walked off towards the exit, but halted just inside the door to hear if there was any response. There was.

'Watch someone doesn't clock your friggin' gob off, love,' was Pauline's parting shot, made, as she thought, into thin air. Bella rubbed her hands with glee. She was going to enjoy bringing this one down a peg or two.

'Random Bag Check' was the latest measure to hit the shell-shocked workers. Each night at the exit to the factory, loutish security guards were given carte blanche to rifle through personal belongings in the hope of coming up with some item of plunder.

'I wouldn't mind if there was 'owt worth pinchin' round here,' remarked Jill as she walked towards the checkpoint with Klepto and Donna.

Klepto fell behind and seemed to be fishing about in her bag. The next minute some objects, hard and plastic, were falling into a nearby waste-bin.

'D'you never learn?' Donna asked her, as they passed safely through the check point.

Klepto merely shrugged.

'What was it?' Jill enquired.

'A few redd'uns.'

'Components?' Donna cast her eyes skywards in disbelief. 'Whatever for?'

'Dunno,' replied the girl with a giggle. 'I just fancied them. I like the colour.'

It was better not to delve too deeply into this mind, Donna decided. Instead she would quiz Jill.

'Kids alright, then?' she asked ingenuously.

'Shouldn't they be?' Jill was on the defensive in a flash.

'They do say they're the ones to suffer, don't they? In a divorce.'

Jill was sick of hearing this tune.

'When you've not got kids, it's easy to jump to all sorts of conclusions.'

'When y'gettin' divorced, then?' chimed in Klepto.

'Soon as the little bits of paper come through. Why else d'you think I'm so chuffed?'

Jill crossed the road towards her bus-stop, eager to escape the rest of this conversation.

'Is she chuffed?' Klepto was asking Donna. '*I* didn't notice it.'

A flash of sateen flickered beneath the nondescript grey of a raincoat. High-heeled turquoise satin shoes teetered out of the toilet cubicle, tottered down the corridor, past the astonished security-guard and into a waiting taxi. Up on the third floor, the twitch of a blind in 'top office' revealed that by one person at least, the departure had not gone unnoticed.

*   *   *

It had been 'Another Bumper Year For Pork-U-Like Products.' So claimed the banner where it hung across the stage, fluttering in the breeze from the air conditioning. 'Introducing the new Pork-U-Pick Range of Gourmet Buffet Foods' – Miss Pork-U-Like Queen 1988 was doing her stuff with the trays of nibbles, persuading suave young executives to put their mouth where their money was and sample the latest range of 'Savoury Nibbles for Discerning Pork Lovers.' Pig seemed to be popping up everywhere – on the stage, in the sandwiches, on cocktail sticks, occasionally dressed in a dinner jacket or a cocktail dress . . .

'If all the world's a stage, then you an' me are only players . . . ' The compere seemed to be waxing lyrical. 'But if Music be the Food of Love . . . there's nowt sweeter on the ear than the tempting sizzle of best streaky, cooked straight from the packet . . .' Cheers and 'hear hears' broke out from the floor, as the poet continued. 'So if yer thinkin' of goin' vegetarian, just wait till you've wrapped yer teeth around a couple of Pork-U-Pick Buffet Snacks – you'll never look at a nut roast again!' More guffaws and roars of approval. 'Alright, now the moment we've all been waiting for – the award for Pork-U-Like Bacon Rep of the Year – if I can just get the envelope open, as they say at the Oscars – goes to . . . Garry Yates from our Eccles and Salford District! . . . a big hand for Garry, please, ladies and gents . . . well done, Garry lad . . . '

As the convention broke into rapturous applause, a woman in a turquoise dress came out of the Ladies' and approached two men on the edge of the crowd.

'Don't y'get sick of all this bacon flyin' around?'

The larger man turned to her, then nudged his pal in the ribs.

'Bread an' butter to us, eh Fred?'

'Oh, not half, Man – an' bloody drippin' toast!'

Manfred had grabbed the turquoise posterior and pinched a good two inches between finger and thumb.

'Eh, Fred! – plenty there f'r a toasted muffin!'

'Oh aye – an' some left over to grill wi' pineapple!'

'She's the right shade for it, eh, Fred?'

Pauline could brook such amusement no longer. Detaching herself from Manfred's clutches, she drew herself up and replied haughtily,

'Yes, well I've just got back from Tenerife, actually!'

'By 'eck, an' here's me thinkin' she's overdone it on the carrots!'

Such disparaging remarks about her hard-earned tan were not entirely to Pauline's taste, but it was simplicity itself to put Fred in his place.

'So y'just missed it, I hear?'

'What's that, then?'

'Salesman of the Year.'

Fred's face went green. 'Hey, was I sick, Man?'

'Sick? Y'were bloody pukin', weren't yer, Fred?'

'I was gutted, that's what. How many packs of streaky did I shift this year, Man?'

'Shift? You've wellied half the pork in Britain round the North-West, haven't yer, Fred?'

'I've had that much pig in the back of my car. That bastard – you ask anyone – beginner's luck. He can't sell.'

'Can he heck!'

'Who was it put Eccles an' Salford on the map?'

'You did, Fred.'

'*I* did, that's who. All the contacts I set up – pig coulda sold himself.'

'Oh, mind how we go now . . .'

The beaming winner was making his way through the crowd in their direction.

'He'll do 'owt for publicity, him. When he finds out yer a famous model, he'll want his picture took wi' yer.'

To avoid such indignity, Fred whisked Pauline and her skirts away to the dance floor. Garry Yates was forced to console himself by having his photo taken with another woman in a turquoise dress, who having posed for posterity, now turned and strolled across towards Manfred.

'Alright, pet?'

'Bella Grout! Long time no see, eh? How's the new job doin'? Y'missin' us, eh?'

'Oh, I'm coping,' replied the unshakable Bella.

'There's nowt like pork for job satisfaction, though, is there?'

Bella seemed unable to lament her passing from the porcine fields, distracted as she was by the sight of another old friend cavorting on the dance-floor with another turquoise dress.

'I see Fred's attached.'

'Too true, he's bloody smitten. Mind, she were after *me* to begin with, but I let her know it wasn't on. Career comes first wi' me.'

'Looks serious.'

'Aye aye, it's bloody tragic. Mind, she'll come in handy for him, Paulette will. She's a model. Just worked a month in Tenerife. Earns summat crucial apparently.'

Bella's eyes brightened. 'That's interesting.'

'So come on, then, sweetheart,' Manfred was dying to hear the latest, 'tell us about this new job, then . . .'

'Eh! Eh! – give over – I'm not a chip supper!'

Pauline had borne with equanimity the gropings to her derrière, the teeth-marks to her throat – but Fred's latest onslaught – trying to reach her tonsils with his tongue – required immediate evasive action. The more so since this was not some 'smoochy' number at a badly-lit discotheque, but a rather sedate waltz in a brightly lit ballroom.

'How d'y'fancy breakfast?' murmured Fred, huskily.

'I beg your pardon?'

'I'm a fiend wi' the middle back streaky.'

'I can't. I've a job on tomorrow.'

Pauline's eyes suddenly glimpsed the clock behind the bar. It was already a quarter to midnight.

'Oh, bloody 'eck!' She pulled herself free of Fred's octopus-grip. 'He'll bloody crown us! . . . er . . . me manager! I'm doin' swimwear at dawn up Blackpool Tower!'

Pauline galloped from the dance-floor, only to collide with Manfred – on his return home from the bar – carrying two glasses of red wine. As a consequence, two people missed out on their next drink, and Pauline's turquoise was now turning a tragic shade of burgundy. She turned to Fred, her face creased in horror.

'Me friggin' deposit!'

Manfred, meanwhile, was attempting to scrub away the injury with a screwed-up serviette. Pauline beat him back with her handbag.

'Gerroff! – yer makin' it worse!' And she ran off towards the exit, muttering 'God, I'm friggin' paggered now!' while Fred stared after her, protesting feebly, 'No, hang about, I'll give yer a lift . . . I've got me Capri . . . '

As if from nowhere, Bella appeared, intent on steering Fred towards the dance-floor, but the rejected lover was too distraught to do more than bemoan his loss and the sad fate of the turquoise dress.

'I wouldn't worry, pet,' soothed Bella, guiding her partner to a quickstep. 'She can always try rubbin' salt in it.'

12.18am. She was almost twenty minutes late, and her fears for survival were gathering every second. The taxi pulled up at its usual spot, just round the corner. She paid hastily – and prayed that Frankie would be fast asleep, dead drunk . . . or even, at this moment, just dead. He was in fact none of those things. His bull-like figure loomed towards the window of their bedroom, making it impossible for this particular Cinderella to sneak into the house – or even into the garden – to change into rags again. Her mind raced – desperate measures were called for. A hundred yards down the road, set back among some trees, was an unlit telephone box, and to this Pauline resorted in order to effect her quick-change.

Two teenage boys, reeling home from a friend's house

and too much home-made lager, found their evening enlivened in a way they least expected. The younger boy, badly regretting that extra tumbler of gin he'd knocked back 'just for the road', suddenly discovered how drunk he really was: the sight of a woman in a disused phone-booth, dressed in bra, pants, dark tights and knee-length boots, took him back with startling clarity to the comic-strips of his childhood.

'Eh, look Baz!' he gasped. 'Wonder Woman!'

But Baz knew of old the wanderings of a drink-sodden imagination, and, whacking his pal across the ears to bring him to his senses, staggered off into the night.

Donna shook the thermometer, noted down the tempera-ture . . . and smiled. It was all going according to plan. As she came downstairs, the strains of Gordon's practising reminded her to make sure the plug was switched off for this evening. She chose a bottle of wine from the rack and put it in the fridge to cool, then turned to find Gordon's arms around her and his face close to her cheek.

'Are we celebrating?'

'I thought we'd have a quiet night tonight.'

Gordon laughed. She loved his laugh. It was deep and full-bodied and it always made her want to join in with it.

'Not much chance of that, love. You'll want to get crackin' with them vol-au-vents, won't yer?'

'What for?' Donna was very slow this morning.

'You've not forgot, have yer? Why else d'y'think I've bin strummin' me fingers hoarse this week? Tonight's our turn for the recital and spread.'

So that was it. Donna felt her heart sink like a stone.

'D'you not remember? Old Percival's coming from Head Office. I might just clinch that promotion at last. How d'y'fancy me as Manager, eh?'

'That'll be nice,' came the flat reply.

'You'd nowt else lined up, had yer?' Gordon was starting to feel anxious now – she looked so downcast.

'Oh no . . . it'll keep.'

She took the bottle of wine from the fridge and regretfully replaced it in the rack. Then, opening the freezer, she dragged out a large bag of frozen vol-au-vents, and, with rather more force than was strictly necessary, flung them down onto the table.

Gordon flinched. He began to suspect what was wrong.

'I don't know – she'll have to get it seen to.'

'Very nasty indeed – I can't think why she came in.'

Heads were shaking, nodding wisely, pontificating solemnly, as Carol May held a cold compress to Pauline's jaw.

'How's it feel now?'

Pauline's brow contracted with pain.

'Just keep it pressed on, love.'

'What's the problem?'

Rex had arrived at Klepto's behest, to view the victim.

Pauline turned a pain-ravaged face towards him.

'Me wisdom tooth's blown up again . . . I . . . I think I'll have to get it fixed.'

'Go to the Dental School – they'll see you without an appointment,' advised Donna.

'Yes . . . I think I'd better,' moaned Pauline feebly.

'Alright, then. Quick as you can.' Rex could see no point in prevaricating. The woman was clearly in agony.

'D'y'want someone with you?' Jill asked with concern.

'Oh . . . no . . . no . . . I'll manage, thankyou.'

Pauline gathered her belongings, and still clutching the cold compress to her jaw, hobbled towards the cloakroom.

Bella, having witnessed the entire incident, now strode up to Rex.

'Was that really necessary?'

'*I* thought so.'

'She could be there all day.'

Rex viewed the woman with utter contempt. 'We're

used to treating the girls with a bit of consideration here. I don't know if that's *another* thing Mr Beachcroft wants to economise on. If so, I'd like it in writing.'

Bella smiled darkly at him. 'I'm sure that could be arranged.'

Fresh air seemed to have an astonishing effect on Pauline. No sooner had she left the factory gates behind, than her swollen jaw staged a remarkable recovery, the cold compress was flung aside and her slow gait changed to a jaunty walk. Was that anything to do with the large cardboard box she was carrying under her arm? Bella moved away from her vantage-point at the office-window and picked up her car keys.

The High Street was quiet for this time of the morning. Something to do with the weather, perhaps. Whatever the reason, Pauline found no queue waiting inside the One-Hour Dry Cleaners, where she deposited her box and its besmattered contents, and emerged into the street again. Bella had no difficulty in picking out the familiar figure as it strolled past the rows of shops, pausing sometimes to scrutinise the latest fashions, finally entering a Fast Tanning and Beauty parlour at the far side of the precinct. Bella edged forward her car a few feet, turned off the ignition, and got out a paper. She was obviously here for the duration.

Rex breathed a sigh of relief. That woman had finally left him in peace for a while. Perhaps now he could get on with the job-in-hand.

'Norma, can we get out last week's overtime figures? . . . and we'll also need to order a cab to take that parcel to the station.'

'No, I don't think we can,' observed Norma, placidly.

267

'Mr Beachcroft says we're to check with Mrs Grout before we order cabs. Apparently some's bin ordered that we can't account for.'

Rex flew into another passion.

'I don't believe this!'

'And Mrs Grout an' I have already been through the overtime.'

'Well, good for you two! I wonder if there's *anything* I can be trusted to do on me own.'

'I could ask Mr Beachcroft if you like.'

Rex was instantly alert to this new tone of Norma's. It didn't take him long to work out exactly what was going on here.

'Word of advice, Norma . . .' he remarked. 'You'll come off worse if there's any tricks to be pulled.'

'I don't know what y'mean,' started Norma, guiltily.

'I think you do, Norma. If y' fancy movin' up in this firm, there's better ways of goin' about it.'

'Like "asking nicely", y'mean?' came the snide reply.

'You could always try it.'

'I did. I'm still here.'

Rex contemplated her with a wry expression. 'Well, don't knock it, love. Y'might soon find yer the only one.'

Bernie was waiting for his favourite as she swung through the factory gates.

'On the mend, my love?' he enquired.

'They can do wonders these days, can't they?' Pauline fluttered.

'Mrs Grout's askin' for you.'

Pauline's face fell. What could the woman want with her this time? Bernie seemed as much in the dark as ever. If there were any complaints about B-Group's output again . . .

'Sit down, Pauline.'

268

Rex's voice seemed almost kindly. He had, Pauline reflected, become quite a different person since Mrs Grout's arrival.

'Tooth feelin' better?'

'Yes, thankyou.'

'Must've been a tricky job,' observed Mrs Grout.

'Yes . . . it took a bit of doing.'

'Must've took a *lot* of doing to require the combined skills of a beautician, dry-cleaner and dress-hire manageress.'

Pauline went white.

'Mrs Grout seems to think you've bin out roamin' the High Street instead of the corridors of the Dental School.'

'Mrs Grout doesn't think. She knows. She had a bird's eye view perched by the curb on Church Street.'

Pauline shot a look of appeal at Rex.

Something in his expression seemed to be urging her to deny it. And Rex knew that if she had, he would have backed her to the hilt.

'Could there have been a mistake, Pauline?'

But Pauline blundered straight ahead and blew it.

'No, but I *had* to, y'see,' she stammered. 'I'd got all wine on it, an' they cost two hundred quid new, an' if y'don't get 'em back on time they charge yer double . . . '

Rex looked away, silently cursing. There was nothing he could do for her now.

'So in fact, this story of a toothache was a complete fabrication.' Bella's voice swelled with triumph.

'Well . . . no . . . not entirely . . . I mean, I have had the odd twinge . . . '

But Bella wasn't listening. 'Norma, could you pass me that file, please?' She turned to Rex. 'There *is* only one option for deliberate absenteeism compounded by calculated distortion of the facts? One week's suspension without pay?'

Pauline almost fell off her chair.

'I take it that's your usual procedure?' Bella pressed.

'We've never found ourselves in this position before,' returned Rex, drily.

'Well, I wonder whose credit that's to?' sniffed Bella. Then, turning to Pauline. 'You'd better collect your stuff. You can return a week tomorrow.'

'Yeah, but . . . I can't . . . what's me husband gonna say?'

Pauline dithered as Rex held the door open for her.

'I'm afraid we're playin' by the book these days, Pauline.'

'Say that again!'

The whole bench had downed tools in a state of shock.

'I've bin suspended,' repeated Pauline. 'One week without pay.'

'For what?' demanded Jill.

'On me way back here, I nipped into the cleaners – an' madam there piped us comin' out.'

'I don't believe this!'

'If that's not the final friggin' bale to break the friggin' hump!' Queenie was almost philosophical. Something like this had been on the cards since February.

'And what did Rex say?' Donna asked.

'Well, what could he say? It's madam rules the roost here – hand-in-beak wi' bleedin Beachcroft.'

'I've bin waitin' for this,' Queenie confirmed. 'It's bin comin' now for six friggin' months an' here it is, landed like a shower of concrete.'

'Well, what we gonna do about it?' Jill was up in arms already.

'I think the dice are down this time, girls,' Carol May lamented.

'I don't see why they should be.' Jill turned to Pauline. 'You don't have to take this, y'know. You're shop steward.'

Pauline seemed to warm to the idea. 'That's right. I'm shop steward. *I* don't have to take this.'

Queenie poured scorn on Pauline's posturing. 'Oh, wadder-yer-like, you? We've heard it all before. Yer all piss and wind like the barber's cat!'

Jill rose to Pauline's defence. 'It's victimisation. She could call us out for less.'

'Oh, I could,' concurred Pauline. 'Oh, no bother.'

Queenie looked cynical. Whatever the injustice, Pauline had a knack of bringing these things on herself, and Queenie wasn't sure she wanted to weigh in on her behalf.

Jill, on the other hand, was a different kettle of fish. 'We've been too soft with 'em!'

'Soft?' Pauline took up the cudgels. 'They've got away with murder. All this cuttin' back, takin' liberties.'

'I suppose they think they can take us for coconut shies as long as they fancy tossin' bricks at us.' Jill was determined. 'Well, they can bloody think again.'

Pauline was really finding her voice now. 'I've not worked me nails down to the knuckles for this firm just to get lobbed off sideways by some snidey white-collar harassment tactics. They can bloody think again. I don't think they realise who they've meddled with.'

'No,' rejoined Jill. 'But they soon will do.'

In the bustle that followed, the ranting, the table-thumping, the final resolutions, one person alone failed to see what the fuss was about. Watching quietly from her corner, Klepto now leaned across to Queenie and whispered, 'What's happenin' now?'

Queenie scowled across the table to where Pauline sat preening her ruffled feathers.

'What's happenin' now is that gob-of-the-north there's just gegged us in on another hiding to nothing!'

Rex looked up as the knock came at the door.

'Come in.'

Jill marched in and handed him a piece of paper. He flicked through it, then glanced up at Jill with an expression which she swore meant 'good for you'.

'Well?' demanded Bella when the emissary had departed.

Rex turned to her with a smile. 'It appears that unless Mrs Smethurst is reinstated immediately . . . we've a strike on our hands.'

Pauline was not looking forward to this phone-call. What if Frankie probed too deeply, wanted details of the cause of the suspension . . . ? Or rather suspensions plural – for she'd decided it would look better if she were not the sole victim of the company's injustice.

'Hello? . . . Frankie? . . . I might be a bit late tonight, love . . . '

The ensuing explosion almost made her drop the phone.

'I've called 'em out, love . . . we've had that much thrown at us this year, an' now they're callin' for suspensions . . . I've told 'em, we won't stand f'r it . . .'

Frankie seemed to find her excuses implausible. It was time to turn on the righteous indignation.

'Well, that's nice, in't it? – I put the union first like you've always said, an' all I get is suspicion . . . if I didn't know how busy y'were, I'd ask yer to get down here an' support us . . .'

Another pause. Then a change of expression.

'You *will*? . . . oh no, y'don't need to, love . . . I know how pushed you are . . . no, really . . . I don't want to put you out . . .'

Pauline cursed. The phone had been put down. Frankie was on his way. Never had her bluff been called in a more vexing – and potentially disastrous – manner.

She looked up to see Bella watching her.

'Yer a very foolish little madam. You do realise this strike's doomed from the word Go?'

'That's a matter of opinion,' flashed the new militant.

'I'll have this lot back at work tomorrow if I have to drag 'em there myself.'

'I wouldn't bank on it,' sneered Pauline. 'My husband's on his way with a load from Agecroft. He was on the lines

272

during the pit strike. He's used to shiftin' big lumps of coal.'

Bella surveyed her enemy with undisguised hostility. 'We'll see who shifts first, then, won't we?'

'Pork-U-Like Packers? Yes, will you hold? I have Mrs Grout for you.'

Bella took the phone from Norma's outstretched hand.

'Hello? Sales Department, please . . . Have you got Fred Basnett there? . . . Bella Grout . . . Just a quick word . . . '

She glanced across at Norma who had returned to her typing. The secretary was looking down, but her ears told her some mischief was definitely afoot.

'Hello, Fred . . . alright, love? Look, I've been thinking . . . I might be able to put a spot of business your way. Why don't you pop round with Manfred about five o'clock? . . . that's right, love, use the main entrance. I'll see you there . . . '

The picket-line was looking quite impressive by the time the buzzer went for the end of work. Makeshift barriers, placards, even the odd banner had been cobbled together. It would look well on any 6 o'clock News, reflected Pauline, feeling meanwhile that she could have done without the extra weight provided by Darren, Jason, and more to the point, Frankie. It was bad enough for folk to see what gormless layabouts your sons were, without their father muscling in and quizzing you about the minutest detail of this suspension business. Presently a few handbags were snatched up out of harm's way, as the dog came strolling through the gates accompanied by none other than Chunky.

'What friggin' kept yer?' snapped Queenie, who was well out-of-humour at finding herself here at all.

'I bin down the allotment, feedin' me tubers,' he replied amiably. 'What's it all in aid of anyway?'

Jill stepped forward. 'It's in aid of . . .'

She got no further. Pauline elbowed her way over, interrupting loudly, 'This company goin' too far, thinkin' they can treat us like scum, bring in people over our heads, run this shop like a Russian labour camp, hand out suspensions wherever they fancy . . .'

'Oh, I see . . .' Chunky was overcome by the sheer force of the blast. 'Righty-ho . . . count me in, comrade.'

Queenie scoffed volubly, found herself a seat and broke out a pack of cards.

'It's friggin' diabolical, that's what!' shouted Pauline, anxious not to let the momentum slide, or Frankie slip in another of his awkward questions. Now the main body of the workforce began to filter down from upstairs, unaware till this point of the existence of any strike.

'Get over here!' Frankie urged them. 'Make a stand against this bastard management victimizing loyal members of the workforce!'

'So who's bin copped for what?' persisted Chunky to Pauline.

'Copped for friggin' nowt,' Pauline assured him hastily. 'People nippin' out on their lunch break. 'Course, managment likes to think they own yer leisure as well as yer eight hours' graft.'

'Well, they can think again,' asserted Jill.

Now a barrage of catcalls arose from the strikers as Bella and Bernie were seen approaching the picket.

'Now, now, girls – I'm just doin' a job of work,' argued Bernie as he was greeted by cries of 'Scab!'

'Don't get involved,' Bella advised him. 'We'll have this lot licked soon enough.'

'Her?' shrieked Pauline. 'She couldn't lick a thre'penny mivvi!'

'I shouldn't bet on it, love,' remarked Bella smugly to herself. 'I've a few reinforcements of me own underway.'

The orange Capri swung round the corner and drew up

just inside the factory gates. Bella smiled viciously as she went forward to greet the visitors.

'Reception party, eh? She shouldn't've bothered, eh, Fred?'

Pauline heard the voice, looked up, saw the faces, and went rigid with shock.

'Don't mind this shower,' Bella was urging. 'You come through.'

Frankie threw the might of his bulk forward and blocked their path. 'Yer comin' through my fist if you trip any closer.'

Bella played her trump card. 'You might know one or two folk here, actually . . . '

Manfred had been well primed. The sight of Pauline's ashen face seemed to fill him with malicious glee.

'Bit out the way for Blackpool Tower, eh, Fred?'

'Take a wrong road or what, Paulette?' came Fred's taunt.

Carol May and Jill clicked simultaneously. Familiar as these two faces had been, they couldn't quite place them. Till now.

Carol May glanced across to see how Pauline was taking it.

Pauline had fainted.

A gasp went up from the crowd. The girls clustered round their stricken comrade, fanning her face, loosening her clothes. For one hopeful moment, it seemed as if she would recover – Donna was rolling back the polo-neck to let in more air, when she felt Pauline's hand fly up and pull the collar to her chin again. Next minute, alas, the invalid had faded, but her head continued to burrow into the folds of her jumper, leaving no second glimpse exposed of the purple mark on her neck.

Frankie leaned over his wife, quivering with anxiety.

'Y'gonna make it, love? It's Frankie, love. Darren, get off yer arse an' fetch yer mam a cushion.'

'What's come over her?' wondered Donna.

'I'll tell yer what's come over her.' Frankie never missed an opportunity to leap on his soap-box. 'Them bloody pits of a management in there! Skin the workers – that's their game. Out all hours, she is – every night with the union, fightin' for better deals . . . '

It was as well the power of his own oratory carried him away, or Frankie might have noticed the gapes of sheer amazement from the rest of the girls.

'She's a martyr, that woman! She wants a bloody medal!'

Frankie bent to help the trembling Pauline to her feet. 'C'mon, love, I'm takin' yer home. Yer havin' a week's rest – an' we'll see who fancies arguin' wi *me* about that.' Then saluting the crowd with a gesture of 'solidarity', he swooped Pauline up – a feat in itself – and carried her towards the gates, cheers of applause ringing in his ears. Pauline discovered she had not actually died – this nightmare really was happening – but opted to remain comatose till the car was well on its way home.

'Don't worry, love!' Jill had shouted after her. 'We're solid here. Bloody solid.'

But once the excitement had died down, it was clear that the strike was by no means solid. Already three-quarters of the factory – workers not on their immediate groups – had walked past, oblivious to the noble cause they were championing. Now a few half-hearted pickets were beginning to warm to the attractions of a hearty supper and a night in front of the box.

Bella, meanwhile, was reissuing her invitation to Fred and Manfred.

'Tea and cakes in my office?' she smarmed.

Any desire for an almond slice was held in abeyance by the approach of Chunky.

'Alright, you two – hop it,' he invited.

'Now hang about . . .' Nobody spoke to Fred Basnett like that. Except apparently they did now . . .

'We know your sort – bloody strike-breakers – bloody management toadies. If I were you I'd leg it sharp before I ly in me top picket to see yers off.'

'Oh aye?' Fred sneered. 'An' who's that when he's at 1ome?'

Out from between the pickets slunk the malevolent hape of a bull-terrier, fangs bared, a low growl rising in ts throat.

'Ah, well now . . . perhaps another time, eh, Man? Ne'll come back when they're a bit quieter.'

'Aye, why don't we, Fred? No sense spoilin' good suits, h? We'll be in touch, eh, love,' he called out to Bella.

Bella's face was grim. 'Don't imagine you've done erself any favours there,' she assured the strikers as Fred nd Manfred beat a hasty retreat. 'You've a lot more to)se than madam there's to gain.'

'Oh, is that right, doll?'

Queenie pushed forward. This woman really had it oming to her.

'Now cop this, motormouth – I want yer two parts shut, :os yer givin' me earache. If I were you, I'd fly that riggin' arse out fast before I wipe its smile off on me foot.'

Bella returned a sneer of contempt. 'We know who'll ave the last laugh, don't we?' And seizing Bernie by the leeve, she stalked back into the factory, leaving the trikers to decide whether they'd lost or gained their oint.

Donna now made her way to the fore. 'I'm sorry, I'll ave to go now . . . '

'You'll what!' exploded Queenie, born-again champion f lost causes.

'I'm sorry, but I didn't bank on there bein' a strike when made arrangements. I've a supper to lay on.'

Jill was incredulous. 'You've a what?'

'Gordon does his organ tonight, an' I've a spread to see),' explained Donna patiently.

'Well, you sneakin', snivellin' snot-ravelled scab of . . . '

'No, Queenie,' Donna interrupted. 'I think you'll find that technically I am *not* a scab. I am *not* attempting to work. I am merely signing off picket duty for this evening. Needless to say, you're all welcome to join us later if you feel like it.'

Simon apparently *did* feel like it, as moments later he was caught trying to sneak out through the delivery entrance. It was Klepto who spotted him.

'Eh! Where d'y'think *you're* goin'?'

'I thought she said we could . . . '

'Yer meant to be showing solidarity.'

'Yeah, but . . . me mam's gonna pagger us . . . well how long do we have to stop for?'

'As long as it takes,' Jill announced.

'What takes?'

'Management to come to their senses.'

And Jill, who was becoming a regular Joan of Arc, snatched up the banner and held it firmly at the head of the picket. Behind her, less committed faces looked at each other and wondered if this was all such a good idea after all.

Gordon suits a bow-tie, thought Donna, as she paused from arranging the bowls of olives to watch him run through his latest virtuoso piece.

'Someone looks pretty good tonight,' remarked Gordon as he pulled out all the stops and pedalled away with his feet. Donna felt a rush of embarrassment. She knew she was 'in face' today, and the new dress suited her colour to a 'T' – even now, disguised as it was, beneath the rather overblown frills of her hostess apron.

Back in the kitchen, laying out the plates and serviettes, she came across the *Mother and Baby* magazine she'd bought earlier in the week. No point sighing over wasted opportunities. She tidied the magazine away, and then thought – to hell with it! Out came the wine, out came the corkscrew. Soon she and Gordon were toasting their first glass to each other, At any rate, it was better than a picket-line.

Most things were, at that precise moment. The late English summer, never predictable at the best of times, had decided to give them a foretaste of winter – so here they stood, in the deepening gloom, shivering in gale-force blasts, while gusts of rain pelted them from every angle.

'I could murder a pork kebab.' Klepto emerged from beneath a sodden banner. 'I wish we'd gone to Donna's.'

Jill treated her to a glare as icy as the current temperatures.

'Well, I don't see why we're all sat here soppin' while *she's* nobbed off on a week's holiday.'

The card school ground to a halt. It had to be admitted that Klepto had a point here. Queenie was asking herself why the thought hadn't struck her before, when Rex emerged from the factory entrance and came towards them.

'Do yerselves a favour girls. Go home.'

'Oh, there's management talking.'

'I can see which side *he's* on.'

The murmurs of discontent soon died away. It was plain to see that Rex was no friend of Bella's at this moment.

'It's a nice gesture, but you won't get her back here before the week's out.'

'It's not just about Pauline, is it?' Jill retorted.

'I know what it's about.' Rex looked as weary as any of them. 'You're not the only ones feelin' sat upon. But don't make the mistake of thinkin' yer indispensable. It appears we're none of us that any more.'

'Why, what's old Smiler got up his trouser-leg this time?' Queenie demanded.

'See this lot?' Rex held out a file full of letters. 'Job applications. Dozens of them.'

'What jobs?'

'Yours if yer not back by Monday.'

Yelps of protest broke out again in the ranks.

'As far as *I'm* concerned, Pauline's on a week's holiday,' Rex continued. 'If *you've* any sense, you'll go home, get some tea, an' be clockin' on at nine tomorrow.'

Then, with a glance at Carol May, he walked to his car, got in and drove away into the rapidly falling darkness.

'Well, now what?'

Klepto's question set them all a puzzle.

'I dunno . . . go home, I suppose . . .' Jill suggested. 'Unless someone's got a better idea . . .'

Donna was wheeling a trolley around Mothercare. She had five hundred pounds to spend and knew exactly what she was after. Nothing pink or blue, of course. Pastels were in this season: lemon yellow, mint green, apricot . . . .

A round of applause broke out near the cash-desk and looking up she saw Gordon leading the cheers, along with Mr and Mrs Frobisher from Accounts, Gwendoline, the branch secretary, Mrs Percival, wife of the Area Manager . . . Now she came to look more closely, Mrs Percival didn't appear to share her enthusiasm for the peach-striped all-in-one sleepsuit – in fact she didn't seem to share her enthusiasm for anything – in fact, if it came to that, they didn't appear to be in Mothercare at all, but in Donna's front room, with Mr Percival condescending to give his seventh encore of the evening. One thing remained constant, however: Mrs Percival's frown.

'Bravo!'

'Marvellous stuff!'

'Encore! Encore!'

It would be ungenerous to suggest that the reason for his popularity was somehow linked to the fact that Mr Percival was the most senior member of staff here tonight – or that the fact that he held the key to many a promotion or preferment had any bearing on how much his music was appreciated. Nevertheless, an eighth encore was being talked of.

The Area Manager turned to Gordon, who hovered beside the organ, waiting in vain for his call to arms.

'Not hogging it too much, am I?'

'Oh . . . no, no, no, no, no, please . . . it's really marvellous . . . eh, Donna?'

Donna came down to earth with a thud.

'Oh . . . yes . . . marvellous . . . really.'

Mr Percival paused to re-focus his concentration. He had a serious, low-key – not to say deadpan – style of playing, which under different circumstances would have sent its audience rollicking with laughter. Now, however, his first touch of the pedals produced only the most reverent silence. Donna settled into her chair and tried to retrace her daydreams back to the cot department.

'You'll be one of those 'women's libbers', I suppose?'

Mrs Percival's remark – less a query than an accusation – startled her beyond belief.

'I'm sorry?'

'All career and no children,' came the biting reply.

'Oh . . . no . . . I'm hoping . . . I mean . . . we're hoping . . . '

Donna hardly knew *what* she was hoping except that this woman would disappear through the rug into the cellar.

'No good hoping at your age,' persisted the dragon. 'Get on with it before it's too late.'

'Excuse me . . . '

Donna rose, tearful, trembling, and abruptly left the room.

'She didn't mean it like that.'

Gordon was tearing out handfuls of tissues and thrusting them into Donna's face.

'Come back in again, eh?'

'Why?' she flashed. 'Will it cost you promotion if I don't?'

Gordon was astounded. 'Is that what you think?' He was making for the door already. 'I'll clear them out now. Let's get shot of the whole tribe of them. I'm sure we can find better things to do with our evening.'

'No, hang on . . .'

Gordon was already turning the door-handle.

Donna had begun to thaw slightly. 'We needn't go that far . . . As long as they're out by eleven o'clock.'

'Eleven?' retorted Gordon. 'I'll have 'em sent packing by ten-thirty!' He grinned at her. 'That suit yer, Miss?'

Donna grinned back at him. He stole his arm round her shoulders and gave her a hug. Further developments were halted by the ring of the doorbell.

'Well, who'll that be? We're all here, aren't we?'

'I'll go,' offered Donna.

'Any tea goin' gash?'

The sight of six bedraggled figures plus dog was the very last sight with which Donna expected to be greeted when she opened the front door.

'What's happened?' she gasped.

'Strike's off,' announced Jill.

'How d'you mean?' Donna could scarcely credit her ears.

'Oh aye, we soon got *that* one sorted!' vaunted Queenie.

'Go'way, then, girl – where's all this scran?'

'Er . . . just a few latecomers . . .' ventured Donna, as Queenie & Co erupted into the room and without any attempt at ceremony fell like vultures upon the vol-au-vents. The dog, to general dismay, had entered shaking its sodden coat, and in attempting to leap onto the sofa, had, by an accident of miscalculation, landed on Mrs Percival's lap. Queenie, mistaking the look of horror for concern about the dog's welfare, hastened to reassure her.

'Nah, nah, not to worry, doll – he likes a bit of tweed.'

Mr Percival, meanwhile, continued his dignified and measured performance, oblivious to his wife's mounting distress, which was made all the keener by Chunky's arrival on the seat beside her and Queenie's offer of a half-empty can of extra-strong lager. Gordon glanced across at Donna. Here were all his dreams of promotion going up in smoke. Queenie, meanwhile, could see nothing but mirth in the whole performance, and, leaning over to Mrs Percival, scuppered Gordon's last shreds of hope, by digging her in the side, pointing to Mr Percival, and spluttering through a mouthful of vol-au-vent, 'Is that real, or does it come free with cornflakes!'

Someone was having a real clear-out. Creams, lotions, pills, tablets, sachets, packets – all manner of health and beauty preparations found themselves hurtling downwards towards the bottom of a dustbin. A hand waivered slightly, then the lid was slammed tightly on. The high priestess, having completed the ultimate act of sacrifice, turned slowly and walked into the house.

'You come in and rest, love,' boomed a man's voice, ill at ease with such tender tones. 'You've had a narrow escape. Yer nerves must be bloody shredded.'

Not so shredded, thought Pauline, that I wouldn't do the same again to get out of this bloody quilted housecoat an' into a decent gridful of make-up.

Queenie was starting to get bored. That old lunatic was still at the organ, the old bat with a gob like a burst wellie still kept giving her dirty looks, the beer had nearly run out, Chunky was snoring, the dog had disgraced itself in somebody's handbag . . . she shifted in her seat. She would have to think of livening things up in a minute. Mrs Percival forestalled her. Looking up at Donna who was passing round the chicken drumsticks, the Area Manager's wife suddenly remarked,

'You've been trying for some time, I take it?'

'I'm sorry?' Donna was quite taken aback by such impertinence.

Gordon hurried in, anxious to smooth the waters.

'We don't think of it as "trying" – we look on it as enjoying the practice.'

'You should get yourself seen to,' Mrs Percival pursued. 'What's the problem? Infertile? Frigid?'

Donna calmly put down the plate of drumsticks. 'I don't really see that's any of your business, actually.'

The whole room gasped as if the breath had been knocked out of it. Donna looked over at Gordon.

'Well, that's torn it now,' her face seemed to say.

Gordon's mouth was grim – until quite unexpectedly, it broke into an enormous smile. From her vantage-point on the sofa, Queenie decided the time had come to weigh in on behalf of the home side.

'Oi! Liberace!' she hissed. 'Don't yer know any Bay City Rollers?'

Gordon, faced with the serious prospect of no job at all, did not behave in the manner expected of a man about to be sacked. He actually laughed aloud. When Mr Percival suddenly ceased playing and turned to address Queenie, Mrs Percival began to fish for her handbag in anticipation of a swift departure. The fact that the handbag had inexplicably disappeared, detracted not one iota from the hush that had fallen on the room.

'I beg your pardon, madam – do I take it something a little livelier is called for?'

'Too right, pal – before we *all* nod off!' retorted Queenie. Whereupon Mr Percival returned to the keyboard and launched into an old music hall song, with which Queenie – much to the surprise of old Mother Percival – was so familiar, that she trilled through ten verses without a break. Soon, there was no quelling the eager songstress, nor her fellow choristers who called for more, nor the dog whose howling provided a novel accompaniment in the upper register of the scales

284

Gordon was laughing openly now, urging Donna to relax and do likewise. Mrs Percival observed the shy smile which flickered at the corner of Donna's mouth, and could resist no longer.

'So how will you manage with a baby on an Under-Manager's salary?' she sniped.

Mr Percival, still keeping his eyes firmly on the music, remarked casually,

'No reason why they should have to.'

Birds of the Wild . . . 'You should be so lucky,' muttered Pauline as she laboured to fit a Ptarmigan's beak to the underside of a Snowy Owl's wing. Jigsaws had never been her cup of tea, and Frankie's idea of diversionary therapy seemed singularly ill-judged under the circumstances. As she sat up in bed, sipping a cup of tepid milk, the concerned husband stuck his head round the door and nodded with approval at the wan figure smiling weakly up at him.

'Now, if y'want 'owt else, just shout our Daz. I'll be back later. I'm tellin' anyone who calls yer havin' no more excitement of any sort till I see yer fit. Peace an' quiet's *your* prescription. You rest up f'r a couple of months, then if I think yer up to it, we might chance a few dominoes down the Workin' Men's . . .'

Pauline's heart sank. So it had come to this. The former model lay propped up in bed, bereft of make-up, barred from leaving the house, and under sentence of utter boredom for at least three months. It was her own fault – it was she who had turned over a new leaf, she who had promised to reform, who had sworn to herself that never, never again . . .

The front door slammed shut. Frankie could be heard burping on his way down the path, then the gate swung open and the footsteps trudged their way down the street and out of earshot. The temptation was too great. Pauline leapt out of bed, flung on her quilted housecoat and started up the stairs.

*   *   *

Night had fallen on the palm trees. Shadows rippled across the still branches; the silent sea lay motionless in the deserted bay. Then, in the distance, a door creaked, a tiny pinprick of light appeared on the horizon, a pair of goggles clicked into place – and another ultra-violet dawn began to break.

CHAPTER EIGHT

October

Carol May was used to getting mistaken for her own daughter, but this morning she felt like her own mother. The stress of the last few months had taken its toll, and the woman who looked at herself in the mirror this morning saw – not the enigmatic, sensual, blonde of indeterminate age – but a raddled, care-worn housewife on the wrong side of forty-five. To be fair, that was *before* the make-up went on – but more and more the fatal flaws (not to mention the contributing factors) were proving impossible to conceal.

Colin shambled into the kitchen to clear the breakfast table. Recently he'd taken to surprising her with a few rounds of burnt toast on a Sunday morning – a treat which unsettled her, less on account of the inedibility of the fare than for the reasons behind this upsurge of marital tenderness. Colin was not an astute man, but it didn't take a Sherlock Holmes to deduce that the untouched breakfast had little to do with the fact that the toast resembled a sheet of carbon. Carol May was staring out of the window, sucking on a cigarette – her fourth already this morning.

'Off round yer mam's again today?' he ventured.

'Y' don't object, do yer?'

'I'll run yer up there if you like.'

'No, no . . . I'd sooner walk. I like the exercise.'

Should he leave it at that, he wondered. Was now the right time to broach the subject he'd been trying to get round to for the last fortnight? There never seemed to be a 'right moment' for anything these days.

'I've bin on to Harry Phipps about his caravan.'

'Oh?' Carol May showed not a flicker of interest.

'I thought y'could use a break. Y've bin lookin' a bit dog-eared lately.'

Thank you, thought Carol May. Try not to swamp me with compliments. Aloud, her reply was in a milder vein. 'You go. I can't afford the time off work. You can do without me, I'm sure.'

'I thought we'd have a quiet week together. We've a few things to discuss.'

Carol May barely flinched, but her mind was racing. Does he know? Is this it?

'What things?' she enquired casually.

'Surprise for yer.'

'Please, Col – I'm not in the mood.'

'There's more redundancies comin' – I thought I might take one this time.'

Carol May sensed there was more to come.

'I've bin thinking we might do that move to Lvtham St. Anne's we used to talk about.'

'But I've a job here,' protested Carol May.

'I fancied startin' me own little business – I thought we could mebbe run it together, eh?'

The sheer idea of exiling herself to some old-age-pensioner's seaside resort, struggling to set up a new business at his age – at *her* age – to leave behind a home, a job, family, friends, more than friends . . .

'What's brought this on?' she asked.

'We could use a change, I thought. How's it appeal to yer?'

'I don't know – I can't get me head round it that fast'

'No, well, we'll think on, shall we?' He paused for effect. 'Get ourselves used to the idea.'

Jill awoke with a start – and instantly wished herself asleep again. Anything to avoid having to confront the evidence of her own eyes – with all its implications – and the thought that at any moment the door could open and Sharon walk in on them . . .

The shape in the bed stirred beside her, turned over and went back to sleep. If only she could get him out of the room before Sharon realised he'd been there.

Sharon did *not* approve. She had made that abundantly clear these last few weeks. Sharon was at that awkward age where she saw too much, understood too little, and asked all the wrong questions. Like the one she was asking now . . .

'What's *he* doing here?'

She was standing in the doorway, looking accusingly at the intruder.

'Ssssssshhh!' Jill motioned her to be quiet.

'Y'promised me he wouldn't be here any more. I'm tellin' me dad.'

'Let's leave yer dad out of it, shall we.' If only we could, thought Jill.

'I hate you.'

Jill knew this was no exaggeration. 'Look, pet, I know it's hard for you . . . '

'You don't know,' flashed the child.

'It's hard for us all. Yer a big girl now, sweetheart. These things happen.'

'Why do they?'

'Because people start wanting different things.'

'I don't,' scowled her daughter. 'I just want the same. What *d'you* want, then? Yer own way, suit yerself – not us, not me dad.'

'Come here . . .' Jill was trying the gentle approach.

'No.'

'Come here.' This time more insistent.

'What?' The face was sullen, the mouth curled.

'It hurts me too.'

Sharon's face broke into a smile. 'Good.'

The door slammed, the footsteps stamped down the stairs. Jill turned anxiously to her companion. He was beginning to stir, now he was waking. Dazed with sleep, the eyes still sought her unconditional approval, her unequivocal love.

'Is it today?'

Jill took his face in her hands and kissed him on the forehead. 'Friday's yer birthday.'

Nicky pulled back the covers. 'Is me dad comin'?'

'I don't think so, sweetheart.'

'He doesn't like us now, does he?'

How many hours last night, last week, last month, spent trying to convince this child that his father still cared, that he hadn't abandoned them. As if she could be sure of that herself . . .

' 'Course he likes you.'

'Why's he never phone us?'

'He's very busy, love.'

Nicky dived beneath the covers again.

'Where y'goin'?' Jill asked, peeping beneath the sheets.

'I don't like bein' awake.'

The covers were pulled down over his head again. Jill bit her lip and tried not to weep. If she could just explain to Sharon how impossible it was to leave this child sobbing alone in his own bed, night after night, calling for his father, blaming himself . . . but Sharon only wanted to hear one thing – that Jill would hand in her notice and beg Ray to come home. If only she realised how that would complicate more than it solved.

'Don't forget, there's yer party!' Jill was determined to bring some cheer to the day. 'All yer friends coming – all them presents.'

Nicky emerged from the covers.

'If I could just have that denim jacket I might be alright,' he remarked slyly.

'Oh, might yer?' Jill was alive to his tactics, but right now they had all her sympathy.

'Perhaps he'll phone on me birthday.'

'Perhaps he will.'

Nicky considered the matter a while, then turned to his mother.

'If he doesn't, then we'll know for sure, won't we?'

'What?'

'That he *never* wants us back.'

'There you go, Mr Buckley. Y'can't get away from it, can yer?'

The security-guard unlocked the gates to let Rex out of the empty factory, and nodded wryly at the armful of files which had just been collected from the manager's office.

'You've got yer work cut out, eh? Fine way to spend a Sunday afternoon.'

'You can say that again,' returned Rex, sounding almost as if he were looking forward to the prospect.

'Don't overdo it, eh?' pursued the joker, as Rex walked round the corner to where his car was parked and flung the files onto the back seat.

'That's it, is it?'

Rex turned to Carol May who sat waiting in the passenger seat.

'That's what?'

'Yer alibi.'

Rex turned the ignition and sped off down the main road. 'Well, what *d'you* think? I've gotta give her *some* excuse for pissin' off on Sunday afternoon.'

Rex's driving always reflected his present mood, Carol May noticed. Right now it was impatient, fast and erratic. She bit her tongue for several minutes, then a succession of ignored red lights compelled her to speak.

'I'd rather we weren't discovered wrapped round a lamp-post together.'

Rex's response was a conservative 56mph in a 30mph zone.

'Is there some problem?' enquired Carol May, tartly.

'Oh no, no problem . . . apart from this place doin' me head in – her at home, her at work, you . . .'

His temper, like his speed, was rising steadily.

'I don't get it. He does sod-all for yer, he doesn't even

know yer there half the time. I've asked yer to leave him . . . '

'And live where?'

'With me.'

'And Stella, and the littl'uns. That'll be snug.'

Rex swung the car up on the curb and snapped off the engine.

'You think it's all mouth, don't yer? I've told yer – I'm leavin' her, I want a divorce. I want a new job, an' I want you with me. Now what've *you* got stashed away here that makes stoppin' where you are so bloody tempting?'

Carol May was silent. She frequently asked herself the same question.

'Right, then.' Rex took her acquiescence for granted. 'So I give her the elbow, then you'll sling *him*. Is that a deal?'

'I'm not makin' any promises.'

'What's up? Y'still don't think I'll do it. Y'don't trust me or what?'

Carol May was almost bitter. 'What do *you* think?' she challenged.

'Right, then.'

The key jerked in the ignition and the car suddenly took off down the street.

'What the hell are you playing at?'

Carol May was growing tired – not to say nervous – of such histrionics. 'Where are we going?' she persisted.

The answer finally came, like a threat, through clenched teeth. 'I've got something I wanna show you.'

The car pulled up outside a newly-built ranch-style bungalow. For a moment Carol May sat puzzled, then something clicked. He'd done it already. For months now he'd been promising to find them somewhere to live for when they left their respective spouses – and here it was – what the popular press would describe as a 'love-nest'.

'Come on.'

Rex got out of the car and was beckoning her to follow. She would try not to get too excited. She wasn't at all sure she'd be doing the right thing, but still the temptation was extraordinary . . .

Halfway up the path, she stopped dead.

'What's the matter?' Rex was fumbling with the keys and looking round with impatience.

Carol May shook her head. 'Oh, no, I really don't think so . . .'

Inwardly she was seething. The nerve, the sheer impudence of the man – to bring her to his own house, the home of his wife, his children, his whole other life. She turned and was heading for the car when Rex caught up with her and steered her back towards the front door.

'She's out. Y'don't think I'd've brought you here with *her* still there?'

He pulled her inside and closed the door behind them.

'Why are we here?'

'I told yer – there's something I want yer to see. Wait there.'

He left her standing in the hall and ran upstairs to the bedroom. Where was it? He had it all prepared. How could it fail to convince her?

Downstairs, Carol May had wandered into the living room – to meet with something of a shock. Stella had execrable taste, Stella was slovenly, Stella had no idea how to make a place feel welcoming . . . so where was the evidence for these claims of Rex's? Clearly he'd forgotten the catalogue of failings he'd been laying at Stella's door these last few months. For here was a home that was furnished with taste, with care, with loving attention to detail. And none of it was Rex's – Carol May was sure of that. Care and attention he had in plenty, but most of it was lavished on himself. What else had she heard? Stella was boring, Stella was thick . . . well judging from the Open University textbooks scattered across the table, she was unlikely to be either of those. One thing she knew already – Stella was not bad-looking. She picked up a photograph from the mantlepiece. Rex and Stella smiling, dipping down beneath showers of confetti on their wedding day. Nearby, one of last year's holiday snaps – Stella in a sunhat, laughing at Rex, who held his four-year-old daughter aloft. Another photo, this time more recent. Rex at the christening of his three-month old son . . . Carol May could almost name the date, nearly six months ago now . . . She had already been seeing him for over a year.

'Now who's joking?'

Carol May had barely time to feel the pangs of guilt, of pain, of jealousy, when Rex re-appeared. She took the letter he was holding out to her.

'What's this?'

'Me resignation.'

Carol May glanced up at him, then down at the piece of paper. Yes, it was certainly a letter of resignation, but so what? He hadn't sent it yet. He might never send it. He was full of bluster and bravado, but rarely had she known him to carry out his threats or promises.

'I've a mate in Milton Keynes. I could walk into a job tomorrow.' He corrected himself. 'We both could.'

'Could we?' Carol May failed to be impressed.

'Or you could please yerself – I can earn for both of us – y'could spend all day gettin' yer hair done if that's what y'fancied.'

Carol May cringed. Sometimes this man seemed to have not the faintest conception of who or what she was.

'What's worth stoppin' here for?' he demanded, coming up behind her, slipping his arms round her waist and kissing the back of her neck.

She resisted barely five seconds before turning and surrendering to his mouth. He was hungry for her, his desire overpowering what feeble show of resistance she could muster, and gradually she felt herself being eased gently backwards, downwards, till her body sank into the cushions of the sofa and his hands were groping the buttons on her blouse. Sharply she pulled away from him.

'What's up?' Her abruptness had startled him. 'She's not comin' back – she's out till late.'

Carol May had glimpsed the christening-photo over his shoulder.

'I'd rather book in somewhere.'

'But we're here now . . .'

He was pulling her down on top of him, unbuckling his belt, now reaching beneath her skirt . . .

The sound of a key rattled in the front door lock. Rex seemed to freeze with horror.

'Oh, shit! – now what? – now what!'

He cast about the room in desperation. Where could she hide? Where should he put her? At that moment a cupboard, a coal-hole would have done. He flung her handbag and coat towards her.

'Christ, what're we gonna do?'

Carol May hadn't moved a inch.

'Why don't you tell her?'

Her face was ashen, but her eyes were like ice.

'Are you kiddin'?'

Rex was almost dancing on the spot with panic.

'Anybody in?' Stella's voice rang in the empty hallway.

Rex buttoned his shirt and ran out to meet her.

'I forgot these.'

Stella came out of the kitchen carrying a pile of books.

'Back out, then?' Rex was desperate to get her through the front door.

'You're back early,' she noted. 'Y'could've had the kids after all.'

'No, no . . . I'm off round to Bernie's in a sec. Just nipped in to pick up some files.'

'I'll see you later, then.'

Stella kissed him and went out. Rex watched her walk down the path and get into the car, then turned to find Carol May standing silently behind him. Her eyes were dead, absolutely devoid of expression, except, he thought, for a shadow of contempt.

'I'll tell her tonight.'

He had to say *something* to make up for the humiliation, the indignity, the miserable figure *he'd* cut in the whole fiasco. But Carol May didn't appear to hear. She was combing her hair in the mirror.

'Look, what else can I say? I'll have me case packed an' be on yer doorstep by tomorrow night.'

Carol May put down her comb. She was weary to the backteeth of all this bluster. Once-and-for-all she would call his bluff.

'Alright, then. Tomorrow night.'

Rex seemed to reel with the shock. 'Yer jokin'?'

He could hardly believe what he'd heard. For months they'd entertained themselves with this little game. He would make these grand gestures, these extravagant offers – she would be touched, but naturally it was always understood that she would turn them down. So what was she playing at now?

'I'll see you tomorrow, then.'

Carol May picked up her handbag and walked out.

The Monday morning rush to clock on had subsided of late into an orderly and subdued procession. When Bella Grout stalked the corridors, lashing them with a 'No talking!' or a 'Get those legs moving!', anyone could be mistaken for thinking they'd been transported to Colditz – except that in this case, there seemed no early prospect of an escape. Two months ago, the sight of a sour-faced woman bearing under her arm a crimped and beribboned apricot miniature poodle would have sent gales of derision ringing through the factory. It was a mark of this woman's thrall that this morning the sight was greeted only by the odd nudge and a few muffled titters.

The luckless Simon was now jiving his way down the corridor – and into his latest humiliation. These days the persecution no longer came from Queenie – she was civil, almost comradely in the face of the common enemy – but from Mrs Grout herself. Turning the corner, Simon found himself staring into the muzzle of an apricot ball of fluff.

'Just the person I was looking for!'

Simon shrank visibly at the sound of Bella's voice.

'This is Beulah. She wants walking four times a day, ten minutes a time.'

'Oh, yeah, pleased to meet yer, doll,' was Simon's attempt at drollery.

'She's in season,' appended Bella.

Simon hastily dropped the paw he'd been shaking.

'Now I'm havin' her served on Friday, so you'll have to carry her when yer out to make sure she keeps away from other dogs.'

Simon was wilting already. Here was yet another 'little job', designed to make him appear extremely foolish in front of everyone. He glanced up at the clocking-on procession. Klepto grinned back sympathetically.

'And in case you're in any doubt,' rejoined Mrs Grout. 'Two thousand pounds, that madam's worth. Her puppies go for five hundred pound apiece.'

'Hey, no problem!' Simon made a vain attempt to look impressive. 'Yer lookin' at Fort Knox – y'know what I mean?'

'I'm lookin' at someone who'll be docked an hour's wages if he doesn't clock on inside thirty seconds.'

Bella sailed off into the office carrying her precious canine under her arm. Queenie stared after it with lip curled.

'It's sights like that make yer change yer mind about vivisection.'

On their way to the bench, Klepto ventured to pose the question which had been bothering her for some minutes.

'How's she mean – "served"?'

This term, as applied to an apricot poodle, seemed to puzzle her. Queenie was happy to enlighten her.

'She means . . . that scrap of fluff gettin' its beef-an'-two-veg on a silver platter, cordon bleu, an' red-hot out the microwave! Mind you . . .' She glanced round at her workmates. 'I bet two thirds of this bench is so friggin' starved, they dive at a scrap of cold pastie.'

'Two-thirds?' Donna gave a superior smile. 'I wonder what calculator *you're* using.'

Queenie was on the alert at once. 'Hey, don't tell us Liberace's hit them high notes at last!'

Donna's reply was a satisfied smirk which seemed to say, 'Wouldn't you like to know?'

Now, with the sound of the buzzer, the group dived for their soldering irons, and set to as if their jobs depended on it – which indeed they did. Simon, approaching the bench to refill the component trays, now leaned across and whispered to Klepto, 'I don't need it – y'know what I mean? I'm a skilled worker, I in't a bloody mongrel porter.'

'Tell her y'want danger money,' advised Klepto in all seriousness.

'Now then, ladies, let's show a bit of bustle. We're under scrutiny!'

It could only be Bernie – and yet, these days, even he had aligned himself with the underdog's cause and wielded his whip-hand much less frequently than of old. Mrs Grout had usurped him in that role.

Pauline gave Bernie a sympathetic pat across the buttocks. 'Cheer up pet – only another twenty years to retirement,' she joked.

'Well, I've got to say it, Pauline . . .' – Bernie was in a "confiding" mood today – 'when you've bin here as long as I have, yer entitled to think of yerself as "management" – and I do pride meself on bein' a bit of a "kid-glove" specialist – firm but fair . . .'

'Oh, definitely,' Pauline was nodding.

'But you've got to ask yerself, what's it all worth, when a woman like that can walk in here an' treat yer like some spotty school-leaver paid tuppence ha'penny to empty bins. I might've expected better, Pauline.'

'Y'should join the union, pet,' came the predictable reply.

'Oh aye, lad,' joked Queenie. 'It'll do bog-all for yer – but at least y'get a bit of company to lick yer wounds with.'

'Telephone call for Mrs Fox! Telephone call for Mrs Fox!'

Norma's voice rang out across the factory.

'Alright, girls,' muttered the avuncular Bernie, spotting Bella issuing forth on her rounds. 'Let's not give her the satisfaction.'

Simon shuffled awkwardly down the corridor clutching a lead, attached to the end of which was a peach-coloured rug on four legs. Suddenly the door to the office flew open and Rex appeared, yelling, 'Simon! Get in here now!'

'Now what've I done,' mumbled the hapless Simon, scurrying through the door with his head down, in constant expectation of a beating.

Two minutes later the whole factory floor was in uproar. Simon had taken leave of his senses and was actually *collecting* componets, instead of distributing them. And not merely collecting – actually snatching them out of busy fingers, sweeping them off bench tops, piling them into trays and bearing them away to the dispatch department.

'What the friggin' hell's goin' on?' demanded Pauline.

'Don't ask me. Orders from the top – know what I mean?'

The sight of Bernie conducting himself in a similar unorthodox manner convinced the girls there was something seriously amiss, but Queenie was too familiar with the workings of the company to expect anyone to bother informing the workers about it. Seeing Norma rush past on her way to Simon's office, Queenie slid out of her seat and followed her.

'Are they all off their mongs, or what?' she hissed.

'The components – they're bein' sent back.' Norma's voice was deathly.

'Back where?'

Norma lowered the volume still further. 'Korea. They've called off their partnership with us.'

'Go 'way!'

Norma nodded ominously. She knew only too well what this could mean – but before she could enlighten Queenie further, Bella Grout's shadow fell across the threshold.

'I presume you do perform *some* function round here?' she enquired of Queenie.

'Just popped in to see what's what.' Even Queenie was chastened these days.

'Then I should pop back to your bench an' pronto, or "what's what" might be a sharp drop in yer wages.'

Queenie slunk off, visualising a dagger between the Executive Managerial shoulder blades.

Bella now turned on Norma. 'To save you this fraternising with the shop floor, I've an errand for you.'

Norma found herself marched under armed escort back to the office. 'To save you the temptation of any more chin-wagging,' Bella informed her.

Gone were the days of co-operation and confidences. Norma now saw herself for what she had been all along: Mrs Grout's dupe. A source of inside information, which, once plundered to the hilt, was now cast aside and treated like any other casual employee. Norma was stung – but she had learned her lesson.

'You can nip out to the shops and get a can of lunch for Beulah. She has the Gourmet variety. And there's a list of shopping you can pick up for me while you're there. Take the money out of Petty Cash.'

Norma was bristling, but Rex's arrival with armfuls of papers, halted further discussion.

'And where's all that supposed to go?' snapped Bella, seeing the debris deposited across her desk.

'Perhaps we'd better get a skip,' remarked Rex, drily.

Norma was rifling through the Petty Cash tin, and looked up with a satisfied smile.

'I'm afraid I can't get the shopping, Mrs Grout.' She

waved a handful of IOUs from the tin. 'Petty Cash is already owed £26.42.'

'How much?' Rex exclaimed.

Norma found the IOUs snatched from her hand and secreted inside Mrs Grout's purse.

'Well, since you seem so short of something to do,' snarled the gorgon, 'you'd better sort out Beulah's litter tray instead.'

Norma looked down at the tray in the corner, then at the orange apparition in the basket, then straight in the eye at Bella.

'I think you'll find that's not actually in my contract,' she observed calmly, and glancing at Rex with a gleam of complicity, she attended to her filing trays instead.

Rex's face was buried in Carol May's neck.

'I've told her,' he whispered.

Carol May pulled back from the embrace and looked to see if she had heard correctly.

'What did you say?'

Rex straightened his tie and lounged back against the wall. They had come to their upper-floor retreat in the lunch-hour, and Rex was diverting his thoughts from the Korean pull-out with plans for the future with Carol May.

'I told her I'd something to tell her . . . and we'd talk about it when I get in tonight.'

Carol May was torn between fury at his endless dithering, and an inexplicable surge of relief that the crisis had yet to break.

'So where we gonna celebrate?' Rex demanded.

'Aren't you bein' a bit premature?'

'I've told yer – I'm comin' out of that house with me suitcase packed. I can book into a hotel till we've sorted somewhere to live. Now when y'gonna tell him?'

'We'll cross that bridge when we come to it.'

Rex burrowed into her neck once again.

'Tell him tonight,' he urged. 'Get it done with. Will yer?'

'I'll see . . .' murmured Carol May, feeling herself weakening already beneath his shower of kisses.

'Mr Beachcroft's here to see you.'

Bella Grout's strident tones rang across the empty floor.

'If it's not too great an inconvenience.'

Rex and Carol May had leapt apart and were now attempting to salvage some shred of dignity from the situation. Bella stood aside to let Rex pass out of the room.

'I believe this floor's out-of-bounds to workers,' she reminded Carol May, then swept away downstairs, leaving her to contemplate her indignity in private.

The limousine roared away from the factory, almost carving up a group of workers as they tried to re-enter the gates at the end of lunch.

'No, hang on love!' came Pauline's sarcastic shout. 'You've only took *half* me leg away with yer!'

'Who was it!' wondered Klepto.

'Bloody Smiler try'na do a Nigel Mansell over us.'

'I wonder what *he* wants.'

Pauline laughed bitterly.

'Probably dropped in to tell us we're goin' into partner ship with Stockport bloody County!'

Norma was crying in Rex's arms. Rex was dabbing her eyes with a handkerchief and trying to offer some scrap of consolation, but they were hard to come by and difficult to swallow. Whichever way you looked at it, a disaster was a disaster.

'I think we'd better get the girls together in the canteen.'

Norma nodded tearfully, blew her nose, and went out to the shop-floor. Rex reached for the phone. This could hardly have come at a worse moment. It was too soon to

302

assess how it affected his plans, but for the time being, all he knew for certain was that a state of emergency had been declared.

'Hello? . . . Stell? . . . listen, love, I've got some bad news for yer . . . '

Queenie was in no doubt about the outcome. The only uncertainty seemed to be the 'who's, not the 'if's'.

'Here we go, dolls – red, black, white, spotted – who's next in line for geggin' their own breed of junk on us? I'll give yer 5–2 the Yanks, 6–1 the Krauts, 7–1 the Nips, 100-1 outside the Brits . . . '

'He's more likely to tell us we've gone over to soldering bloody condoms, love,' quipped Pauline, bitterly.

Rex's arrival put a stop to further speculation, and an expectant hush now fell on the gathering.

'Ladies, gentlemen . . . you probably know by now that our Korean partners Yongchon Electronics have pulled out of the deal they made with us six months ago . . . '

'Best news we've had all year' – 'Thank God for that' – came a few ill-informed murmurs.

'A few minutes ago, Mr Beachcroft notified me that as from 5.30pm this Friday . . . '

'Here we go, here we go . . . ' chanted Queenie.

' . . . this company will cease trading.' He paused to let the gasp of horror subside. 'The usual redundancy and severance benefits will operate. I'm sorry, girls. That's all.' He turned and walked out of the canteen. Not a sound was uttered. No one moved. Then pandemonium broke loose.

A bevy of grim faces stared dolefully at each other as they huddled together on what had been their favourite tea-time retreat and sun-spot – the top platform of the outside fire escape. Now they had gathered here to lament their fate, numb with disbelief, speechless with shock. For each and every one of them, in its own particular way, this shut down spelt disaster.

'They *can* do it, can't they?' ventured Jill after a pause.

'You can tell *she's* never worked before!' scoffed Pauline. 'It used to be the number one pastime round here, givin' yer three days' notice.'

'How much pay-off do we get?' asked Klepto hopefully.

'Don't build yer hopes up, doll,' warned Queenie. 'Y'won't catch old Smiler delvin' too deep in his wallet. Friggin' shrapnel, it'll be. Enough for a night's good bevvy, an' a piss-in-the-wind to jangle yer pockets for a couple of weeks.'

'I had meself down for a life sentence here,' moaned Jill.

'Didn't we all, love?' echoed Carol May.

The muttered tones of this requiem were shattered by the foghorn roar of Bella Grout as she stood glaring up at them from the stairs.

'Get down here this minute! We don't close for three days – in case yer in any doubt, some of yer.'

Jill rose dejectedly to her feet. 'No doubt at all, love,' she uttered wearily.

The dining-room was dark except for a single anglepoise lamp trained on an open text-book, over which Stella was poring, with a notebook and pen beside her. A single place was laid at the table. It was gone ten o'clock. Stella had eaten, the kids were in bed, this was the hour when she could finally get down to some serious study. It was useless to wait for Rex. Eight o'clock meant 9.30 at the earliest. She was quite accustomed to 'carrying on regardless'. And today had, after all, been something out of the ordinary.

In the hallway, Rex flung down his briefcase and tore off his jacket. He'd been wrestling with decisions for four hours in that hellhole of an office, pestered with endless cups of black coffee and murmurs of sympathy from Norma.

As ever, he had failed to come to any firm conclusion. Right now he was tired, hungry and spoiling for a fight.

'Alright?'

Stella looked up from her books and smiled.

Rex felt his temper kindle. He needed an argument, not sympathy, if he was to engineer things in the direction he wanted them to take.

'Well?' he snapped. 'Y'not gonna throw a fit, then? Ask us what the hell we do for dosh now?'

Stella smiled back peaceably. 'I daresay we'll think of something.'

'Oh! "You daresay." That's very reassuring. That's made my day, that has, Stell.'

'Well, it's come at the right time, anyway,' she remarked. 'You getting ready to resign again.'

'Y'what?' Rex started in disbelief as Stella held out a piece of paper to him.

'You left it on the sofa.'

It was his letter of resignation.

'Your style's improving,' observed his wife.

Thank God Carol May couldn't hear this, Rex thought. Thank God she didn't realise how often he soothed his wounded pride or dented self-confidence by knocking off yet another resignation letter. Stella was right, though – his style *was* improving.

'Perhaps *I'll* go back to work,' she suggested casually.

'You?'

'You might recall I was a senior manager before I met you. You could stay home with the kids a while.' There was a twinkle in her eye. 'Y'know – take things easy.'

'Oh, yer a real comic, Stella,' snapped her husband.

Stella seemed undaunted by his vileness of temper. She watched him a while in amused silence as he stalked about the room, cursing loudly, crashing the glasses as he poured himself a drink.

'I've been on to me dad,' she said at last.

'Oh, an' what's The Expert's view of it, then? How's it my fault this time? Where've I managed to put my foot in it yet again?'

Stella waited for this fit of petulance to disperse before adding calmly,

'He's prepared to back you.'

Rex turned on her with a snarl of contempt.

'I know his kind of help. It comes gift-wrapped with two ton of bolts an' shackles strung between the lines. No, I do *not* wanna go cap-in-hand to him, an' end up payin' with four trips a year plus bloody Christmas to miserable bloody Glasgow – *and* have him watchin' over the books so I can't even piss without gettin' his signature first.' He paused. Should he mention it now? 'Anyway, I might have other plans.'

'Oh?'

'I might not stop here at all. I'll have to go where the jobs are.' He was sizing up to say it, but his courage kept failing him. 'You could stop here till I've something sorted out.'

'Could I?'

Stella's tone was innocent enough, but Rex took it to contain a hint of accusation. Again this was the moment to confront her. Again he lacked the courage to face her head–on.

'Look, I don't need this hassle.'

If he could just inflame the argument once more, he might be able to work himself up to such a pitch that telling her would be the best weapon he could use.

'Christ, what d'you have to give for a quiet life!'

Stella put down her pen and gave it serious consideration.

'Now what had they used to tell us at Sunday School? A pure heart, was it? Or a clear conscience?'

'A what?'

Rex flushed guiltily. Stella appeared not to notice.

'I've had enough of these for one night,' she replied, starting to clear her books away.

'What's that supposed to mean? – "clear conscience"? *my* conscience is clear,' protested Rex.

'Well, that's alright, then, isn't it?' returned Stella with a smile, and giving him a peck on the cheek, she gathered up her books and went upstairs.

Rex flung himself upon the sofa and bit his nails. Once again he had failed to come to the point.

Carol May put down her knitting and looked at the phone.

'Why don't you ring?' she chafed, under her breath.

The back door banged. Too late now, anyway. Colin was home.

'There y'go.'

He came in and tossed her a pile of leaflets.

'What's this?'

'Brochures I sent for. So we know what we're lookin' for. Now we've nowt to keep us here.'

Carol May flicked through the bumph – estate agents' superlatives singing the praises of life in Lytham.

'I can't concentrate now.'

Carol May threw the papers aside and picked up her knitting.

'Turn-up for the book, though, eh?' persisted Colin. 'You an' me both coppin' for redundancy at the same time?'

'Yes, isn't it?' returned his wife flatly.

The telephone rang. Carol May was two feet away from it but moved not a muscle. Colin stared at her in surprise.

'Y'not gonna answer it?'

'It won't be for me,' she assured him, though she knew perfectly well who was calling. Colin shook his head and reached for the phone.

'Hello? . . . who? . . . oh, hello, mate, how y'doin'?' He placed his hand over the receiver and whispered to Carol May, 'It's Harry Phipps about his caravan. What shall I tell him?'

307

'Tell him I'm dead,' muttered Carol May, rising in sheer frustration and pushing past him to get out of the room.

'We're still deciding . . . it's a question of dates . . .'

She heard Colin's voice doling out the bland excuses, then, feeling the atmosphere of the house too cloying for her throat, she pushed open the door into the garden, and leaned against the wall in the darkness, gulping in the cold, autumnal air.

Bernie rolled Simon his first cigarette, sat back in his chair and sighed.

'It's a blow. It's cut me to the quick. You see, lad, I've invested in this company – emotional investment – of the very dearest kind.'

'Hey, don't tell me,' nodded the boy between gasps. 'It gets yer right there – y'know what I mean?'

'I've not told Nancy yet,' continued Bernie. 'She's very set on the Canaries this year. I honestly can't see us stretching to it. And that's *without* worryin' who's gonna give the likes of yours truly his future daily slice.' He shook his head dejectedly. 'An' for the life of me, I can't see how we could've made it run more efficient – that's what really eats me – I had 'em humming like little tops.'

'Me mam's goin' up the wall,' admitted Simon. 'She had us down f'r'a future here. I kept tellin' her – I says, Mam, it in't no "future" here – I just like the company, y'know what I mean? – I know where I am.'

'And where you are this moment . . .' intruded Bella, ' . . . is skiving on company time. For which the usual procedure – correct me if I'm wrong – is minus one hour's wages.'

Bernie hastily stubbed out his cigarette. Simon almost swallowed his.

'Oh, hey, we in't got nothin' to do anyway,' he moaned.

'If that's the case, why don't I find you something to do?' offered Mrs Grout. 'I don't really care what it is, as long as I don't see you sitting on your great backsides for the rest of the week.'

Bernie frowned after the departing dragon and loosed another sigh.

'It's all wrong, y'see. Manners cost nothing. I've not put ten years into this place to get spoken to like that.'

Then he packed up his cigarette tin and shuffled out, having aged a good ten years in the last two days.

His place was swiftly taken by the watchful Klepto, who'd been hovering outside waiting to snatch a moment with Simon.

'I've bin thinkin' . . .' she ventured. Simon flushed. 'Y'know . . . like . . . when we're shut . . . well, I might want to send yer a Christmas card.'

'Oh yeah! Hey! No problem,' blustered the boy.

'So . . . you could, like write yer address down in me book if you wanted . . .

'Okay, why not, let's go for it!'

Simon had 'gone' over two-thirds of the way for it, when his hand stopped short and he laid down the pencil.

'Er . . . no . . . it's me Mam, see – she gets funny about letters comin' . . . '

Klepto's face fell. She had been mistaken, then. Ah, well, we live and learn . . .

'Hey, why don't I get *your* address instead – y'know, like, I could send *you* a postcard from Barbados – y'know what I mean.'

Klepto's heart warmed to the idea, but almost immediately she was shaking her head.

'Oh . . . well . . . no, see, 'cos me Dad . . . he reads all me letters . . . '

'Well, I dunno, then . . . maybe we could . . . ' Simon hardly dared utter his suggestion.

'What?'

'Y'know . . . like . . . meet?'

Klepto's face lit up as if this were a stroke of sheer genius.

'Oh yeah!'

309

'Then we wouldn't need the hassle, y'know, like addresses an' that . . . '

'We could meet . . .' Klepto eagerly pursued this line of thought. ' . . . an' if we met, we wouldn't need to write . . . 'cos we could just *say* . . . what we woulda wrote!'

'Yeah! Right!'

Suddenly it was all too much for them. Simon coughed self-consciously, Klepto shifted from foot to foot, they both grinned foolishly, then without another word, Klepto ran out of the room.

This time it was Simon's turn to sigh.

'God! – me armpit's friggin' baked!'

Jill and Queenie were dragging piles of chairs across the floor. 'If I fancied being a cart horse, I'd get Him Upstairs to double me oats!'

'No talking!'

Queenie spun round to the hiss of Bella's voice. The woman stood watching her, arms folded across her ample chest.

'If you moved that great backside a bit instead of giving yer mouth the work-out, we might have a bit of order to show to the receivers when they come here on Monday. But then, I've never known you give a toss for this firm's reputation, so I can hardly see a sense of pride developing now.'

Queenie's fingernails were starting to twitch. As Bella swept away up the corridor, Queenie was muttering after her between her teeth.

'Right, doll – you've just signed yerself up for a swift lash of guerilla warfare!'

Jill, who had witnessed the brief encounter, rubbed her hands with glee.

'I can hardly wait,' she beamed.

Rex's office was unusually deserted when Queenie stuck

her head round the door fifteen minutes later. Couldn't be better, she observed to herself.

'Right, fur-bag! – let's shift them lallies outa that box before I skin yer f'r' a bog-seat cover!'

And grabbing the somnolent Beulah from the cushioned splendour of her basket, she stuffed the beast under her arm and marched off towards the front entrance.

Back at the bench, B-Group watched this exodus and permitted itself a quiet snigger.

The 'Flying Ashtray' was parked halfway up a grass verge with its front bumper in a display of peonies. Queenie opened the back door, threw in the sacrificial lamb, glanced round the carpark and whistled.

As if from nowhere came a tornado of filthy paws, mangy tail and mangled snout – though, miraculously, no handbags – and vaulted breathlessly into the back seat. Queenie slammed the door shut, and casually strolled back into the factory, humming one of her favourite hymn tunes.

'You've not seen Beulah, have yer?' Simon was scampering round Queenie like a scalded cat. 'It's legged off somewhere, an' *she's* gonna freak the arse off us when she finds out.'

'Ooooh, no doll. Last time *I* seen it was out in the car park.'

'Car park!' Simon was beside himself. 'I'm paggered if she catches it cruisin' around by itself – there's half the neighbourhood's dogs queued up out there!'

'Tell you what, doll . . . ' Queenie had her arm round Simon's shoulders. 'We'll go an' sneck it out together, eh? See it's come to no harm.'

Which was how the whole factory-floor came to a standstill, to watch the unbelievable spectacle of Simon and Queenie leaving the building with their arms round each other.

Simon felt the tears rushing to his eyes. The poodle had completely disappeared. He had visions of finding it beneath a mountain of Alsatians, he could picture the mortgage he would have to take out in order to repay the two thousand quid, plus puppies – that made four, maybe five grand . . . his lip was starting to tremble . . .

'Alright, lover, out y'come now!'

Queenie had dispatched Simon safely round the corner before unlocking the back door of the 'Flying Ashtray'. Out bounced the dog, wagging its tail, strutting magnificently. Queenie peered into the red fur of the seat. At first she thought the poodle was dead. The bliss had been too much for it – it had expired in rapture against a tumble of furry dice. But then a paw fluttered, a dishevelled head, bereft of ribbon, raised itself, Queenie reached in and scooped the victim out on to the pavement.

'Over here, Simon!' yelled Queenie. 'I've found her – the minty little madam!'

Simon had to be disuaded from kissing Queenie's foot.

'Oh, hey, you've saved me life – y'know what I mean?'

'Best get it back to base,' commanded Queenie, piling the twitching heap of fur into Simon's outstretched arms.'

'Well done, pal,' she muttered to the dog. 'You've got it right for once!'

Back at base, Bella was wreaking storm-damage throughout the office, while Rex and Norma continued to attend to their business as best they could.

'You must've seen something,' she foamed. 'Prize-winning pedigrees don't just melt off the face of the earth.'

'No, I dare say not,' remarked Norma, to no one in particular.

'I shall just have to call the police, that's all. Dogs like that, they're worth their weight in gold.'

She was already dialling 999 when Simon stuck a bedraggled head – not in fact his own – round the door.

'Just took her out f'r'another breath of air,' he panted.

'What've you bin doing with her! She looks like the Wreck of the Bismarck!' Bella seized her trembling pet from the arms of its minder and bore her off towards the ladies toilets for re-grooming.

Norma repaired to her office duties. 'D'you know, I've always hated filing,' she declared, tipping several trays of paper into the bin. 'Till now.'

'Thought what y'might do next?' Rex enquired.

'Oh, I shall soon get fixed up,' Norma assured him. 'I wasn't plannin' on stoppin' here much longer anyway.'

Rex looked up in surprise. Norma was becoming quite a revelation these days.

'There's no real promotion structure, is there,' she was saying. 'I really feel I've bin wasted these lasted few months.'

'Is that a go at me?' Rex felt most things *were* these days.

'Well, if yer interested,' rejoined Norma. 'I don't really think y'know how to delegate actually – but aside from that, there's only one seat I've ever really fancied, an' that chair was never comin' vacant if I hung on fifty years.'

Rex laughed bitterly. 'Don't kid yerself. I doubt if *I'd've* stuck around much longer.'

'Oh, I've always had you down for a stop-here-till-you-drop merchant.'

Rex found himself laughing at the sheer insolence of the girl.

'An' what makes you think you could *do* my job?'

'Oh, I've watched *you* do it long enough,' she replied. 'There doesn't seem to be any great mystery.'

Rex laughed aloud. 'You've got a nerve.'

'Thank you,' said Norma, obviously regarding this as a compliment.

A tap came at the door.

'Who is it?' Rex demanded.

Carol May came into the room and sat down.

'Oh . . . er . . . Norma . . . could you . . . er?'

Norma knew her job too well to be asked twice.

'I'm just nippin' out for some milk,' she announced as she skipped through the door.

Rex was almost cowering before Carol May, who stared ahead, determined not to meet his anxious gaze.

'I've bin wanting to talk to yer all day . . .'

'In future,' Carol May interrupted, 'if "in future" holds any interest for you – you will do me the courtesy of getting in touch if you can't keep to arrangements.'

'What could I do?' Rex lied. 'The place was bedlam last night – she threw a wobbler when I said we're gettin' made redundant.'

'An' put the phone out of order?' supposed Carol May.

'Look, there's no problem – I'm telling' her tonight. I'll meet yer at half six.'

Carol May would not be drawn.

'I'll do it this time,' he swore.

'If, for some reason, it slips your mind . . .'

The door opened suddenly and Bella strode in with the regroomed Beulah. Rex found himself completely thrown.

'Yes, well, we'll see what we can do about that holiday pay . . .' he flustered to Carol May.

'Dear-oh-dear,' taunted Bella as she returned to dog to its basket. 'We really *are* scraping the barrel now, aren't we?'

Carol May rose to her feet and continued icily as if there had been no interruption, ' . . . perhaps you'll have the decency to phone this time.'

And without pausing to look at either party, she walked out of the room. Rex cursed silently and pretended to be tidying some papers.

'Wages'll be down this week,' announced Bella triumphantly.

'What?'

Rex wondered if now would be an appropriate moment to garotte the woman.

'There's a few out there think this shut-down's a good excuse to skive for the rest of the week. Their pay-packets'll tell 'em different.'

'Don't you ever give it a rest?' flared Rex.

'I do my job,' returned Bella coolly. 'I generally find it quite rewarding, given proper co-operation.'

She seized her clipboard and sallied forth towards the shop-floor.

Rex leaned across to Norma's intercom mike, and calmly announced, 'Telephone call for Mrs Fox. Telephone call for Mrs Fox.'

Out on the factory floor, Bella was still trying to work out why such an innocuous message should produce such a startling effect on the workforce.

She had not really thought how she would put it. She would probably get Rex to stop at a call-box on the way to the hotel, so she could give Colin the news when he got in from work. Notes in plenty had been tried and ripped up. The thought of Colin's face when he came home and found an envelope waiting on the table . . . She looked down at the small weekend case she was carrying. It was as well Colin hadn't come in while she was packing – she probably wouldn't be here now if she'd once more glimpsed that wounded expression, that look of sheer bewilderment . . .

The car came round the corner and pulled up across the road. She was running to meet it when suddenly she halted in amazement. Strapped to their seats in the back of the car sat a five-year-old girl and a nine-month-old boy. Carol May steeled herself to retain the last vestiges of civility.

'Y'should've warned me – I'd've dug out a rattle.'

She climbed in beside Rex and abruptly snapped on her seatbelt.

'I dunno what's she playin' at,' Rex was seething. 'She just dumps them on me, says she's off enrolling for some

315

bloody course or other. I dunno what her game is. I dunno what goes through her head sometimes.'

No, I bet, thought Carol May. Aloud she remarked, 'So y'didn't tell her.'

'Well, how could I? I didn't get chance to open me bloody mouth. She waltzes in, tells me she's back later – an' I'm left with these two skrikers to cope with.'

'I see.'

She turned to look at the 'skrikers' who were blissfully 'otherwise engaged', one with a bag of Smarties, the other with his thumb.'

'Look, we'll just have to make the best of it,' Rex frowned. 'Where d'you fancy goin'?'

Carol May turned to him with a faint smile. 'The Wendy House?'

Nicky put the phone down guiltily as Jill came in.

'What d'you think you're doin'?'

'Ringin' me dad.'

'I've told yer, we've no money to waste runnin' up bills.'

'I just wanted to tell him you've lost yer job.'

Jill laughed at the irony of it. 'I bet that perked him up no end, did it?'

'He wasn't there.'

'No, well he's probably gaddin' off round the town, swillin' his wages down the back of his throat.'

'No, but he doesn't live there any more. The man said he's moved.'

'Moved?'

Jill couldn't remember anything about changing digs in the last conversation she'd had with Ray. Mind you, it *was* over four weeks ago now, and it had hardly been a social call – more a resumption of hostilities.

'He lives here now,' said Nicky, pointing to the number he'd been given. 'But when I phoned there was only a lady there.'

'What lady?' Jill wished she hadn't sounded so curious.

'She said it's her house. Me dad does live there, though. She said she'd give him the message.'

'That's big of her,' snorted Jill.

'Why? Who is it, mam?'

'Y'better ask yer dad next time you speak to him.'

'I asked her if he was comin' for me birthday.'

'An' what did she say?'

'She said she didn't think so.'

'No, well I don't expect he will now,' Jill observed sullenly.

'But who is she, mam?'

'How should *I* know?'

'She said she felt she knew *you*.'

'Well, one-nil to her, then.'

Jill knew she was getting nasty, but there was nothing she could do about it.

'She didn't sound very old.'

Jill felt her temperature rising.

'Oh, I'm sure she's barely seventeen!'

'D'you mind bein' old, mam?' asked Nicky after some consideration.

'I didn't used to,' came the subdued reply.

'I like you old,' announced Nicky with a grin.

Jill felt a smile starting to force up the corners of her mouth. 'Thank you,' she said.

'Can I have that denim jacket?'

Jill tugged his hair affectionately. 'We'll see.'

Nicky grinned broadly and ran out into the garden hallooing at his friend across the fence. Jill sat in silence, gazing at Ray's new phone number.

The nights were drawing in, but it was still light enough to enjoy a few beers out of doors in the beer-garden of a picturesque riverside pub. Or perhaps 'enjoy' was not quite the word. Carol May sipped her orange-juice and gazed out across the serene expanse of water, now

317

glimmering with the reflections of lamps along the water's edge.

'Lauren, don't play with that!'

Rex's voice shattered her comparative tranquility.

'Lauren, I said don't play with it . . . Lauren, put that down an' get over here now!'

Carol May glanced across and saw that the child was playing with an empty beer-glass on a neighbouring table.

'She's not doing any harm.'

'She's to learn to do as she's told,' Rex insisted, grabbing the girl by the wrist and dragging her across to their table. 'Now sit still.'

He re-arranged the baby, Daniel, awkwardly across his lap and pulled the girl into line beside him on the bench.

The child looked across at Carol May and smiled shyly.

'Drink this,' ordered Rex, irritably pushing her orange-juice towards her. But the girl was edgy – perhaps she sensed her father's nerves – it was, after all, almost three years since he'd accorded her the privilege of being looked after by him. Whatever the reason, her hand was unsteady, the glass slipped – and sun-fresh, whole-fruit orange-juice was soon trickling down the leg of her father's newest acquisition from Next.

'Oh, Christ! – now look what y've done, you stupid madam!' He leapt to his feet, dumping the hapless Daniel on to Carol May.

'I don't believe this! I've only had this suit two weeks. Gi's a tissue or something!'

Carol May calmly handed him a handkerchief, then watched in silence as her lover danced a jig of rage round the beer-garden scrubbing frenziedly at his suit. Lauren started to cry.

'It's alright, pet,' Carol May assured her.

'Christ, they're bloody pests, these two,' stormed Rex – though Daniel appeared content to suck his thumb and uttered not a peep until Carol May handed him back to his father.

'Oh Jesus, now *he* wants changin'.' Rex turned expectantly to Carol May.

'Well, don't look at me,' she disclaimed.

Tempted almost to argue the point, Rex wisely thought better of it, and applied himself to the mysteries of the 'changing bag'. Cotton wool, zinc and castor oil, wetwipes, disposable nappies . . . the paraphernalia came tumbling out on to the table and Rex scrabbled about in it, trying to decipher what happened where. Carol May at first remained impassive, watching with amusement as the man bungled about in foreign territory. But when she saw him place the baby on a cold table top and start to tug at its nappy, she began to be less amused.

'How d'you work these things?' cursed Rex, trying to fit a nappy half-way up Daniel's back.

'I think it's the other way round,' remarked Carol May soberly, then seeing him stick the sealing-tape to the baby's thigh, she seized the child from his fumbling hands and took it upon her knee to complete the change without subjecting it to further distress.

'Is this the treat *I'm* down for one weekend in four?' she enquired.

'How d'you mean?'

'Presumably you'll want *some* access to these.'

'Oh too right, I will. D'y'think I'm havin' them forget who their dad is?'

And overcome by a surge of paternal affection, he ruffled Lauren's hair and tipped her a handful of change.

'Here y'are, sweetheart, go an' get yerself some crisps.'

The girl wandered off, bewildered by her father's sudden change of address, and glad to purchase a few moments of peace in exchange for pretending to enjoy crisps. Meanwhile her father was disposing of her mother as if she were some toy he'd grown tired of – which, essentially, she was.

'Stell can have the house. Mind, she might fancy pissin' off back to Glasgow – give them two miserable beggars at home the treat of tellin' her how they knew this'd happen.'

319

'How will she be off for money?' This was no idle concern of Carol May's. She didn't like to think of little Daniel traipsing round with holes in his rompers.

'She's stewin' in it,' Rex assured her. 'Her old man's stashed – an' tight-fisted to match. I know. I used to work for him.'

'I didn't know that.'

'He owns a loada firms up in Glasgow. I did two year's for him.' He paused. 'It's where I met her,' he added, almost incidentally. 'It'll make their day, me dumpin' her. They can say they saw it comin' eight years back.'

Carol May felt sick. Would he one day be disposing of *her* with so little tenderness?

Lauren came running back – without the crisps.

'Daddy! Daddy! Look who it is!'

A man and a woman in their early forties, faces tanned like hide from too many Marbella summers, were strolling towards them.

'How y'doin', mate? – hello, Danny boy! – God, he gets bigger every day – who does he look like, eh? – Stella not with you, then?'

The man steam-rollered his way round the table, pumped Rex's hand, tossed a fiver at Lauren and proceeded to make Daniel be sick by bouncing him up and down on his lap.

'Stell's enrolling on some course or other . . . ' mumbled Rex.

'Oh, she finally decided, did she?' shrilled the woman. 'Good for her. She could be runnin' this country in five years!' and she dug her husband in the ribs, chuckling with laughter at her own joke. Now she noticed Carol May.

'Oh . . . hello . . . you must be . . . ?'

'Er . . . Carol May . . . Nigel . . . Sylvia . . . ' mumbled Rex, unable to postpone the introduction any longer.

'When y'gonna come round for that bite of supper?' Nigel urged, deciding Carol May was too old to warrant a serious flirtation. 'Mind, Syl, you'll have to shape up a bit to beat that thing Stella knocked up f'r us last time. I wonder he's not fat as a pig the stuff she dreams up. Yer a bloody lucky bugger, y' know that?'

Rex smiled a feeble disclaimer and kept his eyes averted from Carol May.

'Thought about goin' away again this year? Y'can always join us at the villa, y'know.'

'Oh, well, no . . . we've not made up our minds yet . . .' Rex broke off. 'Well, as a matter of fact, Stell an' I aren't exactly . . . '

To her horror Carol May realised that Rex was actually comtemplating some announcement. She leapt in, heedless of how foolish it made her look.

'I never think two weeks holiday's enough, do you? Y've only just got there an' it's time to come back.'

There was an awkward pause. Nigel and Sylvia sensed that Rex had been somehow sidetracked, but couldn't quite put their finger on the how or why or where he'd been intending to lead them in the first place. Sylvia now turned to Carol May.

'You work, do yer, pet?'

'Just about,' came the wry response.

'I know just how y'feel, love – when y'get to our age, it plays havoc with the old bones, doesn't it?'

Carol May flinched but forced a smile in reply.

'I've bin goin' to these aerobic classes,' Sylvia went on. 'Tried to get Stell to come along, but she doesn't need to, does she? – figure she's got, makes yer sick.' She turned to Rex. 'Can't think why we've asked yer to come to the villa with us – Stella always puts me to shame when we get on the beach . . . ' Then, to Carol May, 'Y'know what she's like – makes y'feel about ninety, doesn't she?'

This was the final straw for Rex. Feeling honour-bound to champion his mistress, and goaded by circumstances into making the move he'd been so long incapable of, he turned to Nigel and Sylvia .

'Actually, Stell and I won't be goin' away together at all . . . '

321

Carol May was speechless. How could he do this to her? It was the wrong place, the wrong time, the wrong people . . . nothing was turning out the way she'd imagined. She flashed him a look which begged him to keep silent. He misunderstood, thinking she was urging him to get on with it. So he did.

'As a matter of fact, Carol May and I have known each other for some time. We've been thinking it over and I don't see why you shouldn't be the first to know . . . '

Carol May was already on her feet.

'Excuse me . . .' she interrupted, reaching to shake hands with Nigel and Sylvia. 'It's very nice to have met you. I mustn't miss the bus.'

Then she turned, and forcing herself to walk steadily, she almost ran out of the beer garden and flagged down a passing taxi.

Muttering barely coherent instructions to the driver, she leaned back into the corner of the cab and began to weep.

Rex was sprawled out in a chair, having drunk a great deal of whisky and smoked a great many cigarettes by the time Stella returned from her evening class.

'I thought you'd given up,' she remarked as she emptied the ashtray.

'I thought I'd give me lungs a treat.'

'Kids to sleep okay?' Stella had no wish to enter a full-scale shouting-match. Rex, however, seemed all geared up for it.

'There's no mystery, is there. I can put me own kids to bed without the aid of an instruction leaflet.'

'Have you spoken to me Dad yet?'

'What would I want to say to him? You've already told him where I said he could stuff his offer.'

'No,' replied Stella, calmly.

'No what?'

'I didn't tell him.'

'You what?'

'I thought you could tell him yourself when you've finally made yer mind up.'

Rex was pacing the room like a wounded boar.

'I don't believe you sometimes!'

Stella put down the ashtray and turned to him.

'What you "believe" isn't the issue, is it? Either you take his offer or you don't. If I were you, I'd get on and a make a decision . . . instead of behaving like a spoilt ten-year-old who couldn't get his second slice of cheesecake.'

Rex was dumbfounded. Stella was full of surprises, and none more than this sudden attack – he could hardly call it an 'outburst – it was too calm and measured for that. And what exactly did 'cheesecake' refer to? He had his suspicions, but he wouldn't tempt fate by asking to be enlightened. He was taking refuge in a sixth glass of whisky when the phone rang. Stella picked it up.

'Hello . . . yes, he's here . . . hang on . . . '

She held the phone out to him, daring him to take it. He knew it was Carol May. After the evening's catastrophe, how could he blame her for calling him at home?

'Is it . . . ?'

He could barely bring himself to ask, let alone utter her name. Stella smiled at his squirms of discomfort, then handed him the receiver.

'It's me Dad.'

Rex was almost drunk with relief, but this was no time for desperate behaviour. Something had to be salvaged from this debacle.

'Hello? . . . yeah, fine Ron – you've heard about our little misadventure, then . . . ?'

Stella slipped out of the room and softly closed the door.

Nicky was opening his birthday cards. It was Friday morning, the postman had delivered no news of Ray, and Jill was beavering to convince herself that it was no bad thing. Nicky counted up his pile of postal-orders – he was

323

an acquisitive creature and the wise relative knew that cash would always be preferred to the Dinky toy – while Sharon put on her most peevish frown – the one she wore for digging up the litter Jill always thought she'd tidied away – and commenced her assault.

'Mam . . . y'know this bird of me dad's?'

'What sort of an expression's that?' snapped Jill.

'Well, she is, isn't she? His bird?'

'I've no idea what she is – an' I've no particular wish to.'

Sharon watched her mother's face closely as she slipped in the next lance.

'Perhaps me dad'll want us to come an' live with *them* when yer divorced.'

Jill reacted perfectly.

'You'll do no such thing!'

'I'd like to live down south,' Sharon mused. 'Folkestone's near London, in't it? Rick Astley lives in London.'

'An' who might *he* be when he's at home?'

'Aw, mam!' Sharon was appalled at her mother's ignorance sometimes.

'Wembley's in London. Is Wembley near Folkestone, mam?' piped up Nicky.

'I doubt it.'

'Would we be allowed to come an' see *you* sometimes an' all?'

Jill was on the verge of stamping her foot.

'Neither of you are going anywhere!'

'Me dad'll say you can't support us,' Sharon volunteered. 'Janice Gibb's dad got *her* 'cos his new wife's a dentist an' her mum's an alcoholic.'

'Well, I am *not* an alcoholic. Yet,' retorted Jill, feeling that a large brandy might not go amiss at this moment. 'An' as far as I can see, yer dad wants shot of *all* of us, so y'better get used to stoppin' here.'

Nicky returned to the task of hunting out more bounty from between his birthday cards and Sharon began to lay waste her cornflakes.

'You wouldn't *really* want to pack off to Folkestone, would yer?' Jill ventured after a pause.

'*I* would,' said Nicky cheerfully.

'*I* would,' agreed Sharon, with venom.

'Oh, fine,' breezed Jill and wondered whether brandy went well on top of Rice Krispies.

Stella held out the gurgling Daniel towards Rex.

'Kiss for Daddy.'

'Mind his hands – this suit's just back from the cleaners.'

Lauren came bounding up. 'Can *I* have a kiss, Daddy?'

'If yer careful.'

Rex leaned across to receive his customary parting kiss from Stella. She danced out of reach, then turned to confront him.

'Well?'

Rex knew exactly what she was talking about.

'Yer Dad's a right bastard. I knew there'd be a catch.'

'Hardly a catch,' replied Stella. 'Just good business.'

'Good for who?'

'You're the expert.'

Rex was starting to get impatient.

'Look, do I get a kiss or not?'

'Do you deserve one?'

Here it was, the little-boy-lost expression. It never failed. Except that today it did. Stella treated him to a mere peck across the cheek.

'Is that it?'

'You'll have to earn the next one.'

She turned to give Daniel his second helping of Baby Porridge. Rex stood fidgeting on the spot, feeling he ought to say more. In the end he settled for less.

'So . . . I'll see yer later then?'

Stella flashed him the smile of someone who's just played a winning hand.

'Of course you will.'

'Don't tell me you're preparing for siege?'

Rex had arrived at the factory to find Queenie an
Pauline lugging in crates of beer and trays of sandwiches.

'Oh, go'way, doll,' Queenie roared. 'If this place i
gettin' shot of me, I'm leavin' scars it'll *never* get over!'

And she was about to heave an armful of vodka bottle
on to her tray, when Rex intervened and relieved her (
the burden.

'I don't like to see a lady overladen,' he smile
urbanely.

'Not much,' remarked Queenie to herself as sh
watched him disappear into the factory.

Queenie was right to talk about 'scars'. The factory wa
already reeling under the weight of streamers, balloon:
beer-crates and refreshment tables which now occupie
the whole of the factory-floor. Futile had been Bella
protests that the working week ended at 5.30pm and n
before. Rex had overruled her – and even if he hadn't, 15
irate women were more than a match for one extremel
unpopular Executive Manager. So when Queenie strod
on to the shop-floor at 9.30 in the morning and peele
open her first can of lager, everyone could rest assure
there was going to be a long hard day's drinking ahead.

Bella, indeed, was already packing both briefcase an
dog-basket prior to an early departure.

'I see no point in hanging about,' she announced. 'I'
obviously not needed.'

'That never stopped yer before,' observed Norma, in
voice not quite low enough to be misheard.

Rex was sitting at his desk, apparently concocting a li
of names, having been too preoccupied to notice th

retiring Bella, until he found a hand thrust into his face, which, he deduced, he was expected to shake.

'I can't help feeling you've brought it on yourselves,' pronounced Bella in tones of triumph.

'No doubt,' replied Rex, drily.

'I trust you'll find yourself something to suit your capabilities, Norma.'

'I don't doubt it, Mrs Grout,' countered the secretary. 'And the same to you too.'

So ended the reign of Bella Grout in the office – but her sojourn in the factory wasn't quite over.

Queenie leapt out in front of the departing figure and saluted her with a can of lager.

'Excuse me,' sneered Mrs Grout.

'No, hang on, doll. I nearly forgot yer prezzie!'

'I'm sorry?'

'Yeah, y'know' Queenie's voice was laced with sarcasm. 'One of them "tokens of our esteem," like.'

'It's really not necessary,' insisted Bella, eager to evacuate the sinking ship with all possible speed.

'Nah, it's done, though,' Queenie reassured her. 'It'll, like, creep up on yer – an' land on yer mat with a bossin' great wallop in about three months' time.' She paused to give Beulah's ribbon an affectionate tweak. 'Cheers, doll – you've turned out the bezziest little time-bomb in years!'

Bella turned to watch Queenie reel back down the corridor, then she herself made her way towards the entrance, wondering whether the woman was talking utter nonsense, or whether there had been a grain of truth in what she'd said. Glancing down at Beulah's ribbon, she noticed it had come undone. And then a terrible suspicion began to dawn . . .

Bella emerged into the car-park in time to see her company car being driven out of the gates at high speed.

'Where d'you think you're going with my car!' she trumpeted.

'The company's car, I think.'

Bernie had arrived behind her left shoulder and was smiling benignly at the set of car-keys left dangling from her fingers.

'Why don't I relieve you of those?' he suggested with impeccable politeness. 'You'll enjoy the walk on a day like this.'

Rex flung down the pen and read through the short-list. It was not satisfactory, it was not even enough, and then there was the question of whether he should even be doing it at all. He glanced out on to the factory floor, where the party was hitting its peak. Within half an hour it would start to turn sour. He'd seen enough of these farewell thrashes to recognise the pattern: fun and games, early inebriation, carefree optimism, lingering nostalgia, rising hysteria, ultimate despair. There was Donna now. She was still at the optimistic stage, and cheerfully declining God knows how many drinks, so she might make it through to 5.30 without hitting the tears. There was Queenie, jiving with Simon – that was definitely optimism, though one misplaced stiletto could tip them over into hysterics. There was someone already approaching the final stage. Carol May on her fifth gin and soon the handkerchiefs would be out. Christ, what was he doing in here? He was reading the shortlist yet again, he was tearing the paper and folding it into his top pocket. He was making a decision which would be irrevocable.

'Game for a quick turn?'

Bernie had approached Donna and offered his services as a dancing partner, but Donna reluctantly declined.

'I don't think I'm up to it, Bernie. That punch has rather ambushed me, I'm afraid.'

'Y'alright, doll?'

Queenie had noticed Donna's flushed complexion and leaned across with concern.

'I'll just get a glass of water,' Donna replied and headed off towards the toilets.

'There's a turn-up, eh? Miss Prim gettin' tanked up! She'll be paintin' her toenails next!'

It was Pauline, not Queenie who made this remark – and she was justly repaid by having Bernie approach and claim her for the next slow dance.

'Better snatch a last spin with me favourite shop steward, eh?' he cooed, mouth puckered against her neck. 'Where am I to send yer Valentine next year, then?'

Pauline's bottom jaw dropped. '*You* sent that Valentine?'

''Course it was me. Who else d'y' think it might be?'

Pauline grimaced in the direction of Rex's office and vowed that in future she would never trust the evil wiles of a man who set out to ensnare innocent women.

Rex stood in the doorway of his office and watched the party teeter into its second phase. Carol May, helping herself to another drink, glanced up, caught his eye, then looked away. Rex walked back into his office and shut the door.

Hours later, it seemed, Norma appeared on the threshold sipping a plastic cup of Vintage Cider.

'Can I get you something? A few vol-au-vents?'

Rex shook his head.

'I should make the most of it while I'm here,' pressed Norma. 'I might not be so cheap in future.'

Rex seemed to focus his thoughts. He looked at his watch, glanced at the party, took out a folded sheet of paper from his pocket and handed it to Norma.

'There *is* something you could do for me, actually.'

'Yes . . . that's right . . . Mrs Harris . . . I'm sorry? . . . I'm sorry, would you mind repeating that . . . ?'

Donna let the phone drop from her hand and sank to her knees on the floor beneath the call-box. On the other end of the line a voice was still talking, but Donna heard nothing. Sobs began to catch at her throat, not quiet tears, but great gasps of emotion, racking her body with their convulsions. It was in this state that Queenie found her, coiled in a heap on the floor, her face awash with tears.

'Hey, doll, what's happened?'

Queenie feared the worst – whatever that was.

Donna gulped. 'It was positive.'

'Y'what?'

Donna began to laugh. 'It was positive.'

Queenie's mouth fell open.

'Hey . . . y'mean . . . ?'

Donna nodded, burst into a fresh bout of sobs, then almost went into early labour as Queenie's shriek of delight was heard halfway across the county.

'Hey, dolls – Gordon the Organ struck Top C at last!'

The girls stampeded to offer congratulations, advice, last year's baby clothes, and even the hope that if it were a boy it would be named after Bernie.

'Well *you've* timed it nicely, you crafty madam,' sniped Pauline. 'You'll not be sat round twiddlin' yer thumbs like the rest of us.'

'Oh well, I'd always planned to come back to work,' replied Donna. 'I thought we could've organised a crèche.'

'Oh aye, an' friggin' Smiler would've bought yer its first potty!'

'Oh well,' observed Jill philosophically. 'Things turn out a sight different than yer ever expect.'

Queenie rounded on her and gave her a long hard pinch on the cheek.

'Wash your gob outa that great sag, girl. If we're leavin

here without a job, let's at least be sluiced enough to float a friggin' warship!'

The inevitable sing-song was starting up, to be followed in due course by the inevitable conga. All this Carol May saw, though join in she could not. Even without the seventh gin, there was a weight upon her which made her too heavy-hearted for dancing. The singing had reached a stage when ear-plugs could be issued, when Norma tapped Carol May on the shoulder. An onlooker would have heard nothing above the rising din, but closer scrutiny would have revealed that Carol May had repeated 'Up there?' and Norma assured her, 'That's what he said.'

Rex was out of his office. Carol May could guess where, and right now he could rot there for all she cared. Too cowardly to do his own dirty work – he'd sent Norma, of all people, to pass on the message. She would not be drawn.

He could wait for her upstairs till next Christmas. She would not shift a foot towards those stairs.

Norma dodged round an advancing plate of sausage rolls and whispered in Jill's ear. Then a conga reeled past and swept them both up in its train.

Scattered streamers, torn party-hats, discarded beer cans . . . the tell-tale debris lay strewn across the floor. Out in the cloakrooms, addresses were exchanged, phone numbers scribbled on the back of hands, birthdays remembered, reunions planned. Some women wept, others trembled on the brink of hysteria, some shrieked with laughter in order to keep the tears at bay, or the feelings of loss or the impending loneliness or the lack of purpose. A few die-hards clocked off – as if it mattered. A few cynics tore their cards into shreds and left the pieces scattered across the floor. Some were embracing, some were shaking hands, others just nodding. All were saying goodbye.

*   *   *

Carol May looked up to find the party was dissolving around her. The floor was almost deserted now, except for a few lingering sentimentalists who couldn't bear to see the last of what had been their life for the past twelve or so years. Queenie had gone . . . and Pauline . . . and Jill . . . and Donna and Klepto . . .

That really said it all. They'd take it for granted she'd keep in touch, of course. Well, maybe she wouldn't now.

Slowly she got to her feet. Her shoulders were beginning to ache. Old age creeping up, she laughed bitterly. One more drink. And then she did the very thing she'd sworn not to do. She went towards the stairs.

If I go up here, it's like an admission. I'm admitting that I can't exist without him. If I can't exist without him, then I can't stay with Colin. If I can't stay with Colin, then I may as well divorce him. If I take one more step, is that what I'm saying? I suppose I'm saying I *will* leave my husband for him . . .

Carol May's resolution was shattered by the noise of clattering heels on the stairs behind her. She wheeled round to see Pauline stumbling towards her.

'What's the big idea, then? D'y'know?' Pauline was too drunk for this sort of exercise.

'I'm sorry?' Carol May looked blank.

'Have *you* bin sent for an' all?' asked Pauline.

'Sent for?'

'Hey, come on, pet, shift it.' Pauline had already overtaken her. 'I'm frigged if I'm missin the best bit!'

Carol May watched with astonishment as Pauline disappeared through the door at the top of the stairs. What in Heaven's name could Rex be thinking of, asking her there at the same time . . .

She had reached the door. She paused, took a deep breath, and walked in.

*　　*　　*

The fourth floor was utterly derelict. Carol May knew that already, so it was hardly a shock to her. But to the twenty-nine others who now stood there, gazing around them in confusion, it had an almost nightmarish quality. Who were they all? Jill, she could see among the crowd, and Queenie . . . there was Norma . . . and Bernie . . . Donna and Klepto stood with their heads together, talking nervously . . . there was Simon . . . and Pauline the latecomer was just inside the door . . . and she herself, Carol May – the last to arrive.

Rex saw her slip through the door, and immediately he breathed again. He looked at his watch, as if eager to make a start.

'Ladies and gentlemen . . . you're no doubt wondering why Norma's sent you all up here . . . '

There was a ripple of assent. Rex continued.

'I'll make it short. I'm settin' up in business. The same business as downstairs – it's what I know best. I've hand-picked thirty workers to join me in settin' up the new venture. We'll have a new Company Secretary and Deputy Manager . . . '

Bernie took a step forward. At last his moment had arrived.

'Thank you, Norma,' Rex was saying, shaking the hand of his new second-in-command. Norma beamed at the astonished assembly. Now it was her turn to step forward.

'If you want the other twenty-nine places, they're yours for grabs.'

There was an explosion of delight, of relief, of sheer amazement. Rex went on with his speech.

'Now we won't be on big money to start with – it's more like a family business – long hours, lotta graft – but when the rewards come in, we'll all get our fair share . . . '

Queenie looked cynical. Where'd she heard that one before?

'Now, I know it doesn't look much right now . . . but I

333

think with the right effort, the right attitude, we could get in there together an' make something really special.'

He glanced across at Carol May, desperately seeking her approval. She returned his look with a blank stare.

'So . . . if we're all game for that one, perhaps Norma, you'd like to sort us out something to celebrate with . . . ?

Norma emerged from behind a pillar bearing a tray of plastic cups and some bottles of warm pomagne. It wasn't much, but it was a fairly appropriate accompaniment to the occasion.

Rex suddenly found himself accosted by a subdued Bernie.

'I'd like to say, I'm very grateful . . . very decent of yer . . . I suppose I'm not everyone's idea of the One-Minute Manager, but it's good of you to have me along for the ride – very much appreciated . . . '

He put out his hand to shake Rex's. The manager broke away with almost indecent haste, and pushed through the clamouring and grateful crowd to where Carol May stood motionless by the door.

'You *will* take it?' he asked, petrified at the thought of being rejected, man and job, by this woman who captivated and enthralled him.

Carol May stared at him. At that moment she seemed to feel nothing but contempt for him.

'Say you'll take it,' he pleaded.

Carol May knew then it wasn't him she despised, but herself.

'What do *you* think?' she flashed.

But the suspense wasn't over yet for Rex.

'Look, there's something else I didn't mention before . . . '

But even as he spoke, he knew it was too late. The door had opened. Carol May looked round. And saw Stella. She was wearing a stunningly cut suit, she looked confident, she looked beautiful . . .

Rex stepped forward to meet her. 'Y'got here alright?'

'Fine, thanks.'

There was just one flicker, the merest acknowledgement of Carol May. No malice, no envy, no pity. Just a
look. Then Rex put his arm round his wife's shoulders and
led her towards the rest of the crowd.

'Ladies and gentlemen . . . I'd just like to introduce my
wife Stella . . . my partner and fellow-director in our new
venture . . . '

Nicky was modelling his new denim jacket and making no
attempt to help with the clearing up of debris from his
birthday-party. Sharon slammed some empty coke cans
and cake-spattered plates on to a tray and marched out
into the kitchen.

'Shane Vickers said he'll come back later,' she called
out.

'Aw, I don't want him to,' protested Nicky. 'I wanna
watch me new videos.'

'That's a fine way to talk about someone who's just
bought yer a birthday present,' reprimanded Jill.

'It was dead cheap, mam,' Nicky argued. 'It only cost
eight quid. He bought the cheapest of everyone . . . Billy
Smith bought £15.75 . . . Darrell Connelly bought £12.50
. . . Paul Cooper bought . . . '

'I don't want to know how much they spent!' snapped Jill.
'There's things a sight more important than what stuff
costs.'

'Yeah, but he's a cheapskate, though, isn't he. An' his
trainers are only plastic.'

'I suppose I should be grateful you'll wear that jacket.'

This produced the hoped-for response. Nicky beamed
with gratitude and *almost* gave his mother a kiss.

'See, it's not true, then, is it?' Sharon sneered, coming
in again with a tray. 'I want never gets.'

'Sometimes,' Jill replied, almost to herself.

Sharon now applied herself to table-clearing with such

gusto and racket that the rap on the door was almost lost in the commotion.

'Aw, mam, it's Shane Vickers – tell him I've gone to judo.'

'I don't see why I should have to tell lies for yer,' complained Jill as she opened the back door.

There was a parcel on the doorstep. Jill bent to pick it up wondering why on earth the giver hadn't stopped to say hello. Then she recognised the writing. Now she was running into the garden, down the path, towards the gate, on to the road.

'Ray . . . ?'

She called again. The figure halfway down the road halted, stood silent, impassive, waiting for her to catch up with him.

'Ray . . .'

His face, turned aside from her, was neither angry nor smiling. Now she was here she didn't know what else to say.

'Ray . . .'

He turned round and looked back at her.

'Yeah . . . ?'

THE END